Praise for *The Final Child*

"*The Final Child* is such an elegant, well thought-through thriller. It takes the idea of victim and turns it on its head and breaks your heart in the process. I was sucked in for the first half and then whipped through the second half with my heart in my mouth. A fantastic follow-up to *After the Eclipse*."
SOPHIE DRAPER, author of *Magpie*

"This beautifully-written novel is haunting and heartbreaking, disturbing and bittersweet. You won't be able to put it down!"
ROZ WATKINS, author of *The Devil's Dice*

"Yet another stunning thriller from Fran Dorricott. I couldn't turn the pages quick enough."
JO JAKEMAN, author of *Sticks and Stones*

"Fran's writing just gets better and this novel is expertly plotted to keep you turning those pages all night. Parts of this are inevitably heartbreaking, others are full of hope. If you love your crime fiction pacey, well written and full of suspense this is perfect for you."
ALEX CAAN, author of *The Unbroken*

Also by Fran Dorricott and available from Titan Books

After the Eclipse

THE
FINAL
CHILD

FRAN DORRICOTT

TITAN BOOKS

The Final Child
Print edition ISBN: 9781785657900
E-book edition ISBN: 9781785657917

Published by Titan Books
A division of Titan Publishing Group Ltd.
144 Southwark Street, London SE1 0UP
www.titanbooks.com

First edition: September 2021
10 9 8 7 6 5 4 3 2 1

A CIP catalogue record for this title is available from the British Library.

Printed and bound by CPI Group (UK) Ltd., Croydon, CR0 4YY.

This book is dedicated to my family.
Thank you for everything.
I love you all.

"Each unhappy family is unhappy in its own way."
Leo Tolstoy, *Anna Karenina*

1994

3 July

Michael (6) and Jeremy (4) Taylor are abducted from their bedroom in Lincoln in the middle of the night.

18 July

Michael's body is recovered near Saint Mary's Christian Centre, Edmonton Lane, Lincoln.

6 October

Jeremy's body is recovered on the grounds of Foremark Reservoir, Derbyshire.

1995

21 June

George (7) and Jacob (7) Evans are abducted from Sheffield.

17 July

George's body is recovered on the banks of the River Derwent, Derbyshire.

1996

5 July

Morgan (9) and Paul (5) Bailey are abducted from Chesterfield.

1997

24 June

Morgan Bailey's body is recovered in Abbey Park, Leicester. She has only recently died.

2 August

Charlotte (8) and Hazel (6) Davies are abducted from Leicester.

1998

3 June

Randeep (9) and Jaswinder (7) Singh are abducted from Burton-on-Trent.

13 October

Alex (9) and Jillian (7) Chambers are abducted from Little Merton, Derbyshire.

31 October

Jillian stumbles out of the Moorway woodland. She is alone.

Jillian

EVERYTHING WAS SCREAMING. HER legs, her ears. Her blood. The air was so cold even her skin was screaming, her muscles so tense she could hardly move. But she had to run. She'd lost so much time already.

The woods were thick, the path invisible through the tangles and the thorny bushes. The way she had come looked identical to this. She stumbled, driving her lungs to *breathe*, her legs to hold her just a while longer. Her head was throbbing, bleeding and scabbing over from where she'd fallen. She could feel the blood getting cold, welding a patch of hurt onto her skull.

She pushed harder still, her legs trembling with the effort as she reached a narrow gap in the trees. She was panting, could taste rusty bile in her throat. Her lungs ached. The sun had barely risen and the sky was tinged with amber through the tops of the trees, but the rain that fell was cold and hard.

Big, fat droplets of water landed on her frozen skin, soaking her to the bone. She couldn't feel them anymore. It had been raining all night. She'd woken in an icy puddle of leaves, forced herself to move even though it hurt. Her whole body was caked in freezing mud. She couldn't remember exactly what had happened. She recalled terror and wading through water so cold it stole her breath, an ocean of black muck waiting on the other side to pull her down. All she knew now was the belly-cramping fear of the dark place behind her. But at least she was standing, moving, going, *going*...

She stopped at the bottom of a small slope. Just for a second. Just to catch her breath. There was no way around it; she would have to go up and over, or risk doubling back. She couldn't do that. She didn't know if she'd been followed. Glancing around, she felt like a rabbit caught in a snare. She'd seen one of those once. With Alex.

Alex.

She choked back the sob that threatened to break free. She had to be silent, or as quiet as she could be as she ran through the ragged trees. What if somebody heard her? She wouldn't be taken back. Not ever. It was too late now. She'd come so far...

Tears were on her cheeks and they were warm. Almost welcome. She let them fall as she blinked in the grey-gold light. A sudden snapping of twigs made her start, her heart thudding louder and louder, and she knew she couldn't stay, not even to think of Alex. It didn't matter if she couldn't go on. She had to. *Now*.

She bit her lip, steeling herself for the short climb, and then threw herself against the rain-sodden branches, the twigs that sliced and bruised her aching legs, that drew thin arcs of blood across her palms. Her short hair plastered to her forehead, she could hardly see, but she hauled herself up, up, up. Alice back up the rabbit hole.

Then she was upright. Running. There was a path. A burst of laughter bubbled in her throat. The woods weren't endless. The trees thinned, became grass and rocks and dusty white gravel. There was a Pay and Display machine. It was a car park.

She froze as she saw the woman. Fought back the scream and the wild laughter that followed. But the woman was just a stranger, a jogger in trainers and a soaked t-shirt, dappled with sun and sweat and—

The world began to sway. She fought to stay upright, but her legs were numb, locked and jelly at the same time. The jogger cried out, some words that she didn't understand, couldn't process.

The ground rose up.

"Alex," she mumbled. "Alex."

ONE

SEPTEMBER 2016

Harriet

I SAT WITH MY back to the window, listening to the rain lashing against the dark glass. Uncharacteristically, I'd left the curtains open earlier, too focused on my computer screen to close them, and now there was a draught. I'd been gazing at my notes and transcripts all evening, the cursor blinking at me stupidly. It was time to call it a night, but I couldn't. It was like being able to see something out of the corner of my eye, but every time I shifted my head it disappeared.

I contemplated my empty glass of red wine, the silt collecting just above the stem. My mouth tasted ashy. I scrolled back through my notes again, right back to the top. To where everything had started. With Michael and Jeremy Taylor. Six and four years old, stolen from their beds in 1994. The first known victims of the serial abductor known as the Father.

My cousins.

I'd written most of these pages years ago, diary-like bits of interviews with parents of the other children, names I remembered from my childhood like a death bell toll, rambling nonsense that had helped me to process what had happened to them. It had been a pet project, this book, a catharsis. The early chapters showed that – they weren't for anybody else's eyes. But recently a new challenge had arisen. And now I didn't know what to do, didn't know what I believed any more.

How did other people separate themselves from their own history enough to write about it?

My aunt and uncle are worn out, I'd written. *Tired from years of being asked the same questions.*

The lines on their faces are an echo of the suffering they carry deep in their hearts. To go on after the deaths of both of their sons, knowing they might never learn what exactly happened to them, has turned them into shades.

My family talk about my cousins a lot. About prankster Michael and sensitive Jeremy. I've never asked questions before. But now I realise how much there is I still want to know.

"You were only little when they were taken," my aunt says when I tell her I want to write a book about Jem and Mikey. "Only four. The same age as my lovely Jem, but you seemed so much older. I wish you could remember him. I wish you could remember them both."

The thing is, I won't ever forget them, even though I don't remember. That's how I know I need to write this book. Not just for me. Jeremy and Michael, and all of the other children, deserve to be remembered.

Eventually I ask the question that's been simmering inside me for a long while now: "Michael and Jeremy were the first pair of siblings to be taken by the Father. Did you ever think that was important?" My family talk about significance all the time – perhaps there might be some significance in this.

"They were the first." My aunt repeats my own phrase to me, as though this answers my question. *"But it didn't feel like a trial run. Or it if was, he was lucky. Everything was too — careful. Like it was all planned. Otherwise there would have been more evidence, wouldn't there? But I'm sure it's just easier for me to rationalise it that way, rather than think that it might have been my fault."*

I'd first written these notes years ago, when I was at university and struggling to process my childhood. Now I thought about the way my aunt had spoken: *it didn't feel like a trial run.* Sombre, resigned. I hadn't thought much of it at the time, but now I knew better.

I'd let life get in the way. University, graduation, getting a job in the real world; I'd been ready to let this book go. But it was easier to see with hindsight that I might have missed something.

I scrolled through the old interview chapters I'd typed. Nobody else had ever mentioned it before my aunt. Nobody had mentioned that the abductions felt practised, or that the longer the Father's identity remained hidden the less likely it was that he was personally connected to any of the children he stole. That it might have always been, right from the very start, *random.*

But what if we were wrong about Michael and Jeremy being first?

I moved to stare at the piece of paper on my desk. The one that had drawn me back to the book, to the interviews, to the ghosts of children. Just a hunch. Was I imagining things? The similarities? Was I just seeing what I wanted to see?

The rain continued to pound the glass. Even now I didn't like curtains left undrawn at night. A hangover from my childhood. I hated the way darkness haunted the glass, turning it into a black mirror. I didn't like unguarded open windows, either. They invited trouble.

My mind buzzed. I got up and shut the curtains, poured myself another glass of wine. I opened up my web browser and, tongue between my teeth, began to type into the search bar.

I'd made a decision. It didn't matter if it was my imagination; it didn't matter if it was a hunch. I *would* take my meagre information to somebody official. The police still involved with Jem and Michael's case, perhaps. But tonight it was still just me and my thoughts.

At some point I'd have to interview *her*, too, if I wanted to make another go at this book. She was the final child, after all. I couldn't explain why the thought made me so nervous. Perhaps it was the idea of coming face to face with somebody who had survived what neither of my cousins had.

Perhaps I was worried she might tell me more than I was ready to hear.

TWO

31 OCTOBER 2016

Erin

HALLOWEEN WAS JUST ANY other day. I got through it most years by spending the evening too drunk to think, but it was getting hard to find drinking buddies these days who didn't have to get back to relieve a babysitter. It didn't help that I'd let the anniversary creep up on me, or that I'd started a new job in the last year. I loved the office, loved the people, but they were mostly older, and I wasn't sure what was worse: spending the evening alone in a club full of eighteen-year-olds or having dinner with Karen, who lived in the most suburban neighbourhood in Burton.

I couldn't face either, but especially not the hordes of kids who would no doubt be knocking on Karen's door for fistfuls of chocolate. It would make me think of Alex, and that defeated the point of going there for dinner in the first place.

Last year had been different. I'd had a girlfriend, and colleagues I could call on for a last-minute night out. But I hadn't spoken to any of those colleagues since I left the job – abruptly, and without saying goodbye. I couldn't figure out how to explain what had gone on there, why I'd needed to leave, without telling them who I was, so in the end I simply didn't tell them. It was a clean, painful break.

This morning I'd told myself I wasn't going to let it get to me, but it had been a lie. I'd been jumpy and emotional all day, ignoring my desk phone in case I burst into tears on the call. My office buddies avoided me; I could tell most of them were itching to ask me what was wrong but I'm sure my expression warned them off. At midday I opened a stock photo zip folder, and the first image showed a young brother and sister holding hands in the woods. I made it to the bathroom before I felt the tears start, and I stayed there until I felt like myself again.

When I got back to my desk I buried myself in my latest design project, headphones in and blinkers on. I worked that way until long after everybody else went home, waiting until I was ushered out by the cleaners before I decided what to do next.

Mum had offered to pay for a takeaway, but I didn't think I could face that either. She would want to talk about Alex, about the anniversary; she'd want to tell me again how lucky it was that I came home. It's what we'd done over two weeks earlier when we marked the abduction date, something my mum and dad had always done together as a way to honour Alex, before Dad died. We'd watched the appeal on TV, the detective chief superintendent on the news, marking the anniversary of the date my brother and I were taken, asking again for any information. *Anything at all*. Normally I did my best to help her make sense of things, but this year everything had snuck up on me and I just wanted to forget.

As I left the office I was struck by how dark it was. The streets were so empty. My house would be cold, and lonely. I wasn't ready to go home and sit alone. Instead I drove to the gym, which I just about remembered how to get to. It was the sort of membership that might as well have come with a stress ball and a bottle of wine – I hadn't been in six months. But I stayed for two hours, working my way through every machine, twice, until my whole body ached and I couldn't do any more. I showered slowly, brushed out my long hair and applied a comforting layer of makeup in the spotty mirror.

And it was still too early to go home. I left the gym, ignoring the instinct to check behind me as I got into my car. It was silly. There wouldn't be anybody there. Then I drove to town. It was my last resort.

There was a gig on at The Rock, the cheapest – and only – live music venue in Arkney, and only passable if you didn't value your eardrums. It was a small pub off the beaten track, a squat building that didn't fit with the old-fashioned village vibe of the rest of Arkney. Instead it had only one big window at the front, and a dark, sweaty, smoky room in the back. Even despite the smoking ban, it still seemed to reek of stale cigarettes. It was the kind of place where the spilled-beer smell stuck to you, even after a shower. Where you came home with random bruises from strangers' elbows and chewing gum stuck to your shoes.

I loved it.

It was so far removed from the safety of my little terrace house that I often came here after a bad day, at least until recently. The noise was amplified by a hundred when they had live bands on; the room was too small, the speakers too big. The sound blocked everything else out until all that was left was darkness and white noise.

The band tonight was one I hadn't seen before, and normally I wouldn't stay to watch. But tonight I wasn't there for the music. I just needed oblivion, to get away from the niggling voice at the back of my mind. The one I'd been ignoring all week. Maybe longer.

I ordered a drink from the barmaid who always seemed to serve me. She didn't say anything as she slid over a double rum and Coke, just gestured to her watch, which I knew meant Monica was meant to show later. They were friends. I felt my stomach tumble.

I hadn't spoken to her in over a month. We'd called it off. Or, rather, she had. As far as I'd been concerned it was only casual anyway, and I'd always made that clear. Somehow things had got all tangled up, though. She said I was too distant, too hard to read. I'd never been in it for the long haul. I never talked about my family, didn't have enough friends outside of work. I was stuck in my ways... And she, obviously, was perfect.

I knew it was a bad idea to wait for her tonight. Either we'd end up getting into a steaming row in front of everybody – or I'd end up going home with her. And both of those were bad. But I didn't want to be alone, so I took my drink to the back room and waited.

The band were already setting up and a small crowd had formed.

I sat at the back of the room on a table, my feet propped on a chair that was tucked underneath. I sipped my drink and patiently waited for the room to fill, occupying myself with the general din of people having a good time.

I settled back, relaxing against the cool wall and letting the alcohol buzz settle over me. It was just a Monday. Could be any other Monday.

I was on my second drink and the band had started by the time she showed up. She was beautiful in an effortless sort of way. I took in her golden-brown skin, eyes lined with day-old kohl, her dark hair that was braided and cut differently than when I'd last seen her, and felt a familiar thrill. I tried to look away, but I knew she'd seen me.

I hadn't dressed up, just wore my usual work wear of leggings and a t-shirt, but she looked stunning. She wore a skin-tight little green dress, her arms adorned with orange bangles. This wasn't a *thing* any more, I repeated to myself, even as she headed straight for me, a beer in one hand and a rum in the other.

"Hey. El said you were here."

She met my gaze for a second, as if daring me. I felt the pulse of the music in my ribcage, and thought again of my empty house. Tomorrow I would be brave again, but tonight I needed help. She was as willing to make this mistake as I was.

I took the drink.

We watched the band until the end of the first set, both

pretending that we were just friends, that there was innocence in tonight's meeting. I knew that Monica thought it was a bad idea too – saw it in the way she checked her phone repeatedly, flicking the home screen on and off. But in the end we both knew it was going to happen. And we both wanted it to.

We left just as the band started up again, their heads swaying to a mistimed guitar riff. Monica's car was older than mine, a beat-up green Ford, but I liked it. She cranked the heating up full as we peeled out of the car park and drove to her house, a small semi-detached she shared with a flatmate – absent tonight – and a cat. I didn't like cats, but I'd always made an exception for Monica's fluffy tabby, Savage.

We tumbled into Monica's bedroom, throwing aside shirts and socks and pants and bras with abandon. The rum was good, the night was cool, the silky sheets cooler still. Monica's tongue was like electricity, sparking life back into my skin. Her breath was hot, her fingers cold, the rhythmic movement of our bodies an exorcism of the ghosts of the night.

Afterwards, she offered me a cigarette. Her brown skin seemed to glow in the light that filtered in from the street lamps. We lit up and the air above us quickly became wispy and sort of grey.

"This doesn't mean I forgive you," she said.

"I know."

"And it doesn't mean we're getting back together."

"I know that too."

She rolled over and propped herself up. "Are you kidding me? You're not even gonna ask if I wanted to?"

"You were very clear last time I saw you. I'm not girlfriend material."

"This doesn't bother you at all?" she prompted.

I shrugged. Already the memories were creeping in, the distant buzz of the rum fading. I realised that I felt just as hollow and irritable as before. And I still had to go home to my empty house.

"This was a bad idea," I said. I stubbed the cigarette out angrily in her ashtray. I wasn't angry at her, just myself for thinking it would work.

"You're too damn right." She shook her head. "What's got into you tonight?"

"I'm sorry." I sighed. "Look, I'm going to go. I'm sorry about all of this – and before. I'll call you later, if you want. I have some stuff I have to do tonight."

Monica said nothing, just watched me underneath heavy eyelids as I got dressed quickly, shoving my feet into my shoes with more force than necessary.

"I'll call you," I said again.

"Please, don't."

Monica's house wasn't far from The Rock, which I was grateful for. A fifteen-minute walk was enough to drag me the rest of the way to sober without feeling like I needed another drink to reward the effort. Why had I let myself lash out like that? It wasn't me. I was usually so good at being *normal*. Sure, I got sad this time of year, but that was understandable. Some people knew I'd lost my brother – they just didn't know how, and I was good at encouraging them not to ask. But most people never knew, and that was fine by me. It meant I could pretend nothing had ever happened.

The trick-or-treaters were long gone now, all tucked up in bed. I lit a cigarette and stood beside my car for a moment, smoking in the darkness. The street lamps made everything look like melted gold, but my mind focused on the shadows. How big they were, how deep. They seemed to hold multitudes. I pulled my jacket tighter.

I'd been feeling antsy for days. The anniversary had crept up on me, insidious. It felt like something was behind me, like eyes on the back of my neck. It was absolutely ridiculous, given that I was as safe and well-adjusted as I'd ever been. I had a good thing going, a job I enjoyed, coworkers I could definitely manage to tolerate. There was nobody out there taunting me from the shadows. The Father was dead and nobody even really knew who I was. I had no reason to be antsy.

And taking all of that out on Monica had, as I'd thought, been a stupid bloody idea.

I shivered and climbed into my car. Tomorrow would be a long day after a sleepless night. As I pulled out of the car park I made sure to double check the shadows either side of the road, locking my car doors just in case.

EXCERPT

Jeremy & Michael Taylor

Abducted: Lincoln, 3 July 1994

Two days before Michael (6) and Jeremy (4) were abducted from their home in Lincoln their mother took them to the zoo. Jem loved the zoo – the monkeys especially. He said they were like his older brother Mikey, who liked swinging from ropes and bars at the playground.

"They had such a good day," their mother, my aunt, remembers. "It was the first time we'd been that year, but usually we went to Twycross a few times through the summer, and the boys absolutely loved it. I think there was a new activity trail, and we didn't stop all morning."

Her face clouds as she recalls what came next.

"I like to remember what they enjoyed," Auntie Sue says. "Like how Jem used to make those silly bracelets out of beads and thread for his toys. He made them for us, too, but the toys got the best beads, the best thread. I like to think about the good stuff. It helps me to stop thinking about – the other parts. Afterwards. Like I love to remember how Jem always, always smelled like chocolate. Didn't matter whether he'd just had a bath, or been playing football with your Uncle Greg. He could have been swimming in the ocean and he'd still smell like chocolate.

"The boys used to watch TV together on the weekends. They played tag on the street most nights.

They were running around playing tag at the zoo that day, while we ate our lunch. Jem fell and Mikey, bless him, picked his brother up and carried him back over to me going shh, shhh the whole time. It was adorable."

I try to only think of Michael and Jeremy smiling, happy, playing tag and laughing at monkeys.

Sometimes it's hard.

THREE

1 NOVEMBER 2016

Harriet

I TOOK MY MEAGRE information to the detective my aunt and uncle had mentioned. Her name was Godfrey. She agreed to meet me for a quick coffee on my lunch break so I could explain what I'd found. I hadn't really asked permission from Sharon for the long lunch, but she did it more often than she should as well, and I knew she was in a manager's meeting which would probably run over into the early afternoon.

I fought an unfamiliar, nervous energy as we both sat down, the detective giving me a polite handshake.

"Two children," I said when Godfrey gave me the go-ahead. "Siblings, like all the others. They're in the right age range, seven and nine. The right sort of location, not far from the others. And it happened around the right time, just a year before my cousins."

Detective Godfrey steepled her fingers. She was in her fifties, with curly brown hair that she'd scraped back into a bun. It was hard to tell from her face what she thought of my hunch, but the first thing she'd said when she met me was, "Ah yes, you were the journalist."

"I had a look before I came out to meet you," Godfrey said now. "But these boys were reported missing in the spring. All of the other abductions happened during the summer or autumn."

"Yes, but this might have been the first time, right? Perhaps not everything was the same. Jillian and Alex were as late as October, so an early abduction isn't outside the realm of possibility."

"They had both also run away before." Godfrey dumped some more sugar into her coffee and stirred it.

"Well, yes," I said calmly. "I saw in the paper that they were runaways, but other things fit, don't they? They were last seen at night, their bodies weren't found. No clues or other evidence."

"They weren't biological siblings, either," Godfrey added. It felt like she was one step away from counting my failings on her fingers, a list of all the reasons my theory didn't fit. "One boy was from Birmingham, one from Manchester. They'd both run from group homes *and* fosters before."

Her tone confirmed her lack of conviction. She had the same information I did, but clearly we had different interpretations. Where she saw holes, I saw possibilities. The detective glanced at her watch, casually.

"I know. I know they weren't blood relations – they had different surnames and that's why I didn't connect them right away, because I'm sure I've probably seen information about them before – but they were still living in the same house, sharing a bedroom. And I know they'd run away before, but they weren't found this time," I explained. "The other times the boys turned up, not very long after they'd run away, but this time they just disappeared. As if somebody had taken them."

"I'm not denying there might have been some foul play, but the Father took his victims right from their beds." Godfrey shook her head. "Both together, at night. There's no proof here that these boys did anything but leave the house of their own free will and then get into some trouble later."

"Can you at least look into it? Just... *confirm* I'm not right? They were last seen somewhere in Staffordshire, I think, on the border. The article mentioned a bus station or something?"

"Yes." Godfrey softened a little. "Of course, we'll have a look at the old footage from the bus station, double check everything. I know the fact that it was only a year before your cousins were taken makes the timing seem right here, but often with these things there are any number of ways of looking at the facts. These boys were out on their own, in the middle of the night, with no money or transport. It doesn't mean there's a connection. But I'll look into it. Obviously I can't make any promises, but I do appreciate the time you've taken to talk to me."

And that was it. It was out of my hands. I'd achieved all I could – at least as far as official tracks were concerned. But there was still something niggling at me about the whole thing.

Handing it over to the police had made me feel worse, not better. Like now it was out of my control.

But maybe there *was* something I could do about that.

I had new interviews lined up with a few of the parents

over the next few weeks, to catch up and go over their original chapters. I wanted to start pulling the interviews into something real and book-shaped, and I wondered if any of them might have anything they wanted to add.

Now maybe it was time to talk to Amanda Chambers and her daughter. In the beginning, when I first started working on the book, I hadn't had much luck with either of them. Mrs Chambers had said she wasn't in a very good place, and didn't feel comfortable talking to anybody she didn't know. I hadn't pushed it. And, I realised, I'd been reluctant to talk to her daughter anyway, so it had felt like fate had somehow intervened.

It had been years, so perhaps I'd have better luck this time. I found Mrs Chambers after a good bit of digging. She answered my call on the third ring and, much to my surprise, didn't immediately put the phone down. I arranged to see her after I finished work – at her suggestion. It wasn't lost on me that yesterday had marked the anniversary of her daughter's escape, but if anything that seemed to make Mrs Chambers more willing to talk.

I headed straight there from the office, found the house and sat in my car staring out into the dim evening. It was getting late. Almost seven. I was surprisingly nervous.

Eventually I managed to drum up enough courage. I stepped into the cold night, smoothing down my wild hair, patting at my shirt, tucking it into my dark jeans. Mrs Chambers met me at the door; she had bottle-blonde hair, pronounced crow's feet at her eyes, and a warm if apprehensive smile.

"Miss Murphy, right?" she said.

She let me in, then led me into a small lounge with a tiny inglenook fireplace.

"Do you want a drink?"

She made me warm tea, a little milky for my taste, and we stood for a moment sipping at our drinks. The friendliness she'd displayed on the phone was still there, but now it was hidden by a bundle of nerves.

"So you…" She gave me a once-over, assessing. I imagined that she must have dealt with a lot of press over the years. "You're a journalist?"

"A writer," I corrected. "Former journalist." She arched an eyebrow but waited for me to explain. "I wrote for a few publications, small online ones mostly, after I graduated, but I didn't stick with it formally. I appreciate it's not a glowing record but – as I mentioned on the phone earlier – I'm working on a book, more of a personal project. It's abou—"

"The children." Mrs Chambers nodded, popped her mug on a floating shelf next to the fireplace. Framed above were pictures of her children: a young Jillian, short white-blonde hair that stood up in tufts and wide blue eyes; her brother, Alex, not looking at the camera but off into the distance, his own hair a sandy blond and his cheeks just losing their childish plumpness.

"Yes," I said. "It's about the children. My cousins – they were Jeremy and Michael. Taylor, I mean. The first…" No matter how many times I told this story, it was still hard. "Anyway, I wanted to write the book about them, and the others, because – well, I was tired of the same old rubbish. Stuff about *him*. Not *them*. You know?"

Mrs Chambers nodded. She had made no move to sit down, and so we both stood awkwardly.

"I was hoping I could talk to you about Jillian, and Alex. Especially Alex. To get an idea of what he was like, the sorts of things you might want the world to know about him, if there is anything in particular. I'd like to talk to Jillian, too—"

Mrs Chambers shook her head, suddenly full of emotion. She coughed, a wet hacking sound. Then, "No, sorry. She won't want to talk to you. I know she won't—"

"I don't want to make her," I said quickly. "I don't. Ultimately it's up to Jillian. But—"

I was interrupted by the sound of the front door as it opened and shut. There was a brief pause as Mrs Chambers looked at me, and then at the door.

"Mum?"

A woman came into the room. She was small, thin, with long blonde hair that had been dyed darker at the tips and pale skin, black smudges of makeup under both eyes like warpaint. It was the first time I had ever seen her and I was shocked by how solid she was, how strong, her movements fluid and surprisingly confident.

"Oh – hello," she said when she saw me. Her gaze flicked between her mother and me. "Sorry. I didn't realise you had company tonight." She gave me a smile and a small wave. "I'm Erin."

"My daughter," Mrs Chambers explained. Erin, *Jillian*. She'd changed her name. No wonder she'd been harder to find.

Jillian waited expectantly, and when her mother didn't introduce me I had to force myself to speak.

"I'm Harriet. I'm here to talk to your mum about a book I'm writing," I said. It came out colder than I'd intended it to, as though the effort of explaining myself had bled all of the emotion from my words. "I'm a writer."

Instantly Jillian's expression closed up. She shook her head, shooting her mother a look I recognised as panic.

"I was just about to tell your mum about the project," I forged on. "I used to be a journalist. I've interviewed the other families, but my cousins—"

"We're not interested," Jillian said.

"Your mother wanted to hear me out. I wanted to tell her that I'd found something recently – that I think they might take another look at—"

"Please, don't. *I'm* not interested. Look, Mum, you do whatever you like, and I'll see you later."

Jillian turned to leave, but just then Mrs Chambers began to cough again. She bent double, her face going very pale. Then she grasped at the shelf on the wall, knuckles going white, and leaned against it. But the shelf didn't hold, and I watched in what felt like slow motion as it came away from the wall, her mug of tea tumbling to the floor.

Mrs Chambers sagged, one hand going to her chest as she let out another strangled cough. Jillian froze. I rushed forward, grabbing Mrs Chambers' elbow as gently as I could and guiding her to the sofa.

"Mrs Chambers, I'm sorry – are you alright?"

She looked like she was having trouble breathing. I glanced around the room, noticing a pack of tissues nearby along with a blue inhaler. I reached for it, and she nodded.

She took the inhaler quickly, giving herself a few puffs before allowing herself to sink back into the cushions of the sofa. Jillian still hadn't moved. Her eyes were glassy, her jaw tense as she'd watched it all unfold.

Once Mrs Chambers had given herself a couple more puffs her cheeks began to flush pink again.

"Can I get you a drink?"

She nodded.

I left them in the lounge and headed towards the kitchen, where I fumbled through finding a glass and filling it with water. I searched the surfaces for something to mop up the spilled tea, the rhythms of helpfulness soothing the hammering of my heart.

"Uh…"

I turned around at the sound of a voice. Jillian stood in the doorway to the kitchen, her arms crossed defensively but her expression warmer now.

"Thanks," she said. "For – you know. Helping."

"It's okay."

"She's had a chest infection. She gets pretty wound up but I've never… I've never seen that happen before. I just froze."

"It's okay," I said again. I was calmer now. "No harm done. Is she alright?"

Jillian nodded. "I think so." She blew out a breath. "I'm sorry for overreacting before. I just… You've not been hanging around here recently, have you?"

A look flickered in her eyes, like fear. I shook my head.

"No. Tonight's the first time I've met your mum. I'm sorry if I caused any of this. I just wanted to talk to her. She asked me to come round."

Jillian nodded but she seemed distracted.

"I'll take the water through and then I'll go," I said.

Jillian followed me back into the lounge, where she took the tea towel I'd found to mop up the tea and laid it aside, finding instead some kitchen roll and a bottle of carpet cleaner. I gave Mrs Chambers her glass of water and she sipped at it.

"I should get going," I said. "But I would still like to talk to you when you're feeling a bit better. Is that okay?"

"Yes." Mrs Chambers nodded. "Please. I want to tell you more about Alex. I'm going away soon though, on holiday. Maybe when I get back?"

Jillian didn't look at me as I left.

Out on the street the air was cold, refreshing after the warm house. That had not gone according to plan. I was still looking for my car keys when I heard the front door open again behind me.

It was Jillian. She stepped onto the path, arms folded again. She didn't look much like the photos I'd seen of her as a child, when she'd been boyish, with her shorn hair and fine-boned, angular face, but I'd spent a long time studying all of the children and I could just about make out the resemblance: the same sharp jaw, the same eyes, clear and blue like the ocean.

"Thanks again," she said.

She glanced over my shoulder, as though she was looking

for something – or someone. But the street was dark and empty behind me, limned with gold light from the street lamps. The shadows pooled. Jillian pulled her hoodie tighter around herself.

"It's okay. Like I said."

She turned to go again.

"Jillian," I said quickly. "If you change your mind, and you want to talk to me – for the book, or just because – then here's my card. My number's on the back."

It was an old business card; it still said *journalist* on it, even though it had been a while since I'd even tried to get something published. *Insurance underwriter* didn't have the same ring to it. I held the card out to her, creased from my handbag, and she stared at it for a second before taking it.

"My name is Erin," she said. And then she went inside, closing the door swiftly behind her.

At home I flicked the kettle on. The flat was cold and sterile. I'd moved in six months ago but hadn't bothered to decorate properly.

The only thing I'd managed in the lounge was getting my photographs reframed to match the wooden shelves. My favourite picture of me and my brother Thomas sat on the mantel next to one of my cousins and my aunt and uncle taken a few months before Jem and Michael were abducted.

The thought occurred to me as I poured a small glass of wine that I could put up some fairy lights easily enough. I could make the flat feel more *me*. I could knit something new, a nice throw or a blanket, as it had been months since I'd picked up my needles. Or I could go back to karate if I wanted to get out of the house more. But lately I'd been so focused on the book that I hadn't wanted to do either.

I didn't want to write tonight, though. I knew that without talking properly to Jillian and her mother the rest of the pages would sit on my laptop gathering dust, just like they'd done five years ago, when I'd given up on it last time. Jillian had answers to questions I had been desperate to ask for a long time.

I glanced up at the photo of Thomas and me. In it we both grinned, gap-toothed and wild. He'd moved to Australia two months ago and, what with one thing and another, I'd not spoken to him properly in three weeks, just mistimed Skype calls and short, messy emails. I missed him more than I thought possible.

I sighed. I'd messaged him to tell him I was writing the book again – I knew he'd be supportive – but I hadn't told him about what I'd found, or that I'd spoken to the police. I didn't want to put too much weight behind my theory until I had more proof.

It was for the same reason I was glad I hadn't had a chance to explain myself to Jillian and her mother tonight, to tell them about my hunch. I wasn't even sure how seriously the police were taking me. I'd done my research, but in the end all I had was what little I'd found on the internet, an old newspaper article, and a vague suspicion about a decades-old crime.

My phone rang. I picked it up and set it on speaker.

"Hi, Mum."

"Hello, sweetheart. You sound tired. Are you alright?"

I smiled. "I'm fine. It's just been a long day." I'd gone straight from the office to Mrs Chambers' house, and it was only now that I realised I'd forgotten to eat dinner.

I grabbed a microwave meal from the fridge and stabbed it mercilessly while my mother talked. It was probably time I started cooking again too. I'd become lazy recently.

"You really ought to come walking with me one weekend," Mum said. "We hiked up Thorpe Cloud this time. The views are stunning. I think you'd like it. We could go to Dovedale. See the river. It would do you *good*. All that fresh air out there and you're always stuck indoors—"

"I like being indoors," I muttered. "Besides, I'm too busy."

"You've been saying that for ages." Mum sighed dramatically. "I know you work, but you've got your weekends. What are you filling them with anyway? Not that book again? You know how I feel about you bothering your aunt."

I felt myself ruffle but I refused to let her hear it. She had dealt with Michael and Jeremy's deaths in the same way she had dealt with my father's death and Thomas moving across the other side of the world: by throwing herself into her *own* life. Hiking, yoga, volunteering, the five adopted dogs she now doted on, holidays with friends and an army of boyfriends. My mother had a better social life than I did.

But writing this book had stopped being about catharsis the moment I started to suspect everybody had been wrong about Jem and Mikey. Now it was about facts.

"Yes," I said carefully. "But Auntie Sue is fine with me asking her questions. It's not like I'm the only one, and I think I've actually got something here—"

"Are you hoping to sell it?" Mum asked.

"Well, maybe? I don't know. Eventually, I hope. I'm not really doing it for the money or anything like that. It's just—"

"Because you know, sweetheart, those things are normally done on proposal, right? I'm worried that you're wasting your life on this. Why don't you set it aside like you did before? Get back into the journalism game if you want to write something. There's no deadline on this, so no hurry. You could do with spending more time with your friends too, getting yourself a job you *love*, maybe meeting somebody…"

The microwave pinged just in time to prevent me from saying something I'd regret. It didn't matter that there wasn't a deadline, that I wasn't under commission in some news office any more; there was something burning inside of me that drove me onwards, and I knew I wouldn't settle until it was done, even if that meant proving myself wrong. I'd taken a break once before and regretted it.

"I just want to finish it," I said, wishing now I'd just told her I was freelancing again. "Thomas would agree with me if I could get him to bloody well call me back. It's his fault anyway. He's always banging on about the boys. Both of you are. Is it any wonder I want to write about them?"

"Of course he'd agree with you. He always does, and he *always* likes the things you write – even those daft unicorn stories you used to tell."

I snorted despite myself. Contrary to Mum's memory, those stories had been *Thomas's* creations. I'd always been more interested in the grisly side of life. Once, when I was nine or so, Thomas bought me a book about the Whitehall murders. We hid it from my mother. I had nightmares for weeks but it didn't stop me poring through the whole thing with morbid excitement.

"Anyway," I said, "I made contact with Jillian Chambers and her mother today. I don't know how receptive they will be, especially Jillian, but I'm proud of myself for reaching out. I've been putting it off for ages."

"Don't you think you ought to leave her alone?" She said this gently, as though she thought I was pestering.

"I can't, Mum. It's important. And honestly, she seemed a bit spooked tonight. I actually just want to make sure that she's okay."

This was the truth. I *was* worried about her. Because Jillian Chambers had been afraid of something.

FOUR

4 NOVEMBER 2016

Harriet

A FEW DAYS LATER I called in sick at work. The sun was barely even up, the treetops sprinkled with bluish gold light as I climbed into my car, the windshield spidered with a patina of frost. I couldn't stop thinking about the book, my hunch, about Jillian's strange question about me hanging around, how unsettled she'd seemed. I hadn't slept properly in three nights.

I thought about the little I knew about Jillian. While drafting the early parts of the book I'd returned again and again to her and her brother, Alex. The survivor, and the last victim. All the information I had dried up after her abduction and then escape in 1998, even though it was in the news and in the press often enough. The original investigation had been huge – I remembered it vividly. Searches, information appeals, Crimestoppers and police interviews. It eclipsed everything, and like the disappearance of Madeleine McCann, people had never stopped talking about it.

Jillian and Alex had vanished eighteen years ago, stolen from their beds just like my cousins, and eight other children. By the time Jillian was found she had been missing for over two weeks. And when she turned up with a concussion, a badly sprained ankle and cuts on her feet, and a severe case of hypothermia, but somehow miraculously alive, she had no idea what had happened to her brother, or how she'd managed to get away from her captor. She didn't know where she was, or where she'd been held, and couldn't remember anything that had happened to her.

Since then, she had remained hidden from the public eye. She had never been interviewed by the press, so the information I had was limited to second-hand sources. When I was younger, I had been frustrated by this, the way she'd disappeared without giving any of us the answers we craved. But obviously it wasn't that simple. She had been a child, scared and hurt, her memory either gone or locked up tight. Now I was frustrated by the journalists; I was angry about the newspaper and magazine articles that weren't about the murdered and missing children but which instead gave space and time to *him*. The lure of the unknown, the unknowable.

The Father – as the press had named him – had abducted twelve children between 1994 and 1998, starting with my cousins. He took siblings, always in pairs, often boys but not always, right from their beds while their parents slept peacefully down the hall. The abductions happened in the summer or early autumn. The children always shared a bedroom, disappearing like ghosts out of their window, as if Peter Pan had reached in and taken them. They never seemed to have put up a fight. Those that were found had been injected with insulin, their deaths quick, and they were always wearing new pyjamas.

Jillian Chambers was the only person who could tell the truth about what happened – and she couldn't remember it. I realised now how hard this must have been. To cope she seemed to have done her best to disappear from the world, to become as little like that angular, boyish-looking girl she had been as possible. To vanish, just like her brother.

Even now the thought of what had happened to Alex Chambers filled me with dreadful fascination. The same as it always had whenever the Father took another pair of siblings while I was growing up. Thomas and I hadn't really been aware of the details, but it was hard not to notice the way parents at school did that apologetic sidestep whenever they saw my mum and dad, the way people looked at my aunt and uncle if we went out for Sunday lunch and they were recognised.

My aunt and uncle had been lucky – if you could call it that – to be able to bury both of their sons. Some of the children who were taken were never found. Auntie Sue always held a little prayer circle in her garden when another pair of siblings were taken.

The abduction I remembered most vividly was during the summer of 1997. Charlotte and Hazel Davies had been abducted on 2 August, not six weeks after Morgan Bailey's body was discovered in a shallow grave in a park in Leicester. She'd been missing for eleven months.

I was seven years old. It was the first time I was really aware of what was happening. The news of the girls' disappearance, the lack of new police leads, made headlines right up until Princess Diana's tragic death later that month. Afterwards too. More children missing, more children gone.

My aunt held a prayer circle a few days after the girls were taken. She made hot tea and baked a sponge cake for her church congregation and we all ate and drank solemnly in the garden, wilting under the sun while praying for the girls' recovery. For their bodies to be found, at least, so their family could bury them.

I'll never forget the hot, itchy material of my dress, sweat on my back, how Thomas and I had been planning to play in Sue and Greg's fountain to cool off but our parents had stopped us. We needed to be serious for a while. We had both sulked, refusing to say *amen* to my aunt's prayers because we still didn't really understand, then, what it all meant.

Foolishly – and just for a moment each time – over the months that followed I would often be plagued with fear over whether mine and Thomas's sulks had been the reason neither Charlotte nor Hazel were ever found. Even though I knew that was ridiculous, the thought still bothered me from time to time.

I'd been thinking about it again when my phone rang at eight o'clock this morning. It was Molly Evans. I felt a surge of excitement at seeing her name, already contemplating the possibility of an excuse to miss work at some point.

"Hello, Harriet love." Molly's voice still sounded exactly the same, even after five years. She spoke so quickly it was hard to keep up. "I'm sorry to call out of the blue, and so early. I was thinking about you last night, and that book of yours. I just wondered… are you still working on it?"

"Yes," I blurted quickly. "Actually, I am. In fact, I was going to give you a call. I have a few more questions."

"Oh that's good. That's really good. I'd love to talk some more. Well, I'm actually calling this morning because – I had this thought last night. There's going to be a memorial at the weekend. I know your aunt and uncle don't usually bother but I wondered if you might want to come?"

"I—"

"And then I thought, well why don't you invite her round to tea? So that's why I'm *really* ringing. Do you want to pop round sometime? I can give you the details of the memorial if you're free this week… And I can answer your questions, too, two birds one stone and all that. Oh and I have some more lovely pictures of the twins."

"That would be great," I said earnestly. I checked my watch. It still wasn't too late to claim I wasn't feeling well and get out of the whole day of work. I wasn't the only one who'd ever taken a sneaky Friday off, after all. "Is this afternoon too soon?"

As I pulled up to the small semi-detached house in Sheffield I'd last visited over five years ago, I had the feeling that very little had changed. The same lace curtains hung at the window, the same weedy plants grew in a garden that had gone bare for the winter. Even me. I glanced down and realised that

I was probably wearing the same sort of outfit. The same black jeans, winter boots, plain button-down jacket.

Molly Evans was the mother of George and Jacob, the children who were taken in June 1995, just a year after Mikey and Jem. Molly had always been the most ardent supporter of my book.

The doorbell was old and made a squeaking sound as the metal pressed inwards. It was the same one they'd had last time I was here. Back then I'd come to find out the details you don't get from the kinds of newspaper articles that circulated after the children were abducted. I came to ask the questions I didn't want to ask my aunt. I'd expected resistance, but Molly was a talker.

She was the one who had first told me how the Father got his name.

"A writer in the newspapers gave it to him," she'd said, a pained look on her face, "because he looked after our children. He clothed them, fed them, brushed their hair, made them clean their teeth. He kept Morgan Bailey for almost a year, you know, before he killed her. We don't know what he did with them, all that time. But he looked after them."

I still shuddered at the thought, that somebody could masquerade as a parent like he had.

Molly answered the door. She was in her fifties, with a head of dyed black hair that was almost blue and a nose so hooked it made her look like a witch.

"Hello—"

"Harriet!" she exclaimed. "It's been so long. I'm happy to see you. Come in, come in." She welcomed me inwards, wafting her arms ineffectually as though she wasn't sure whether she wanted to pet me or give me a hug. "So, you're still writing about our babies?"

She acted as if months had passed since my initial interviews, not years. I felt my face flush in embarrassment. Molly led me into the lounge, where a large TV was playing a muted sports channel. A small dog yapped at my legs – a different one than I remembered, but no less irritatingly cute.

"I'm sorry," I said. "Things have been... Well, it's more difficult to write about than I thought. What with graduating and working and then... I recently changed jobs again. But I started writing again recently. I think I've found some new information. Has anybody been in touch with you yet?"

"No, I'm so sorry, my love, but I expect they'll come and chat with us in due course. I'm glad you haven't given up on us. Would you like a cup of tea? Andy – Andy! I forgot to tell you, but come and see who's here."

Molly bustled off and poked her head through to the kitchen. When she returned it was with her husband, who was distinctly less pleased by my appearance. Andrew Evans had aged faster than his wife. The skin around his neck had started to sag, and his cheeks were gaunt, as though he didn't eat enough and exercised too much.

"It's Harriet," Molly said. "You remember. The *journalist cousin*. She's back onto writing that book about Jake and Georgie, aren't you, love?"

"Yes, I—"

"Nice to see you again," Andy muttered.

His wife continued to bustle, straightening things that didn't need straightening, and eventually disappeared to make that cup of tea. Mr Evans sank onto the sofa and a haunted look passed across his face.

"We told you everything we remember about what happened," he said slowly.

"I know." I smiled my best reassuring smile. "But when your wife called I thought it would be good to have another chat. I really want to get this book right, and do George and Jacob proud."

I sat on the sofa near Andy and waited quietly for his wife to come back.

When she did it was with a tray bearing three large mugs filled to the brim with steaming, strong tea.

"So, love, you said on the phone that you had some more questions."

"Yes. I've written a lot more. But it's been so long since my original interviews that I should talk to everybody again. In case there was anything else you want me to add. Anything we didn't talk about before."

Andy let out a small sound, like a deflating balloon, but his wife just nodded.

"Like what?" she asked. I suddenly realised I didn't know what else I wanted to ask. Except...

"Like... Jillian Chambers," I said slowly. "I'm going to try to talk to her."

"Jilly." Molly's mug slipped and tea sloshed onto her harems. "Poor girl."

"She's a bit reluctant at the moment."

"Well I should think so," Andy said. "She went through a lot. More than any child should. I'm not surprised she doesn't want to go over and over it with strangers."

"Do you know her well?" I asked, trying to hide the heat in my cheeks.

"We used to know her, but not well," Molly said. "They'd never come out to us in Sheffield – we only ever saw them when everybody got together." Molly set aside her tea and reached for the little dog as he darted between her legs. She lifted him onto her lap and rocked him like a child. "We all— Do you remember I told you about the group we started?"

"The therapy?" My aunt and uncle had mentioned it as well, but they'd never been. They preferred to spend their reflective time in church.

"Yes. We still meet sometimes. Less often now, but if there's an anniversary or if there's some kind of milestone… It's not easy to get everybody together since we're all spread out and people have their own lives, of course. But it's nice to have somebody to talk to. Jillian and Alex's mother came with her husband to a few different sessions – oh, years ago. Right in the beginning. But… well, things got a bit heated. Not naming any names, but a few folks didn't like, uh… they didn't feel comfortable sharing their loss because they felt like it was different for Amanda and her husband…"

"Because of *Jillian*?" I asked, unable to stop the incredulity in my voice. "You mean because she survived?"

Jillian had shut down, refused to talk about her brother's

disappearance, but who could blame her? The thought that she'd been ostracised from a group that might have helped her to cope simply because her mother and father hadn't lost as much as the other parents… God.

I wasn't entirely surprised, though. Some of the parents were – well, they were hard work. Andrea Davies had been hostile with me at first, and I wouldn't have put it past her to behave badly without considering how her actions might hurt a little girl, and Randeep and Jaswinder's father could come across very judgemental when he felt threatened.

"Well, when you put it like that," Andy said. "Sounds awful."

"It *was* awful." Molly glared at her husband. "After that we kept in touch, but Amanda never came back to the group. She hardly even goes to the services unless they're down in Burton or Derby. Jillian never came back either. Maybe you could mention the memorial…? I'd love it if Amanda or Jillian felt like coming along."

"How could they treat her so horribly?" I asked, my brain still caught on what she had said about the other parents.

Some of the families hadn't been able to bury one, or both, of their children, but I couldn't believe that they would push out the Chambers when they needed help. We were all in the same boat, surely? Poor Jillian might never have been able to really talk about what happened to her with people who understood; perhaps that was why she'd been reluctant to talk to me.

"I think…" Molly sighed. The dog wriggled and she put him down. "I think they felt like their loss was more *righteous*. It's partly why we stopped going to the meetings as often. I'm sure that's why your aunt and uncle don't go. There are some people there who were martyred by a lack of knowledge—"

"Because their children weren't found?"

"Exactly. And they think they suffered worse than the rest of us. As though burying the empty coffin of one child isn't as bad as both. Did they think I wanted to bury one of my children and not the other? Aren't we *all* suffering?" Molly blinked back tears.

"We don't want to suffer any more." Andy's voice was thick. He stared blankly at the silent TV screen. "We want to *live*. To stop thinking about all that pain, all that anger he caused."

"I know," I said quietly. "That's why I need to write this book. So the world remembers the children instead of him. That's why I want to talk to Jillian."

AFTER

Mouse

THEY CREMATED HIS BROTHER. The boy sat on the front row of a small, empty crematorium with Mother but they didn't touch.

The coffin was tiny, wooden and polished. The boy wanted to touch it, to see if the wood was cool against his skin. Like Chris had been.

He wondered how hot the flames would get. It was the kind of question he would have asked if they'd been at the house. The sort of question his father would have answered.

He resented the man at the front of the room who was talking about sadness. As if he knew what they were feeling.

The boy was surprised by how little he missed his brother. Maybe it hadn't sunk in yet. Maybe they would get home and he'd be sorry that he was on his own now. He wasn't sure. He didn't really understand how it was all supposed to work.

He shifted in his seat. His stomach rumbled uncomfortably. Mother tensed slightly as though she wanted to swat him but she didn't move. Didn't touch him.

After it was done they all filed out of the crematorium and into the snow. It was still freezing, the sky a solid block of grey. The few mourners stood together for a minute or two and he stood with them while Mother spoke in hushed tones to a man he didn't recognise.

The boy waited patiently as one of them pinched his cheek. Another one patted his head. Mother saw this and smiled hollowly, grief painting dark circles under her eyes. She came over to join them, shaking hands with the cheek-pincher.

Then everybody was gone and it was just him and Mother again, snow creeping around their ankles. He knew there would be a long ride home in their rusty old car and then dinner at the big table with only the two of them.

He wondered if she might notice him more now.

FIVE

Harriet

I'D BEEN CHECKING MY phone all day, hoping Jillian might decide to call me. I'd played our conversation over in my mind, wondering if she'd think it was my fault that her mother had collapsed. Talking to Molly today had made the guilt worse, and I wanted to apologise.

Searching for *Erin* Chambers – which, I reminded myself, was her name now – I'd managed to figure out that she worked for a marketing company in Burton, in an office block not far from town. She was credited with the revamp of their website, and it looked like she was good at her job.

The address of the office wasn't far out of my way. In fact, I reasoned, by the time I'd made the hour and a half journey from Sheffield to Arkney to get home, going a bit further south to Burton, just to check on her, wouldn't take long. I didn't want to freak her out, but I had no other way of getting in touch without bothering her mother and it seemed like the office might be the most neutral territory I would find. I'd rather have to apologise for scaring her than spend the evening worrying whether she was alright.

By the time I got there it was just starting to get dark, the evening developing that smoke-tinged quality of blueness and the shadowed trees dancing against the sky. I sat in my car, holding a cigarette between my fingers but not smoking it. Daring myself to drive away and forget this whole thing. She'd phone me if she wanted to talk, wouldn't she?

But then, there she was. And I still hadn't driven away. She looked pale, drawn. She buttoned her coat up tight, glancing nervously down the street before heading right towards the car park where I waited. Rather than let her get close enough to scare, I made sure I wasn't subtle, slamming my car door and waving at her.

"Jillian?" I called.

She frowned, stopping in front of a car.

"What are you doing here?" she asked.

"I'm sorry for just turning up," I said. "I wanted to apologise for the other night. I know it must have been really jarring, and it's not how I wanted to meet you. I've left a message for your mum too. I didn't mean to upset her and I hope she's alright." *And I'm worried about you.* I had to stop the words before they tumbled out, too.

Jillian didn't move, but her stance softened.

"Okay, apology accepted," she said.

We stood together, still and silent. I tried to work out why that hadn't made me feel any better. Jillian was still wary, like a cat, but there was something warm between us. I tried to grasp it.

"Do you think you would talk to me?" I prompted. "About what happened to you?"

"Why?"

The word was heavy. But she didn't turn away, and I wondered if she was hoping I'd ask her again.

"I know you probably just think I'm some sort of leech. But I'm not in this for the money. My cousins – they were abducted by him, too. I've spoken to everybody else, Jillian. *Erin*, you're the last one." I ignored the embarrassed heat in my cheeks and held her gaze.

"My name is Erin. And what makes you think I care?" Her eyes glittered with a kind of quiet steel that made her beautiful, and I thought of what my mother had said. Was I only doing this because it made me feel better, or could it help her too? Was my new information worth dragging up the past?

"Don't you want your voice to be heard?" I asked.

She laughed. "My voice? Since when has anybody listened to my voice?"

"I want to hear you," I said. "I know you don't know me, but I'm not trying to upset you. I'm trying to help."

Jillian – Erin – levelled her gaze at me.

She was still unsettled, her eyes flicking to the bare space behind me every few seconds. She shivered in the chill of the evening.

"What do you want from me?"

"There's a memorial," I said. "This weekend. I'm going to

go and I wondered if you might want to come with me. We can talk, or not, that's up to you. But I wanted to offer, just in case you're *ready* to talk to somebody. I don't know exactly what you've been through, but I'm a good listener."

Erin took a short, sharp breath. Her cheeks were pink, her blue eyes icy in the gathering dark.

"Tell me the details," she said. "Then I'll decide."

SIX

4 NOVEMBER 2016

Erin

APPREHENSION FIZZED IN MY belly as I drove home. I'd been fine until Harriet Murphy showed up, so why did I need to talk to her now? I'd forgotten how much I hated being *Jillian Chambers*.

I swerved out of a roundabout. It was dark now. Even the shadows seemed to have shadows. I let my thoughts sizzle and pop, because maybe my annoyance that Harriet had turned up uninvited − at my office of all places − would override something else. Something deeper.

Fear.

The fear I'd felt for days, that unsettled feeling that had started before Halloween. Mum wouldn't be much use if I told her; she saw Alex − boys and men that looked like him, anyway − at least ten times a year, in supermarkets and banks. She was always on the phone to Wendy, the liaison officer we shared, about one thing or another. But this wasn't like that. I didn't know what it was, but for the first time in years I was jumping at my own shadow.

There had been a time, in the early days after I first came home, where everything frightened me. The dark, the shadows that bright lights cast, candles and fire and thunderstorms. I was frightened to pet dogs in case they barked and I jumped, frightened to watch TV shows with even the most cartoonish of villains. But eventually that wore off, the edges dulled and I could manage it. I learned to channel the fear, started making candles and listening to rain-sound playlists like white noise. When year after year followed with no new abductions, no mention of the Father, I convinced myself finally that I was safe. He was gone.

Then there came a day where I had a realisation, like the cementing of an idea that had been growing for some time. He was dead. He must be. I could never explain the certainty I felt, waking up one morning and realising I had slept without nightmares, realising I hadn't thought about Alex in a few days without flinching. It had been like an awakening. The Father must be dead because it was as if the spell he had cast was broken.

Now it felt like going backwards, like that old fear rising again. Even though there was no reason why it should. I was jumping at loud noises, feeling the hairs prickle on the back of my neck every time a stranger walked too quickly, or laughed in the street. And I hated myself for it.

Maybe I was working too hard. I'd been doing a lot of overtime on a website design for a new client, long days and not enough exercise. Except I didn't *feel* overworked. I liked my job, liked the control I had when I was designing and the pride over finished projects.

No, this fear had nothing to do with being overworked or tired. It was something else. Like a shadow following me wherever I went. Could Harriet Murphy help? I didn't want to talk to her about Alex, about me. I didn't want to be interviewed for her book. But there was nobody else I could turn to. My colleagues didn't even know I'd had a brother, never mind that he was dead, and none of my friends these days knew the truth. They didn't know who I really was. I kept a firm line between my social life and my mother, wary that one day she might accidentally tell them more than I wanted them to know – a line I'd drawn as a teenager and never really allowed to lapse. For the most part it worked, helped me to stay 'normal', allowed me to be like everybody else. But now I realised I didn't have anybody to talk to.

Except Harriet.

Maybe it was time to face the questions I'd avoided since I was a child. Maybe Harriet would have the answers. And she wasn't like the others; she wasn't police, but she wasn't really press either. She was sort of… calming. I thought back to the way she'd reacted when Mum had her asthma attack the other night. How confident she'd been. How I'd frozen. Alex – he wouldn't have stumbled like that. I pushed down the guilt.

The truth was, there were a lot of things that I didn't know, and maybe Harriet could help. I remembered the night we were taken only in smudged shadows of memory. First: Alex and me, together, huddled somewhere in the dark. Red and grey and fear. Then, only me. Darkness and cold. And then a jogger in the weak morning sunlight, calling an ambulance as

I collapsed. There was nothing in between. No memory of the weeks I had been gone, or what had happened to my brother, how I'd come to be without him.

I often thought about it. What had happened? We'd been together, and then we weren't. I must have made him angry – the man who took us. Alex couldn't have, he wasn't like that, but I could have. Maybe I'd cried, or maybe I'd screamed too loudly. I'd thought about it hundreds, thousands of times, but the problem was I just couldn't come up with a theory that stuck. Nothing felt right. Like the truth was fighting away my feeble attempts at an answer, while remaining steadfastly hidden.

Whatever had happened, it felt, now, like I'd spent my life running from it all, but it hadn't seemed that way before. Before it had simply been about moving on, getting over it, learning how to be myself without Alex. But perhaps that's why I was feeling so unsettled. Perhaps Harriet could help me to make sense of my imagination, the feeling that wherever I went somebody was watching me.

I pulled up outside my house and counted to ten. I'd sleep on it before I agreed to anything. I wasn't going to let some random writer with a pretty face overturn all the decisions I'd made since I was a kid – not without thinking it over first.

I got out of my car, the night misting with my warm breath. Within seconds I noticed that something wasn't right. My neck prickled.

My bedroom window was open.

I rarely slept with my window open. I usually tried for an hour or two when it got unbearably warm in the summer, but the paranoia, that horrible feeling like spiders on my skin, flared up before long. *Unsafe*. Open windows and unlocked doors were unsafe. If I opened any windows, while I was cleaning or if the day was warm, I always shut them soon after. I thought back to last night. Had I opened the window without thinking? Forgotten to close it? What about this morning? My blood hummed. Something wasn't right. I wouldn't have forgotten.

It had to be Mum. She had a key and a habit of stopping by with bits she'd picked up at the supermarket, but she'd never opened the window before – and her thoughts on safety were similar to mine. Besides, she should be on her way to Skegness now, not taking time out of her holiday to check on me. And why would she have opened my window in November anyway?

My stomach clenched and my hands balled involuntarily.

The door was still locked. Maybe Mum had turned the heating up and then made herself too warm? Maybe she'd had a headache and needed a lie down with some fresh air? I knew I was grasping at straws but the reasoning helped me to stay calm.

Inside, the house was cold, the heating off and the lights untouched. I inched inside. I heard the door creak behind me and the hairs on my arms stood to attention. But it was just the wind.

If it wasn't Mum who had been inside, it must have been somebody else. A burglary or something. Anger started to override the fear in my gut as I looked at my house with new eyes. The TV in the lounge was still there, but it was an old bulky thing. I didn't have much else worth stealing except a bit of cash and jewellery, and my laptop in my bedroom…

I crept up the stairs, frightened by the sound of my footsteps on the worn carpets. As I reached the upstairs hallway I realised that I should just call the police. It was their job to check if stuff was missing – or at least help me do it. If I'd been burgled then somebody could still be inside my house. But, I reassured myself hollowly, everything looked normal. The bathroom was empty, so was the spare room. Everything exactly as I'd left it. Except it was cold in here, freezing.

Somebody had been in my house.

Icy panic swallowed all of my logic and reason. I reached for my mobile phone.

"Nothing's missing?"

The policeman who had been tromping around my home while I searched it wore a friendly expression on his young, clean-shaven face. He'd been nothing but kind, polite and business-like but his words nettled me. As if I was wasting his time. His partner was outside, checking the perimeter of the house.

"No, it doesn't look like it." I'd ticked off all of the obvious stuff. TV, laptop, cash, jewellery, all where I left them. "I mean, nothing obvious anyway. Maybe he was startled."

"It's possible. Neighbourhood like this, all the houses pretty close together, it's easy to spook a thief."

I nodded, absently rubbing my hands over my arms, my skin prickling. The police officer had had a good look around inside, too, checking windows and door jambs. He'd looked

64

for fingerprints, but I knew most of the ones he'd found were mine, smears of lotion after a shower or sticky with dust from where I'd been cleaning and needed to breathe fresh air.

"So, what happens now?" I asked hesitantly.

We were in the lounge, and the police officer had just finished making a few more notes. He looked up and gave me a reassuring smile.

"House-to-house enquiries," he said, indulging me. "Check with the neighbours, see if they heard or saw anything. I'll leave you my details and you can get in touch if you find anything is missing later. Smaller things, especially, aren't always obvious right away. Check your electronics again, that sort of thing. Officers from the Burglary Unit will take over from there."

I nodded again. I felt stupid.

"I'm sorry," I said. "I really thought… Thank you for coming."

I watched out of the window as the officer talked with his partner out on the drive before they both climbed into a car. Once they were gone I made myself a shaky cup of tea in the kitchen. It was late, and I stood drinking it beside the kettle, body still too tense to move. I sighed as the warmth thawed my limbs, glad I'd turned the heating right up to push out the icy night air.

Finally I headed upstairs. I was bone tired, my whole body aching with the exhaustion after all that adrenaline. I couldn't help myself, peering into each room as I passed it. Bathroom, spare bedroom, even the airing cupboard, before I finally came to my own bedroom. I'd thrown stuff around a bit as I searched for the jewellery I knew was there, but since I hardly ever wore any I'd made a bit of a mess trying to find it.

I didn't want to stay here tonight, I realised. It felt like my privacy had been invaded, even if that wasn't true. Even if I was imagining it. I should probably just grab some stuff and go and stay at Mum's. I didn't fancy sleeping in my old bedroom, but her sofa was comfortable enough. I'd just chuck some stuff in a bag and I could leave.

But coming into the bedroom now I was struck by something. Something I hadn't noticed earlier because I was looking for what wasn't there that should be, not something that *was* there and hadn't been before.

There was a child's doll sitting on the bed, her dress pooling in her lap, her glossy curls a little bit wild. I frowned. Something about it was familiar but I couldn't place it. Where had it come from?

I was too tired to question it. Too tired to do more than quickly grab a clean top and some underwear, my hairbrush and my phone charger, and then hurry out to my car. I'd call my mum from the road.

I hardly slept. Curled up on Mum's sofa with the lights on all night, candles burning on all surfaces, it felt like I was inside a shrine. The candles made me feel like I was safe, somehow, the flames a mark of warmth. I'd made some of them from scratch for Mum over the last few years. She liked to save them, like ornaments, but I lit them all, even despite the migraine that made my vision swim. Making candles was one of my favourite things to do; the balance of scents, the way the wax looked as it softened. I let the TV trip from episode to episode of one mindless show after the other because I couldn't sleep but I didn't want to think either.

The following morning I received a visit from Wendy. She'd been with us since Jane got promoted a few years ago, but it was clear she didn't intend to stay a liaison officer forever either. I'd hoped she wouldn't call today, but in the end I realised that had never been an option.

My head was splitting from the after-buzz of the migraine and it felt like a hangover.

"Erin, are you alright?" Wendy asked before she'd even got in the door. She shrugged off her coat and headed straight for the kitchen to make tea, like always. I followed with a barely repressed sigh. I just wanted to be left alone.

"I'm fine," I said firmly, convincing myself. "My head is killing me but what else is new. I hate migraines. Look, I think I made a mountain out of a mole hill, but I'm okay now."

It didn't sound like I believed what I was saying, but I was determined to try. I wasn't Jillian, and I wasn't going to let myself get freaked out over this. Erin was *fine*.

Wendy turned, halfway through opening the teabags.

"Well, I'm glad your mum called me even if you didn't," she said. "She kept going on about how she should come home, forget the holiday. I told her to stay where she was and that I'd stop in."

I leaned in the doorway.

"Thanks. Honestly. Her coming home early would be the worst thing for her. And for me. She's been on about that holiday—"

"For ages." Wendy handed me a cup of tea in Mum's favourite mug. "I know. That's why I told her to stay. I'd have driven over to Skeggy to see her today but they've got me running through some blurry old CCTV bus station footage so I've not really got time. I said I'd pop round here though, make sure you were okay…" She gave me a look that wrinkled her nose so the dark freckles danced on her pale brown skin.

"I swear I'm alright." I held up my fingers in a Scout's honour sign. "The officers last night were great. Nothing was broken, not even the window, and whoever did it was long gone before I got there. I'm *fine*."

We headed back into Mum's lounge and I turned the TV off.

"And you haven't noticed anything strange recently?" Wendy asked. "Anybody hanging around? None of those true crime nuts, or anything like that? You know you can talk to me."

Truth be told, I'd been avoiding Wendy for a while. She was younger than me by a year or so, and had been a fresh recruit when she was first assigned to my case. It felt like she was always trying to make up for that – she was too friendly, too *much*, always ON all of the time.

I didn't need a friend.

"Why wouldn't I have told you?" I asked.

"People get embarrassed, think they're wasting time, but anybody that's been following you or bothering you is worth mentioning."

I shook my head. "No. Not even journalists this year, which is great. Well, aside from one but she's totally harmless. After last time – people finding out, you know, me moving here, I thought it might be harder to hide. But so far they've left me alone. Which is good because I like this job and I like my house even more." The last time somebody found out who I was, that I was *little Jilly Chambers*, it was a co-worker. They wouldn't let it drop. They asked me questions – inappropriate questions – and got angry when I wouldn't answer them. They threatened to write a blog and tell everybody in the office who I was.

I had a meltdown, properly freaked out because they wouldn't stop texting and calling me. They'd created this whole forum dedicated to the Father's crimes and they sent me photographs from the newspapers, photos I had never wanted to see. That was why I'd moved house, changed jobs. It was why I didn't really have any friends any more, and nothing like that had happened since.

Wendy's expression said she wasn't convinced by my *I'm totally fine* routine. I sighed.

"Alright, I *have* been feeling creeped out recently," I said. "A bit on edge. But I thought that was just me."

"Creeped out?"

"Yeah. Like, I've had this weird feeling the last few days that somebody is following me, but whenever I check there's nobody there. But – you know what it's like. Mum gets all sorts of paranoid around this time of year, seeing Alex everywhere, and I thought it was just rubbing off on me."

"Yeah, I get that." Wendy had wrinkled her nose again at the mention of my mum. She always made out that she was just as impatient with her as I was, as if she wanted to be my friend, but I never knew how much was an act and how much Mum's over-the-top personality genuinely annoyed her. "But it was definitely just a feeling, yeah?"

I paused. Had she noticed something I hadn't realised I was doing, a tic or a flinch that betrayed the fact that I hadn't told her everything? I stopped pulling at the threads on my jeans.

"There *was* something else. Something I found in the house when I was packing some stuff to come here. I went into my bedroom and, on the bed, there was a toy…" I shrugged, feeling weird now I said it out loud. There must be a plausible explanation, right? "A doll. Just sat there, you know?"

"Are you sure it's not one of your old toys?" Wendy asked.

"Well, no. I'm not sure," I admitted. "It doesn't look like mine but it's… I dunno, it's familiar. Like I've definitely seen it before."

"Maybe your mum left it for you? You told me last time I saw you that she'd been clearing out a lot of old stuff. Maybe she found it and thought you'd like it. And it only unsettled you last night because you were already upset."

Wendy didn't seem afraid, and that helped to settle the worry inside me. This was stupid. Imaginary people bringing dolls into my house…

"Yeah, you're right," I said, relief making my whole body relax. "That makes sense. She did say she'd been doing that. She probably left it before she went on holiday. She maybe even left the window open herself, you know. An accident or something."

I felt like such an idiot. But I wouldn't let myself make a big deal out of it.

"We all make mistakes. Are you sure you're okay?" Wendy gestured, and suddenly I realised she'd seen the candles, lined up like a dormant army on the mantlepiece. "Do you want to talk about any of it?" She put her tea down on the table and leaned in. "I mean – the police coming to your house. Did that conjure any memories?"

"About…?"

"About Alex, and what happened?"

"Do we have to go over this again?" I rubbed my hands over my face. "I'm not going to remember anything new."

But maybe Wendy was right. Maybe that's why I'd been so spooked about the doll. The police had unsettled me, all those echoes from my childhood. I should have known she'd find a way to talk about it, though. After all, that was literally her job. How would I ever be able to move on when there was always this to come back to?

"It might help to go over things again," Wendy suggested. "See if last night shook anything loose. It does happen sometimes."

This was the routine I hated: sympathy, questioning, *remembering*. Always the same.

"Okay. Well, obviously we were taken in the middle of October so it's a similar time of year now, which probably explains why I freaked out. Except it's colder this year…" I let the memories come to me slowly. Half of the things I remembered had been examined so many times, by experts and myself as well, that I wasn't sure what was true any more.

"We went to the park after school the day it happened. Played out for hours. I remember falling from the climbing

71

frame and biting my lip. It bled and Alex came to help me. Or maybe – maybe that happened before. Anyway, we played for ages."

"Where was your mum?"

"She was there for a while, then she sat in the car for a bit, where she could see us."

"And later on, after you went to bed?"

We shared a bedroom, with bunk beds. Alex wanted his own bedroom but Mum insisted that we share until we were old enough. Which meant that until *I* was old enough to look after myself, Alex was stuck with me.

I remembered being put to bed that night, the darkness of the room, the cool air snaking through the open window. We knew we weren't supposed to open it, because of bad things that had happened to other children, but it had been too hot that night, the heating on for too long or the night unseasonably warm. And bad things only ever happened to other people. I remembered the curtains trembling like leaves, and the faint sound of something soft, a thud against the wall, a rustle like somebody opening a bin-liner. The faint smell of rubber.

"There was a smell."

"A smell?" Wendy asked. I jolted back to myself.

"Yeah, uh, I don't know what. Like – rubber gloves? Like the kind dentists wear. Not strong."

"I don't think you ever mentioned that before."

I felt my heart stutter in my chest.

"What?"

"The smell. You've never told me about a smell." Wendy

was one step away from gleeful. Like this was part of some big puzzle for her.

"I don't know." I shook my head. "Maybe I'm making it up. I probably told Jane about it. I just know it was dark, and confusing, and I woke up at one point – and then I was so tired again." I felt myself getting defensive, fists clenching.

Wendy leaned over and laid a hand on my knee. She'd done this before, and I hated it, but I didn't move. Instead I said something to distract her.

"I broke up with Monica," I blurted. "Or she broke up with me. I don't know. I'm just a bit of a mess. Can we call it a day, please? I'm tired of going over this stuff, and I have a headache."

Wendy pulled back, sympathy morphing her face.

"Sure," she said. "That's fine. We can talk again some other time when you've had chance to process. I've no doubt the police will be in touch soon about last night anyway."

I nodded, but I wasn't thinking about that. I was thinking about how I needed to talk to somebody else. Somebody who wouldn't try to be my friend.

I needed to speak to Harriet Murphy.

SEVEN

5 NOVEMBER 2016

Harriet

THE MOON WAS JUST rising when I pulled into the car park of a pub in Arkney town centre. It wasn't a place I'd been to before but I'd driven past it enough times, and it was somewhere between Jillian's house and mine — how funny, I thought, that we'd ended up living in the same town. This place was a chain pub; although it was quaint from the outside, perfectly matching the surrounding area with its uneven beige stone walls and peaked roof, inside it was inconspicuous and busy, gaudy carpets and beer stains and all.

I'd been surprised when Jillian called me this afternoon. She'd sounded tightly wound. I was meant to be having dinner with Mum tonight but I couldn't ignore the desperation in her voice. The memorial was tomorrow, but clearly whatever Jillian wanted to talk about couldn't wait.

The pub was crowded, as I'd thought it might be, filled with young families, the children running around bundled in hats and scarves to ward off the chill night air. Out back I heard the fizz and pop of distant Bonfire Night fireworks.

I headed for the bar, ordered myself a large soda and lime. Then I turned to survey the tables and booths, feeling nervous again.

Jillian – *Erin* – was already here. I spotted her almost immediately, tucked away in a corner booth and boring holes right into my skull. I took another sip and then headed to her table.

She looked tired. Nervous. Her blonde hair was plaited back from her pale face, and her dark eyeliner was bolder than I'd seen it before, perhaps to distract from the circles under her eyes.

"Erin," I said, forcing myself to use her name. She wasn't Jillian any more. "Sorry I'm late."

"You took your time," she said by way of greeting, but she gave me a shaky smile.

I climbed into the booth. Our knees knocked together and I spilled my drink, a puddle forming in the centre of the table.

"Shit," I said, wiping the spill. "I'm sorry. I came as soon as I could."

"Yeah, well… Thanks. I know it was last-minute."

We looked at each other. Erin's eyes were startlingly blue but hooded, as though she wasn't giving me her full attention. I took a deep breath.

"What happened?"

Erin bristled.

"I don't mean to pry. It's just… on the phone you sounded a bit shaken up."

"I don't really want to talk about it yet." Erin shrugged.

She sipped at her own drink – it looked like Coke, maybe rum or whisky too, though she was probably driving – and held her hands tightly around the glass as though she was trying to stop them from trembling. "You said you wanted to talk to me about this book you're writing. Well, go on then."

I shook my head. "Look, let me be honest first. I'm not a journalist. I'm not even really a writer. I haven't got a contract or a publishing deal. I have a day job, I work in insurance – somehow they've not fired me yet. I *am* dedicated to this book, though. It's important to me. I just wanted to throw that out there before we got into anything. But... off the record, I do want to ask – is something going on?"

Erin didn't reply, but she didn't flinch away from me either.

"Alright," I said. "You obviously don't have to talk to me, but I think this will work better if we're both honest with each other. You invited me here."

She didn't answer. I regrouped. "The book..."

"Yes?"

"It's meant to be, well..." I'd been working on my pitch for this project, honing it so that I could explain it again to the parents I had plans to re-interview, but at the sight of Erin's faintly hopeful face my words got jumbled. "It's about you. Them."

"Them?" Erin shifted. Mechanical. "The... children. Alex?"

"Alex, too." I nodded. "It's meant to be this... sort of a celebration of life. Like, aren't you sick of the world only seeing the man who hurt your family? I want to write about their lives, not just their deaths. I want this book to show the world who they all were. And who you were, and *are*."

I could see that Erin knew what I meant. I didn't have to explain to her about the countless lists on the internet of 'most notorious serial killers' or 'top ten unsolvable crimes'. This case was still everywhere, but all they ever cared about was *him*. The Father. Not about the lives he destroyed. Those were just footnotes.

"Why do you need me?" Erin asked.

"You are one of them." I said this simply, but as carefully as I could. "You deserve this just as much as they do, not least because of how brave you've been, because of how you survived."

"Survived?" Erin's face blanched, whether with anger or fear I couldn't tell.

I forged on, cursing myself inwardly, "As for why *now* – that's on me. For a long time, writing has been the only way I've been able to process things, my own family's loss. Losing my cousins made me want to do something. I started writing this book about the children the Father had hurt as a way to deal with that pain, that loss. I grew up knowing more about the theories around the abductions than I knew about the children he'd hurt. And I'm sure it was the same for you—"

Erin lunged. She was leaning halfway over the table before I'd even realised I'd upset her.

"You're doing this out of some misplaced sense of self-righteousness?" she hissed. "You think just because you're related to *them* that you have any right to tell *my* story?"

My hands went clammy. "It's not like that. I want to *help*."

"Help?"

"It's not just the book," I said quickly. "It's – this, too. Why we're here. You called me, remember? I wanted to make sure you're okay."

Erin sank back into her seat, glancing around us.

"Something is going on with you, isn't it?" I said. "What happened?"

"Nothing."

"Something did," I pressed.

Erin's expression didn't change but she made no move to leave either. Her eyes sparkled with what might have been the beginnings of tears but her lips were resolute – it was a look more akin to fear than anger. I felt my skin prickle again.

"It's nothing," she said. "Just… it doesn't matter. I've been having this feeling, recently. Like somebody is watching me. But there's never anybody there. I convinced myself it was all in my head, because of the anniversary. And then… last night, I got home, and somebody had broken into my house. Or, maybe they didn't. I don't know. I *thought* somebody had but I've calmed down since then. The police came and nothing was missing…"

"Oh, god, Erin. I'm sorry. Are you okay?"

"I'm fine," she said. "I just thought that talking to you might be – helpful. That you might know more than me. That maybe it's because I'm winding myself up, you know, and maybe I could do with learning more, opening up more. To somebody impartial. Sort of."

"Erin… if you're ready to talk to me, I'll tell you everything I know."

"Everything?" she asked.

"Yes. If somebody broke into your house——"

"Somebody *did* break into my house."

"If somebody broke into your house," I continued, "do you think it's a possibility that it's connected to who you are?"

"Well, yeah, I guess…" she said. "But why would it be? It seems a bit extreme for even the most crazed theorists, and mostly I get left alone now the Father's dead."

The conviction on Erin's face was startling. I had theories about what had happened to stop the abductions, but never anything concrete. Maybe prison, or death *in* prison, but I wouldn't swear to either. Erin, though, seemed sure about this.

"I'm not saying it's definitely connected," I said. "But it's probably a good idea for you to have as much information as you can get, right?"

Erin drained the last of the Coke and rattled the ice cubes thoughtfully.

"Okay," she said. We had reached some kind of truce. She leaned back. "So tell me… what did you say to make my mum freak out the other day?"

I steeled myself for her reaction.

"I didn't really get far enough to tell her anything, but I wanted to say that the police might have a reason to look into certain things in your case. Because I told them that I don't think my cousins were the Father's first victims."

It wasn't exactly how I'd wanted to tell her, but there wasn't ever going to be a right time. And now that the words were out in the open I felt instantly lighter. But with the swooping sense of relief also came the other thought, louder now: what if I was wrong? And what did it mean if I was *right*?

"What the hell do you mean, *not his first victims*?"

"It's − a hunch. But, look. Everybody thinks Mikey and Jem started this whole thing. They were the first recorded pair of siblings to disappear with the Father's M.O., right? Siblings, the bigger ones small for their age, taken from their shared bedroom in the middle of the night, the window left open, their bodies later found injected with insulin, dressed in pyjamas that weren't their own… My aunt and uncle are asked constantly if they knew anybody who would have wanted to hurt the boys, because with abductions of children it's usually somebody the children know. But everything felt so practised. No evidence left behind. Like he'd spent a long time planning. Or maybe it wasn't the first abduction."

"Right…?"

"Well, I found something that might be connected. I found an article, just by chance, about this pair of runaways from Derby. In 1993 two boys went missing from a foster home − that's a year before my cousins were taken. At first I didn't think anything of it, because there are so many differences, and they didn't even have the same surname. They ended up at the same foster home six months apart. They were from Birmingham and Manchester originally but they were absolutely inseparable once they found each other. The foster mother was caring for a few other kids at the time and she said these two had been a bit of a problem. Once they were together they misbehaved, got suspended from school for skiving, mouthing off at teachers, that sort of thing. Nothing serious but the school came down on them hard.

"A while later they disappeared in the middle of the night. Just upped and left. The foster mother didn't notice anything strange *before* they left – in fact they seemed quite happy to be out of school – but they'd run away from foster homes before, and even made it to various cities before they were found, so nobody suspected it was going to be different this time. The older boy ran away three or four times at various points before this, and I think the younger one ran away from his previous foster home after a fight at school with an older boy.

"They were last seen hanging around outside a bus station on the Staffordshire border, but nobody ever confirmed where they were headed because if they bought tickets it was with cash and the cameras never caught them getting on a bus, although they could have left on foot through one of the blind spots. They were flagged as high risk at the time. So they weren't taken from their bedroom, but they were never found so I can't count out other similarities."

I saw the gears turning in Erin's mind. I lifted my chin, waiting for her to look at me again.

"Why do you think they're connected?" she asked eventually. "If the boys weren't actually related to each other, and there are so many differences—"

"I don't think that's the point," I said quickly.

"What *is* the point then?"

"They were still siblings," I said. "In all but blood, anyway. The older one small for his age like all of the Father's victims.

They were thick as thieves, so as good as brothers even if not biologically. Their bodies weren't found but a lot of the Father's victims weren't found. It's almost like… an earlier, untested version of the same pattern.

"The children were too young to have disappeared that easily by themselves. When kids go missing at that age – wilfully – they're usually found. These boys had been found within hours when they'd run away before, separately."

"How old were they?"

"Nine and six."

"And nobody ever connected them to the Father before?" she asked. I was surprised that she looked less afraid than she had earlier, that steeliness back in her gaze.

"No," I said. "Even I wouldn't, except I have a *feeling*. I don't know. The location, and the fact that both boys went missing at the same time and neither was ever found…"

Erin twitched.

"I think the police will look into it in any case," I said. "And that could change things, couldn't it?"

EIGHT

Erin

I WATCHED HARRIET LEAVE and tried to keep it together. I'd thought talking to her would help but it hadn't. It was like the world I'd built was crumbling to the foundations. I didn't know what to believe. Harriet had wavered between conviction and insisting that it was just a hunch. But there was an intensity to her I couldn't shake; it was like the first numbing drop of alcohol – it made me want more, to know more, to understand. And that was something I'd never wanted before.

Once she left I stumbled outside into the beer garden where the fireworks had just finished. The sky was thick with smoke and tinged orange by the bonfire. It looked like hell on Earth, the air speckled with ash and stars.

I stood underneath the overhang of a large oak tree and inhaled the scents of frying onions and candyfloss. I'd only had one drink and yet somehow I felt as if I'd had ten. What Harriet had told me, about those missing boys, it swirled in my head. Round and round and round… It wasn't the reassurance

I'd been hoping for. What had I even hoped to achieve?

I folded my hands under my armpits to ward off the cold, regretting that I didn't own any decent winter boots. I thought about the book Harriet was writing, all of the interviews she'd probably done. Was I ready to get involved with all of that?

I could just keep on as I was, going to the office, chatting with colleagues, making candles in my spare time – but would I be able to ignore it now? Now that I'd realised that's what I'd been doing. *Ignoring* it, not moving on. Not really.

No matter what had really happened last night, this spooked feeling that I couldn't shake was real enough. I'd spent so many years avoiding the truth that it had become like a ghost. It haunted me. I needed to know what had happened to me. I needed to remember.

But what if I was wrong about Harriet? How did I know that I wasn't just a meal ticket to her?

The truth was, I didn't know. But it didn't *feel* that way. When she looked at me, it was like she was seeing me. I wasn't just a victim with a capital V. Nobody who knew my past had looked at me that way in a long time. She didn't just pity me, and she wasn't crazy either. Even when she talked about those missing children, it wasn't with the same fervour I'd seen from the crazies on the internet or my ex-colleague Jeff. Not like the people who had built entire websites around theories that the Father was still alive and living in rural Perthshire, that he was in prison in America for trying to start a cult, that he was a time-traveller…

It was part of the reason I'd ignored it all. The information that was in the newspapers, their best guess of what happened to me during the weeks I'd been gone. I didn't look for information on the other children, the other victims. It was all just guesswork anyway.

As a teenager I hadn't been interested in learning about the other children, not even when my mother paid for therapist after therapist so I'd have somebody to talk to. I didn't want to talk about it. I didn't want to read about it. In fact, I was so actively not interested that any mention of the Father or his victims produced bouts of impossible sickness that had me hanging my head between my knees.

In recent years he had popped up on most of those 'Top Ten Creepiest Unsolved Crimes' lists on Facebook and Buzzfeed, and I'd avoided those too. I didn't want to risk seeing Alex's face staring out at me, forever my big brother, but now frozen as a child. Worse, I didn't want to see my own face, the me that wasn't me any more.

About a year ago I decided to open one of the lists. I was surprised by the amount of information I'd managed to absorb even without trying, but it was probably inevitable considering the scale of the investigation.

Twelve children stolen over five years. Always in pairs, always siblings.

Gender and race varied, although he took more boys in the beginning. The children were from all over the Midlands and the North, ranging from four to nine years old. A few true crime nuts focused on the fact that most of the places were right off the motorway – but that didn't mean a whole lot considering the ground covered.

Sometimes their bodies turned up. Sometimes they didn't. The bodies that were recovered had been found with extremely high levels of insulin, leading the police to believe that he injected them with the overdose to kill them. Some of the internet nuts linked this to the Beverley Allitt case in 1991, where a woman had murdered four children and attempted to kill more still. But there was no more to connect the Father's victims to Beverley Allitt than there was to link them to Harold Shipman. It was all just wild conjecture.

That hadn't stopped the crazies from suggesting everything from the Father being a disgruntled male nurse to him being a cult leader, though.

It wasn't the manner of death that haunted me so much as the period between abduction and death. Like what happened to Morgan Bailey, whose body was found almost an entire *year* after her abduction, yet she'd only recently been killed. She'd been alive all that time.

Morgan was the one who kept me awake at night. It was always the same thought, too. *That could have been me.* Whatever happened to me, at least it was over quickly.

Long after Mum stopped us going to the group therapy sessions I still couldn't think about the other families without that familiar pang of guilt deep down. Why had I survived when their children, when Alex, hadn't?

Even now, watching the embers of the fire as they tumbled into the night sky, I wondered if it was worth this, just because some bastard had decided to try to scare me. Was it worth seeing all of the families at the memorial tomorrow? Was it worth dragging up all of those old memories, of the days after I had woken up in a hospital room without my brother, no idea where we'd been for the last few weeks and no way to find him?

What else was there to know? I had survived and Alex had not. That was all there was to it.

I felt a prickle on the back of my neck. The shadows were long and the night was still. I stood away from the crush of bodies around the bonfire. The tree shaded me from the mizzling rain, and I had darkness to my back where a long fence ran the length of the beer garden.

I glanced around swiftly, taking in smiling, shadowed faces I didn't recognise. My shoulders tensed and a churning in my gut made me peer into the darkness behind me. I felt somebody watching me, eyes creeping along my spine. But when I turned there was nothing to see except mud and shrubbery, the shadows of the trees smudged by fairy lights strung between lamps.

I shivered, rubbing my arms with my hands. I wanted to light a cigarette but I had no intention of sticking around long enough to smoke it. I was just on edge, I told myself. Spooked by the fact that somebody might have been in my house.

In the end I paid half a fortune for a small burger with burnt onions and walked quickly back to my car while shovelling it in my face. The shadows seemed to swim with human-like shapes that looked suspiciously like my nightmares.

BEFORE

Mother

THE HOUSE WAS EVERYTHING she had ever wanted. It needed dedication and inspiration but she was lacking in neither. She had always liked a challenge. It was why she had married Jack. She saw no shame in admitting that she liked being needed.

The house was no different to their marriage.

They moved in over the course of three days, both blessing and cursing the old lady who'd left it to them in her will in such a state of disrepair that there was a leak in the ceiling in the kitchen and three broken upstairs windows. Their meagre belongings didn't even fill half of the space.

The boys were as happy as she'd ever seen them, Mouse running shrieking between the rooms with Chris-Bear crawling after him. She and Jack carried their boxes from the van with one eye on the boys. They left everything stacked up against the wall in the front hall.

"We can't leave them there," she said, lifting Bear onto her hip.

"I know," Jack said. He swiped a kiss on her cheek but his attention was elsewhere. Then he disappeared into the basement, his tool-belt gripped loosely in his fist.

It was left to her to shepherd the boys into their bedroom that evening after a rushed dinner of spaghetti hoops on toast. Jack still hadn't reappeared from the basement, and after yelling for him to come and eat she'd left him to it.

But it got darker and he still didn't emerge. Had he left the house? She hadn't heard him leave, but she wasn't going to run around looking for him. He'd been moody recently, even the prospect of a fresh start making him irritable. She didn't fancy being shouted at after their long day.

The wind picked up outside, whistling down the side of the house. There was a sharp crack from the roof, then another from the ground. She jumped.

Just a roof tile. Another one. She'd have to mention it to Jack so the boys didn't get hurt in the garden tomorrow.

"Father?"

One of the boys was out of bed. He was in the hall in his pyjamas, his brother's bear tucked under his arm and his hair mussed with sleep.

"Hush, Mouse," she said. He jumped, his eyes glittering in the dark. Mouse always wanted his father when he had a bad dream. "He's not here," she added. Where was he? "You'll have to make do with me."

Even in the big bed he wouldn't settle. Every noise made both of them startle, every jump shattering her peace that little bit more.

"Lie *still*, Mouse."

He couldn't. Or *wouldn't*. Rain drummed a steady pattern of white noise behind her eyelids and in her chest, a soothing sound – until Mouse wriggled again. She reached out and slapped his thigh. Only enough to make him understand she was serious. He made a little mewling sound, which was pitiful really. Then he quieted.

In the morning they would sort the roof tiles and the leaks. Jack would have mellowed and they'd all have breakfast together in the kitchen. She might even make eggs if she could find the good pan.

In the morning everything would be perfect.

George & Jacob Evans
Abducted: Sheffield, 21 June 1995

The first time I spoke to Molly Evans about the twins, George and Jacob (7), in late October 2009, she told me how much George loved to sing.

"Oh, that boy was never quiet," she said. "He sang from the moment he woke up to the moment he went to sleep. He used to drive us mad. We'd always be yelling *Georgie, quiet!* but it never made a difference. It was like we'd been given a bird instead of a boy."

"What did Jacob make of all the singing?" I asked.

"He liked it. He used to hate it when people told Georgie to shut up. He had this little harmonica Andy got him, and he played it when Georgie sang. He didn't like confrontation – he was ever so gentle – but I think he felt like it was his job, you know, to look after George.

"They loved being outside, those boys. We got them out of the house whenever we could. There's a big park not far from here that we always used to go to with a whole bunch of adventure play equipment. They remodelled it the spring that the boys were taken. And we played out there more than ever before. It was marvellous…"

"Did any of their friends use the park too?"

"Not really," Molly said. "Most of them lived nearer the school, but George could make friends with anybody.

I remember this one time, there was a boy who'd lost his mum, and the boys looked after him until she found him. That's the sort of children they were." She sighed. "Maybe they were too trusting, but I couldn't have changed them."

NINE

6 NOVEMBER 2016

Harriet

THE NEXT AFTERNOON I got a text.

I'll come to the memorial. Can we go together? Mum's on holiday.

I hadn't dared to believe she'd come. Not after what I'd told her last night. *I don't think my cousins were the Father's first victims...* I'd expected her to freak out, but I'd been wrong.

I drove to Erin's house a good five miles below the speed limit, faintly nervous. I hadn't been to one of these memorials in a long time, and I hadn't really thought about how it would feel, seeing so many of the parents I'd interviewed all in one place.

Still, I thought, it would be worse for Erin. I remembered what Molly had told me about the therapy group and was surprised to feel anger towards the people I'd been writing about for so long. I knew they weren't perfect. I'd spoken to them after the worst days of their lives; some of them had been polite, friendly even, some immediately welcoming, but others had been outwardly hostile even after inviting me into their homes. I'd seen in them the same grief wrapped in anger I recognised in my uncle, in

Thomas and myself too. But it was different knowing Erin now, knowing that people had pushed her away.

When I pulled up outside Erin's house she was already waiting. I saw the curtains twitch in one of the downstairs windows and she stepped out seconds later in smart, dark jeans and black trainers, her jacket buttoned up tight.

I got out of the car.

"My car's a piece of shit," Erin said by way of greeting. "Been crapping out on me. Thanks for the lift." She eyed me cautiously, as though she wasn't sure how to act around me. Then she said, "Come on, let's get this over with. The service is in Chesterfield, right? That's, what, forty minutes?"

She checked her watch. The sun was already getting low in the sky and Erin's nervous energy was contagious.

When she climbed into the car she smelled of perfume and cigarettes.

"Did you stay at your house last night?" I asked.

"What's it to you?" Erin raised her eyebrows, a small smile on her lips. I liked the way she raised one side more than the other.

"I just wondered if it was safe." I shrugged. "You know, with what you told me—"

"Honestly, it was nothing. They didn't even take anything." Erin held her hands in her lap, perfectly still, watching as the trees and cars passed. "It might have been a prank or something."

"Why would somebody break into your house as a joke?" An interrupted burglary was one thing, but a prank? It seemed to me like Erin didn't know what she thought – or she did and didn't want to talk about it.

"People aren't very nice," Erin said simply.

"Well, no…"

"Maybe somebody found out about Alex and me and wanted to make a point. It's not the first time I've been the centre of somebody's attention. In my last job I had a colleague who went a bit overboard with all these weird theories. I wouldn't put it past people. I don't know. It happened, the police are dealing with it, and I'm not worried any more." She paused. "But no," she added. "For the record: I didn't stay there. I've been crashing at my mum's house. Okay?"

I drove on in silence. I had so many questions I wanted to ask, but I couldn't bring myself to do it. It seemed like Erin felt the same. The air in the car was stuffy, the heater blasting.

After a while she finally broke the silence.

"Those boys," she said slowly, "the ones who – went missing before. I've been thinking about them. About everything, to be honest. I just don't understand how it happened. Children are hard to just – *take*. And if you try to take two at the same time… They're not light. Not easy to carry, especially if they're not willing."

"They're not," I admitted. "But all of the older children were fairly small for their ages, like you. Short, skinny. There was a theory about how he might have lured them, maybe with sweets or threats, but without proof it's hard to say exactly how he did it. It could have easily been a bribe or a threat. Either way he must have been prepared…"

It felt wrong to be discussing this with Erin. But she had raised the subject, so I tried not to shy away, knowing she was probably thinking of the person who had broken into her home.

"He chose the children at random, didn't he?" Erin said. I noticed the phrase *the children*, not *us*, the distance she put between herself and them.

"Yes. From the North and the Midlands. A variety of ages, different genders and combinations. Different skin, hair, eye colours. Earlier on they looked a little more similar, lighter hair and skin, small dark eyes. But by the end there was no pattern to the children or the locations. The only things they had in common were that they were small and that they were siblings. Always a pair, always taken together and always found separately." *Or not at all*. I felt the words I hadn't said hovering between us.

Erin had fallen silent.

"I'm sorry," I said. "This must be hard."

"Yes," she said. "But it's okay. I'm – I think it's time to try."

I cleared my throat awkwardly.

"It's just so clinical," I said. "The whole thing. No DNA or trace evidence. Taking children from their *beds* feels personal, but nobody has ever been able to figure out a connection between them. I mean the parents were home during the abductions. That takes some serious balls, doesn't it?"

Erin grunted.

"Thing is, those foster brothers… if they were somehow connected, there could be something which the police missed. That's partly why I wanted to talk to you and your mother. I wasn't sure if you might remember anything important, anything that might confirm it."

"Well I don't remember anything at all," Erin said. She sounded tired, as though she'd been up half the night wracking her brains. "So realistically you might as well leave the police to it."

"I just wanted you to have a say. I know I'd want to, if it were me."

Erin didn't look at me. She fumbled with her phone, sent a couple of quick messages, and the only sound for the rest of our drive was her gentle tapping on the dark screen with her fingernail. By the time we reached Chesterfield she hadn't spoken at all in nearly fifteen minutes.

As we slowed into the town traffic I cast a quick glance in her direction. She looked solemn. I couldn't tell whether she was regretting being here, but I couldn't help the words that came out next, as insensitive as they might be.

"You haven't asked me the boys' names," I said quietly.

Erin looked at me and blinked.

Oscar and Isaac, I thought, as loudly as I could.

"That's because I'm not sure I want to know."

TEN

Harriet

"HARRIET…" ERIN SURPRISED ME by speaking again as we pulled into the small car park on the hill near Chesterfield train station. I turned off the engine and spun to look at her. She took a small breath. "Are you going to write about this?"

"I don't know," I said. I surprised myself with my honesty. It felt like we'd broken some invisible barrier that had been between us. "I'd intended to."

"Oh," she answered simply. "Okay."

Together we got out of the car. During the daylight hours this small tarmacked space would look down over the trees and a winding stretch of road, but in the evening it was cast in long, greyish shadows. I felt the tension at the bottom of my spine as Erin fumbled around in her pockets, pulling out a cigarette and a plastic lighter.

I was glad the Crooked Spire wasn't far. I could see the church already, the point of the spire reaching up to pierce the sky, twisted and lethal, as though a monster had gripped its point with a melting grip and wrenched it around. It appeared through the trees, black and looming.

"Why now?" Erin asked. She'd pulled her hood up although it wasn't raining any more. "The memorial, I mean. Why today?"

"They do them quite regularly," I explained. "Or they used to. Less so, now. I think in the early days it was a way to connect everybody. Before Facebook and everything... But everybody's so scattered that it can be a bit difficult to organise. I think this one is — to remember everybody. To mark the — well, the end of it all."

I didn't say *to mark the day you came home and the kidnappings stopped*, but I knew we were both thinking something like it. Erin had said that the Father was dead. She believed that, even though there wasn't any proof. What did I believe?

I wanted to believe that he was dead, but that seemed too neat. If anything I was more inclined to side with the theorists who assumed he was arrested for another crime — burglary or breaking and entering seemed likely considering his preference for climbing through windows. What that meant for Erin's safety, though, I wasn't sure. One theory I'd liked for a while suggested that the Father might, in fact, be the notorious Edward Slater, arrested for a string of arsons in Derbyshire in early 1999, and who had later died in prison. But I wasn't sold completely. Why move from kidnapping to arson?

"I've never been to one of these," Erin said quietly, startling me out of my thoughts. "Not even once. I told my mum I was coming." She trailed off and came to a standstill just outside the churchyard, her cigarette tip glowing as she inhaled deeply. "God, I'm a mess. This is really hard. I – thank you." She shrugged. "Yeah, thanks. That's what I wanted to say."

A crowd had already gathered outside the church. Nobody seemed to pay any attention to Erin. With her hood up and her long hair darker at the ends she looked nothing like she had as a child. The trees were heavy with yellowing leaves, the castoffs scattered about the big grey cobbles like confetti, crushed under the weight of many feet.

There were faces I recognised, and people that said hello to me. I hadn't seen most of the parents in years but they all remembered me. Some had aged better than others; a couple of parents came tonight with children who were now much older than their siblings had been when they'd died. The thought filled me with an overwhelming sadness. I looked over to see if Erin was okay, but she hung back, her hood obscuring her face.

Some folks I didn't recognise. A man with sandy hair stood back, watching with sadness lining his face; a woman blew her nose into a clean white handkerchief. People had begun lighting candles already. Tea lights in some places, but thick pillar candles in others. The leaves in the centre of the path had been swept towards the edges, a pathway of lit candles in glass jars leading to the church itself.

The effect was eerie. The guttering candlelight was yellow and cast strange shadows. It reminded me of the creeping silhouettes in cartoon monster movies. I leaned over, watching as Erin clenched her fists tight.

"Alright?" I asked.

She nodded tensely, but I could tell she was lying. I stepped a bit closer, hoping it might help.

I spied Molly Evans by the doors to the church, but she didn't see me as she ducked inside.

I'd never been in the church before – I wasn't even sure if they did regular services here. I'd always assumed that the crooked spire was a tourist trap now, but the musty smell of old bricks and beeswax as we stepped inside made me reconsider.

"I read that the Devil himself twisted the spire," Erin whispered. Her voice trembled as she walked half a step behind me into the dimness. "The stories say he landed there, and when he tried to flee from – I don't remember what – his tail wrapped around it and melted it into a spiral. I wonder if he meant to do it."

Finally Erin dropped her hood. Her eyes darted about the room as she took in all of the different faces. I wasn't sure whether she recognised any of them, but they certainly didn't notice her.

"Are your family here?" Erin asked.

I shook my head. "They don't come."

"My mum goes sometimes but mostly they make her very upset. I'm glad she's not around tonight. Let's sit at the back."

Something about Erin's expression made me sad. How hard must it have been for them over the years? Especially after Erin's father died. There didn't seem to be much softness between her and her mother, the space tinged with sadness, but I could tell from Erin's tone that she loved her more than she'd admit.

* * *

Afterwards, the crowd spilled out into the night. Some of the candles had already burned down. We'd lingered for a good five minutes afterwards, watching people leave. A few of the parents saw me, and came to chat. Morgan and Paul Bailey's mother gave my arm a squeeze and promised to be in touch. Nobody noticed the silent Erin, who hung back near the door, her phone still and black in her hands.

"Are you okay?" I asked again when we were alone.

She didn't answer.

The air was so cold it made my lungs ache. We stood under the trees, watching as the final parents drifted across towards the road or the town centre. People spoke very little, but the smiles that passed between most of them were warm.

There were a few people who looked official. Police, probably. I'd noticed them during the service, and now they stood out among the mourners. One, a young woman in a dark suit, with pale brown skin and curls, came to stand beside us.

"Hello." Erin knew her. "Harriet, this is Wendy. Uh, she's a liaison officer."

"Harriet – Harriet Murphy, right? You're the one who called in and spoke to Godfrey about Operation Moray recently." Wendy gave me a once-over. "Journalist?"

"Harriet is writing a book," Erin said. Then she turned fully to the officer. "Have you heard anything about the break-in?"

Wendy shook her head. "Not yet," she admitted. "But they'll only get in touch with me if they find something. They'll touch base with you as often as you asked them to."

"Can you tell us anything about what I told Godfrey?" I asked. "About the boys I—"

"Not at this moment in time," Wendy said. I wasn't sure whether she meant because of where we were, or because she didn't have anything to tell me. "Is there anything else you've noticed since, anything missing?"

"No." Erin shook her head emphatically. "Nothing was taken. At least I still haven't noticed anything."

Wendy turned back to me, reaching into her pocket and pulling out a card, which she handed over.

"Erin, give me a call if you need to. And, Miss Murphy, it might be useful if we could have a chat sometime soon."

She left us, then, catching sight of somebody else she wanted to talk to – I thought it might be the Davies' mother, but it was now too dim for me to tell.

"I wish they'd tell me more," I said.

"I don't." Erin rolled her eyes. "Wendy's a nut but she's nice enough. Just very – pushy. Do you want a cigarette?" She pulled a packet from her pocket, along with the plastic lighter. I took one gratefully and we stood smoking for a moment in silence.

Suddenly footsteps sounded behind us. Erin spun a fraction faster than me, her body tensed to run, but she didn't move. It was Molly Evans, her big coat buttoned up tight and a woolly hat pulled down low. Erin dropped her cigarette and stubbed it out.

"I'm glad you came," Molly said. It was directed at both of us. She turned to Erin, then, and I shifted my attention elsewhere, pretending to stare at the gathering night as the candles melted down. "Hi," she said uncertainly.

"Hello. Thanks for inviting me. Harriet told me."

"I thought it was time. Your mother's said before she'd like you to come to these things, but you weren't ready…"

Erin shrugged but didn't deny it. They spoke for a while longer, awkward pleasantries that I didn't feel I should intrude on. Molly wasn't her usual bubbly self, though, and the eventual lull in the conversation made me pay attention.

"Anyway. I wanted to… I, uh…" Molly made a wet noise in her throat. She looked nervous.

"Yes?" Erin breathed.

"This might sound odd, but I just thought I'd ask… Do you ever feel like somebody is watching you? I know it's all in my head, but I just wondered if either of you ever feel like that? I wonder if it's because I'm a bit emotional. You know, as if my brain is inventing a reason to feel anxious. Andy tells me I'm being silly."

"It's not silly," Erin said. She tried to smile but it didn't work. "It's probably just – the long nights." She looked at me, an expression I couldn't read. "But if you're worried you could talk to Wendy about it. You know her too, don't you?"

Erin pointed her out and Molly nodded, visibly relaxing. "You're right, love," she said. She flashed a smile that seemed more confident. "Probably just time to touch base. Anyway, I'm glad to have seen you. You can keep in touch, if you'd like. Harriet has my number."

We watched Molly go. Erin started to walk back to the car, head down and shoulders hunched. I ran to catch up with her.

"Hey. Aren't you going to tell me what that was about?"

Erin lifted her head. "What what was about?"

"Not telling Molly about your break-in?"

"That's not got anything to do with this," Erin said. "She just wanted reassurance. It's like that, sometimes, I think. You just get a bit overwhelmed and need somebody to talk you down. God knows I've done the same for Mum enough times. She'll be fine now. She can talk to Wendy. Anyway, I don't think what happened to me is very serious. It just shook me up a bit. Can you take me home now, please?"

"You don't have to pretend it's not a big deal to you, Jillian."

I realised the slip as soon as the name left my mouth, but I couldn't catch it in time. Erin froze. I felt heat flood my face. She'd been Jillian to me for so long that sometimes it was hard to remember.

"I'm sorry," I said quickly. "Erin. I didn't mean to use that name again. Can I buy you a drink to make it up to you? I'm really sorry…"

"Yes," Erin blurted, then smiled as though she'd surprised herself. "God, yeah. I could do with something to take the edge off. Where?"

"I actually don't live too far away from you," I said. "We could go local."

ELEVEN

Harriet

I CHOSE A BAR I'd been to a couple of times before, right on the outskirts of Arkney. The area around it had a sort of measured old-time feel to it, nice stone buildings and cottages with thatched roofs. The bar was close enough to both our houses that I could park up and we could get taxis home if it came to it. It was the sort of place I'd call a 'nice clothes' bar, classy and small, with a food menu and a big window strung with industrial-looking lightbulbs. We ordered something each, small meals that came on wooden boards, and Erin made a comment about the choice of desserts. When the food came, Erin devoured it with gusto, guzzling down her rum and Coke like she'd not been fed or watered in days.

I laughed.

"What?" Erin demanded. "Never seen a girl eat?"

"Never like that." I realised I was still grinning. "But there's definitely something quite amazing about it."

"Shut up." Erin rolled her eyes.

She polished off the last of her drink and ordered another. I sipped at my wine, letting the alcohol numb some of the questions in my mind. What was I doing? It wasn't a good idea to be here, especially not with alcohol involved. If I wanted to help Erin then I had to keep a clear head. Yet when the second glass of wine Erin had ordered for me turned up I drank that too, wanting to relax.

Erin's phone was on the table, and she checked it several times during the meal. After the second glass of wine I felt brave enough to ask her about it.

"Are you waiting to hear from somebody?" I asked.

"Huh?" Erin glanced at her phone and then back at me. "Oh, it's not important. Just – a friend."

Jazz music played in the background; it should have been soothing but it was too loud. The room was dimly lit, too, small candles on all of the tables, and it all felt a bit much. Erin didn't seem to care, though. She ordered another drink for both of us, and then scooted around to my side of the booth so we could talk over the music.

"Why did you come and see my mum the other day?" she asked, her glass halfway to her mouth. "I mean – why now?"

"It was the article," I said, slowly. I was suddenly very aware of how close she was. I could smell her cigarettes and her perfume, musky and warm. Some of her eyeliner had rubbed off, and I realised how pale she was under her war paint.

"Because you just found out about those boys?"

"Yes. I've wanted to write this book for… for years. I started it when I was at university. And I kept adding to it. I interviewed the families when I was in my first and second years, in between my English classes. And then I did a Masters in journalism. I had all these ideas about how I was going to change the world. You know?" I shook my head. Drank more wine. "I showed some of the book, as it was then, to my tutor, just transcripts and notes to myself and stuff. It was a mistake. He told me I'd never get anywhere by navel-gazing."

Erin snorted in surprise. "What? He said that?"

"I know. I was young. I took it to heart. He must have meant that it was too much about me. The book, I mean. What I'd written. And he was probably right. But there are plenty of books out there that do the same, combine autobiography with other things. And like…" I felt my throat begin to swell as I thought of how much my brother had shielded me over the years. "I just feel like in some small way it's my story too?"

Erin was silent. I watched as she rattled the ice cubes in her glass and I worried I'd upset her. I'd made it about myself again. I hadn't meant to. I—

Then she lifted her chin and I realised she wasn't mad. Her blue eyes were glossy with unshed tears and she gave me a small smile.

"I read some of the stuff you wrote on your blog," she said. I swallowed my surprise. "Yeah, I found it. I saw the one you wrote about that girl who went missing during the solar eclipse last year. And that journalist who found her. It was… sensitive. That was you, right?"

I felt my cheeks flush.

"But you're not a journalist any more," Erin went on. "Right? You stopped?"

"Yeah. I – I did it for a while. Did the Masters, graduated, got a job with an online news outlet. Did some small pieces. Mostly fluff. But it was… it was so exhausting. It's so competitive and I couldn't write what I wanted and…" I sighed. "I guess I gave up."

"Why do you have to do this?" Erin asked. "Why now? Why not just leave it alone?"

"I tried, but I can't let it go. I'm not… I'm not as strong as I want to be, but I'm trying. I'm not pushy enough to make it as a professional journalist, but this isn't about that. I tried to get in touch with – the foster brothers' mother…"

"It's okay," Erin said. "You can tell me their names."

I blinked. This was an offering. A gesture of trust.

"Oscar Tyrrell," I said. "And Isaac Higgins."

She nodded slowly. "Go on."

"I tried to call their foster mother and she shut me down. I thought about giving up then, but I just can't. The children… Growing up, I didn't feel like I could escape from them. And it wasn't just Jem and Mikey. It was all of them, like I was connected to *all* of them. And my brother used to help me deal with it. But we grew up, and I guess we started to let our guard down, and I realised how much it had impacted everything. He moved away recently, and when I found that article – I was pulling Mum's floors up, of all bloody things, and I found the newspaper underneath, padding the floor – I wanted to tell my brother about this hunch because it seemed important. And then I thought, well, other people should know, too. About *all* of the children. Do you… understand?"

"Yes," Erin said softly. "I get it. But not everybody is like you. Not everybody wants to talk all the time. I always just wanted everybody to let me forget it in peace."

She finished her drink, checked her phone as if to signal that the conversation was over, and then looked back at me. Her eyes were glittering again, but this time it was different. Mischief was written all over her elfin features.

"What?" I asked.

"This is getting very maudlin," she said. "And I demand that we get over ourselves. You promised to make it up to me."

"And what exactly do you suggest?"

"We should do what I always do when I want to relax. Two words." She wiggled her eyebrows suggestively and, just for a brief, golden, confusing second, I wondered what it might be like to kiss her. I swallowed.

"Two words?"

"Live. Music."

This time Erin chose. We left my car and walked to a small pub with an even smaller back room. Erin buzzed with her characteristic nervous energy, but something else hummed between us as well. I tried to forget the memorial, the book. Just for tonight. Erin looked at me expectantly as we found our way into the back of the building, a band already on stage. The music was loud, filling everything. My heart, my lungs, my ears. It reverberated in my chest.

As soon as we got settled I saw Erin relax. Like the person

she'd been in the bar – my place of choice – was only a shadow of her real self. Here, I stood tensely, arms by my sides, but she melted into the space in the room, swaying in time with the music. This was her element.

The music was something I didn't recognise, coarse and grungy-sounding, guitars and drums and low voices. It wasn't my sort of thing but it appeared to be Erin's. I watched the fluid way she moved her body, limbs like water, and found myself smiling.

The song changed, this one with a faster beat. I let myself get swept up in the music, pushing all thoughts aside. I closed my eyes, felt the sound inside my head. Felt my own pulse, the alcohol buzz under my skin.

When I opened my eyes, Erin was watching me.

"You're staring," I said.

"I'm not. I'm drunk." She smirked, that one corner of her mouth lifting.

"Slow down then," I said.

The music was loud, and Erin leaned in when she said, "I don't want to."

I swallowed, brushed my hair back off my forehead. It was warm in here and I felt the heat flushing in my face, my chest. I drank a swallow from my glass of water, and Erin tipped her head back, exposing her throat.

"You're not a journalist any more," she said, changing track. "But you've got a blog. So what do you *do*?"

"I'm an underwriter. Insurance, like I said before. It sounds boring but it's not that bad. I'm quite good at it, which I'm sure is the only reason they put up with my shit." I shrugged. Until recently I'd been writing on the side, freelance stuff, but lately I'd let even that tail off. "It pays the bills."

"I love my job," Erin said. This was quieter, and I had to lean in again to hear her. My pulse jumped even as I did. "It's just an office thing. You know. But I get to mess with websites. Photoshop, some social media. All sorts. It's creative. I like how I can start the day with one thing and end with something entirely different. Or how, sometimes, you can fiddle with the same thing for hours and hours and it looks like you've done nothing – but you know you've made it better."

I realised that she was offering me something. Something personal.

"I make candles, too." She laughed at herself, as though she'd said something funny. "God. I'm such a nerd. But I love the smells, the whole process. It's like – alchemy? Or something magical. So yeah. I make candles."

"I – I knit."

It felt like bonding.

"Jumpers?" she asked.

"Yeah. Sometimes. Blankets mostly. I love baby blankets. I sell them on Etsy."

I waited for Erin to laugh, although I wasn't sure why she would. But considering the way she'd laughed at herself, I was surprised when she just nodded.

"Cool. I like blankets." Then she sighed. "I need a smoke. You coming?"

I downed the rest of my water and left the glass on the edge of the crowded bar. The place was heaving for a Sunday night. But it was still early, really. We stumbled out into the night. There was a small patio to the side, just next to the road and the car park, tinged with silver lamplight. It had been raining again, on and off, and the concrete was slick. We were the only two people out here, cushioned from the wind by a wall, Erin humming to the faint pulse of the music as she patted her pockets for her cigarettes.

"Let me."

I grabbed my own packet and handed one to her. She lit it before saying, "I didn't think you had any, the way you were so eager to smoke mine." But her smirk was real.

Something had shifted, tonight. I felt it in the way she stood closer to me, the way she didn't flinch when I spoke now, like she had done sometimes before. It was as if she had always expected a question she couldn't answer, and now she didn't care about saying that she simply didn't know.

I didn't want to ruin the mood, but I had to ask, "Erin, do you really, honestly, not remember anything about what happened to you?"

She didn't react, just smoked a bit longer. Eventually she sighed. "No," she said. "And you can write about that if you want. I don't have a fucking clue. Alex and me... we had a great childhood. He really looked after me. I remember these nights where we'd get home from school and Alex would say we should go hunt for berries or make homes for the field mice that he said lived in the park. He wouldn't even ask Dad sometimes; he knew when we could get away with it without trouble. My memories are happy, you know? And then, some bastard took us both, and he – he kept me for nearly three weeks. Something happened in those woods. Something that meant I made it and Alex didn't. I don't know why we weren't together. I wouldn't have left without – I don't know if I was dumped there, if he decided he didn't want me after all... I don't know.

"But that's *over two weeks* I can't remember. And after that things were shit, pretty much universally, for a long time. Dad – he wasn't the same after. He drank quite a bit, used to just sit and watch TV. He always watched a lot of TV but it was different, you know. Or maybe I noticed it more – without Alex to drag me outside to play. Anyway, Mum just soaked up all of that sadness..."

Silence fell again. I thought about all the years I'd spent wondering if Erin remembered more than the press knew. Wondering if the police might be holding something back. But now I realised that wasn't what had happened. She'd banged her head, and she'd forgotten it all.

I probably knew just as much, if not more, about what happened to her than she did.

"You know," she said, giving a wry laugh and finishing her cigarette, "if I had the choice between the woods and certain death? Even now? I think I still wouldn't choose the bloody woods ever again."

"Fuck, Erin. I'm sorry, I—"

Before I knew what was happening, Erin had leaned towards me again. Closer this time. Too close. Her lips grazed my cheek and my heart leapt in my chest and I stumbled away. My body ached to stay there, next to her, to feel her solid warmth against my arm. But I couldn't. This was meant to be *business*.

"No," I said. More bluntly than I meant to.

Even in the dark I could see Erin's blush. Her expression changed from its smirk to something else, embarrassment unfolding.

"I…"

"I don't think so. I don't…" I pushed away from the wall, my tongue twisting in knots.

"I'm sorry?"

"You've – we've been drinking. I can't. It's not right…"

"I'm not actually that drunk."

I was already walking, my feet tripping over themselves to get some space as much as the rest of my body hummed to stay next to her. Guilt wrapped itself in my chest. I didn't know what I was doing; I didn't know how to feel. I'd never thought of being with *anybody*, never mind a girl like Erin. And now it was all I could think about. But it was the alcohol, that blunt emotional honesty. Laying everything bare.

I stopped. Turned.

"Wait," I said. Hope flared in her eyes, but that only made it worse. "No, I mean… will you be able to get a taxi okay?"

For a second I thought Erin might swear at me but she didn't.

"I'll be fine," she said quietly.

"I'm – I'm sorry. I just… I'm trying to be professional and…"

"Harriet, it's – it's fine. Whatever. Okay? I'll get a taxi home. Thank you for dinner."

TWELVE

Harriet

I MADE IT ALL the way back to my flat before I checked my phone. I hoped by the time I got there Erin might have texted me. Might have… said what? Something. Anything. I felt like the world's biggest idiot – but I wasn't sure whether I was angry at myself for letting my guard down or for not kissing her back.

It was the wine. The stress of the memorial. Erin probably hadn't meant anything by it. But I was supposed to be the one who was in control; I was the one who had come into her life and disrupted it, so I should be responsible for what happened.

I tried to push down the feeling that grew in my chest, like I'd blown it. Not just for myself, but for the book. We'd finally been getting somewhere – Erin had opened up about herself without prompting, and that was important. And now I wasn't sure if she was mad at me.

I made coffee and drank a full cup before I could face my office and all of the notes and files within. It was really late, but knew I wouldn't be able to sleep for a while. I shot another quick email to Thomas, noticing he'd finally replied, with no real content. *Sorry Sis. So busy ADVENTURING. Saw a spider the size of my FOOT yesterday. Getting settled at the new job, Jessica says hi. You sound busy. Will Skype in a few days, ok? Lots of love, Tom.*

I went back to work. It was no good wishing that he'd be my sounding board, so I had to do this myself. I laid my scrapbook images out like a tarot spread, pictures and newspaper clippings for each of the missing pairs of children. I started with Jeremy and Michael. They were abducted on 3 July 1994. The photos I'd chosen for my file were the ones they used in the press. I had other pictures, ones my aunt and uncle had given me, which would go in the final book, but when I was writing I preferred to use the official media pictures; it made it easier to separate myself from them. Author from subject.

My cousins both had hair like burnished gold, that glorious autumn shade between brown and blond, smiling in their school pictures. Michael had a cheeky grin, one dimple.

I laid their photos to one side and read my initial notes. The boys were found three months apart, Mikey first on 18 July, two weeks after their abduction. My aunt and uncle said the autopsy suggested he'd probably been dead around a week. Jem was found on 6 October, miles and miles away from his brother, and he'd probably been dead for around six weeks. There was a suspiciously high level of insulin in Mikey's body, and although the tests were inconclusive the same was suspected for Jem. The theory was that they had been injected with it, and this is what had killed them.

They had both been dressed in pyjamas when they were found, but they weren't the ones they'd been wearing when they were taken. The police tried to identify the clothes, but they were store-bought from a large chain and had been on sale for months.

The boys both seemed well-fed, clean. Cared for, except they were dead.

Next were George and Jacob Evans – Molly's twins. They were taken at the start of the summer of 1995, almost a year after Jem and Michael. Only George was ever found. It had taken dental records to figure out which of the boys had died; he'd been injected with insulin, like my cousins, but his body had ended up in the River Derwent, which had left him in a bit of a state.

Morgan and Paul were taken in July 1996, a year after George's body was found. Morgan turned up almost another full year later. She had been healthy, but her body was more badly bruised than any of the other children. When she'd died, she hadn't gone quietly. But the bruises hadn't led the police anywhere – publicly at least. No handprints or weapon imprints of any kind that they could confirm. All we knew was that they occurred perimortem and hadn't had time to heal. Like the other children, Morgan had died from an insulin overdose. The autopsy had confirmed that she had been alive, and eating, less than a few hours before her body was found. Unlike the other children, though, he kept her alive for eleven months before finally killing her.

Charlotte and Hazel Davies were taken two months after Morgan's estimated date of death, disappearing from their beds in August 1997. Neither of them were ever found. And less than a year later, Randeep and Jaswinder went missing from their home in Burton.

This was where the pattern changed. Randeep and Jaswinder were abducted on 3 June and by 13 October the Father had struck again, stealing Erin and Alex Chambers on a warm autumn night. Two pairs of siblings in four months.

Auntie Sue said that at the time they wondered if he was *devolving*. Losing patience. Everybody was hoping it would mean he would slip up, make the sort of mistake that might allow the police to nail him. When Erin escaped it made people feel almost hopeful. But there was still no helpful evidence.

I recalled the tension, the summer following Erin's return. Everybody waiting with baited breath. Windows locked, curtains drawn in my house immediately after dark, official warnings on how to keep children safe. And then, when nothing happened, the relief. The same again the following year, and the one after that, until even the ghostly memory of Morgan with her eleven long months of captivity seemed to fade. The Father was gone. Finished. Perhaps licking his wounds after Erin's miraculous escape? Or perhaps locked up for arson and then dead in prison, like I'd once hoped.

But it was too late for all of the children he had hurt, and the broken families left behind. I thought about Morgan, the way she had been held away from her family for all that time before dying anyway. It wasn't fair.

I sat back, checked my phone. Nothing. I hoped Erin had made it home alright. I should have watched her get into a taxi.

I stared at the sheets of paper in front of me. I still, even days later, couldn't figure out exactly how Isaac Higgins and Oscar Tyrrell fit into all of this. They'd gone missing in 1993. But, like Detective Godfrey had pointed out, it hadn't been during the summer. It had been early March.

I kept coming back to the same things: how did the Father choose the children? And why did he take them at all? But I couldn't focus. Tonight all I could think about was Erin's face after I turned away from her. It was just a kiss on the cheek, but something about it had scared me. Maybe in a good way.

I didn't want to mess it up.

A sound outside the door of my flat made me jump. The empty study seemed to echo around me. I laid my notes aside and stood hesitantly. Listened. For a long while I heard nothing but my own breathing.

Then it happened again.

It was like a knock at my door. A single one. Knuckles on wood. I tiptoed out into the hall, and then towards the door. The spy hole was misty, but I peered through it anyway. I caught glimpses of shadows, the warped knot of my doormat kicked too far away from the door, my neighbours' neat and tidy across the hall. They were on holiday.

"Hello?" I said. "Is anybody there?"

No response.

I undid the latch and slowly opened the door. I didn't know what I expected, but the entry was abandoned. Silent. My heart thudded and I let out a short breath of relief.

And then I noticed the lift. It was going down.

THIRTEEN

7 NOVEMBER 2016

Erin

I'D WOKEN UP THIS morning with another migraine and decided to work from home. I chucked down a couple of strong painkillers and a cup of tea, and lit a few unscented candles before settling on the sofa. But I was jumpy, and the residual headache wasn't helped by Wendy, who'd texted me checking in mid-morning and sent me into another spiral of worry about the break-in. I couldn't reconcile what I thought had happened. Was it an interrupted burglary or a prank? I wanted to believe it hadn't happened at all, that I'd made the whole thing up, but I couldn't get past the idea that I'd never have left that window open.

And then there was the doll. Mum said she didn't remember leaving it there, but she'd had a box full of things for me to sort through. Had I found it and put it in my bedroom? I didn't think that was possible, that I might have forgotten something like that, but how else could it have ended up on my bed? Perhaps the police officer had found it somewhere else and moved it. The uncertainty gnawed away at me.

I wasn't getting anywhere with my latest website project anyway; my head was all over the place. I couldn't stop thinking about last night, too. The way Harriet had reacted. The feeling of embarrassment was worse today – perhaps because I'd had more to drink than I thought. But I had no reason to be embarrassed. It wasn't like I had to worry about Monica any more. Our relationship had been casual for a long time before it ended anyway.

I'd sent her several messages over the last few days. The only response she'd deigned to give me was a single text which just said *leave me alone*. I knew better than to push her but I couldn't help feeling bad about the other night.

My brain kept coming back to Harriet. I hadn't even kissed her properly, so why did I feel so embarrassed? Perhaps it was because it hadn't happened and I wanted it to.

The painkillers had taken the edge off my headache but the migraine made my brain feel too woolly for work. I found myself drifting back to what Harriet had said about her cousins and those other boys. I needed to know more. I needed to find out if Harriet's hunch was more than a hunch.

I did a Google search for the runaway foster brothers. I'd let her tell me about them over dinner, but I didn't know why. What was I hoping for? Did I want them to be connected to Alex and me, or was I hoping that it was all in Harriet's head? Why was I torturing myself?

I started my search with their names: *Oscar Tyrrell and Isaac Higgins missing*. There were a couple of articles, old newspaper links and references to the case on a few blogs. I waded through it all, but found little more than I already knew. The boys had run away from their foster home in the middle of the night, were spotted at a bus station the following day, and after that they were never seen again.

I tried every search I could think of, across various websites and social media. I even trawled through Reddit. I managed to find another newspaper article, more recent, which led me to Facebook.

There was a page, last updated in 2009, created by the boys' foster mother, Jenny Bowles. It was a cross between a self-help page for parents whose children had run away from home, and something else. Something angrier. I scrolled through the posts, noticing that the more recent ones Jenny Bowles had posted were different from the early ones. The later ones were less about her children *running away* and more generalised, about her loss, her anger. Almost as if she'd changed her mind about what had happened to them.

And then I found an address – a *home* address – and a contact number. The page asked for all kind mail to be directed to a residential address in Derby. "Your warm wishes have supported me through my tough times. Thank you. P.S. NO INTERVIEW REQUESTS."

Derby. That wasn't far from Arkney.

My stomach twisted as I realised I wanted to talk to her.

Half an hour later I pulled up outside the address I'd grabbed from the Facebook page. I knew it was a risk turning up without any confirmation that Jenny was still living here, but after last night I felt a strong urge to confirm what Harriet had told me.

Google Maps led me to an area just outside of Derby city centre. The address was for a block of flats, newer than a lot of the properties around it, which were a bit run-down and grubby. I parked in the courtyard. Then, on second thought, I pulled back out onto the road, tucking the mirrors in and hiding my valuables in the glove box before stepping out.

I peered at the list of names next to the door and felt a flutter of excitement, or fear, when I saw the little white sticker marked *J Bowles*. I pressed the buzzer.

Nothing.

I held it again, this time for longer.

Finally, something happened. There was a faint crackling sound on the other end and then a weedy female voice came on the box.

"Yesss?"

"Sorry to bother you. My car broke down outside. I was wondering if I could come inside to use your phone? Mine's run out of battery." I wasn't about to make the same mistake as Harriet.

There was a muffled sound, followed by a click. Then a long exhale.

"Okay... Come up a floor. The door's open."

Another exhale. Another click. Then the door buzzed. I followed the stairs upwards until I hit another corridor, a dark blue carpet leading me down a short hallway towards a door at the end. I knocked quickly but didn't wait. The door swung open to reveal a brightly lit entrance hall painted a cheerful blue.

"Hello?" I called.

"In the lounge, duck." Another exhaling sound.

I followed the sound off to the left and into a small sitting room. It was decorated in shades of gold and brown paisley. Not exactly tasteful but lived in. There was a sofa against the back wall; the woman sitting on it was probably in her late sixties. Tightly curled grey hair framed her face and her eyes were very blue.

I spotted the source of the breathing sound immediately. Hooked up to her nose was a tube which ran down to a canister sat on the floor. She regarded me with a shrewd gaze and then smiled when she decided I didn't pose a threat. I wondered if she made a habit of letting strangers into her flat when she was so clearly unable to defend herself.

"Excuse me not getting up, duck," she said. "You said your car broke down?"

I didn't flinch. It was too late to change my story now.

"Yes. Just outside. Can I borrow your phone to call AA? As I mentioned, my phone battery died, and I don't know the area very well."

Jenny Bowles gestured towards a vintage-style black handset sitting on a table beside the sofa. I thought fast as I tried to figure out how to play this.

I eyed the phone and then decided. I dialled the number of my landline, hoping that it looked like a legitimate number for a car repair should anybody bother to check. When the number went to voicemail I did my best to sound like I was having a conversation with somebody.

I glanced around. Across the mantelpiece of an electric fire there were photographs. Too many for me to see which ones might be Isaac and Oscar.

After I hung up I turned to smile at the lady again.

"They're sending somebody out. Said it would be about twenty minutes." I let this hang in the air and kept my face expectant yet friendly.

"Do you want to stay while you wait?" she asked. Very trusting. I wondered if I looked more sympathetic than Harriet, with her glossy red hair and intimidating stare. I wondered what she'd say when I told her I'd come here.

"Thank you," I said. I gestured towards the photographs on the mantel with one hand. "Are those your family?"

"My children." She let out an exhale sound again and smiled. "Lots of them. I've had lots of babies over the years." She paused. "They're all my babies; fostered or adopted, but all mine."

I sank down onto the sofa near her, my hands pressed between my knees. I didn't know how to ask her about Oscar and Isaac. In the end, I didn't have to.

"They're all up there," she said. "Even the two that were taken from me."

"Oh?" *Yes.* Not only had she asked me to stay but she *wanted* to talk. And that phrase. *Taken from me...* I tried to keep my face sympathetic but vaguely disinterested. "I'm sorry...?"

"My boys. We thought they ran away..."

"And – you don't think that now?"

Jenny shrugged. "It doesn't matter what I think. I'm an angry old woman." She turned to me and reached out; her arthritic fingers latched onto my arm with surprising strength. "You should never get old. It sucks the hope out of you."

"What happened to them?" I asked. "If you don't mind me asking…"

"I lost them. They were there, one minute. Arguing before bed – playfully, like brothers do. And I put them to bed like I always did. And in the morning they were gone."

"You don't think they ran away in the night?"

"I expect they did. But I don't think they meant to stay gone. They were good boys, both of them. I think they were… testing boundaries, but something happened."

"I'm so sorry," I said. And I truly meant it.

Jenny smiled. "You seem like the kind of girl I'd have liked for a daughter. Friendly. You know you shouldn't trust strangers?"

I almost laughed. "I know. I don't normally. This was sort of unavoidable."

"It's always unavoidable." She sighed. "Always. I said *that* was unavoidable. Except of course it wasn't at all. If we'd only known…"

"What could you have done?"

"Something," Jenny said simply. "Everything. I would have done *anything* if I'd known somebody would take them from me."

"Do you think… they were taken by somebody they knew?" I asked tentatively.

Jenny looked at me with the first hints of suspicion but didn't hesitate when she answered.

"Could have been. Always can be, can't it?"

Jenny was lonely. I could tell, despite the photographs, that she was on her own a lot of the time. The place was clean, but empty. She was desperate to talk, to tell her story, but probably didn't want the pressure of *explaining* herself like she would have to with a journalist.

"Yes," I agreed. "It's a scary thought, but it's true."

"Do you have any siblings?" Jenny asked suddenly.

I flinched.

"I… I did. I do." I didn't know what else to say. But Jenny clearly wasn't done.

"Siblings," Jenny Bowles said again. "They protect each other. They *should*."

I felt my heart in my throat. Jenny had spoken with such force, such raw honesty, but her meaning was masked.

"What?" I asked stupidly.

That seemed to bring Jenny back to the cheerful old woman I'd met when I first arrived. She withdrew her hand from my arm with surprising speed and fixed her smile again.

"I suppose you'd better go," she said firmly. No mention of my car. Of the AA that was meant to be coming to fix me up. I felt a slither of guilt worm up inside me.

"Yes. Look, I'm sorry—"

"Don't apologise, duck. These things can't be helped."

I left the way I came, only now the hallway felt darker. I found myself checking the shadows. I started to feel my skin crawl, like it used to when I was nervous as a child. I scratched at my arm, feeling it prickle like there were little needles underneath, the skin getting red and sore. I'd fought so hard to overcome this habit, the scratching, the raw skin, the nervous desire to run nails over flesh when it felt like there were a thousand bugs underneath. I clenched my fist and forced my hand away.

By the time I made it to my car my heart was hammering in my chest and my palms were sweaty.

It felt like drowning, like a whole lake full of water sitting on top of my head, panic holding me down. I realised that Harriet was right. All of the thoughts I'd been ignoring since she told me about the boys just crashed over me like a wave, all of them at once. If Oscar and Isaac were taken by the Father, did that mean the police might have new leads? Would it even matter?

Siblings should protect each other. I wondered what Jenny meant. I'd failed Alex, but how did she know that? Was she talking about her boys, or somebody else?

I couldn't remember where I'd put my phone. It took me several long minutes to remember that I'd stashed it in the glove compartment. When I found it, I saw I'd a missed call and a text. Both from a number I didn't recognise – until I saw it was the same number I'd called to reach Harriet.

The text simply said *I'm sorry about last night. Call me? I can make it up to you – again.*

I ignored it until my hands were steadier. I dialled Monica's number instead, needing to funnel some of my nerves into something that wasn't – whatever this was.

She picked up on the third ring, as though she may have been holding her phone. I don't know why I rang her, except that I wanted to hear a familiar voice, even an angry one.

"Mon, hi."

"Erin, I can't talk to you."

"Why not? I know I was a bit shit but there's a lot going on. I've got… some personal stuff—"

"What, and I don't? Look, it's freaking me out, okay. You need to get this to stop. I understand. But the least you could do was talk to me if you're seeing somebody else, Erin. I don't care what you've got going on but leaving gifts at my house is fucking *weird*."

"Hang on—"

"No, Erin. It's not cool, okay? I get the picture. You're not available. *Stop calling me*."

The call disconnected.

BEFORE

Mouse

THE DOCTOR LET THEM go home but he didn't feel better. Mother herded them into the car and Chris started to complain immediately. *I'm tired, I'm cold, I'm hungry* – it was never-ending. Why couldn't he just shut up and deal with it like the rest of them had to?

By the time they got home Mouse was feeling even worse and Chris was doing his head in.

"Little Bear, your brother is poorly, we've got to try to be quiet." Mother was doing her usual simpering thing, her immaculate hair pulled back in a neat bun and her smile mechanical. She must have learned it when she was an actress. That was a lifetime ago, now. Before she got married and had children.

She cocked her head to the side and made her eyes all wide and for a second it always seemed real – really real. Like she actually cared. But it had been an act since Father left. Mother told them at first he was in the basement, and then that he was working, and then that he was living in the grounds of the big house. Mouse didn't know what to believe.

Chris didn't shut up until they fed him. Cheese sandwiches cut into triangles without the crust and cake for dessert. Chris ate it all but Mouse couldn't keep anything down. He hadn't been able to since dinner last night. Mother said it would be better if he ate something he could throw up easily and the doctor said the feeling would pass, but so far it hadn't even gone away a little bit.

It had been this way since they'd moved in, though. Since Father had stopped tucking him in at night. There were random evenings where he sat down to dinner feeling fine and by the time he went to bed he was ready to puke up his guts. *Spores. Mould. The damp. Milk allergy. Maybe it's the bread.* Mother rolled her eyes and waved her hands and petted his head like he was a dog while he underwent test after test after test.

"There, there, Mouse," she always said. She held him tight and he smelled foreign worlds on her work uniform. He knew she worked in lots of places, with lots of different people, and sometimes she liked to just drive and sit in her car for hours before picking him up from the childminder. She stared at the people on the street outside the houses where she visited people who needed to be cared for, tears striping her cheeks. She'd done it once while he was in the car – she'd forgotten he was there.

"Mother's here," she always said when he was sick.

But she wasn't. Not really. She was on another planet half the time, her thoughts stuck in some loop of Back Then. Once or

132

twice he'd caught her watching tapes of her old performances on video. She got dressed up for it, eyeliner and eyebrows and face powder. She wore heels and a dress even though she never left the bedroom and she always sighed dramatically when she saw her own face on screen.

The woman on TV was different. Not really Mother. It was so different to how she was now that he couldn't believe they were the same person. It wasn't just that she was younger or that she looked kinder. It was everything; the way she spoke, the way she moved, the willowy strength that had faded to dumpy force over the years.

If he challenged her about how much she'd changed, she got angry. Once she had hit him. She might be distant when she was alone with him but in public her act fooled everybody. All she had to do was channel the way she treated Chris *all* the time. The doctor always said that he'd never seen a more devoted mother, even if *the boy* didn't appreciate it.

He didn't want to appreciate it. He hated her. She was plastic, merely a stand-in for the mother he remembered. As though she had forgotten that he was as much her son as Chris was.

Tonight it was one of those nights where she didn't leave him alone. It was always this way when he got unwell. She stayed with him all night, only relinquishing her bedside vigil when Chris had a night terror and started to cry. She rushed to Bear's aid and the room was quiet and dark after she left. Peaceful. He liked it better when she was gone, none of that fake sympathy.

He lay in bed and thought of Father. Of what he would do when he found out how Mother was acting. He imagined that he would get very, very angry.

That *was* something he could appreciate.

EXCERPT

Morgan & Paul Bailey
Abducted: Chesterfield, 5 July 1996

When Morgan (9) and Paul (5) were abducted from their ground-floor bedroom in the bungalow where they lived, the family hadn't been planning to live there much longer. The house had been too small for a growing family.

"I was pregnant with Sarah then. We were looking at houses," Vera Bailey explained, "but we hadn't found anywhere yet. In the end we moved for a different reason. A fresh start, you know."

Vera's youngest daughter was born in October 1996, just three months after Morgan and Paul were abducted. When I visited Vera's house – a spacious cottage in Calow – she was alone, but her house was filled with photographs of her children.

"We like to have them with us. It was so important for Sarah growing up, to know about her brother and sister. We didn't want her to feel like she was eclipsed by them, obviously. It's not like that. It's – God, it's hard to explain, isn't it?"

We took a short break while Vera made tea. When she was ready to talk again she told me a little more about Morgan and Paul. "Morgan was the typical older sibling. She loved to boss Paul around. Not in a mean way, she just liked to be in charge. She was very bookish, loved to read, she was quite girly too. Barbies and, what were those little things? Polly Pockets? She had loads of them.

"Paul loved playing with Morgan so much – loved everything they did together. Barbies were actually his favourite kind of toy. Dolls, anything where he could dress them up or do their hair." Vera smiled at the memory. "They used to take dolls everywhere. Paul's favourite was this baby doll with a little pink dress, you know the life-sized ones? When you sat her upright her eyes opened, and when you laid her down they closed. He used to rock her and feed her and everything."

"Did Sarah like dolls?" I asked.

"Nope." Vera laughed. "Sarah would never be caught with dolls. She was all about climbing trees, building stuff, trucks and diggers and cars. Probably – probably better that way, to be honest. She's a mechanic now."

Talking to Vera I could see plainly the spaces in her life that her older children had left behind.

"I didn't ever want Sarah to feel like she didn't know them," Vera said later. "And that was – that was hard. It was hard because we didn't mourn them like we wanted to. After all that time we thought Morgan was dead. We thought they both were, because some of the others – died quickly. We thought she was like them. But she wasn't, was she? And Paul… We were wrong once, what if we were wrong about Paul being dead too?"

This, then, must have been the hardest burden to bear. For eleven months Vera had mourned her daughter and her son together, only to find out that Morgan had been alive all that time. And they'd never know what happened.

"Morgan was such a good big sister. She'd have loved Sarah. So would Paul. He'd have wanted to dress her up and comb her hair and everything. We joked he'd either become a hairdresser or an actor when he grew up. Morgan used to punch anybody who told him that dolls were for girls. She'd always say, 'Yeah, and getting smacked is for bullies.' I knew we shouldn't encourage it but it was so damn reassuring, knowing that whatever happened they'd look out for each other.

"That's why I thought they'd be – together. It was almost easier, at first. Knowing that Paul and Morgan were together. Even if we never found them. Then when that poor family found Morgan in the park, and she was... Once we buried her, it made it harder to mourn Paul. We couldn't go to the cemetery and see him. And every time we went it just... it compounded the fact that they weren't together any more.

"We just kept thinking, when they found her, over and over, *why there, why then?*"

She didn't have to say the rest but I knew what she was thinking: *and what happened to Paul?*

FOURTEEN

7 NOVEMBER 2016

Erin

I CALLED HARRIET.

"Hey," she said on the second ring. "Uh. Are you okay?"

"I'm fine." I had no idea what Monica had been talking about but I didn't want to think about it right now. I could barely keep it together as it was.

"How—"

"I'm sorry," I said.

There was the awkwardness between us again. It felt like last night was a year ago, a lifetime ago. When we'd been comfortable, when I'd wanted to talk. And I missed that already, that closeness I hadn't had with anybody for a long time. I knew I shouldn't care – Harriet was still essentially a stranger – but I was shaken by the morning, by my cryptic conversation with Jenny Bowles and how it felt like I knew even less now than I'd originally thought. And I wanted somebody to talk to. Somebody who understood.

"Listen," I said, before Harriet could say anything else. "I need to get out of here. I need to do something." I blew a breath out, unsure even as I said it where I was going with this. "I want to remember. I'm tired of being broken."

"You're not—"

"I am," I cut her off. "It feels like it sometimes, anyway. And I don't want to be."

The silence felt static between us. I imagined Harriet, sat at home or in a small office, her hair like fire. I imagined her face – thoughtful, like when I'd told her about my candles. Her canines exposed when she smiled, pointed like a wolf.

Eventually she said, "I've got an idea. If you're serious about me helping you to remember. But you won't like it."

My stomach tumbled but I shook myself. "What did you have in mind?"

Harriet picked me up from my house since we'd both finished work early. We didn't speak much at first, a tension between us that neither of us was willing to address, but as we drove we settled into a comfortable silence. Forty minutes passed, the trees and road signs tumbling by. I didn't ask where we were going – despite everything in me saying I should, I didn't want to know. I wanted to trust Harriet to make this decision for me, to not have to be responsible for once.

But as we pulled into a car park, the Pay and Display machine the only sign of human life, I began to regret my decision. There were no cars here, no dog-walkers out today. It was the same view that haunted me at night sometimes and I felt my mouth go dry. The sun was low, the sky tinted lilac-grey.

"Here?" I said quietly.

"I told you you wouldn't like it," Harriet said. "We don't have to stay. I just – it might be useful to jog your memory. I thought, after what we were talking about last night…"

"Do you think this will achieve anything?" I asked. "I mean, really? You think if I show you how I supposedly stumbled out of these woods after nearly three weeks away from home I'll suddenly remember everything that happened to me while I was gone?"

"Supposedly?"

"*Supposedly*. I don't remember anything meaningful. Just the darkness, and being terrified. Before I saw that bloody Pay and Display sign, that jogger, it's all a jumbled mess. They've been trying to get me to remember for years, Harriet. The liaison officer, therapy, all sorts of shit. I told them to pack it in because there's nothing real in there."

Harriet was quiet for a moment. The motor was still running, the heaters blasting out too-warm air.

"Have you been back here since?" Harriet asked.

"Why would I? It's not exactly my favourite place." I scowled as I remembered. "Actually, that's not true. The police brought me. They wanted me to retrace my steps because the dogs couldn't track me. The rain was heavy and they couldn't see, and I think one of the dogs got caught in some kind of trap? I'd run through a – a bit of the river, like across the flood plains where the mud had just… Anyway, it was still raining when I came out of the woods and I couldn't

140

remember which way… They never figured out where I'd come from – only that there are a few farms and old houses nearby and it could have been any of them. Or none of them. There are a lot of roads, so I might have come from one of them. The only CCTV is near here, I think, and obviously that's not where I started out. I think they tried to use those number plate recognition things but they never figured out if I came out of a car or a house or what."

"But you've never been back here on your own?"

"I've only ever come when they made me. I'm not even sure I want to be here now."

"Do you want to leave?"

I blew out a breath, digging around in my pockets for my cigarettes and lighter. Reassured by their presence I shook my head.

"No. It's fine. I guess… maybe it'll shake something loose."

We got out of the car and picked our way carefully across the packed earth that formed a path into the trees beyond the car park. I knew that a wooded patch stretched for miles beyond here, right up to a small golf green to the east and a few farms and big, old houses scattered up to the north and west, towards Stanshope and Wetton. But it felt like the trees were endless. They were tall and dark, like an army of ghosts.

I shivered.

I led the way, although I didn't know where I was going. The air was warmer in the cocoon of the woods, the wind relegated to a gentle whistling sound. Clusters of oak trees and silver birches surrounded us, blocking the sky and the way ahead. The light was weak and grey; it was darker in here than it had been in the car park, a feeling encouraged by the rich blackness of the soil underfoot. It would be so easy for the woods to swallow us whole. We probably had less than an hour before it got dark.

"Have *you* been here before?" I asked. I lit a cigarette, needing to do something with my hands.

"What?"

"Have you been here before? In these woods?"

"Yes," she said. "A few times up at the other end. I used to live quite close. I came with my brother and my dad when I was a kid – for the golf course."

"Why would you come here? It's a horrible place."

She shook her head.

"No, it isn't," she said.

I felt the words like a punch and Harriet looked at me with panicked eyes.

"I don't mean it like that," she added quickly. "Obviously it's a horrible place to you. I just mean, it doesn't *have* to be. It's just trees and dirt and grass, farms and fields. But of course it's horrible for you – because of what happened."

The air had chilled again. I rubbed at my arms half-heartedly, trying not to let myself get angry.

"But this place," Harriet continued, "didn't have anything to do with the awful thing that happened to you. Just like my aunt and uncle's house didn't have anything to do with Jem and Mikey being abducted—"

I turned, unable to control myself now. "Do they still live

there, then?" I snapped. "Do they feel happy there in that house?"

"Yes, actually." Harriet shrugged. "I think they like knowing that they've got all of their memories, still. And Jem and Mikey's favourite places. The tree out front they used to climb, the fountain in the garden they used to throw tennis balls into. It makes them – all of us, really – feel close to them… It's how we dealt with it, I guess."

"That's not how my parents dealt with it," I said. "We stayed in the house for a while. Until we could afford to move. I hated it. Hated that bedroom. I had nightmares – every night. I fell asleep in the bathroom a lot. When we moved it was better. Like a fresh start." I shrugged.

We'd left the dog walkers' path now. It would be so easy to get lost in here again tonight and the thought made me want to shrink into myself. Despite everything I was glad of Harriet's presence by my side as the shadows lengthened, as the trees made our footsteps echo. It felt like being watched by a hundred pairs of eyes.

"You might have come from that way," Harriet said then, gesturing towards a smaller dirt path that branched off. It was covered in tangles of leaves and undergrowth. "The other way leads up towards the river round that loop. It rained heavily the couple of nights before you were found, and there were flash floods and a couple of mud slides in the area. They couldn't find any trace of a car, but given the state you were in when you were found the police surmised that you probably travelled a decent distance on foot."

"I can't have come that far," I whispered. But we didn't

know how long I'd been walking before I collapsed in the car park. It could have been hours.

I let myself head towards the smaller path. Harriet followed a few steps behind.

"No," she agreed. "But the police searched all of the houses and farms nearby. One of the theories at the time was that you were dumped here and he drove away. You had a pretty nasty head wound and people said that he maybe thought you were… going to die." She went quiet.

"Go on," I prompted.

"The police canvassed the area, talked to everybody who lived nearby, but never came up with anything solid. Either the folks had alibis or they were too far away, or the houses were empty. There are a few properties north of here that fit the bill for the isolation, but there was no evidence that anybody had had any children there. I think they even used, like, thermal imaging or something? The dog-trap situation was a problem."

"They never knew when exactly I left him," I said quietly. "How long I'd been out here, away from Alex. There was a two-week window and I couldn't tell them anything. Maybe we were in one of the farmhouses just temporarily or something and he let me go. Or maybe, like you said, I was hurt and he thought I was gonna die anyway. Who knows?"

I felt the panic rising inside me. The trees were too tall, too close. I sped up, stumbling, my breath coming in spurts. Then I felt Harriet's hand on my shoulder, warm and solid.

"Let you go?" she asked. "What makes you think he let you go?"

I fought the panic. "I was seven years old, Harriet. Alex was – older. He was well-behaved. Maybe I made the Father angry. Maybe Alex was better than me."

Better. It was the first time I'd realised that this was how I'd felt, all that time after I came back, this was what I was afraid of. What if Alex was dead, and I wasn't, because he was better than me somehow?

"How do you know you didn't just escape?"

A laugh that was painful and full of *everything* burst out of me. "I just do, okay."

"But *how*? You were the only one who was found alive. You could have been at a service station and managed to get away. Maybe in one of the lay-bys. There's a petrol station not far from here with a decent-sized parking area, no cameras, and we know he travelled across counties often, so he probably had to refuel at some point and maybe you managed to run. Maybe you thought you could get help—"

"I wouldn't have done that!"

My voice shattered the ticking quiet of the wood, startling a dark bird that dove out of a tree with a fractured *caw*.

"I wouldn't have left him," I said, this time more quietly.

I *couldn't* have left him.

"You might not have had a choice."

"Stop," I said tiredly. "Please stop. Let's just walk, okay?"

I cut blindly through the thicker undergrowth where branches and brambles caught at my jeans, ignoring the path now. I

145

shook them off, anger still simmering, hiding the fear beneath. The woods seemed to groan around us. Wind tossed the leaves. It felt like the dips and hollows were trying to catch me, drag me right back to the darkness.

I reached a spot where there was a steep incline. I looked up at the bank, with its golden leaves and hidden traps just waiting to suck me down.

"Are you going up there?" Harriet asked. "You'll kill us both. It's got to be a forty-five-degree angle."

I clenched my fists inside my coat pockets, and then pulled them out and started to climb. Harriet let out a bewildered sound but followed. We scrambled up, my weak ankle screaming as I grabbed onto roots and branches and rocks.

When we emerged at the top, where the land evened out and the trees stretched dizzyingly high above, I felt a sickening twist in my belly. Like a shadow at the corner of my vision.

"I…" There was nothing special about these trees. Was there?

I closed my eyes against the beginnings of twilight, tried to remember how this might have looked at night. I pictured silver-gilded shadows. I felt sweat bead on my back and the hairs rise on my arms.

And then I remembered sliding, darkness, brambles and bark clawing at my bare hands and my back as I fell. The smell of fresh dirt all around me. My whole body wet, trembling, hands and feet like ice…

"Erin?"

Harriet was at my side. I opened my eyes, saw the weak

silver-grey light of the early evening and the autumn-jacketed earth again. I lifted my hand to my face, almost surprised to find it clean of blood and dirt.

"I'm fine."

"Did you remember something?"

I spun. Harriet's green eyes were alight with curiosity. I wanted to be angry with her. I wanted to *want* to slap her away for being so transparently excited. But I couldn't deny the excited lurch in my own stomach. I'd remembered something.

But it was just a feeling. Nothing real.

"Just the darkness." I unclenched my hands and stepped away.

"Is that all?" she asked pointedly.

"I think I fell. I was soaked, maybe from the river. I fell down there." I pointed down the hill we'd just climbed. I could almost feel the graze at the base of my back, the thudding in my skull.

"That's a long way down. Especially for a kid."

"I know. I think it's why——"

"Why you don't remember. Your head injury. It makes sense. I always wondered if your injury had happened before, if that might be why you were in the woods. I thought maybe… that might be why he left you." Harriet grimaced. "I'm sorry if this upset you. But I'm glad, I guess if that's the word, that you didn't remember something worse."

I swallowed hard. "Hey," I tried for a light tone. "Remember last night when I said I'd never take the woods again, even over certain death? Next time hold me to that."

Because I wasn't sure there *was* anything worse than this. I'd been running. Why would I have been running if I hadn't left Alex behind? I couldn't fight the thoughts any more, the fears that had eaten me alive for eighteen years.

If I'd escaped, and left my brother behind, what did that say about me?

FIFTEEN

Erin

ON THE DRIVE BACK to my house my thoughts returned to Monica. What had prompted her to freak out like that? And what were those gifts she was talking about? I hadn't thought much of it earlier – in the light of day – but it was getting dark now, and tension bubbled deep inside me. I texted her again, but got no response.

"Thank you," Harriet said. "For your patience today."

I surprised myself by laughing. "Thank you for driving. Pity it was a waste of time."

Harriet shrugged. Again there was that humming static between us. It felt less like awkwardness now, though, more like a different kind of tension.

"Will you be okay staying here tonight?" she asked hesitantly as we pulled up outside my house.

I snorted to hide the feeling in my chest. I knew I should go and stay elsewhere, but where was there I could go? I didn't want to sleep at Mum's again. I refused to be driven out of my own home.

"I'll be fine," I said. "But thanks."

She left soon after and the air felt empty when she was gone. A neighbour closed the boot of their car and I jumped, heart slamming in my chest. *Stupid*. Stupid arsehole for breaking into my house to scare me. Stupid Monica, not texting me back. Stupid Harriet for taking me back to those woods.

Inside I poured myself a drink, put on a TV boxset in the background, and busied myself with cleaning. The place was still a bit of a mess from when I'd thrown everything about while checking if anything was missing – and it hadn't exactly been spotless before. I lit homemade candles over the mantelpiece, glad for their glowing warmth. Something about candles soothed me, although their naked flames had frightened me once.

Over the years I had figured out how to love them, their light so soft and yellow, and the ones I'd made recently smelled like a pine forest, fresh and green, which reminded me of Christmas. It was like overcoming that small fear had allowed me to feel like an adult, Erin instead of Jillian...

When it got late enough I blew out the candles and snuck upstairs to my bedroom. I lit more upstairs, ones in jars. When I climbed into bed I left a couple burning on my bedside table to hold back the dark.

It didn't work. My dreams were plagued by shadows all wearing Alex's face. The sky was just beginning to get light when I started to consciousness. I had been dead asleep, the most recent dream leaving a residue like a low moaning sound I could hear deep inside my chest.

"Hello?" I called into the dimness. The candles were still

burning, their light casting writhing shadows. I slipped from my bed, unsure what had woken me. A cold draught snaked around my bare legs. I grabbed a hoodie from the back of a chair and threw it over my shoulders.

My heart was pounding. I couldn't tell whether I'd been woken by a noise or just by my dreams. I pushed my nails tightly into the palms of my hands and grabbed my phone. Crept out into the hallway. The house was still and quiet now. I was going mad.

Then I heard it again. A clatter that was like somebody walking on the lino in the kitchen. I had definitely locked the door, and all of the windows were shut tight. Maybe I'd accidentally shut a neighbour's cat inside – that had happened once in my old house...

The stairs opened out into the hallway. There was nothing down here. Just the burnt-down stubs of the candles I'd blown out hours ago, standing like sentries on the mantel.

I headed for the kitchen. The worktops were limned with silver moonlight, spotless and shining where I'd cleaned them earlier. The tap dripped. The window was open, just a crack – its little silver key no longer sitting in the lock. But that wasn't what caught my eye.

I lifted my phone and started to dial.

Right in the middle of the floor somebody had arranged candles into the shape of a heart. Not my candles. Thick red ones. The red wax had run off, coating the linoleum floor with puddles that looked like blood. Their wicks were still lit, the fire still going.

It was a message.

"You don't share the house with anybody?" the police officer asked. He was a different one than the last one, and younger still. He had a scab under his nose where he'd nicked it shaving and I stared at it.

"What? Uh, no, just me." I rubbed my hands on my knees.

"Looks like a prank to me," he said, his tone verging on unkind.

"No, but…"

"There isn't any sign of anybody breaking in. Maybe somebody has a key? Do you have a key for that window?"

"Yes, but nobody else has one. There's… I mean there should be one in the lock but there isn't." I felt my cheeks flush. When was the last time I'd had company? Would Monica have done something like this, to fuck with me? Jesus, maybe it was her in the house the other night, too.

"Just seems funny to me. A flaming heart. I bet it's somebody you know. A joke. Really I should give you a warning." The policeman shook his head as if I was a drunk teenager who'd been caught stealing a traffic cone. He wandered back into the lounge and catalogued my candle-making supplies laid out on the dining table.

"Those *are* mine," I said, attempting to make my tone light.

"It's not funny. It's a waste of resources." The officer frowned. "You mentioned you had an open case with us."

"Yes. Another… break-in."

"Right. Well, here's my card. Give me a call if you find

anything is missing. Otherwise, Miss Chambers, I suggest you get all of your window keys back and tell your friends to stop playing jokes on you."

I didn't know what to say to that so I clamped my lips shut and folded my arms. Anger rose inside me. It wasn't a joke, and I wasn't wasting their time. Was I?

After he'd gone I wandered back into my kitchen. The candles still sat there in that stupid heart shape. I stared at the window. Then, angrily I stomped back upstairs to bed, where I knew I wouldn't be able to sleep.

SIXTEEN

8 NOVEMBER 2016

Harriet

"DID YOU HEAR WHAT I said?"

Sharon peered at me over the top of my computer monitor. It was after 1 p.m., and most people had settled back down at their desks already. My salad sat in a Tupperware pot in front of me, hardly touched.

"Sorry, what?"

Sharon rolled her eyes. She liked doing that – rolling her eyes, shrugging her shoulders, waving her hands about like a child wafting at a bee. It just added to the impression I had of her, which was that she had no idea what she was doing either. She'd said as much, once, about how she wasn't sure how she'd ended up in this job but she was good at it. Like me. It meant we usually got along fine, even if she was my manager and she was meant to know better – and take less of my shit.

"I said you don't look well. Are you okay?"

"Sure, just tired. Headache." I hadn't stopped thinking about the woods since yesterday. And how awful I'd felt leaving

Erin outside her house last night. How afraid she'd looked. There was something else going on, too. The way she'd kept checking her phone, as though she was desperately hoping for a message.

"Earth to Harriet?"

"What?"

Sharon leaned in, her acrylic nails clawing either side of my computer terminal as she gripped the other side of my desk.

"Go home, H," she said. "You're no use to me like this."

"But—"

"You've been distracted recently – and you've not taken a holiday all year. I'd rather you take some time now than in January when I actually need you. Take your laptop home if you have to. Just keep in touch."

It felt like a dismissal, but perhaps it was a blessing. I hadn't taken any holiday because it hadn't seemed worth it. She was right, so I didn't argue.

I threw my work laptop and uneaten lunch in the boot of my car and pulled out of the parking space, not really sure where I was going to go. I had more interviews lined up for later this week but I couldn't even really think about those now. It was all Erin, fear after her break-in and remembering my own worry after that lift trick the other night… It was probably nothing, but to get into the building you needed a key.

My phone rang and I'd accepted the call with the car's Bluetooth in seconds.

"It's me." Erin's voice was strained.

"What's up?" Alarm hummed through me.

"It happened again," she said. "I think. Somebody broke in through my kitchen window. While I was sleeping. They were gone when I woke up. There was this shape made out of burning candles in the middle of the room."

"Erin, that's awful!" I exclaimed. "Did they take anything? Did you tell the police?"

"I called the police, yeah. An officer came and had a look, but he said it was probably a joke. I couldn't find the key for the window, so he said it might be my – friends. He told me off for wasting police time. Like a *caution*, if you can believe it. I just want to—"

"What? A caution?"

"Just a mild one, but maybe he was right. The officer said there wasn't any evidence of anything except somebody leaving candles in my kitchen. Who does that unless it's a prank? He found my candle-making stuff and I guess the police didn't find anything last time either because it was like this guy definitely thought I was some dumb student or something."

"Erin, do you want me—"

"I need to get away from my house," Erin blurted. "I've got to think about things, calm down. I'm so angry. I need to distract myself."

I thought for a second. It had been my suggestion to go to the woods yesterday and I wasn't sure whether that had helped – but Erin seemed to have recalled *something*. Was it worth trying something similar? Maybe afterwards she'd feel ready to talk about what had happened and it might help her to calm down.

"I think I have another idea for something we could do," I said. "But—"

"As long as it's not the woods," Erin said, "I'll try anything. I just want to get these memories out of my goddamn brain. Are you at work? If not, can you please come and pick me up?"

I knew from the original missing person's case that Erin had grown up in a small detached house right on the edge of a village called Little Merton, about half an hour's drive from the car park where she'd turned up after her abduction. The village was like a smaller version of Arkney, most houses built in the last twenty years. Like Arkney, too, it had a sort of false quaintness to it. Houses styled as if they'd been built much longer ago, little parks dotted between rows of biggish homes. A safe place to raise a family.

I'd googled the property before leaving the office car park, only to find that it was currently up for sale, and the sellers were eager. The building had lovely golden brick walls and a chocolate slate roof, two little circular windows downstairs making it look like a gingerbread house.

I sensed Erin growing tenser as we drove. She knew before I told her where we were going. She'd probably known it was on the cards from the moment she opened up the other night, maybe even before that. It was, after all, the last place anybody had seen her brother. Except maybe her.

I thought of her disbelief when I'd told her that my aunt and uncle still lived in the same house Jem and Mikey had been taken from, and wondered whether that was strange. I'd assumed the way Sue and Greg dealt with things was – well, *normal*. But maybe we were the strange ones?

As we pulled to the end of the street where Erin had spent a lot of her childhood, I slowed the car – the house just out of sight. Erin's expression was closed.

"Do you…" She wrung her hands together, worrying her bottom lip between her teeth. Her hair was wild, her makeup darker than usual, as though she'd applied a fresh layer right before I picked her up. "This morning I remembered what Molly – Mrs Evans – said. About feeling like she was being watched. I just brushed it off before, but do you think I ought to talk to her…?"

She looked at me hopefully.

"Maybe?" I said slowly. "Or I guess you could talk to your liaison officer again, right? Maybe you just got subconsciously affected when she said it to you," I said, partly to reassure her and also partly to quell the growing disquiet inside of me. "The break-in shook you up, and Molly sensed that and that's why she talked to you but that's made you feel worse?"

Erin sat silently for a moment, her gaze fixed on a point outside the car where a small bird was hopping between branches in a hedge. I wondered for a second if I'd offended her, but she made no move to leave.

"We don't have to do this," I said. "We could get something to eat instead. Just take your mind off things—"

"I want to see it." She didn't look at me, but she wasn't avoiding my gaze. The awkwardness between us was secondary to Erin's fear. "I think you're right. It might help. I've been so determined to block everything out, but it's different now. I've only been back on this street a couple of times since we moved out in… 2000, I think? A long time. I wonder if they'll let us have a look around."

"I called ahead on the way to come and get you," I admitted. "It's for sale. I asked if we could look around. I didn't tell them who you were."

"Well." Erin let out a long breath. "Let's do it then."

There was a big tree out front. It had great gnarled boughs that stretched way up in front of the house, blocking the view from the neighbours' windows. The current owners had strung it with fairy lights, plastic solar-powered bulbs like the ones Mum had in her garden, though right now they looked sad and unloved in the grey daylight.

"I learned to ride my bike down here," Erin said. She gestured at the street. It was probably the most personal thing she'd told me yet. A story without a punchline. "Alex learned and then he helped to teach me. He was… He was good. He was always better at stuff than I was. Could ride with no hands. You know – kid stuff. He…" She stopped. "Never mind."

"What?"

"No, it's nothing. I was just thinking about something he said once. He said he taught me because nobody taught him and he didn't want me to hurt myself. But that can't be right. Dad must have taught him."

I handed her a cigarette, not wanting to push her. I'd bought a new box this morning, on the way to work, subconsciously

159

picking up the brand she seemed to favour. She took the offering. Neither of us spoke until we were finished.

"I don't really remember what Dad was like when Alex was around," Erin said eventually. "But I know he was different. He died quite a few years ago now, while I was in sixth form. He had a heart attack, totally out of the blue."

"I'm sorry."

Erin shrugged. "It's fine. I don't think about it that much any more." She frowned. "I guess I'm just a cold-hearted bitch." She laughed but it was forced.

"Do you want to talk about last night?" I asked then.

"Off the record?"

I ignored the pinch in my chest – that this was what she still thought of me.

"Yes."

"It... What if it wasn't a prank, Harriet? I heard somebody in my house, in the middle of the night, and came downstairs to burning candles. These fucking red candles. It wasn't funny. It triggered... not even a memory. Just this *feeling*. Like I should know who left them. And why."

I tried to hide my reaction.

"Were they candles you made?" My voice sounded tight.

"No," she said. "I guess that makes it worse, huh. Somebody brought their own."

"You're right. That's not funny."

Erin shook her head. "But the policeman – he didn't believe me. And I'm worried it's some kind of message."

"A message? What do you mean?"

160

Erin wet her lips nervously.

"In my bedroom, before, there was a doll on the bed. I don't know where it came from. I told Wendy and she said it was probably my mum who'd left it. But Mum said it wasn't her, unless it was in with some other stuff. I hoped it was her, that she'd just not remembered. Maybe it's part of the same thing."

"What kind of doll?"

"I don't know, just a doll. Like the kind you have when you're a kid. I don't remember having one but I thought maybe I'd forgotten. It was… it was familiar, though. Freaked me the hell out." She rubbed her arms.

"Do you think the same person left the candles?" I asked.

"I don't know," Erin muttered again. "I don't know what I'm saying. It doesn't matter. Can we – can we just get this over with? I already feel shit enough."

Baffled, I let her lead the way.

"It just doesn't look the same," Erin said sadly. "I don't know what I was hoping for. What do you think of it?"

The owners had left us to it. They'd shown us around downstairs, but now they abandoned us to trudge up to the bedrooms without supervision. They were clearly eager to sell.

I glanced around at the beige carpets, the magnolia walls. It was like the whole house had been stripped of any character. It was hard to imagine what it had looked like once upon a time, when two small children lived here instead of a couple with kids long grown up.

"There's – a significance. To this house," I said. I tried to choose my words carefully, but Erin still blanched.

"Significance…? I thought we were just here to see what I remembered."

I hadn't been prepared for how little she knew.

"This is the only known sighting of the Father," I explained. "At least, that we know about. People have theorised that, like the first, the *final* abduction is just as important in solving these sorts of cases—"

"Sighting?" Erin fixated on that word. *Oh…* I realised. She really didn't know *anything*.

It had started to drizzle. One of the windows was open and the air tasted like fallen leaves and mud. Erin's face was a map of heartbreak.

"Your dad," I said quietly. "He saw something. He didn't know what. He was drunk. He said he saw a shadow in your bedroom, by the window, when he went to use the bathroom. He told the police he thought he'd been dreaming. But when he went to check on the two of you the next morning you were gone."

"My dad…?"

"I'm sorry. I thought you knew. I mean I thought you must know…"

"This is what I mean," Erin murmured. "I don't know anything. You know *everything*. How can there be so much I don't know? I didn't… My dad." She frowned. "My dad. Jesus."

"Did you remember something?"

"No. No, not like that. But after I came home Dad tried to talk to me. He – he was trying to explain, I think. Maybe. I don't know exactly but I was impatient with him because he started to drink more. I hated it…" She let out a huff of laughter. "I didn't really get that it was a problem, you know? Before, I mean. I didn't like it when he drank, he'd just sit for hours in front of the TV with beer after beer, but I didn't really allow myself to admit that until afterwards. I think Alex understood it better than me, and he shielded me. Maybe all those times he took me out of the house to play… maybe he was protecting me.

"And when Dad tried to talk to me I just, like, totally shut down. I didn't want to hear what he had to say. I don't know if he was going to apologise or… or maybe it wasn't about that at all. Maybe it was something else."

She stopped. Her expression shifted again, something unreadable passing over it.

"Did you and your dad get on before that?" I asked, thinking of my own dad. We'd never been super close, but he was always easy to talk to.

Erin shrugged: "I guess, yeah. He was fun. You know. Most of the time. But he got belligerent when he drank. Alex…"

"Did Alex get on better with your mum?"

"Alex got on with everybody," Erin said. "I just can't believe Dad saw something and I never knew. I can't believe I never let him talk to me."

"You can't beat yourself up about that," I reassured her. "You were a child."

163

Erin raised her chin and looked me straight in the eyes as she said, "Yeah, but so was Alex."

She sighed and turned away, heading for the bedroom at the end of the hall. The one, I realised, which had been hers. And Alex's. Perhaps the last place she ever remembered seeing him alive. I hadn't missed the tears welling in her eyes.

I decided to give her some privacy.

I stood in the front yard, breathing in the autumn smells. So many questions swirled in my head that I felt dizzy, the large tree in front of me giving me a sense of vertigo as I gazed into its thick branches.

I couldn't imagine how Erin felt. Knowing that her father had seen something the night of her abduction and been too drunk to properly comprehend what it was – understanding as an adult, too, that his drinking was a problem.

I lit a cigarette, watching the greyish smoke plume upwards to coil between the branches of the tree. As I stood I wondered whether it would have been different if Erin's father hadn't been drinking that night. If he'd been able to articulate exactly what he saw. Who was the man who took them? How did he do it?

I gazed at the tree. It was big, with solid, knotted limbs. Easy to climb. I thought of my aunt and uncle's house – they had a tree similar to this out front. A shiver ran through me. Was this how he'd gotten access to the houses of the children whose bedrooms were on the first floor? I'd read true crime junkie posts about the Father's method, and a few had mentioned trees and ladders and bungalows but it had never felt so real before.

Finally I heard footsteps behind me. Erin flew out of the house, her jacket flapping.

"I'm sorry," I started. "I hope I didn't upset you about your dad. I didn't know—"

"Never mind that," she blurted. Up close I realised she was crying. "Can we go?"

"Erin—"

"I think I know what happened. *The window*," she panted. "Alex. Me. God, I must have been stupid. I went first – I don't know why. Maybe I was carried? I felt so light, so strange. But Alex... he came after me.

"That's how he did it," she explained. "That's how the Father got us both out of the window. He carried me. I think he must have said Alex had to come with us if he wanted me to live. Alex was trying to *protect* me. Like he always did."

AFTER

Mother

THE DAYS AFTER BEAR'S death were like a nightmare. She drifted around the house in a fug of gin and tonic and cigarette smoke. She'd quit almost ten years ago but that small fact didn't seem to matter any more. Even the old tapes didn't help her to feel anchored now. She couldn't stop picturing him – all blue and cold, the life frozen out of him by the December lake. She saw it every time she closed her eyes.

Nothing made sense. Before Jack she had been happy, had lived without fear of the future. And then he swept in, wrapped her up in his magnetic plans. It had been grand, at first. She gave up acting – willingly, for him. Or so she thought. Then she had had Mouse and Bear, and she had got all that money and the big house, and her life had shifted again.

In the last couple of years she had begun to think of things as *Before Jack* and *After Jack*, ignoring the time in the middle and the fact that there was no *After Jack* – not really. He was still here, a presence that she couldn't unstick, his shadow falling across everything. Sometimes she wasn't sure he had ever left, like a ghost haunting them. Maybe he *was* living in the grounds, like she'd told Mouse. She wouldn't put that sort of persistence past him.

But since Chris died everything had changed again. Now it was *Before Bear* and *After Bear*. And the After was a black void that sounded like a leaky roof and smelled like dust. Tonight was the worst it had been. One month exactly. She never thought she could hold such pain as she had inside right now, like a thousand jagged knives.

They had spent the evening sitting quietly by the fire. It was cold, snow frosting the grass. Mouse was quiet, even for him. She wondered if he was sick again, but she didn't have the energy for that. When she put the boy to bed he was solemn, watchful. And when she looked away she could have sworn his expression morphed into something like thunder clouds.

There had been an incident two days before. A dead cat in the back garden. Not one of theirs – they didn't keep pets any more. She'd cried when she found it and made the mistake of asking Mouse if he knew anything. She hadn't meant it in a bad way, she just wanted to make sure she wasn't a bad mother.

But in asking she had breached some sort of truce they'd reached since Chris died and now Mouse wouldn't speak to her. Wouldn't look at her except if she asked him a direct question. It was only her duty to ask, wasn't it? But the boy had taken offence. She felt like she couldn't do right by him at the minute.

She rolled onto her side. She'd been plagued by indigestion and lying on her back was uncomfortable. The darkness in the bedroom was soothing. She could virtually taste the silence of midnight outside. She thought about going back to work tomorrow. She couldn't bear the thought of all those sympathetic questions. *Are you okay? What happened to your son? How's your other boy holding up?*

All the worse because she didn't know the answers. Maybe she should start working for herself, because she couldn't deal with this. She felt like she was one crack away from an avalanche.

The house creaked and settled. She let out a sigh that tasted of old gin. She preferred the darkness despite the shadow – because in the dark she could pretend that everything was still salvageable. That she still had two perfect sons and a perfect marriage and a perfect house. That she wasn't afraid.

She rolled over again and felt *it*. A presence in the room. A shadow darker than the rest. She stopped moving instinctively, her breath trembling in her chest. Her heartbeat stumbled. It was the ghost again; even now he was gone she could have no peace from his control. Was he even really gone?

"Jack…?" she hissed.

The shadows slipped and twisted but she couldn't see anything. Except maybe the outline of something smaller than Jack. Was it Mouse? The curtains twitched. Somehow that scared her more. How much of her fretting had he seen? She closed her eyes and tried not to cry.

This wasn't how it was meant to be. She was going insane.

EXCERPT

Charlotte & Hazel Davies

Abducted: Leicester, 2 August 1997

I have only been able to interview the parents of Charlotte (8) and Hazel (6) Davies once together because the girls' father travels for a living and spends around eight months of every year living in Hong Kong, where his father's family are from.

"Matt's always worked a lot," Andrea told me. "Ever since the girls were small, and even more now. He's back and forth, all over the place. We all went to Hong Kong on holiday once, when the girls were two and four. They hated it. It was too hot for them, too loud. But I always told them we'd go back one day – and they'd love it like Daddy."

Matthew was quiet. He's not tall, fine-boned like both of his daughters, and the quiet house seemed to weigh very heavily on him.

"They never got to go back though," he said. "They never met my father. It was really poor timing when we took the girls to visit – he was out of the country. We thought there would be more opportunities. You know?"

"Hazel was a chatterbox," Matthew said when I asked about the girls. "Talk, talk, talk. She loved, you know, the usual. Painting and art, anything where she could get her hands dirty. We still have some of her old clay figurines. Do you want to see them?"

He came back with three. Two animals and a third I couldn't identify.

"What's that one?"

"We don't know." This, finally, made Andrea laugh. "She was so proud of it though. We think maybe it was meant to be Charlotte."

"Did Charlotte like art too?"

"Yeah, I guess," Matthew said.

At the same time Andrea said, "Oh not really. She'd much rather have been outside."

They shared a look.

"She did prefer being outside," Matthew conceded. "I guess whenever I was home she stuck pretty close to me, and I'm more of an indoor person."

"When Matt was in Hong Kong she was hard to reign in." Andrea shrugged in a way that said she hadn't minded. "She was very sporty. Rounders, football, tennis. God, she loved tennis. She sometimes even slept with this tennis ball she'd doodled on, right under her pillow. Even though I told her not to. I couldn't find it after and it wrecked me. She liked martial arts, too."

Andrea sank into the sofa and her expression changed.

"Sorry." She cleared her throat. "Just creeps up on me sometimes. I was thinking about the martial arts − tae kwon do, she did − and how unfair it was. The reason we paid for her to go was so that she'd be able to protect herself."

"We didn't know that it wouldn't matter," Matthew said.

"No. I know. I know."

SEVENTEEN

8 NOVEMBER 2016

Harriet

WE HURRIED AWAY FROM the house. I held Erin's arm – she looked like she might keel over at any moment. When we reached the car, she leaned against it with her whole weight.

"Sorry," Erin muttered. "I just... Sorry."

"Don't apologise." I waited for Erin's eyes to focus, and then I added, "What exactly did you remember in there?"

"I don't know..." Erin hesitated. "Just feelings. Like flying. Cold air. The window. He was small enough to fit through the open window, but strong enough to carry me, persuasive enough to get Alex to go with him once he had me." She started to shiver. "I don't know why I'm so surprised. I just didn't expect anything to happen. I thought I'd never remember. I lived there for a couple of years after and nothing ever... The nightmares..."

"Come on," I said. "Get in the car. I think you need a drink."

Erin didn't argue. We drove in silence to a pub I knew. It

was small and compact, and more importantly it was dark inside. I settled Erin in a booth before getting us both drinks. When I returned she seemed a little more put-together.

"Drink this," I said, handing her a glass. "It'll help."

She sniffed the brandy suspiciously, but took a big mouthful anyway.

"Do you want to talk about it?" I pressed gently.

"Yes. I think so." Erin sighed. "I'm just going over and over it in my head. Why I'd go with a stranger out my goddamn bedroom window. And now it makes more sense. He drugged me. I was never sure about that before, but the smell of gloves, like latex, over my nose… Maybe he put something in my mouth. I think Alex was alert. Like… like he was worried about me. I've never been sure about the drugs before. But he must have needed me docile to convince Alex."

I felt a tremor of excitement shoot across my face, even though I tried to fight it. *I knew it.* There was a small segment early on in my book about the logistics of the abductions. How one person might manage to steal two small children without alerting anybody, without leaving any trace. The trees out front, latex gloves: it all fit together. I'd theorised in my notes that the Father must have subdued one or both of each of the pairs of siblings in order to get them out of their houses unnoticed.

"There's no need to look so pleased with yourself," Erin snapped.

"Sorry. But I knew there was no way he'd get you out without subduing at least one of you. The police wouldn't release any details from the tox panels they ran, but I knew he

173

had to have done something more than just offer you sweets in the middle of the night—"

"I guess I could ask the police to tell me the results. But I was gone nearly three weeks so surely the drugs wouldn't have still been in my system anyway? Nobody ever even talked to me about it. I always just assumed he'd lured us out. The name they gave him didn't help." Erin slumped in her chair. I found myself wanting to reach for her outstretched hand; I wanted to massage the warmth back into her fingers. "Everybody assumed he was *kind* to us. That maybe he knew us already or something. But if he subdued one of us, that means we didn't go entirely willingly. I never understood why they thought that he was kind. Didn't he abuse one of the girls?"

"Morgan Bailey was beat up pretty bad," I said. "He kept her longer than anybody else they found. But Morgan and Paul were the third pair he took and the name the press had given him had already stuck, probably partly because Jem and Mikey were looked after until they died. It took the press long enough to *publicly* connect the first couple of abductions in the beginning anyway, what with them being in different counties, and the children being different ages. The police held loads back, including the window information, when they talked about Jem and Mikey's abduction because they didn't know it would happen again. When the media latched onto it, there was hysteria."

"I can't help thinking that the police missed stuff because everybody was looking for the wrong thing." Erin finished her brandy with a mournful shrug. "Everybody was looking for a man who we knew. A father figure. We didn't want to go, Harriet."

"It seems so ob—"

"Obvious?" Erin let out a stringy laugh. "Is it, though? I remember people, so many people – even Wendy – asking me, 'Do you know who would hurt you or your brother?' and it's the same now. The police asked me if I know who would break into my house. If I fucking knew, I wouldn't have called them!"

"I understand, Erin."

"No, shut up a second."

I clamped my lips shut but I didn't take it personally. Erin was animated now.

"So he drugged us," Erin went on. "I don't know what the police thought about that, but what do you think? *Does* that change anything if he used one of us to lure the other one out?"

"I..." This was so far beyond the parameters of my book that I was momentarily stunned. "I don't know. We know he always took siblings, perhaps that's why. So he could get two children with the same ease as taking one. But why would he need so many?" It sounded callous even as I asked it, but it was a valid question. Why take two at a time?

Erin scrunched her eyes up tight.

"I just don't get it," she said. "There's got to be a reason. All of the kids shared bedrooms, right? You don't find that accidentally. So he was *looking* for pairs of siblings, children who shared a bedroom, so he could take two at once. Which makes me think it's not just about having two kids – the sibling element is important."

I kept quiet. Erin didn't want me to fill the silence.

But something did, anyway. A faint buzzing began. Erin jolted, patting around her pockets as though she'd been stung.

"Mum?" she blurted, answering her phone in a swipe. "Are you okay?"

A pause. A release of breath.

"Oh, god, sorry. I'm just… It's fine. I'm just jumpy. I'm glad you're okay. Are you having a nice holiday?"

Erin's hands were shaking.

"They're meeting again tonight?" The tentativeness of Erin's voice made me pay attention again. Her eyes sought mine across the table, cold and blue and nervous, but a spark of hope within. "And Molly – she sounded okay, right?"

A pause.

"No, it's nothing. Don't worry. Give me the details for later? I think I want to go."

She put the phone down, stared at me for a moment, then shook her head as though dispelling a cloud.

"The therapy group," she said. "Do you know it? They're meeting tonight. Some of them said they needed a chance to talk, after the memorial. They invited her but obviously she's on holiday… I should go. Maybe they can help me figure out who's breaking in to my house. Maybe it's even one of them – I don't know. I wouldn't rule anything out now." She clenched her hands into fists.

I knew I couldn't just abandon her now.

"I'll drive you there if you want."

EIGHTEEN

Erin

I GAVE HARRIET THE address. They were still meeting in one of the same churches. There was a rota of sorts, each city or town where children were abducted taking turns to host so somebody didn't always have to drive miles and miles. This Methodist church in Burton was all shiny wood and air freshener. I'd hated it before, even when we were trying it out in all earnestness, trying to talk out our feelings; my stomach fizzed at the thought of going back.

"Are you sure you want to do this?" Harriet asked. "You seem iffy."

"Ugh," I snorted. "Iffy. Have you ever even been to one of these?"

She shook her head. "My aunt and uncle always said they'd rather have parties than sermons. Molly said you'd had a bad experience, before. Did you go or just your parents?"

"I went to a couple, right at the beginning. Well, the beginning for me. They'd been meeting before me and Alex were taken, obviously. We just sort of crashed their circle."

"What are they like?" Harriet asked tentatively.

"Look at it this way. My mum and dad just wanted some kind of closure. They wanted to talk about the son they'd lost, to people who understood. Everybody sits in a circle and there's tea and biscuits, but they're all ratty because they've had to drive a bloody long way to get there, and nobody wants to *not* be there, so sometimes they just get wound up for nothing. My parents found it hard enough because of – me, and what happened, and *they* didn't make it any easier. Except for a couple of them who were nice, like Molly. So Mum and Dad found their own coping methods."

That was all I was going to say on the matter. I was sure Harriet could figure out the rest. Dad drank and smoked more and more until he had a heart attack. From the day I was back Mum became overly clingy. Nervous. Obsessive.

Now, the thought of going back, it made me feel like my skin didn't fit properly.

"Are you coming in?" I asked as we pulled up.

It was already getting dark and Harriet's face looked ghostly white in the glow from the floodlights that sat over the church door. I watched as she chewed on her lip, some internal battle raging. I wanted her to say yes. Even the distance between the church and the car seemed too far on my own.

"I'd better not," Harriet said eventually. "I don't want to… intrude. If I'm there I'll be a distraction. Maybe you can catch them off guard without me?" She must have noticed my face fall because she added, "But don't worry, I'll wait in the car."

"Thank you."

"That's what friends are for."

"Right." I gave her a terse smile, trying to ignore the ticking feeling in my chest.

I couldn't, though. Even as I grabbed my phone and shoved it into my pocket, darting into the brightly lit entrance of the hallway, I was asking myself if that's what this was. Were we friends?

The mood in the church was sombre. There was a circle of plastic chairs already set up, some people I half-recognised and some I'd never seen before sitting in them. There was a table with a paper cloth and a selection of coffee, tea and biscuits by the door, just as I'd predicted.

I glanced around awkwardly, wondering if Molly was there. I could do with a friendly face, and maybe I could talk to her, make sure she was still okay, ask her if she'd been exaggerating before. But I couldn't see her. Instead I was met by blank stares.

A man wearing slacks and a green jumper started to approach me and I felt my insides twinge. I recognised *him*, only he'd been fifteen years younger when I'd last seen him. He was the vicar who ran these Burton sessions.

Now I had to decide. Was I Erin Chambers? Was I somebody else? Too late I realised I didn't have a plan. Would they have seen me at the memorial? Did that even matter? How could I make these people trust me? Did I even want to?

"Hello," the man said. He wanted to shake my hand, but I kept both of mine in my pockets. In one I clutched my phone, in the other my box of cigarettes and my lighter, desperately trying to keep my breathing even.

"Hello."

"This is a closed session tonight."

He didn't turn me away but it was clear from his tone that he expected me to leave.

I brushed back a strand of my blonde hair and said, "My name is – Jillian. Chambers. I'd like to sit in."

For once, being *Jillian* seemed to be worth something. Even despite the grating pain that saying it aloud caused. There was a collective intake of breath.

"Jillian…" the vicar murmured.

The woman closest to me was probably in her fifties. Her hair was impeccably styled, bronze with hints of gold, and her eyes were a piercing silver-grey. I didn't remember her.

"Alex's sister," she said.

Her expression was direct and I felt myself shrinking a little under it. Then she smiled and the spell was broken; warmth.

The vicar stepped back to let me into the circle. It was clear that she was running this thing now, not him.

"I don't think we've met." I walked straight to the woman with the bronze hair but neglected to offer my hand to shake.

"Vera Bailey." She patted the seat next to her and I sat.

"Morgan and Paul's mum."

She half-inclined her head. Paul and Morgan seemed to be the two children the public remembered the most, aside from Alex and me. The brother and sister had been five and nine years old at the time of their disappearance. They were good-looking children, from what I saw of their photographs online. Both had dark hair that was almost black and bright blue-green eyes. I had thought about Morgan most nights after I made it home from the hospital. *That could have been me, could have been me...*

I wondered if Vera had dyed her hair because it was going grey, or if it was because the dark hair betrayed by her eyebrows was more than she could stand to look at in the mirror. I nervously fiddled with the ends of my own hair, the faded brown dye I'd hoped would help me the same way. In the end it had just made me look like a stranger and I'd let the blonde grow back in.

Morgan had died *eleven months* after her abduction. Eleven long months of whatever suffering I had managed to escape. I felt my whole body tingle and itch and I had to stop myself from wriggling in my seat like a child.

"I'm – sorry," I choked.

"We're all sorry," she said. "That's why we're here."

I agreed with that. I decided that, despite my initial feeling towards these people, I liked Vera Bailey. She was direct – but warm. I wondered if she had been here back when we'd first come. I didn't remember her.

"I haven't seen you here before," Vera said.

It was like she had read my thoughts.

"No," I said eventually. "We came years ago. Mum and Dad and me. Then we stopped."

Vera nodded, as if she understood.

The room was filling up now. I was suddenly overwhelmed. All of these faces, half-remembered. I glanced about, my gaze winging from one side of the circle to the other. It really felt like I was her. I was Jilly again.

For years I had been *little Jilly Chambers* or *poor Jilly*. I tried everything I could to get away from her. I grew my hair, dyed it, stopped wearing combat trousers and playing outside. I wore makeup – still did, even now – to hide the circles under my eyes, the sharpness of my cheekbones. I wanted to be as little like the girl who had been stolen as possible. As little like the girl who was Alex's sister. But it wasn't that simple. No matter how many new friends I made, or jobs I started, I could never shake her off completely. My hair came through with blonde roots; my eyes were still the same, hooded and blue; my mum still, sometimes, looked at me like she had looked at Jillian. But it made me feel strong to *try*. To move forwards, or at least sideways, instead of remaining where I was. I'd been two people for a long time, and suddenly being just her – just Jillian – was strange. Eerie. Like I was a living ghost.

I gripped my phone in my hand, cocooned in my pocket, almost praying for it to vibrate with a reason to leave.

"We have a new face here tonight," Vera said when everybody was settled. She smiled at me. A few of the others followed suit. "You might remember her. Jilly Chambers. She and her brother Alex—"

"We know who she is," one woman murmured. I was surprised to realise I recognised her, even after all this time. Andrea Davies. She was the mother of Charlotte and Hazel, abducted in 1997, a year before me and Alex. I vaguely remembered the way it had made everybody nervous. It was like the memory of Princess Diana's death. Something that shook the nation but had meant little to me.

Mostly, though, I remembered the bitter way Andrea had spoken to my parents, while I was stood there watching. The way she'd said we simply didn't have the same experience. Mum had been devastated. Andrea had never been able to bury either of her daughters, and she was angry that my mother, somehow, still had me.

Andrea's expression wasn't hostile now, just tired. She looked sadly at me, and then at Vera.

"She has every right to be here. Same as us," Vera said, before she could protest. As though this was old ground.

Andrea folded her hands in her lap but didn't argue.

"She lost somebody, too," a woman agreed, her tone firm. I turned, catching sight of a lady I thought must be Jaspreet Singh. She was here alone. Randeep and Jaswinder had been taken right before Alex and me. The same year. Just four months earlier. I felt my blood chill at the vague tickling memory, of a child's hollow face in the dark, an old plastic toy clutched between frozen fingers. I shivered. Where had that come from? "And goodness knows we need all the support we can get," Jaspreet added. "People can be cruel."

Andrea shrugged, but I was paying more attention to Jaspreet, to the way she wouldn't meet my gaze even as she defended me, the way she stared resolutely at the tissue she held in her lap. Her hands were shaking, as if she was holding in something else she wanted to say, but she was afraid to voice it.

"What do you mean?" I asked gently.

"That's what these meetings are for," Vera said. "Support."

"That's not what she's talking about though." I leaned towards her. "Is it? Has something specific happened?"

"I didn't—"

"Don't badger her," Andrea cut me off, a little of her old aggression leaking through. "You can't just barge into this safe space and demand people talk to you."

"I'm just asking what happened." I frowned. "Something *has* happened, hasn't it?"

I turned back to Jaspreet. She was three or four chairs away. The vicar, sat to her right, reached out to give her arm a reassuring squeeze.

Jaspreet let out a wet-sounding sigh, but still refused to look at anybody. "It's – it's why I asked if we could meet, actually," she said.

Vera leaned in. "You didn't say there was a reason, Jas."

"I know. It's just… I think somebody has been – following me. The last few days." Jaspreet picked at a loose thread on her sari. "It's – it's not a huge deal, but it's shaken me up. I wondered if it was all in my head, or if anybody else…"

"It's not a reporter?" I asked. Maybe it was a misunderstanding? But Jaspreet was shaking her head. "Or some kind of prank?" I thought about what the police had said to me and a squirming feeling started in my belly.

"I don't think so. It's not very funny."

"Did you tell the police?"

184

"Not yet," she said. She fiddled with the tissue in her lap, picked at her sari some more. "I thought I was just being paranoid. Thursday, he, whoever it was, left a football outside my front door. I brushed that off as just kids, or something. You know. But… Randeep loved Man U, and yesterday I found a football shirt on my washing line."

I thought of Molly, about what she'd said. We'd all been through so much that we didn't know whether to trust our emotions, but this surely couldn't be a coincidence. I fought a shiver. But… the Father was dead. Why would somebody start playing tricks on us now?

I thought back to all of the times I'd felt like I was being watched, even before the doll in my bed, the candles in my kitchen. How long had this person been watching us?

"You've got to go to the police. You've got to tell somebody," I said, panic making my voice shaky.

"What if that makes him angry?" Jaspreet had gone pale. "It's got to be somebody I know, right? Somebody who knew the kids."

I bit my lip so hard I tasted the first coppery tang of blood on my tongue, but I couldn't answer.

"How did you know?" somebody else asked me. A woman with long blonde hair who hadn't said anything before. She had Vera Bailey's fine, pointed nose – a sister maybe, but much younger. Another daughter?

"What?" I said.

"How did you know to ask her if something was wrong?"

"I didn't. Not exactly. I just…" I gripped my phone tighter.

Wished that Harriet was in here with me. "Somebody has been in my house. I thought it was a break-in at first, but nothing's gone. It feels more like a mean trick." *Or a threat.* I didn't say that out loud.

"Did he leave gifts for you, too?" Jaspreet asked.

My blood ran cold at the word *gifts*. Suddenly I thought of Monica. Of what she had said to me on the phone.

Leaving gifts at my house is fucking weird.

NINETEEN

Harriet

I WAS STILL IN the car when Erin tumbled out of the meeting. The sky was dark, speckled with only one or two visible stars, and the floodlights over the church doors made everything sweat silver. Erin was like a ghost, pale and fluid, rushing towards the driver's side where I sat with a cigarette in my mouth.

I wound the window down and tried to pretend I hadn't been watching the door for long minutes already. The darkness was making me antsy. Twice I'd sworn I could see somebody standing behind my car, a shadow in the rear-view mirror, and twice I'd looked to find nobody there. Erin's nerves were rubbing off on me.

"How did it go?" I asked.

"Come with me."

I climbed out of the car, saying nothing, and let Erin lead me away. Nobody else had come out of the church yet, but as Erin forged a way around the back of the building, where a bramble hedge grew and stretched along the side of a small, overgrown grassy garden, I heard the doors swing open and shut and then the sound of voices spilling into the night.

She had a frantic kind of energy about her, as if she wanted to be anywhere but here and yet needed to get something off her chest – fast.

"Sorry, we can go in a minute. I just need to be outside for a minute, away from everything. I need to breathe."

We came to a spot that might once have been a vegetable allotment, earth churned along the edges and tangles of weeds in between. It was too dark to see much, but Erin pulled a lighter from her pocket and lit a cigarette. Then clicked the lighter again so the flame hovered, for a long few seconds, in the darkness.

"Didn't go well then?" I said eventually.

She let the flame die, the golden glitter in her eyes fading. "It was… It was hard, seeing them again."

I could tell she was holding something back. I waited until the sound of engines starting in the car park had faded to a distant hum. Until there was just us and the darkness.

"What happened?"

She didn't look at me. I felt a tide swell in my chest, an emotion I wasn't familiar with. Worry? Or something else?

"I won't write about it. About this conversation." I threw the words out before I could change my mind. Erin blinked.

"What?"

"I think we're beyond that now."

I realised as I said it that I didn't know what I meant by that. Did I mean the book, or did I mean something else?

Whatever it was that was happening between us?

"Are we?" Erin asked.

She leaned closer.

"Yes."

Erin let out a long breath.

"Okay, look. I have this... feeling. I haven't got any proof. I don't know if it's a memory or if it's wishful thinking, but I can't help wondering if this isn't random after all."

"What do you mean? The break-in?"

"All of it. I think he – the Father – was looking for certain candidates. I keep coming back to the sibling thing, how he always took *two* children, when one would have definitely been easier. It must be some compulsion, or there's something about physically getting one kid to protect the other that gets him off." She paused. "I thought he was dead. He is dead. He's got to be. But somebody is out there right now – fucking with more than just me. And whoever it is, something has obviously triggered them."

"I'm not sure I understand." I stepped back, away from Erin's intoxicating warmth, and let the cool wind chill me back to consciousness. "The other families have had break-ins too? Are you saying that it's connected to what happened to you?" I thought of my aunt and uncle, alone with just a collie for company. Were they safe?

"No. Not break-ins. But Molly said she felt spooked, and tonight Randeep and Jaswinder's mum said somebody had left *gifts* for her. Followed her. None of the others have had any problems. But it's like a *selection*," she said the word like a curse. "I don't get it."

"It's like an echo of the Father," I said. "It seems random, but careful. It's probably some true crime nerd just getting his jollies. The randomness is bound to help him get away with it like it did back then—"

"Except I don't think that's why the Father did it," Erin pointed out. We'd bounced back to him again, like an old scab neither of us could stop picking at. "I don't think it was *just* to avoid being caught. Look at the kids he stole. They started out looking kind of similar, didn't they? Your cousins and the Evans kids, all of them were small, white, with brownish hair and dark eyes, and they were a bit younger. Then after that, Morgan. As if something wasn't right at first, and he needed to try something else. A girl. And then *two* girls. And then Randeep and Jaswinder, brown skin and older again… It's almost like he wanted to sample children across the board. The only thing they have in common in the end is that they're siblings, and *around* the same ages."

"So…?"

"I don't know." Erin blew out a frustrated breath. "There must have been something important about brothers and sisters – regardless of gender, or even biology if we bring Oscar and Isaac into the mix. And if it's not biology then it must be the *relationship* he's looking for. Maybe it's a challenge, to see which sibling lasts longer. Whether one protects the other. Or, maybe he hates siblings because his sibling hurt him. I don't know. Morgan and Paul were found so many months apart, it makes me wonder why he'd keep Morgan so long? But then, we don't know how long he kept the others. The ones that weren't found…"

She lapsed into silence.

"Did Jaspreet tell the police about the gifts?" I asked. "They surely get this all the time with people affected by high-profile cases. There are so many awful, obsessive people in the world."

"No. I told her to tell them though. I genuinely don't think she knew what to do about it, since so far it's not been... I mean, it's not actually been harmful. He didn't break into her house or threaten her. It's like a power play, but I just can't work it out. It feels like we're all in this stupid game but only this guy knows the rules. Everything is *calculated*."

"It's okay," I said. "Whoever this person is, they obviously don't want to hurt you."

"We don't know that."

"Yes, I think we do. He could have hurt you when he broke into your house the second time – you were right upstairs – but he didn't."

"What do I do?" There was more fear in her voice now. "I don't want to go home. And I can't stay at Mum's forever."

"You could call the police," I suggested. "Explain that you're afraid. Tell them about Jas."

"You think I haven't thought of that? But if I call them after last night they'll probably just tell me to stop wasting their time again. What proof do any of us have that this isn't just a big, fat, unfunny joke? A few candles and a football shirt? Maybe we're all just collectively losing the plot. Like you said, he could have hurt me but he didn't."

"Come home with me then." The words were out before I could think about them. "Stay at mine. It's safe there, quiet. Get some rest and see what happens when Jaspreet reports the gifts."

I didn't think Erin would agree. But then, she did. And I didn't know whether that was a good thing. The shadows around us seemed to stretch and shiver and I found myself looking over my shoulder as we reached the car.

There was nobody there.

TWENTY

Harriet

MY FLAT FELT HOLLOW and empty after Erin's busily decorated house, where we'd stopped to grab some of her things and her car. The whole rest of the drive, the lonely silence eating me, I'd reconsidered my offer. Thought about taking it back as soon as we arrived.

But I couldn't just send her home alone. So I said nothing. Now, as we came up in the lift to my floor, Erin let out a small whistle.

"Nice place," she said.

Erin dumped her bags unceremoniously in the hallway, not caring about the people in the flat below – or perhaps simply not thinking about them. I watched her eyeing my sparse furniture, the pictures of Thomas, and Auntie Sue, Uncle Greg, Mikey and Jem on the mantel.

"Do you want a drink?" I asked, as much to distract her as anything else.

She nodded, still looking around.

"Tea?"

"Got anything stronger?" she asked. Now she looked at me. I saw a spark of panic in her gaze, as though she felt as out of place here as I felt she was. I softened. None of this was as bad for me as it was for her.

"Sure."

I poured a glass of wine for me, and the last finger of a glass of rum for her, mixed with some flat Diet Coke. She didn't complain. She wandered around my lounge, eyeing the cheap TV which I hardly ever watched, the stacks and stacks of books on one wall.

"Non-fiction," she said, pulling a face. "Politics? History? Who even are you?"

I fought the blush that prickled my cheeks.

"I like research. Facts. Truths—"

"Nothing is true," Erin said bitterly. "Everybody has their own individual truth."

"That means there *are* truths, though," I pointed out. "Just because it's not the same truth doesn't make it exist any less. Anyway I like biographies too, and thrillers." And true crime, but I didn't mention that.

"Figures."

She sank onto my sofa, cupping her glass like it was sacred. She looked exhausted, her face pale and her blue eyes almost silver. I wished, again, that I did have fairy lights, or something other than the stark bare bulb overhead and simple lamps dotted around. Everything was too bright, too clinical.

"I'm not going to lie, this is a bit weird," she said.

"You're telling me?" I took a big gulp of my wine. "But I wasn't going to let you worry about a place to stay—"

"I could have found a hotel or something. Or just sucked it up and gone home." Erin blushed. I noticed, as she knew I would, that she didn't mention any friends she might stay with. Not even the person she'd been texting. She'd been fiddling with her phone again in the car, as though she was hoping for a better offer, but as far as I could tell nothing had come of it.

I thought, not for the first time, how similar we might be, if not for this awful thing that had happened to her. We'd both lost our fathers young, both had grown up with an older brother, although the age gap was larger between me and Thomas. I felt a pang then, sudden and painful, an echo of Erin's loss. What would it be like to lose Thomas? His moving halfway across the world and only being able to Skype was painful enough, but he was still there. I'd emailed him again today, but I wasn't sure if he'd seen it yet.

Erin picked up her phone again. The way she held it made me realise something. She was afraid again, more than the low-key concern of the last few days.

"Erin," I said. "What's going on?"

"You mean aside from all of the shit I've been going through for the last week?" She forced a big gulp of her drink. "Sorry. That's…I just…"

"Just what?" I asked gently. I moved over to the sofa, to sit beside her.

"There's something I want to tell you," she said. "It's – about the phone calls and stuff I've been making. I have... So, I have an ex."

I found a surprised bubble of laughter in my throat, although it wasn't funny.

"Is that what you're worried about? Erin, I'm not—"

"No," she cut me off. "No, I mean... I was worried about her, a bit, before. At first I thought it was because last time I saw her we had a fight. We'd been broken up and I let it get messy. I tried to call her, after. She ignored me but I kept texting, calling, you know. To make sure she was okay. I spoke to her, finally, and she was freaked out. She mentioned something about somebody leaving *gifts*."

"Do you think he's been there?" I asked slowly. "Do you think it's the same person doing all of this?"

Erin's lip began to tremble. "I don't know. Maybe it's nothing. I don't know what to do. I've tried calling her tonight, too. I don't want her to think I'm some psycho who won't leave her alone but God, Harriet, I'm really freaked out, especially after what Jaspreet said. Maybe I *should* call the police – but Monica doesn't know about me, she doesn't know anything about my past, and I don't want to scare her by sending cops to her house if everything's fine. And I don't want to get in trouble again."

For the first time I realised how naive Erin was. She looked like she wanted me to reassure her, to tell her that everything was going to be okay. I reached out and rested my hand on her arm.

"Would you feel better if we went to see her?" I asked.

"That'll reassure you, and me, and we can talk to her, get her to let the police know that something is going on if that's what's happening. If Jaspreet gets in touch too they'll have to appreciate the severity of this. Besides, if he's been leaving her gifts, she might have noticed something useful, something we can tell them."

Erin nodded slowly. "Okay," she said. "Okay. She – she should be at home tonight, I think. She doesn't normally work evenings at the beginning of the week."

"Come on then," I said. "Before it gets too late."

I drove. It was only a ten-minute drive but every second of it seemed to last half a lifetime.

Eventually we came to a stop outside a house. The windows were dark.

"Are you sure she's home?" I asked.

"She should be. That's her car. You won't leave while I nip in will you?"

"I'm not going anywhere."

I turned the engine off. Erin got out of the car and headed to the door. She rang the bell. Waited. Then tried the handle. It dipped smoothly and the door swung open.

Erin turned back towards me, worry in her eyes. I went to join her. The shadows seemed to dance on Erin's face and I fought the urge to look behind me.

"Maybe she left it open?"

Erin shook her head. "She wouldn't."

The street around us was deadly silent, the houses all quiet and dark. Erin didn't move, her lips frozen half-parted as we listened. But there was nothing. Erin gave the door a gentle nudge and it swung inwards.

That's when we noticed the candles.

AFTER

Mouse

HE RECOGNISED THE BOYS but he wasn't sure where he had seen them before. He found them in the potting shed, their hands tied together and their mouths stuffed with old tea towels. One was younger than the other.

They panicked when they saw him but he soon calmed them down. They were both small with black skin and short curls. The older boy was the skinnier of the two. He said his name was Isaac. The young one, around Mouse's age, was called Oscar.

"Where are we?" Isaac asked. Tears streaked his dirty face, snot caked around his nose. It was gross. One of the boys had wet himself and the shed smelled like a barnyard.

"How did you get here?" Mouse asked. The boys didn't move. It didn't matter how hard he tried, they didn't know the answer. It might have been Mother, but he doubted it. Mouse felt excitement tickle his toes. Father must be back.

He thought about leaving the boys there. It was springtime,

and the days were getting longer and warmer without being hot. He could leave them in the shed. Mother probably didn't know they were there; he should check what she wanted to do.

But that wouldn't stop the feeling inside of him. Why were these boys here? He didn't understand. Ever since Mouse's father had left he'd felt like something out there was looking after him. Helping him get what he wanted. Was it his father or a ghost?

Mouse had said it aloud. How he wanted a new brother or sister. Not any old brother, maybe not even just one. Two would be good, to start. He wanted to make sure he got the right kind, one who would look after him and play with him and love him for ever. He'd spoken quietly to himself, deciding how he would choose which brother was better by watching them play together. And now, here was a special present. Two brothers in the shed – just for him.

If Mouse had to choose, he thought the younger boy was better. Oscar said he was only a year older than him, but Mouse had a birthday coming up so that wouldn't last. And Oscar wasn't loud, either. He didn't cry or yell when Mouse untied them. He didn't try to run away like Isaac had. Although the cool thing about Isaac was how small and slow he was for his age. Mouse was strong and big, and the running away had given him the chance to try out a really good punch.

He took both boys back to the house. Mother was in her bedroom with her films going, cigarette smoke so heavy he could hardly see her. He didn't want to bother her. The boys asked when they were going home, but they didn't even know where home was.

Mouse made them sandwiches, cheese triangles with the crusts off and slices of cake, just like Chris used to like. Isaac started to cry. Maybe he didn't like cheese. Mouse watched the brothers from a distance, his stomach burbling and his brain spinning.

Where had they come from? Why were they here? He didn't like either of them, really. Not even quiet little Oscar. He thought of the shed, how nobody went back there. Of how it looked, from his window at night, like a rotten gravestone tooth. They must be a gift from Father, even though Mother had said he was gone forever. Father *had* left him the cat that time. Sick and quiet, and easy to play with. That was fun. It would be just like Father to do something like this, to get back at Mother for all of the times she'd loved Chris best. Father would find it funny to bully her—

A sick thought curled inside Mouse's belly. It was like a sharp bit of ice in Mother's drink. What if the boys weren't a present for him? What if they were *instead* of him? He didn't know why he had the thought but it frightened him.

When the boys had finished their food and wiped their dirty faces, Mouse made sure they were listening.

"There are rules," he said. He didn't care that Isaac was older than him. Mouse knew how to fight, and Isaac was skinny like a twig, so they'd both have to listen.

He closed the kitchen door and led them to the door to the basement, the one that was hidden. The house was old and filled with puzzles like this one, corridors and stairs that went nowhere, doors that opened to bare brick wall. Father told him that it had been two houses, once, like that Frankenstein's monster thing all sewn together.

The boys looked at him and their dark eyes were scared. *Good.* Oscar stepped behind his brother.

"What rules?" Isaac squeaked, trying to be brave.

Mouse thought about this for a minute. He needed rules that would keep him safe. Rules that would make sure they couldn't hurt him, couldn't make the sickness start again. Mother wasn't allowed to like them better. He didn't really want them getting any attention at all.

"No running away again," he said firmly. "Or you'll get it. Don't bother Mother. Don't be loud. Stay downstairs unless I say you can come out. And do exactly – *exactly* – what I tell you."

They shook and cried some more, and Mouse realised he was pleased. The scared feeling inside him had gone, now. He didn't expect the boys to follow his rules exactly, but this way, he could punish them when they disobeyed. And if neither of them made a good enough brother, if they argued or made Mother want to hurt him again, he'd just get rid of them both and it would only be like before.

EXCERPT

Randeep & Jaswinder Singh
Abducted: Burton on Trent, 3 June 1998

Jaspreet Singh was one of the first people I spoke to when I was thinking about writing this book in late August 2009. A few things have changed since then. Jaspreet is no longer married – her husband moved down to London in January of 2011 – and she is now employed full-time as a teaching assistant. She loves to show me photographs and videos of her son and daughter.

Randeep (9) and Jaswinder (7) are always grinning. Pictures, videos, even drawings of each other show that. Always, those big toothy smiles.

"Jas lost both her front teeth a couple of months before they were taken," Jaspreet told me the first time we met, pulling out a big folder of pictures.

"Did her teeth both fall out at the same time?" I asked. "My brother's did. He looked so goofy for ages."

"Yes, but not on their own. Jas and Randeep were playing swingball at the park – you remember that game where the tennis ball is tied to a pole and you've got to hit it back and forth with rackets? We were at a big picnic that my husband's company organised every year, and Jas and Randeep were playing with another little boy and his mum, and the ball hit Jas square in the face. Randeep helped her up, you know, really worried, and then Jas – she was such a brave one – she just picked up the racket and started playing again. The mum apologised since she was playing opposite Jas when it happened and she probably hit the ball too hard, but it wasn't a big deal. Or it didn't seem like it until both of Jas's front teeth fell out." Jaspreet shook her head. "She had this great big gap in her smile after that. That's how I remember her, even now.

"For years she had all her teeth. But those couple of months without them, they're what I remember. I guess because she hadn't got her grown-up teeth yet. I used to think about that every day. How I'd never know what her grown-up smile would have been like.

"I think the same about Randeep, too. Whether he'd have kept playing football, whether he'd have become a doctor. That was his plan. Most kids have lots of ideas about jobs they could do, right? Randeep *always* wanted to be a doctor. But he still slept in his Man U shirt every night, because he said it let him play football in his dreams."

"I'm sure he would have been a good doctor," I said. It probably wasn't the right thing to say, but Jaspreet smiled anyway.

"He'd have made a *great* doctor," she replied.

TWENTY ONE

Erin

I INCHED NERVOUSLY INTO Monica's dark house. There were two red pillar candles at the bottom of the stairs; their faint orange glow made the darkness flicker around us. They were like the ones left in my kitchen. A knot tightened in my chest. Vaguely I knew Harriet was behind me and I was glad I wasn't alone.

The stairs went straight up from the front hall. I knew she wasn't downstairs, the rooms all dark and expectant. I fumbled for my phone, dialling Monica's mobile number. A frozen claw dragged through my heart when I heard the faint trilling of her phone upstairs.

I didn't turn the lights on.

"Maybe it's another joke," I whispered desperately. Harriet said nothing. "There's obviously nobody here."

Together we climbed to the top of the stairs, their creaking the only accompaniment to our breathing.

"Monica?" I tried.

And then I was at the top of the stairs and Monica's bedroom door was open, just as mine had been. It was like with the doll only I knew this was not the same.

Harriet took a sharp breath behind me.

"I'm calling the police."

Monica was right there. A dark mass on the white sheets of her bed. The only light in the room came from a single red candle that guttered by the open window, curtains trembling.

But now her bed sheets weren't white. They were red.

And in the middle of the bed was a small, plain piece of paper. I inched closer, my breath coming in sharp bursts. Just three words. My whole body went into shock and I felt sick. It couldn't be him. It couldn't.

Remember the Father.

I was still shaking. The police station was a hive of activity but I couldn't make sense of any of it. I didn't recognise anybody, even the people I knew I should. I sat numbly in a small room with a big blanket around my shoulders. Somebody had checked me over. Somebody else had brought me coffee which was now cold.

I'd spoken to a handful of people. I couldn't remember what I'd said to any of them. Not even Wendy or Harriet. I vaguely remembered phone calls, panic. Darkness and then lightness and then a bumpy ride where I cried and threw up the minute we came to a stop.

My brain was one big blank spot around the image of

Monica, lying there on her bed. All that blood. The white bed sheets. The window, the moon. The carpet soft and a little damp. The note. *Remember the Father.*

I wanted to be sick again but I didn't have anything left to throw up. I tried to keep my hands still but I couldn't. My arms crawled with invisible spiders.

I didn't know what time it was when the next person came into the room. I glanced up, my body vaguely registering that this was a face I *did* recognise.

"Erin?"

I stared. My heart seemed to be beating incredibly slowly. My ears were full of water.

I blinked blankly at the woman in front of me.

"It's me, Detective Godfrey."

"Oh, hi," I croaked.

The detective's features smoothed out into more of a smile. Reassuring. At least that's what I'm sure she was aiming for. It came across as more of a grimace. Her brown skin looked paler than usual in the bright lighting in the police station. I felt like everything had been washed to within an inch of its life, including the detective. I hadn't seen her in an age. I wanted to break down and spill everything.

What could I tell her that would help? What more could I do than cry and hurl up my guts? He had been there – right there. In Monica's house, just like he'd been in mine. But he was supposed to be *dead*.

All I could think was, *why didn't I tell the police about Monica's response on the phone? Why didn't I tell them about the gifts? Why didn't I push back when that idiot told me it was a joke?*

"I'm sorry to see you again like this. Do you feel up to talking?" Godfrey asked. "We'd like to confirm the sequence of events."

"Did you talk to Harriet?" I asked, panic suddenly filling me again. "Is she okay? Where is she?"

"She's fine. She's still with my colleague. Wendy's out there too, asked if you were alright. She said you get migraines."

It felt like my body was filled with sand.

"How long was Monica dead?" I asked quietly.

Godfrey weighed her answer before she spoke.

"A few hours," she said eventually. "We'll know more after the autopsy."

"It was him. Wasn't it? The same person who broke into my house, who was following the others. You know about all that, right? Wendy said you'd see it on your computer or something, after the second one. I was going to call you…"

"The others?" Godfrey asked.

"The other families," I explained breathlessly. "Of the children. Molly Evans and Jaspreet Singh. I saw Jaspreet tonight. She said she thought she was being followed. That somebody left gifts outside her house. Molly said the same thing about being followed the other night."

Godfrey's lips went thin. "How long has this been going on? Why did nobody report anything?"

"Uh, just a few days." I ran my hands over my face and swallowed the tears that made my throat sticky. "Jaspreet told me tonight – we didn't think it was that serious. I called the police when my house was broken into but they said it was just a *joke*. That somebody was messing with me. I told Wendy about the doll in my bed and she said it was probably mine, brought round by my mum, and I'd just forgotten it and I thought she was right."

I felt a boiling sensation in my blood.

"What doll?" Godfrey asked. Her face was unreadable, but I knew she was angry. A muscle in her jaw corded and she held her pen too tight.

"A child's doll. It was on my bed after the first time I said my house had been broken into. Nothing was taken. The police did fingerprints and stuff but I don't think they found anything. They didn't know who I was. I only found the doll later. Mum said she didn't remember it but I just thought she'd forgotten. I had a lot of old toys at her house still. And then the second time—"

"There was a second time?"

"Yes. The second time I found candles in my kitchen. I didn't leave them there but I don't think the officer who came believed me. He saw my candle stuff and thought it was a prank. My friends messing me around. Because they made a heart shape." I realised I was crying. "I didn't fight back because I didn't think it was that big of a deal. Like yeah it was shitty and I was freaked out, but people *are* shitty."

Godfrey's frown deepened. "The note," she said then. "Can we talk about that?"

"I don't know what it means. I don't recognise the handwriting. It can't be anything to do with what happened, can it? The Father is *dead* and nobody even knows who I am. I don't understand. Why would somebody do this and blame it on what happened?"

Godfrey didn't answer. Every time I said it, it felt less true. But he *was* dead. He had to be. Didn't he?

"Can you trace the note? Figure out the paper and stuff?" I asked. "What if it's a copycat? Or, no, not a copycat. I just mean what if it's some internet psycho?"

"We're going to do our best to figure out how this is all connected," Godfrey said.

"She didn't deserve any of this," I whispered.

"I know. I'm sorry, Erin, but I need to ask you some more questions."

I sucked in a deep breath. "Okay."

"When they asked you earlier you said you'd known Monica McKenzie for a little while. And that the nature of your relationship was fairly casual. Is that right?"

I nodded.

"Now, yeah. We dated for a while. I last saw her properly on Halloween. We met at The Rock and then went back to her house."

"Did she seem normal to you?"

"Yeah." My voice broke and fresh tears appeared on my cheeks unbidden. "I spoke to her on the phone and she was a bit funny with me, but I just thought that was because we'd not long broken up. I didn't know what to make of it."

She had been afraid, not angry, and I hadn't even realised.

"When was this?"

"Yesterday. She said somebody had been leaving her gifts. She implied it was someone I was in a relationship with. I wanted her to explain but she hung up on me. That's why I went there tonight. I didn't think it would lead to this."

"What sort of gifts?" Godfrey pressed.

"She didn't say. But Jaspreet Singh said somebody has been leaving things outside her house, too. A ball, a football shirt. Things her son would have liked. Monica didn't – she didn't tell me what he left for her. I didn't think it was connected..."

Godfrey wrote something down in a small notebook.

"And the last time you saw her, did you notice anything strange? Did you see anybody watching her? Did she say she was worried, or seem upset?"

"No," I said. "She seemed fine. I was the one who was jumpy."

"Okay, what about the Father. Did you ever talk to Monica about him? About what happened to you and Alex? Any theories you might have had?"

"No," I said. "I never talk to *anybody* about that stuff. The only bastard thing that connects Monica to all of this is *me*, and it's my fault she's dead. What if it's him? What if he's back?"

Godfrey paled a little. Or maybe it was the lights as she shifted in her seat. I made sure my eyes met hers and I let her see all of the things I was feeling.

"You still haven't remembered anything new about what happened to you?" she asked softly. "With therapy or Wendy?"

"No. Just... what I've said a hundred times before."

"And the red candles?"

"...What?"

For a second I thought of the ones that had been left in my house but the look on Godfrey's face said she didn't mean those ones.

"Candles. In Monica's house. You don't know why they might be significant?"

"I…" I couldn't think of anything at all except the colour of red blood on white sheets and I felt sick again. "No. They're not mine."

"Were they the same kind of candles that were left in your house?"

"I don't know," I murmured. "I think so, but it's hard to be sure. Both were red pillar candles. I got rid of the ones in my house, threw them away. I'm so – I'm sorry."

Godfrey leaned back in her chair. It creaked and I jumped, my skin prickling. I forced myself to sit still while she asked me a few more questions, the world a blur of guilt and sadness. Eventually she was done.

Relieved, I let myself be led out into the wider building, the buzz growing around me. Now what? Where could I go? Harriet… Had I put her in danger? Monica had known me, and look what had happened to her. But would Harriet even leave me alone if I asked her to? I wanted to call my mum but I didn't want to scare her. I didn't want her to panic and try to come home. I didn't want that on my conscience, but more importantly I wanted her to stay away, to stay safe until I knew what, exactly, was going on.

Fifteen minutes later Harriet showed up with coffee from a machine. She looked exhausted, dark circles under her eyes and her hair wild, but she marched straight for me, thrust a cup of coffee right into my hand, and demanded I come home with her.

I didn't say no.

At Harriet's house I sank onto the sofa while she ran the bath. My arms felt like they were on fire, itching and crawling with hundreds of fire ants. I pushed both sleeves up and scratched at them until my skin was scored with red marks. When Harriet came back I forced myself to stop, but the crawling sensation didn't abate. She led me into the bathroom, which was painted in shades of purple, white borders on everything making it look crisp and bright.

The police had taken my clothes as evidence. They'd been covered in Monica's blood. Harriet guided me towards the toilet and sat me down on the closed lid. She seemed glad of the distraction, glad to be helpful. She took my shoes off while the water ran and bubbles gathered on the surface, also lilac.

She peeled off my socks. My borrowed jumper. My shirt over my head. I didn't have the energy to feel embarrassed but I noticed, somewhere in the back of my mind, that Harriet's neck and face had gone pink. She looked away as I stood up to pull my trousers off.

"I'll leave you——"

"No!" I said. I dropped the trousers to the floor, panic overtaking me. "Please don't go. I don't want to be on my own."

She nodded once and then sat herself on the toilet while I continued to undress, her gaze fixed on the closed door. I didn't care. I didn't want her to see me. I just needed somebody to be here.

"It doesn't make sense…" I sank into the water, felt the heat rush over me and the first wave of feeling return to my toes and fingers. "It must be because of me."

"It isn't your fault."

"Yes, it is. I just wish I could remember what happened back then. What if I know who he is? What if I've seen him on the street – would I even recognise him?"

"I'm sorry if you feel like I've been pushing you too hard," she said, "taking you places you're not ready for."

"No. I asked for your help. Not that I thought it would lead to all of this." I rested my chin on my knees and stared at the water.

"It's okay."

"It isn't, though."

Harriet was looking at me now. Her gaze started at the crown of my head and followed the arch of my back. Her colour was more red than pink now, but she was calm.

Afterwards, I dressed in clean pyjamas. Harriet led me to her spare room. It was furnished more than any of the other rooms, with what looked like home-knitted blankets on the futon, degree certificates on the walls. A desk sat against the back wall in front of a window, curtains shut tight; her laptop was set up haphazardly beneath, folders and notebooks piled either side of it like a fortress.

When Harriet was gone I crawled under the blankets and sheets, shivering despite the layers. Finally, in the darkness, I let myself think about the conversation with Detective Godfrey.

What *was* so important about red candles? They were following me, mocking my own love of candles and fire to cleanse and soothe. Was there something I should remember about them? There must be.

For a long time I'd been afraid of fire; I hated the way the shadows danced when Mum lit the hearth or her scented candles, and for years after what happened to Alex and me I avoided candles. I didn't remember being afraid before. I'd beat the fear, worked hard to turn it into love. But now I found myself questioning that original feeling of dread. Where had it come from?

I was too tired to examine the thought carefully. The darkness swayed me with its heaviness. I bundled up a spare jumper I'd brought with me, using it as a teddy bear, holding it to my chest to pretend that I wasn't alone. Eventually, after what seemed like hours, with the first grey light smudging the sky, I fell into a fitful sleep.

I was running. The trees were like monsters in the black night. The only light came from the moon, silvery and weak. I stumbled over roots and my feet skidded in slick mud.

My breath came in plumes. I ran harder and faster than I ever had before. And somewhere behind me I heard somebody shouting my name.

"Jilly! Jilly, go!"

Then I was inside. Inside a big house with wooden panelling. Clean, but old.

I stopped. It was freezing. The hairs on my arms stood to attention as a curtain fluttered nearby. Somewhere there was a creaking sound. Stairs. All of the windows were open but the curtains were closed. I wanted to curl into a ball.

I couldn't though. I had to keep moving. I had to go somewhere. I had to do something. I just couldn't remember what.

Suddenly there was a big staircase behind me, a door to my right. A long corridor stretched ahead. Brown leaves scuttled with the wind, which snaked around my ankles. I had to leave. Had to run again, but I couldn't find the way out.

The door had disappeared. I spun around until I was dizzy but the only way was the corridor. A basement smell, damp and cool, dragged me onwards.

"Jilly… Jilly, please."

Alex?

I spun around again. His voice had sounded so clear. I peered into the darkness, the floor spilling out in front of me like a map. I followed it quickly, the leaves still bristling with the wind.

"Jilly?"

The voice came from the corridor. There were no lights and the walls closed in on me as I tripped forwards. I wanted to squeeze my eyes tight but something in me made them stay open. I drank it all in.

There were oil paintings on the walls. Or at least they looked like oils, shiny and crackled in places. There were two closed doors, one after the other.

The corridor was long. Too long. I started to run, tugging my body into motion. And then, finally, too quickly it came to an end. I smacked into the door, felt it hard and cold under my hands.

I pushed it open.

In the middle there was an old cot. The sides were slatted like bars but the front was open. It was bigger than a regular cot. Not like the one Alex or I had slept in. The mattress was thin and mouldy, mottled with green and black.

On top of it was a body. A girl, maybe. It was hard to tell. Her hair was short like mine, boyish, and she wore shorts and a t-shirt, both too grubby to identify.

Dark brown skin. Hollow eyes. Skin taut around her cheeks, bitten fingernails ragged, the fingers on one hand broken and twisted, wrapped around an old child's toy. A doll with a pink dress. This face was the same one I'd seen a flash of during therapy. Like Jaspreet, but younger.

Jaswinder.

There were candles, too. Red candles. Four of them on the floor, casting the room in wavering light. One for each us. Four children – now three.

Now there was just Randeep, Alex and me.

TWENTY TWO

9 NOVEMBER 2016

Harriet

I WOKE HOURS BEFORE Erin. I checked my work emails and found one from Sharon, checking in. It took me a long time to build up to calling her. To explain what was going on. As I expected, she flapped and fawned, and somehow that felt worse than her not being bothered. But either way, she said I could take some time.

I put on a pot of coffee. I drank my first steaming cup standing in the kitchen. The caffeine was like electricity and it sent a buzz through my dull limbs. I remembered when a really good karate practice had done the same thing. I hadn't been in almost a year. That was long before I found Oscar and Isaac's news article languishing under my mother's lino. Before Jillian became *Erin*. It seemed like a lifetime ago.

I didn't know what to do. The police hadn't given me any details but I wasn't sure I'd have been in a fit enough state to take them in anyway. All I knew was that Monica knew Erin, and now she was dead. I couldn't get the sight of her lying in that bed out of my brain. But who would have wanted to kill her?

I thought of the note we'd found. Erin thought it was from *him*. The Father. That he wasn't dead after all. Could it be true? Was it possible? If the Father had been in prison all this time, it wasn't completely outside of the realms of possibility. But the question that Erin had asked haunted me as well: *why*?

Why now? Why do this at all? If he'd wanted to hurt Erin, he could have. Easily. So either it wasn't him, or it wasn't that simple.

I wanted to go over my notes again, but my laptop and files were all in the spare room. I couldn't bear the thought of waking Erin, not after everything she'd been through.

I was overtaken by the desire to make sure she was *safe*, a sensation so strong it made me breathless. I wished that she would have gone somewhere other than here, where somebody else could protect her and reassure her. The weight was heavy on my shoulders. But I also knew I didn't want her gone; I wanted her where I could keep an eye on her. I put on another pot of coffee.

It was midday before Erin appeared, her blonde hair mussed and her face shiny and pink with sleep. I noticed one of my notebooks in her hands as she entered the kitchen.

"I found your notes," she said.

I had a lot of them. Newspaper articles, interviews both new and old in longhand, photographs and photocopied chapters from a couple of books on unsolved child abductions and murders. I felt sorry, suddenly, that I hadn't moved them away. Not because I was worried Erin would be angry with me, but because I didn't want her to have to see her brother's face when she wasn't expecting it.

"Are you okay?" I asked gently. "Do you want coffee?"

She nodded. I got up, poured a fresh cup and pushed milk and sugar towards Erin.

She came forward, putting the notebook down softly, as though it was a child. Something had changed, I realised. I wasn't sure exactly when it had started, but over the short time I'd known Erin she had opened up, peeled back the disinterested veneer to expose the fear and insecurity within. This morning it was as if the final walls had fallen. She wanted to know what had happened to her and she wasn't going to give up until she had answers.

"I'm... I've spent so long avoiding it. And I'm – I'm disappointed." She sighed through her nose and began to load up her coffee with sugar and milk. "I was hoping... maybe there might be *something* that made sense to me, once I looked."

"Erin, it's okay. Be gentle with yourself. You've never allowed yourself to ask these questions before."

She wasn't really listening to me. "I mean, how do you abduct that many children and never leave any evidence?" she asked. "It's like now. How did the police not find anything? It must be him. Christ... I know he probably wore gloves or whatever – that's probably what I smelled, over my nose, the gloves... But the rest of it. How do you *do* that? How do you get away with it?"

"A lot of the early crime scenes were a mess," I said tentatively. "Windows open for hours before the police got there, sometimes rain got in. The first couple of cases weren't connected publicly until 1996 because of creating a public panic, but journalists leaked information that they shouldn't have known. The police literally interviewed hundreds of people, but stories conflicted, people misremembered things. Parents trampled through the kids' rooms before calling the police, as you'd expect. Some even lied about leaving bedroom windows open, afraid that they'd be judged for it. It happened twice, I think.

"It took the police over two weeks to connect the Davies girls to the Father because their mother said they'd gone missing in the morning, not overnight, and didn't mention the window right away. The newspapers got involved, reported eyewitness testimony that meant that for a while people were looking out for a green transit van on the motorway, but then that turned out to be nothing, and then Mrs Davies backtracked..."

"Do you think it would have made any difference if none of that had happened?" Erin looked different without her armour – her baggy jeans and smudged eyeliner. She looked vulnerable and *human*. She looked more like the little girl whose photograph had been plastered over all of the newspapers for weeks back in 1998. Young, boyish, overwhelmed.

"No," I said honestly. "I think there wasn't much to find anyway. He probably wore something that limited trace evidence, was prepared. I wouldn't be surprised if he chose more victims than we ever saw, and relied on luck, or rather *opportunity*, as the first step. Open windows, children sharing rooms, large trees out front or ground-floor bedrooms... The Father was clever. Meticulous. You have to know how to plan, to be patient.

Especially as parents got more savvy and the media were all over it. But he's also somebody who knows to subdue instead of fight. Which makes me think he's used to being persuasive. And without a motive everybody is just chasing their tails. I don't think we were ever going to find any evidence."

"I just hope they find something," Erin said. "That when he hurt Monica he made a mistake…" She blinked. "I keep going over everything in my mind."

"Things have come a long way since the nineties," I said. "They'll find who did this. Maybe we should leave the police to do their job."

"How can I trust them now?" She caressed the handle of the mug with her thumb, back and forth subconsciously. "After the way they were with me. What if they missed something? What if he left a clue in my house and none of us realised because we all just thought it was a – a *joke*? Somebody *died*. Who knows what will happen before they catch him? I think he's taunting me, Harriet. He knows there's something in my head that might tell me who he is, but for some reason he *wants* me to remember it. And that's why he killed Monica."

"What—"

"I think he wants to teach me a lesson. I've forgotten what happened to me, to all of us – and somehow he seems to know this. He's tormenting me. I don't think he'll stop now until either he gets caught or I remember."

"Okay," I said. I ran a hand over my face. I felt suddenly shaky. "So if the police don't find any DNA or trace evidence, nothing physical, what about psychological motive? We still have the fact that he took siblings——"

"And Oscar and Isaac," Erin said. "I keep coming back to this in my mind, but what does his obsession with siblings say about him?" She gestured animatedly, her coffee forgotten now. "Did he have a sibling he hated?"

"Or maybe he never had one," I pointed out. "Or he had one and lost them. Maybe he didn't protect his own sibling or maybe he feels betrayed. You could spin this any way and it won't help."

Suddenly a spark of something flickered in Erin's eyes. "Protection..." she muttered. "Did I tell you I went to see their foster mother?"

"What?"

She waved away the look of distress on my face. "I pretended to have car trouble and I went to her house."

"Erin, why?"

"I wanted to see if I could figure you out. And I guess it felt like something I needed to do for myself." She said it simply, but there was a gritty determination there. I realised that she was more afraid, more angry about the police not believing her than she'd let on so far. "Anyway, you said she wasn't helpful when you talked to her. Because you're a writer. Well, I'm not a writer – and she didn't know who I was. I never told her. When I was there she said something weird. I'm thinking about it now and I just... I'm trying to remember exactly what she said. Something like 'siblings should protect each other'. Hang on, maybe I should..."

She pulled her phone out of her pocket, prodding at

223

it mercilessly before holding it up to her ear. My brain was buzzing. Here we were, back to Oscar and Isaac again.

"What are you—" I tried. She shushed me.

I could hear the faint hum of the dial tone.

We waited. The phone rang, and rang. Slowly Erin's eyes narrowed and her lips thinned until all that was left was a grim line.

"Maybe we should try again later," I suggested. "Do you think she's okay? Should we call the police?"

Erin shook her head.

"What would we tell them? That I have a *hunch*? Something tells me they won't believe me. Or take us seriously. But she lives alone..." she said. "Like Monica. We should go check on her, at least. What if she's hurt?"

Erin drove. When we pulled up I didn't have time to register where we were, the building or its tenants. Erin was out of the car before the engine had even died.

"You don't really think she's in any danger, do you?" I asked, more to reassure myself than anything else. Erin didn't answer. It was clear she hadn't thought Monica was in any danger until it was too late.

She marched straight for a buzzer by the door and held it down. It crackled for what seemed like forever. She let go and tried again.

Then, finally, there was an exhaling noise.

"Hello?"

"Mrs Bowles?" Erin blurted, relief palpable. "It's – I'm the one who came about my car, you let me inside—"

"Ah yes. Did you get home okay?"

"Yes, look, can we come up? I have some questions for you."

"Questions? Why would you have questions? Didn't I help you enough?"

"It's about your boys. I want to know about Oscar and Isaac—"

"You didn't have car trouble, did you?" Mrs Bowles asked. "I don't want to talk any more. I don't think it's a good idea to drag up the past."

Erin glanced at me. It was clear she was taken aback. I gave her an 'I told you so' look and shrugged. This was exactly the response I'd got when I'd phoned her.

"I'm sorry if I've made you uncomfortable," Erin said. "But I really was grateful for your help. And I got the feeling you wanted to tell me something, before. Are you… Do you still—"

"Who do you have with you? I don't talk to the press."

I stepped back, scanning the building. I couldn't see any faces at the windows, but they were dark squares against the bright day.

"W-what?" Erin stammered.

"I watched you. Who's with you?"

I glanced at the car, then back at Erin. Eventually I shrugged. She could obviously see us, but it didn't have to mean anything.

"A friend. She's alright, though," Erin fumbled. "She's with me, I can vouch for her."

"I don't think so," Mrs Bowles said. There was a strange

hiccuping sound and then she said, "I don't talk to the newspapers so I think you need to leave."

"I understand. I'm really sorry, it's just—"

"The boys were my life. My children still are my life, ever since I stopped working for other people and started doing what I wanted to do. I used to clean houses and I never had any control. But I had to take charge. *All* of my children are my life. I just wanted to keep them safe. Do you *understand*?"

This was forceful. I felt like we were missing something – and looking at Erin's face it was clear she felt it, too. We were having two different conversations.

"You said something about siblings," Erin tried. "Last time—"

"My children are my life," Mrs Bowles repeated. "If anything were to happen to any of them... I can't have that sort of hurt again. I'm not interested in being in your silly interviews. Why can't you leave me alone?"

"Hurting your children is the last thing we would ever want," I said. I spoke louder than Erin had. More firmly.

It didn't work.

"I have to go now. I'm sorry you got the wrong impression."

The intercom went dead.

Erin sagged against the side of the building, the same shell-shocked look on her face that I was sure I wore. She thrust her hands into her pockets and a frown crept across her face.

"Well that was weird," I said.

TWENTY THREE

Harriet

"SO WHAT NOW?" ERIN asked as we walked through the door to my flat. I threw my keys into the bowl in the hall.

When I turned she was massaging the bridge of her nose. It made her eyes water – or perhaps she was crying. I wanted to step closer, but I didn't know whether she'd want me near her. Or whether she had just wanted me to stay in the bathroom with her last night because I was the only person who knew exactly what she'd seen and she needed somebody, *anybody*, who'd understand.

"We work on what Jenny gave us," I said calmly.

In the kitchen I put the kettle on, waiting for Erin to follow me through. She did, slowly.

"Do you think…" she trailed off.

"What?"

"It just… It felt suspicious. What Jenny said, how she was with me. Before she let me into her flat, she opened up to me. But this time, the way she acted when she saw you there. It was the total opposite. Almost like she was hiding something." Fear danced in Erin's eyes.

"What are you saying?" I flicked the kettle off so I could listen properly. "Do you think she's involved—"

Erin shook her head quickly. "I don't know, I didn't mean that. I don't…" She stopped speaking and flicked the kettle back on. "I'm just wound up," she said after a moment. "I don't know what to think."

We made the tea in silence, my mind going a mile a minute.

"Jenny mentioned her kids," I said eventually. "Her other kids. If she won't talk, maybe one of them remembers the night Oscar and Isaac disappeared?"

"I can't imagine they'd be able to forget it," Erin said. A haunted look passed over her face.

"Right. Even if they thought their brothers ran away, maybe they can help us plot out a timeline for before it happened. We know that everybody else – you and your brother included – didn't have much in common beyond their abductions. We have the windows and the time of year, both of which we don't have for Oscar and Isaac. But you and Alex weren't taken in the summer either, so maybe it's not the time of year exactly that's important. Maybe it's more – I don't know, temperature-related or something. If it's warm there's a higher chance of finding open windows. So, maybe it's opportunity? Except – well, it can't be *purely* opportunity, otherwise you wouldn't all have shared bedrooms with your siblings." This was making my brain hurt. "There's more in common with the cases after bodies were found. Pyjamas that don't belong to the child, insulin overdose as cause of death. Before you were abducted none of you went to the same places, shopped in the same places. You were all cities, *counties*, apart. But if you throw Oscar and Isaac into the mix, in Derby – well, they're basically at the centre of it all, geographically speaking. So maybe…"

"Maybe he was reckless?" Erin frowned. "Maybe the first victims were close to home. So, Derbyshire? And that's why he went further afield when he did it again. Jeremy and Michael were from, uh, Lincoln, right?"

I nodded. "Yes. Then you've got kids as far as Sheffield, and as close as Burton. All over county borders, no real pattern, except that they're within a few hours' drive of each other and near motorways. But if you take Derbyshire as the central point, that would make Sheffield and Lincoln sort of outliers."

Erin's expression was a mask of sadness. I knew she was thinking about Monica, because I was too.

"Where do we start though?" she asked. "We don't know if the locations mean anything, we don't know if the age or the gender of the children really matter. The boys started off looking sort of alike, but in the end, we – all of us – were just… us." She sighed. "Did the pattern evolve accidentally, or was it tailored? We don't even know anything about Jenny's children. They might have different last names, like Oscar and Isaac did."

"She fostered some, but some of the children were officially adopted by her," I said. There was a brief line about them in the very first article I'd found about Oscar and Isaac's disappearance, the one I'd found under my mum's lino. "Hang on."

In my office I rooted through two of my scrapbooks before

I recovered the piece. I'd found it just weeks ago, but it must have been under the lino for years, probably since around the time it was printed. The paper was yellowed, shiny with glue. I wouldn't have noticed it, except that day I'd been thinking about Jem and Mikey. With Thomas being gone that was happening more and more. And there it was, laid amongst other old bits of newspaper which had been used to make the concrete more even. I looked at it, at the date – just over a year before Jem and Michael were taken – and thought, *what are the odds?*

I took the scrapbook back into the kitchen. Erin was staring intently at her phone.

"I'm on the Facebook page again," she said. "It's where I found Jenny's address. There are quite a few followers but I'm trying to scroll back to the beginning to see if any of them match the family photo on the page."

I slid the scrapbook across the table. From Erin's face I realised she hadn't looked at it when she was going through my notes. Gently, I held down the pages so she could read.

"*No Sign of Runaway Boys.*" She read the title of the article, her voice leaden. "They were both under ten years old. How on earth did everybody think they'd actually run away?"

"They had a history of it, I guess," I said. "And it changed things, even though they were high risk."

"There," she said, then. She was gesturing to the piece of the article I'd remembered. "Ms. Bowles had one other foster child living with her at the time of the boys' disappearance, and she has two adopted sons (family pictured)."

The picture was missing, but the caption beneath it was

still there. It listed their names, and ages. Isaac, Oscar, Adam, Jonah and Danielle.

"Jonah and Adam must be the adopted sons, and Danielle the foster," Erin said. "I'll see if I can find anybody with those names on the Facebook page. Danielle will probably be harder to find."

I booted up my laptop and started a Google search. *Adam Bowles* and *Jonah Bowles* got me a whole lot of nothing. Or too many somethings. So many Facebook pages but none of them local, several links that didn't even seem related. I found one reference to a *Bowles Cleaning Service* on a blog about old local businesses that had since folded, which we could link to Jenny at a push, but it told us little besides the fact that it had been a Derbyshire mobile business with a focus on friendly and efficient customer service.

We worked in silence for the most part, breaking away only for a small lunch which both of us picked at. I kept the tea coming as we each followed rabbit hole after rabbit hole and came up empty-handed.

Later on we tried the TV while looking for a distraction, but it was short-lived. We'd caught the tail end of the local news, and there was Monica's face. The sound was muted but we both saw it. Erin turned it off like she'd been scalded as I turned my face away.

"It's no use," Erin said after another long while of searching. We'd been at it for hours, now, comparing profile pictures to the newspaper photo in my scrapbook, trying to narrow down by age, but all we'd found were two Adams who hadn't listed their surnames as Bowles or their location. We couldn't rule them out, but we couldn't contact them easily either, unless we fired random messages into the void. We hadn't found a single Jonah that looked even vaguely the right age. "Either they don't want to be found or they're not there at all."

"We could try the Danielles again," I said. We'd found at least thirty who lived in the UK and could be the right sort of age, but without a surname or updated photo it was almost impossible to figure out who the right one was. "Send them all a message."

"Saying what?" Erin blew out a big breath, then rooted around for a cigarette. "Can I smoke in here?" I didn't normally smoke inside but these weren't normal circumstances. I shrugged and got up to open a window. Erin continued, "We can't exactly message thirty people and say, 'Hey, were you ever in foster care in Derby?'"

"Why not?"

"We just can't," she said. Exasperation made her clumsy, and she knocked her mostly empty mug. We both scuttled back, grabbing phones and laptops and papers. "Shit, sorry!" Erin swiped at the mess furiously with a paper towel. "How will this get us anywhere? It's hopeless. It just feels like it'll never ever be over."

She scrubbed frantically, her neck corded with tension. I reached out – slowly, so she could stop me. She didn't.

"I'm sorry," I said. "Why don't we take a break?"

Erin sniffed, her frown easing. "Okay. God I'm such a mess. Can we get out of here for a while? I'm getting myself all twisted up."

I waited until Erin got up to change before sending private messages to all of the Adams and the Danielles we had found. I could see Erin's point about it seeming endless, but that didn't mean we couldn't try.

The bar was dark and the drinks were cold. More importantly the place I'd chosen didn't have a TV which would be showing the local news. Erin was happy when I chose somewhere small and dimly lit. It felt good to be out of my flat, away from ghosts and grief. We were both content to sit quietly and take stock.

I found us a corner booth. At the bar I ordered myself a triple gin and tonic, searching for the kind of abandonment only clear spirits could give me, and two equally strong rum and Cokes for Erin. I wasn't sure if she wanted two, but she probably needed them.

She was just finishing on the phone when I made it back to the table.

"Sorry, that was my mum." The look on her face was tired, but warm. "She just found out about Monica. I didn't tell her. I… I don't know why I didn't. I guess I didn't want her to worry? Which is stupid, because now she's even *more* worried. Maybe I was in shock. I did think about it, but I never called her. Anyway, she wants to come home, which is exactly what I'd thought she'd want."

"What did you say?"

"I told her she should stay where she is. Apparently Wendy said the same thing. I mean, what can she do if she's here?

I'd rather her stay out of harm's way." A shadow passed over her face. She reached for one of the rum and Cokes. "You remembered my drink order," she said, a little surprised.

"I always remember what a lady likes to drink."

I had never felt this way about anybody before. Especially not a woman. But there was something about Erin that drew me in; she was vulnerable but strong, smart and beautiful, but also so much more than any of those things. At first I hadn't known what to expect; I'd been almost *envious* of the way she'd shucked off her old self, changed her name and moved on from her tragedy, but now I realised she hadn't really managed to move on at all. She'd only hidden from the past, not escaped it.

Erin sipped her drink. Her eyes were darker tonight, smudged with their familiar kohl, but also a touch of uncharacteristic blue.

"Mum said she had a 'friend' staying with her. They were going on a *date* tonight. That's why she called. She said she wanted to come right home."

"Is that – unusual?"

"Well. Yes. My mum doesn't date. But apparently it's some guy she's been seeing for ages and ages and it's quite serious. I mean, he's staying there with her at the cottage, I think. I guess that's more reason for her to stay there. I think if he wasn't there she'd have just turned up tonight wanting to make sure I'm okay. I've got to check in with her as it is. This guy, though… I wonder if she wanted me to meet him. If that's why she kept asking me to go with her." Erin paused, thoughtful.

"I've been avoiding her a lot. Turns out I don't have a clue what she does with her free time."

I thought of my own mum. Her persistent nagging for me to join her hikes. And Thomas, so far away. I knew I should make more of an effort with her, and I didn't even have an excuse not to.

"Perhaps you ought to talk to her more," I said.

"About my brother?" Erin raised an eyebrow.

"I didn't say that."

"No, but you thought it loudly enough." She gave a small laugh, a huffing sound. "I know what you think of me. I saw it the first time I met you. You think I should talk about Alex, like you talk about your cousins, right? Well, you have somebody to talk to – your brother. He understands what you're going through, from the same perspective as you. I don't have that."

"I…" I felt this like a punch to the gut. How I'd been frustrated with Thomas for not emailing me often enough, and here was Erin, never able to talk to her brother again. I felt tears prickle at my eyes and I blinked.

Erin's face softened.

"What's your brother like?" she asked.

"Thomas is, uh, seven years older than me. He's an engineer. He moved to Australia a couple of months ago with his fiancée." I paused. "He's – really funny. Makes a lot of stupid jokes. But he puts up with me pestering him, looks out for me. I can't wait until he comes back to visit. I miss him."

Erin was silent, sipping her rum. Processing.

"I used to talk to him about Jem and Mikey a lot. He was

the only safe person who I could tell, when it got too much. I used to feel like we would never be as good as them? God, that sounds so fucked up. But, like, when we were kids my mum was really overbearing. She got better as we got older, once we were out of the house and she sort of had to accept it, but when we were kids it was all of these *rules.* No open windows, no walking to school; we weren't even allowed to play outside unless somebody could watch us. I think she would have always been very protective, but it was worse because of what happened to them.

"I didn't realise how much we talked about them as adults, either. Until he moved. And now... I've come to realise that most people don't *want* to talk about them outside of my family. Because it's too sad, or they don't know what to say. So, they focus on what they think is safe. They talk about *him.* All those stupid true crime roundups, journalists, whatever, they never seem to care about the victims – or the rest of us. Like it's too unbearably sad for them."

Erin finished her second drink.

"It wasn't like that with me," she said quietly. "They wouldn't leave *me* alone. They followed me everywhere, badgering and poking, wanting to know my story. It was like they didn't understand why I couldn't tell them. Alex was my older brother. He protected me. I think I left him to die, and the worst part is I don't even remember any of it."

"I understand." I let the numbing warmth of the gin soothe my raw nerves, the tension between us easing. "I think I do, anyway. It must be so hard."

Erin rewarded me with a tiny smile. She was flushed, I noticed, from the rum and the warmth. Maybe from something else, too.

"Can I ask you something?" She looked serious.

"Uh-oh." I finished my drink. The alcohol was kicking in now. We were both swaying slightly with the music. It was some loose beat, a type of house music maybe. "But go on."

"Why didn't you go and physically try to talk to Jenny Bowles?" she asked, almost hesitantly. "You said the police wouldn't give you any information, which I get. But, I would have thought you'd have really tried, if you wanted proof that they were connected to – *us*?"

I didn't miss the word 'us'. It was the first time she'd willingly identified herself as one of the children. But I couldn't say anything, or risk losing her trust. I thought for a moment before speaking.

"At first... I didn't know how big of a deal it was, or whether I was making it up. I've always been interested in siblings. When I first started writing the book at university I searched for other crimes, disappearances or runaways that were maybe connected. It was a weird hobby, but I found it soothing going through and discounting them as part of the pattern, as though I was double-checking everything. It frustrates me to think I might have even seen something about Oscar and Isaac at the time, but dismissed them because of their different surnames. I don't know *what* made me think when I found that article...

"Anyway, about two years in I found these sisters who were listed as runaways, and I tried to get in touch with the parents.

The girls were older, sixteen or so, and one had been found dead only half an hour or so before I got in touch. I didn't know... The family were extremely upset, obviously. They thought somebody had leaked it to the press...

"I don't blame them for being angry, but they threatened me." I swallowed. "I was afraid. It felt like a sign that I should stop digging into things that had nothing to do with me. And then obviously that tutor told me my work was juvenile so..." I sighed. "I stopped. But when I found that article about Oscar and Isaac it felt like a different sort of sign. I saw their faces, the way they stood together in that picture the newspaper used, and I didn't even realise they weren't related by blood until I read the article. But Jenny really didn't want to talk to me and I thought about that other family. I guess I talked myself out of it. That's why I took the information to Godfrey before doing anything else."

While I talked Erin listened intently.

"Oh," she said, finally. *Oh*. As though everything we'd been through over the last few days could be summed up in that one word.

"Can I ask *you* a question?" I asked.

She stared for a second, thoughtful, and then nodded.

"When did you decide to change your name?"

For a moment I thought she wouldn't answer, but then she said, "When I woke up in that hospital I knew straight away that I wasn't Jillian any more. Something in me had – fractured. We were always Alex and Jillian, Jillian and Alex. Without him, I couldn't be *me*. The old me." She sipped her drink sadly. "Erin is my middle name. I grew my hair, started wearing makeup as soon as Mum would let me. I tried other things, too, dresses and skirts and earrings, but those things just made me feel like more of an imposter. This way I'm me, but not me."

She got up without saying any more, ordered more drinks. We didn't talk after that. There was a feeling between us that was both cautious and reckless. The later it got the louder the music grew. I watched her fingers, the way she held her glass. Admired the dips of her collarbones when she leaned in closer. I smelled the perfume she had borrowed from my bathroom, musky and warm. I noticed things about her that I'd never noticed in anybody else.

We drank until the world swam. When we left the bar, staggering out into the freezing night, the moon was out, a broad half-circle that made our shadows twine together. The night air smelled like smoke and pine trees. Erin held my arm.

If I had been on my own I might have been afraid. There was a sensation, I felt, like a hand at the back of my neck. It was residual, the image of what had happened to Monica burned into my memory. But the alcohol numbed the feeling, and Erin was close, and the shadows stayed just that: shadows.

At my flat we finished the last of the gin and then moved onto brandy and amaretto, the dregs of liquor bottles I'd had for an age. From a time when I had more friends outside of work to drink with, from when Thomas used to come over and we'd hang out. I'd missed a Skype call from him earlier in the day, but I couldn't face talking to him. I had no idea what

I'd say. It would be hard, I thought, to tell him such important things over a connection that glitched and wavered. I didn't want to have to repeat myself.

I didn't want Erin to overhear.

Both of us were eager to forget. Erin leaned against me as we swayed to silence. She pressed her lips, slowly, to my throat. I felt my body react, the first instinct to pull away, but I didn't want to. And when I didn't move she did it again.

Then her hands were on my back, tracing the waist of my dress, her touch feather-light. I didn't stop her as her fingers hovered on my hips. She waited.

I pulled her closer, until the lengths of our bodies were touching. I could feel her breath on my skin, hot and sweet with cherry alcohol.

She leaned into me. I felt one hand on my back, the other pressed against my thigh. The top of my leg. I loosed a breath that overflowed with want. She responded with a sigh of her own, and I knew in that moment I needed to make her do it again.

We tumbled into the spare bedroom. The futon was less comfortable than I remembered, but I didn't care. Erin pressed me down into the blankets and sheets. Then she was on top of me, her weight comforting and wild at once, setting a roaring wave growing in my stomach, between my legs. Her lips were at my neck and my hands were in her hair, and the blankets I'd knitted tangled around our legs as we moved together.

Afterwards we curled together. The room was dressed in moonlight. It made Erin's hair look like liquid gold. I wanted to kiss her again, but her eyes were closed and I couldn't disturb her. She looked peaceful.

I lay for a while in the darkness, Erin's head resting against my shoulder, and felt the weight of dread start to ease back in.

ON THE NIGHT

Jillian

"YOU HAVE TO RUN."

Jillian replayed Randeep's words over in her head. She was shaking but she didn't feel afraid any more, only numb and empty. Like she wasn't even there. The walls of the well were slick with rain and slippery green moss, but the stones were big and they stuck out, and they were both good climbers. It was deep enough to hide them but she didn't know for how long. It wasn't far enough from the house but neither of them could run any more, not yet.

"Jilly, we need to go," Alex whispered. He was right. If they stayed here much longer they'd freeze. It was raining, every drop of icy water like a needlepoint. Their borrowed pyjamas were dirty and soaked.

Alex held her close. He smelled a little of sweat and panic, and Jillian was almost glad for his buzzing terror because it made her remember: they had escaped, they'd made it this far, which meant they could get home.

"I'm tired," she mumbled. She could hardly see Alex's face except for the weak moonlight. "I don't want to run any more."

"Jilly we *have to go*. We can't end up like Jas."

Jillian thought of Randeep again. How he had helped them to escape. He said he couldn't leave without his sister – but it wasn't too late for them. He told them how his sister had tried to run, two days before Jillian and Alex came. And he hadn't been allowed to see her again.

They all knew she was dead, but Jillian had been too scared to tell him that she'd seen Jas on her first night in the basement. Or rather, they'd seen her body, lit by candlelight. It was a warning. They would have to run, better and harder and faster than Jaswinder had.

"This house is crazy," Randeep had said. "It gets to you. You're meant to be part of the family. You'll eat cake until you feel sick. And then you'll get angry, or somebody will, and the basement won't be good enough any more, and one of you will end up dead. Because you weren't a *Good Fit*. And then two more children will turn up, and it'll happen all over again. Nobody is good enough."

"I don't think we should leave yet," Jillian whispered into the close darkness of the well. "If Jas... We can't do the same as her..."

"Jilly, we can't stay here. We'll freeze. As long as we're moving, that's what's important. Let's GO."

He helped her out first, her nails scrabbling against dirt and stone and grass. She waited. She was smaller than her brother and she could jump back into Alex's arms if she heard anything.

She counted to a hundred. It was clear. There was nobody here in these woods except the two of them. Then she reached down to help Alex out. He was heavy, his body grown after a long, hot summer. He was only two years older than her, but right now that felt like years she'd never see. Her whole body was shaking with cold and exhaustion.

Now they were out of the confined space of the well, Jillian's heart started to pound and sick terror seeped into every millimetre of her. Alex grabbed her hand and they began to run. They didn't know where they were going. Just away.

The trees slashed at their faces, their legs, as they left behind the house and the lake. They knew somebody had drowned there years ago; it was a story they'd heard more than once. Death was everywhere. Jilly stumbled and let out a yelp, her ankle twisting on the slick grass. Alex panicked, yanking her to her feet and pulling hard.

"*Come on!*" he hissed.

The wind picked up. It sounded like a scream. Jillian tried to run faster but her ankle hurt. Alex pulled her again. Her bare feet ripped on twigs and the crackle of autumn leaves.

"Jilly, come *on!*"

"I can't, Alex, I can't." She was sobbing now. They ran so hard their breath was hitched and Jillian felt panic in every bit of her explode into something breathless, a dragon, no a *monster*, that threatened to take her vision too. The woodland floor was jagged and dark, treacherous with hidden dips and skids and—

And then Jillian fell again. Alex yanked her arm so hard the socket was like a firework and she saw stars.

"I can't run any more," she cried. "Alex, I *can't*."

"Come on, you idiot, get up——"

There was that screaming sound again. It made Jillian's bones turn to water. She screeched and scrambled to her feet. It wasn't the wind, it wasn't a monster. It was human – and that was worse.

They splashed through a river, the water up to their waists. It was swollen with the rain, sucking and pulling at their clothes. The mud on either side was trying to bury them alive. Alex gripped her hand tight, and when they tumbled onto the banks Jillian had to spit a mouthful of silty water into the dirt. Alex yanked her back up, and on they went, the trees still closing in around them.

They came eventually to the edge of a slope that led down through trees and leaves, steep and scary. Alex slammed into her back as she skidded to a halt. *We have to go, we have to go. We have to GO.* But she didn't want to. She couldn't. She looked at Alex, his white face streaked with mud.

"I can't," Jillian whispered. "I'll fall. My ankle——"

She wanted to cry. She wanted Alex to hug her, like he'd done when they were very small. But his face now wasn't the face she knew. It was all points and hollows, his mouth open and panting. He was so cold, not like the warm, solid presence she always felt.

"You've got to go," he said. His eyes cleared. "Jilly, you've got to go down."

Jillian felt like time had slowed.

"Alex, help me," she whispered.

And then he pushed her.

EXCERPT

Jillian & Alex Chambers
Abducted: Little Merton, 13 October 1998

"The kids were always thick as thieves," Amanda Chambers told me over the phone when we spoke about Alex and Jillian. "Alex was obsessed with his sister from the moment she was born. He used to climb out of his cot and go and sleep next to her on the floor. We used to call it Alex Watch."

"He was protective?"

"Oh yeah. They used to ride their bikes together on the street. Alex taught her how to ride, to skate, to play cards. I hardly had to get involved." She laughed, and then went silent. "I probably ought to have paid more attention but I was happy that they were keeping out of trouble, out of the house."

"Was Alex a quiet boy?"

"Yes, I suppose he was actually. They were both pretty quiet. Alex especially so, but he had such a smile. He was like an angel. Sometimes I find it hard to remember and I have to find old video or pictures of them together. But it's never the same. Sure you see the dimple, but you don't see what made him *laugh*. Whether he made himself laugh or not. He used to do that a lot. To make his sister howl with him. It was brilliant. It was how he made up for feeling like he had to carry the world, I think. He always wanted everything to be perfect, wanted everybody to be happy."

"And Jillian?" I asked eventually. "What about her? Was she very worried about people being happy?"

"As a kid she was oblivious. She only cared about Alex. Now she pretends she doesn't care what people think, but it's not true. Things were complicated when they were little. I think Alex noticed more than she did, and he shielded her. Sometimes I just felt *so guilty*," she said.

"About the children?"

"Yes. I think about it a lot, even now. I used to talk to my husband about it, before he died, but now I just think to myself… I should have paid more attention. I should have made sure that the windows stayed locked, told the kids more often not to mess with them. I told them, but I didn't go and check every night. I didn't make *sure*. We didn't think it could happen again. Two in one year. It sounds awful, but we thought we were safe. And it felt, when they were gone, like all these dominoes had been lined up and that open window was the first nudge to send them all tumbling down."

After this conversation I asked Amanda to meet with me, so we could talk through things some more. She agreed, but when I asked her if she thought her daughter might talk to me for the book she shut me down.

"No," she said. "She doesn't talk about her brother. I'm not sure she'll ever be ready to do that. I think it'll take something catastrophic to make her see that when we used to call her *lucky* it didn't mean she hadn't suffered. We didn't mean it that way. But I think..." Amanda sighed. "I think we might have messed her up by telling her that. So, you can try but I doubt she'll open up to you."

TWENTY FOUR

10 NOVEMBER 2016

Erin

I WOKE EARLY TO an empty bed, my head muzzy with a hangover. The room was cold, the wind blowing outside. I gathered my senses and glanced around me. There was no evidence of our night together except the duvet and blankets that were bundled on my side of the bed, where I'd been tossing and turning.

The curtains were closed, the window firmly locked, and I got up to look outside. The morning was bright and cold. I knew in another life I would have felt guilty about sleeping with Harriet after what had happened to Monica, but instead I found that I felt better for it. Like a cleansing of ghosts. I ignored the little bleat of guilt at my own callousness; now wasn't the time to let regret win. And besides, I liked Harriet.

I dressed in my pyjamas and then headed into the kitchen. Harriet wasn't there. I made myself a coffee and then wandered down the hallway to her bedroom. The door was cracked and I poked my head through into the dim room. I heard the gentle stream of water from the shower and breathed a sigh.

I showered in the guest bathroom and got dressed. When Harriet finally appeared her hair was still damp at the ends, her cheeks flushed, and it suited her. I crossed the room and lifted my hands to the sides of her face so I could kiss her firmly. She let out a little squeak of surprise, but much to my relief she didn't pull away.

"What was that for?" she asked.

"Sorry. When you weren't in bed I – I thought you'd done a runner," I said.

She gave me a sheepish smile.

"Don't be daft. Unless there's a reason you think I'd abandon you here?"

Now it was my turn to be sheepish. The awkwardness was back; it felt a little like being a teenager again, so many thoughts and feelings about Harriet and Monica and Oscar and Isaac and Alex all swirling in my brain that I didn't know *how* to feel.

"No. No reason." Did she regret it? Was that why she'd been gone when I woke up?

She eyed me cautiously, then took a step back awkwardly.

"Look, about last night..."

"I'm sorry," I blurted. "Really. Look, it's my fault. Okay? I take full responsibility. I was a mess and I needed to let off some steam..."

"Responsibility?" Harriet turned back to me, her jaw firm. Not what I expected. "You say it like it shouldn't have happened."

251

"I thought you regretted it…?"

"Oh, god." Harriet let out a grunt of frustration, then a laugh that sounded like a whole lot of relief. "Okay, look, let's start again."

"Alright."

"I just wanted to make sure that I hadn't… upset you?" Now I realised what the expression on her face meant. She was nervous.

"How?" I asked.

"I've never…" She worked her jaw, another flush creeping. "It doesn't matter. Whatever. We're too busy to be acting like teenagers, let's just forget it—"

I crossed the short distance between us and reached out. I held her arms, and looked into her eyes. Then I kissed her full on the mouth. This time she relaxed against me, kissed me back, and she tasted like toothpaste.

"It was *great*, Harriet." I smiled. "Honestly. You have nothing to worry about."

"Are you sure, because—"

"I'm sure," I said firmly. "I know things are – well, they're complicated. But you know that too. We're adults." I let my smile linger for just another moment, and then I allowed myself to think about those complications again and I felt any happiness drain out of me. I was exhausted.

"Hey," Harriet whispered. "Are you okay?"

"I'm…" I blew out a shaky breath. "I'm okay. I'm just – after what we were talking about last night, I'd really like to go and see my mum? It's a bit of a trek but… I don't want to wait for her to come home. I don't want her to come here. But I want to see her. Make sure she's okay."

"Do you want me to come with you?" Harriet asked. There was hope in her eyes.

And I realised I did.

"She's still in Skegness, it's a long way—"

"It's only a couple of hours each way. I'd rather you didn't go alone…"

"Yes," I said quickly. "If you mean it, then… please."

I called ahead, making sure I knew where I was going and explaining so Mum didn't panic when I turned up, and then Harriet drove. She'd had less to drink in the end and my head was still a bit tender. She didn't speak much on the drive and I was glad, and when we arrived she held up her phone.

"My brother tried to Skype last night," she said. "If you don't need me inside then I thought I could stay out here? Signal's good, and it'll give you guys some privacy."

"Stay in the car?" I fought the trepidation that made my voice and hands shake.

"I won't go anywhere else," she said. "Promise. It'll be fine."

"Okay. But I won't be long, and then we can get some lunch."

Inside her rented holiday home Mum was already making tea. She welcomed me in with a fussy hug and kept pulling at my hair, which had dried messily in the car.

"Is Harriet not coming in? It was nice of her to come all this way. Wendy said you were spending some time with her, which is reassuring given everything… It's all over the news now."

It was like Mum didn't know what to say. She wanted to be

at home, to be able to look after me. I understood that. But her being there wouldn't help anything, and it made me feel better knowing she was out here, away from it all.

"How… are you doing?" she asked then, gently. Awkwardly. "I know you and Monica were – close."

"Oh for goodness' sake, Mum." I sighed. It had been ridiculous to think that one conversation would heal our relationship, even after the last few days. "She was my *girlfriend*. You know that."

"Yes, but… you weren't together." Mum swallowed, and the look on her face made me soften. She was trying.

"No," I agreed. "No, we weren't. It was complicated. I'm not sure how well we knew each other at all. I… I have a lot of feelings about what happened. Mostly it feels like my fault."

I couldn't help it. Tears began to well in my eyes and no amount of biting my lip helped.

"Oh, darling." Mum reached out for me, taking my tea and then pulling me into her arms. She was only the same height as me, but she managed to envelop me, and it was, for a moment, like being a child again. "It's not your fault. The police will do everything they can to find out what happened."

I sniffled until I'd managed to get myself under control. I didn't believe her. What if they couldn't figure it out?

"How are you anyway?" I asked when I could.

"Oh, you know," she said. "I'm alright. I… I was just so worried about you. I wish you'd told me…" She stopped herself. "I'm just glad you're okay," she said.

"I'm okay. Harriet has been a big help. I guess I've been

worried about you too. I hope you're at least looking after yourself here?"

"I'm trying, hon. Nobody knows I'm here, so that makes me feel better about staying. If they publicly connect Monica to us, *you*, at some point the newspapers might try to find me. But I'm keeping the doors and windows locked. I've – had my friend come and stay over with me for a few days too. He was driving out here every day but it got a bit silly."

We settled into an awkward silence. I was brimming with questions that I didn't know how to ask. After yesterday, and after Monica, I realised I wanted to talk. About Alex, about what had happened, but I didn't know where to start.

"Mum… when Alex and me – when we were abducted… did you ever notice anybody paying a lot of attention to us?"

Mum shook her head. If she was surprised that I'd finally broached the subject she kept quiet, although I could see the faint tremor in her hands.

"No. If I had, of course I would have said something. We thought everything was *fine*. The police… At first they didn't want us to think it was anything to do with – *him*. They seemed to think it was something else, because obviously it wasn't the summer and everybody knew… everybody knew he took kids in the summer. And those other children from Burton had been taken. So we thought…" She went quiet for a moment, running her fingernail around the rim of her mug.

"Those weeks you were gone, they were the longest weeks of my life. We tried everything. Your dad – he even saw a psychic. Of course we hoped, but deep down I was – I was afraid you'd both never come home. Afterwards they asked you about it, but you didn't know anything. None of us did. There was no way of knowing if he... if he targeted the two of you or if it was just... chance." She sucked in a breath. I saw a small tear catch in the corner of her eye, where the creases were thickest. She blinked. "I played it over and over in my head, you know. Me and your dad both did. But we never..."

"What about what Dad saw?"

Mum's breath hitched.

"He didn't know what he saw," she said. "He always said he was confused, because it didn't look like anything bad. Just you or your brother messing around. An outline at the window, one of you reaching for the other. Maybe you had a nightmare and opened the window for some fresh air... He said Alex was talking, soothing you, and Alex said something like, 'Don't worry, I'll protect you.' It seemed innocent. Even when he talked about it afterwards, it was like he was grasping at straws. He didn't even think at the time that the window being open was – a problem. I mean... he just didn't *think*."

"Why didn't you ever tell me?"

"You didn't want to know." She shrugged. "And it didn't matter. I mean – it didn't make any difference. By the time we thought it was important it was too late."

She was crying openly now. I felt that old pang. I'd always hated watching people cry. I never knew what to do. Not like Alex would have. He was always good at making people feel better.

"Oh, Mum." I knew she needed a hug, and I wanted to give her one. But even despite the way she'd held me only minutes ago, now the space between us felt very wide and I stood, frozen, as she cried. "I… I think I ought to go."

"You're not leaving again? I thought you were going to stay with me."

I shook my head. This was the last place I wanted to be – I needed to be *doing something*, not hiding. I'd already decided I couldn't go back to work, not yet, and my brain would just go in circles if I stayed here.

"Well, let me come home with you then. I don't want you to be on your own—"

"No, Mum. I'm not on my own. It's okay. *Please* stay here. You need the break and – well, it's probably the best place to be right now. Stay here and try to relax with your friend. Okay?"

"Alright, hon."

I said my goodbyes and headed out to the car. Harriet was still waiting, and she sat quietly until I got in. Then she gave me a small smile, an *Are you okay?* that I felt rather than heard. I nodded.

She put the car into gear and drove.

"Thomas finally showed me his new house," she said, obviously trying to distract me. "It's amazing. Really big, new. Must have cost a fortune but his fiancée's loaded." She paused. "I tried to ask him if he knew anything, about Jem and Mikey that could be helpful, but… it's not like we ever thought this would happen. I didn't even tell him everything before because I thought… I wanted to talk to him face to face. But it's weird, I didn't even know where to start."

I didn't answer, but she seemed happy to fill the silence. The time passed quickly, and I slept for some of the journey back. We stopped at a small pub off the motorway when we got close to home, but we ate mostly in silence before heading back. The day had clouded over now and the light was dim and watery by the time we got back to Arkney. Outside Harriet's building, we pulled into the car park and she swore.

"I gotta park in the back," she muttered. "They've nicked my spot again. Here, take my keys. I won't be a minute."

Outside I shoved one hand deep into my pocket, gripping my lighter and my pack of cigarettes as if they were lucky charms.

Inside it seemed too dark, the sensor lights above my head blinking into action as I stumbled out of the lift. There was something on the welcome mat outside Harriet's door.

A parcel. A small box wrapped in some sort of birthday wrapping paper, red balloons and white cakes. The package had been tied carefully with a red ribbon.

I felt guilt shift in me. Was it Harriet's birthday?

I grabbed the parcel and carried it into the flat, placing it on the kitchen counter.

It must have been nice to have neighbours who'd do something like that. I was barely on speaking terms with either of mine. I knew one of my neighbours loved singing Taylor Swift at 2 a.m. and another regularly practised – badly – on an electric keyboard early on Sunday mornings, but that was it.

I thought about Harriet's call to her brother and felt the cavern of sadness in my chest crack a little wider. I wondered what it would be like if I still had Alex now. An emotion I couldn't place made me pause.

Then my thoughts came crashing together and I knew what had been bugging me all morning, maybe what I wanted Mum to pick up on. What I'd been thinking about since we'd talked to Jenny Bowles again yesterday. She had said siblings *should* protect each other – implying they didn't always.

It didn't feel like she'd been talking about Oscar and Isaac, so she must have been referring to somebody else. I'd thought it was suspicious at the time, but now I knew why. Could it be possible she knew something about who had taken us?

I grabbed my phone and tried Mrs Bowles' number again. It went right to an automated voicemail. I left a message.

"Mrs Bowles. It's Erin again. Car trouble girl. I'm really sorry to bother you, but this is so important. It's true that I'm not who I said I was. But I have an idea that I need to run by you and it's urgent. When you said siblings should protect each other, you weren't talking about Oscar and Isaac, were you? Please call me when you get this."

When I was done I went back to Harriet's notebooks, still spread out on the counter where we'd sat yesterday. I scanned the pages again. It made me feel sick. I didn't know what was worse, that it felt like we weren't getting anywhere or that the police were out there right now, investigating, and I had no control over any of it. I didn't even know what they were doing. CCTV, ANPR – what good was any of that when we didn't know who we were looking for? And how could I even trust that they'd be investigating the right things?

Eventually I heard the door open.

"Sorry," Harriet said. "I had to park down the street *again*.

259

At least we're not going anywhere any time soon. Do you…
Are you okay?"

"Not really. I called Mrs Bowles. No answer."

"She's probably busy. Or she's screening her calls now. I
think we freaked her out pretty badly yesterday."

"Or it's something else." I narrowed my gaze.

Harriet's eyes strayed to the breakfast bar behind me. I lost
my train of thought and spotted the little parcel. I'd forgotten
about it.

Harriet looked from me to the package, and when I showed
no sign of recognition she pointed at it.

"That's not from you…?"

"I thought it was from a neighbour or something." I pulled
up Mrs Bowles' number again. "I found it outside the door. It's
not your birthday, is it?"

Then I heard Harriet swallow. The sound was audible and
it made me look up from my phone. Her expression was frozen.

"What's up?"

"I don't know any of my neighbours," Harriet said. "But I
know the ones opposite are on holiday…"

Both of us stared at the package. Now its red and white
wrapping seemed ominous.

"Family?" I asked.

"No. My mum wouldn't…"

And then I realised.

"It's not for you."

The thought hit me like a brick wall collapsing on my head.
I felt the breath swoop out of me and I gripped onto the edge

of the breakfast bar as my legs went to jelly.

There was no tag on the outside. Just the bow. I tugged at the ribbon. The paper was taped exactly. Precisely. Like something you'd pay somebody to do in a department store. But I knew for a fact that no department store employee had wrapped this.

"Harriet," I said ever so slowly as I snicked the paper with my nail. "We need to call the police…"

"What—"

She stopped when she saw the contents of the box. Red, soupy cotton wool.

And four severed fingers.

TWENTY FIVE

Harriet

THE POLICE TURNED UP with a whole army of people. I took on the role of Erin's protector again, without even realising what I was doing. It was like donning a familiar coat, now.

There were people everywhere. People in suits and uniforms and people with mobiles and clipboards and cameras. We'd stepped out into the entrance hall to warn them that the package had been left on the doorstep, but I had a sinking feeling that whatever evidence might have been there was gone now Erin and I had trampled all over it.

I recognised Detective Godfrey from before, her wild curls hastily scraped back in a way that said she might have been halfway through tying them up when she'd left wherever it was she'd come from.

I hastened to show people into my flat, to get them to do something – anything – to get the boxed parcel out of my sight. They must be fake, right? *This* must be the joke.

Erin's anger burned white-hot, and she tackled the small

detective as soon as she came through the door.

"Are you doing *anything* to stop this from happening? First Monica – now this. Is this just going to keep getting worse? What next?"

She barely let the detective get through into the kitchen to have a look. I hung back, feeling like I was getting in the way no matter where I stood.

"Erin—"

"Jenny Bowles. The woman Harriet told you about. The lady who fostered those missing boys. Did you send somebody to talk to her?"

The detective turned to Erin, paused, and then reluctantly said, "Yes. A few days ago. We've not managed to contact her today—"

"Are these her fingers?" Erin blurted.

"But we just talked to her yesterday," I said, shock making me slow. "She was fine then."

"We'll know more when we've examined everything."

We all knew what that meant. Erin and I were pretty sure these were her fingers. We'd both seen the nicotine stains on the ones in the box, the arthritic knuckles, the fingers twisted and broken.

"When you go through her flat," Erin said, "you'll find my fingerprints." She said it straight but I could tell from the way she gripped something tightly in the pocket of her hoodie that she was nervous.

"You were inside?" Detective Godfrey frowned.

"I went to ask about her boys. Harriet told me about them.

263

She said that she thought they might have been the Father's first victims. Just like she told you. So I went to see if Jenny'd talk to me, but she didn't really."

The detective's face remained impassive.

"I tried to call her again today," Erin added. "I started to wonder if she might have known who the Father was but was too afraid to tell anybody…"

"You think she was being threatened?"

"I think it's possible. She kept talking about her children. Her adopted children. As though she was worried they might be hurt if she told the truth."

Before the detective could ask us any more, a man's voice broke through the general din and our eyes all swivelled his way.

"Here, boss, you might wanna look at this."

He was pointing into the box.

"I don't think so," Erin muttered.

There was a while where we stood, motionless, as the police removed something from the box with what might have been tweezers; somebody took photographs, and placed it into a transparent bag. It looked like a piece of paper smeared with blood.

The detective showed it to Erin.

"It's addressed to you," she said. "Would you mind taking a look? Don't touch it."

Erin took half a step forward. I watched as the colour drained from her face, her expression morphing from anger to fear so slowly it made me realise that one always masked the other.

Her hand was trembling as she gestured at it. I waited a respectful half a second before reading it over her shoulder.

Jilly, the note said. *The basement. The girl. Four red candles. That's how it began. Do you remember what happened next?*

"What does it mean?" I asked.

"Do you have any idea?" the detective said.

But Erin just shook her head. I stepped in, let my hand find the bottom of her back, my touch as light as I could manage. She leaned into me, her whole body vibrating with fear.

Four red candles.

"They're the candles from my dreams," Erin whispered. "I remember them, sort of. In, like, a basement? I remember a girl. I think she was dead. Jaswinder Singh, maybe. It's like he's trying to tease me. I think he *wants* me to find him. But that's all I know. The rest is… nothing."

Hours later, we found ourselves in a hotel room as the darkness thickened. The police were going over my whole block of flats, checking the broken camera system, knocking on doors. There was police tape, interview after interview. *Had anybody seen anything? Heard anything?* There was a resounding feeling that nobody had noticed.

I phoned Mum, who was down in Brighton now staying with some friends and the dogs, and then I emailed Thomas to update him. Erin called her mum and the conversation was stilted, panicked at first and then, eventually, calmer, but the whole exchange was warm, hesitant.

We couldn't stay in my flat, and Erin's house was out of the question, but neither of us felt safe anywhere else and we didn't want to end up in police protection, feeling like we were being watched every minute. It was getting late and we decided to check into a hotel off the motorway, about twenty minutes from Derby, where we were surrounded on one side by fields.

We spoke very little at first, both shaken and unsure. The room was big enough, but cheap, containing little more than a double bed and a TV. We switched it on briefly, but Monica's death had made the national news and Erin quickly turned it back off. If Jenny was missing, or dead, how long would it be before it was her face on there too? How long before journalists discovered we'd been to see her just yesterday?

I'd brought my laptop and my notebooks from home. The police already had all of the facts anyway, but these notes felt personal to me.

Erin looked sick, the dark circles under her eyes a mixture of makeup and chronic lack of sleep. I wondered if going out last night – and then what came after – had helped, or if we'd only made everything worse.

Every set of footsteps past the door made her jump, and even with the curtains closed, the windows firmly locked against the night, I think we both felt exposed.

"What are we going to do now?" I asked eventually. We had a bottle of wine between us and were taking turns drinking directly from it.

"What *can* we do? We're stuck. He's going to keep doing this until he can't do it any more. Until he runs out of reasons, or people. And then he'll either kill me, or he'll get caught. Maybe both. Simple as that."

"Or he'll keep at it until he can make you remember," I said. I genuinely believed that. "He doesn't want you to die. Why go to all of that trouble to break into my block of flats and hurt neither of us——"

"He killed Monica."

"I know." I sighed. Took a sip of the wine and passed it back. "I'm sorry. I didn't mean… I just meant that he obviously has something else in mind for you. There's some other reason that he's leaving you – well, *clues*. I don't know why——"

"He called me *Jilly*. Like he's fucking taunting me."

"You were 'little Jilly Chambers' to the newspapers, weren't you?"

"Yes."

"And they reported all about your escape. So, the Father – if this is him – must have known that you were alive."

"All these years I thought he was dead. I don't know why. I guess it was blind hope. Why else would he just… disappear? But I guess me getting away meant he had to go into hiding. That makes more sense.

"But… if he could have found me again at any time, why now? It's not like we even moved house straight away afterwards. So, whatever happened, I must have been no use after I escaped."

"Maybe he was in prison?" I suggested. "That's one of the theories. I thought maybe it was true, that he got caught for something else. I hoped he might have died there. Maybe he was just released? The timing is surely not a coincidence, though."

"Basically it's on me," Erin snapped, but it was tired. *She* was tired. She gulped another mouthful of wine. "How did this even happen?"

"I don't know," I said softly.

Erin relaxed a little, then. As though the fact that I didn't know either made her feel better. I reached over, gave her knee a gentle squeeze. Now might be a good time to tell her about the Facebook messages I'd sent. On the drive over I'd felt my phone vibrate, and I'd checked it while Erin was in the bathroom. One of the Danielles I'd messaged had sent me a short reply. She'd spent some time in the care system. One of her foster mothers had been a cleaner who looked after several boys, but she didn't remember very much and couldn't – or wouldn't – confirm the details I'd given her.

But I didn't say anything. As the night wore on, and the wine ran low, Erin began to relax a little bit more. She curled up on her side fully dressed and closed her eyes. I sat with my laptop on my knees and listened to her breathing even out. I'd tell her if I learned anything more.

I didn't want to get her hopes up.

TWENTY SIX

Erin

I WAS RUNNING. THE same dark trees, skeletal and tall. Finger-like branches scratching at my face as I stumbled and tore through the black night. I fell, grazed my knee. He was behind me.

I scrabbled to a halt at the edge of the familiar dip. It looked higher now. My legs were shorter. The fear of the unknown at the bottom left my breathing ragged. But I wouldn't let it defeat me.

I fell into the cold darkness. The leaves scratched me, burning against my skin. I tumbled head first, tasted dirt and rotten leaves in my mouth.

The ground was icy and hard. It wasn't the forest floor any more. It was concrete, unyielding under my cheek. Groggily, I tried to sit up.

"Jilly."

Alex's voice was inside my head. I couldn't turn my neck to search for him. Everything hurt.

The smell was mould of a different kind. And dust. Something rusty, too. I realised my lip was bleeding.

It was too dark to see anything. Slowly I was able to lift my head. A cold breeze snaked the length of me. I pulled my legs up, felt something heavy digging into my ankle. I reached down and then yanked my fingers away.

Chains.

I wanted to cry but I knew I couldn't. I didn't have any tears in me.

"Alex? Alex, are you there?"

"I'm here, Jilly."

"Where are you?"

"I'm here. Jilly — Jilly, don't leave without me."

"I won't. I'm here."

Then there was grass and leaves and a burning at my back as I skidded down the slope, tumbling into the darkness in the woods. And I left him behind. He made me leave him. I was meant to go back for him so that he didn't end up like the others. But I didn't.

I blinked. In the darkness there was a light. A warm, hot light that filled me with hope, and then with terror. Basement walls melting to reveal the dead girl, eyes hollow, the fingers on her hand bent at weird angles where somebody had fought her, where she clutched that old doll. And on the floor below—

Four red, dripping candles, wax pooling like blood. Lighting the room that became Jaswinder's tomb.

"Don't look at her, look at them. They're just candles," Alex whispered in my ear. "It's only fire."

Then one burnt out, leaving a trail of smoke behind.

"Alex, I'm scared."

One of us would be next.

"Don't worry, Jilly, I'll protect you."

Four candles… Four fingers. Four children, down to three.

The Father had been speaking to me and I hadn't been listening.

TWENTY SEVEN

11 NOVEMBER 2016

Harriet

ERIN BOLTED UPRIGHT IN bed, fighting the blankets, fighting me.

"Shh. Erin, it's me!"

Slowly the tension drained from her body. She looked into my face, as though she was examining every inch of it in the weak lamplight. She sucked in a shuddering breath. Slowly I loosened my grip on her arms.

"Are you okay?"

She shook her head. I got out of bed and flicked the kettle on. I made tea for both of us and carried it back to the bed in the small white mugs, precariously full. Erin took hers gratefully.

"How about now?" I asked. It was maybe three in the morning, the hotel around us completely silent. I could hear the faint drip of the shower in the ensuite, and the motorway traffic a little way off.

Erin took a sip of the scalding tea, wrinkled her nose at the long-life milk and then slowly nodded.

"I think so."

"Do you… want to talk about it?"

She started to shake her head and then stopped. She stared at the murky tea, eyes chasing the scummy water on top. She had fallen asleep in a chunky cardigan but I saw that she was shivering.

"I had a nightmare," she said eventually. "It didn't make sense, but… I was thinking about what Jenny said, when we spoke through her intercom."

"What do you mean? It was too confusing. Just that stuff about all her children—"

"Exactly. *All* of her children. She was talking like she was trying to protect them, right? Like I told the police, I think somebody was threatening her. But…"

She stopped. I felt an icy dread settle over me.

"I think he was with her," Erin said slowly, the air thick between us. "When we went to her flat. I think he was there the whole time…" She put her tea down hastily on the bedside table, her face going grey.

A thousand questions swelled inside me. "Do you think…"

"He killed her because of us. Because I went there."

"Erin, it's not your—"

"Can you stop fucking telling me this isn't my fault?" she snapped. Then, "Sorry. Sorry, I didn't mean to yell. It's just… it *is* my fault. Don't you get it? All of these taunts… They're messages which I've been missing this whole time. All the work the police are doing, it's all a waste of time if I can't figure out what he wants – because they're never going to find him.

"He doesn't *want* to get caught yet. He's had years to make this plan, he must know how to hide. But now it's different. He wants *me* to find him. He wants me to follow his breadcrumbs. That's why it's no good if he just gets rid of me. He wants me to find him, to find where it all happened."

I had seen Erin afraid before but I had never seen her look so defeated. She pulled her knees to her chest and wrapped her arms around them, folding herself small.

"I don't know all of the answers," I said, "but I do feel like we're getting somewhere with this." She started to argue but I held my hand up. "Let me finish. Look, I sent some messages. I know you didn't think it was worth it, but I did it anyway."

I waited for a second. Erin processed what I was saying but her expression didn't change.

"And?" she said.

"I had a message tonight, from one of the Danielles. One of her foster mothers worked as a cleaner."

"So, that's Jenny?"

"Yes, I think so. She couldn't remember a lot about that time – she was only with Jenny around six months – but she said that the lady who looked after her did some cleaning up in those big houses up in Derbyshire. You know—"

"The ones near where I was found?" Erin sat up a little bit straighter. "But the police spoke to everybody around there, didn't they?"

"They did. But they weren't looking for a connection to two long-missing foster children. They were looking for your brother. Maybe there's something the police missed, or didn't realise was important. They searched the empty houses, spoke to the occupants of others, but they didn't find anything suspicious. Still, might be worth following up?"

"It's not a lot to go on."

"No, but it's more than we had a couple of days ago."

"I know," she whispered. "What about the Adams? Did you get in touch with any of them?

"I sent a few messages," I said. I checked my phone.

"Hey, look." There was a new message from one of the Adams sent an hour or so ago. I opened it, a sort of excitement bubbling inside me.

The message was short, to the point. Yes, he was Adam Bowles. The police had been in touch about his mother and he was considering who he should and shouldn't talk to, pending the official investigation into his mother's disappearance.

Suddenly, the realisation that this man's mother was missing – and probably dead – made the excitement drain right out of me. Although I'd sent the message before what had happened with the parcel, with the fingers, I still felt guilty reading it back. It felt callous.

"What does it say?" Erin asked.

I only now realised I'd turned my phone away from her, stopping her from seeing the unbearable sadness in Adam's message.

"It's pretty vague."

"Can you call him?"

"Right now? Erin, it's the middle of the night."

"I mean… tomorrow." I knew what her expression meant: what did night and day matter when this was life or death?

"I'll send him another message," I said. "I'll just say that we're sorry, and if he feels up to talking… Maybe I'll send a friend request, too, so he can do things on his terms."

"Right," Erin mumbled.

"We will figure this out." I moved a little closer. Erin sighed and nestled into my side, my arm around her shoulders. I held her weight against me, feeling how tense she was.

Outside a branch skittered across the window and both of us jumped.

"How?" she asked. "I'm running out of belief."

I held onto her all night, although neither of us slept very much after that. Eventually we gave up, and Erin got up to shower. I checked my phone. At some point in the night Adam Bowles had accepted my friend request. I fought a surge of hope.

It was one minute past nine, the shower roaring in the bathroom, when I phoned him. I half expected him to ignore my call through Facebook Messenger – he might even be with the police, and accepting a friend request wasn't exactly evidence he was ready to *talk* – but there was a beep as the call connected.

For a moment there was nothing except a buzzing static. Then I heard a muffled sound like a yawn followed by an apology from a male voice that sounded somewhere away from the receiver.

"Hello?"

"Hi. Is this Adam?"

"Yes." A pause. Then a long, exhausted breath full of the weight of the last twelve hours. All that pain and hurt and longing in one. Eventually he said, "You're... Harriet? I saw your message, before..." He sounded throaty, as though he hadn't long woken up. Or perhaps he hadn't slept at all. I know I wouldn't.

"I'm sorry," I said. With everything that had happened in the last twenty-four hours I didn't know what to say. I didn't want to mention the missing fingers which might have been his mother's; I didn't know what the police would have told him, or how much he knew about why I was calling.

In the end, Adam spoke first.

"You're the writer, aren't you? The one they said received..." His voice broke and he took a shaky breath. He knew, then. Which meant the fingers were probably Jenny's. "*God*. Sorry. Uh, why did you want to talk to me before? How do you know Mum? Have you – Do you...? Do you know where she is?"

I heard the sudden swell of panic, the hope all jumbled up inside.

"No," I said quickly. "I don't know where she is. I'm so sorry. But I do want to help in any way that I can."

"How? Did you tell the police everything you know? Do you have any ideas at all where she might be? Can we set up search parties and you write about them or something?"

"I don't think I can give that sort of help," I said. "I've talked to the police, though. I... Did they tell you about me?" I asked. I needed to know if he knew about Erin, too.

"They said you were a writer. I'm going back to talk to them again later, maybe..."

"I *am* a writer. That's sort of how I know your mother. I have a friend – and we'd been talking to your mum about something that happened a long time ago. My friend, in particular, spoke to her because she was involved." I heard Adam's breath hitch and I forged on. "I'm writing a book about children – the victims of a serial killer. I wanted to talk to your mother about your foster brothers, Oscar and Isaac, the ones who ran away, and a possible connection between them and him."

"You think Mum being missing is connected to my foster brothers?" Adam asked, panic back full-force. So the police hadn't told him everything yet. "But they ran away such a long time ago. Why would they…" He paused. "Wait, you said you're writing about a serial killer. You don't think…"

"I think it might be easier if we talked about this in person," I stopped him. "Please. I don't want to jump to any conclusions, the police already have all of this information but—"

"Which serial killer?" he asked.

"Adam—"

"Who is your friend?"

Erin was out of the shower and brushing her teeth. It wasn't fair to ask this man to talk to me without giving him something, some truth. I had wanted to tell him in person, to test his reaction, but his mother was missing and he was our best lead.

"Her name is Jillian Chambers," I said quietly. "She was abducted by the Father."

The silence was deafening. Then I heard a muffled sound, like a voice asking if Adam was okay. He swallowed audibly.

"Okay," he said eventually. "You're right. Let's talk in person. After the police… I'm meant to be going to the station soon, to talk more, I don't know." His voice was muffled, as though he was covering his face. "That's in Derby. Are you near here? I'm in a hotel. Should we…? I don't know. How can I even help? All of that stuff with Isaac and Oscar was a long time ago."

"I know. I'm not expecting anything. But after you've spoken to the police maybe we can talk more, that's all. Maybe it will help."

"Right." His voice broke again. "I'll do anything. We can talk after – the police…"

We agreed a time and place and I put the phone down.

Erin appeared, hair in a towel, fresh tank top and clean jeans, her eyebrow raised in question.

"Who was that?" she asked.

"Jenny's son. I've arranged for us to meet him later. He's in Derby—"

"You arranged to meet him? Harriet, we don't even know him. He could be anybody. I…" She blinked tears from her eyes furiously.

"I was trying to help. I thought you'd want to talk to him, to make sure somebody asked about Oscar and Isaac."

"You should have talked to me first." She pulled the towel from her hair and began to comb it angrily with her fingers. "How do you know it's safe? It's one thing to refuse protection while we're here, together, but if we just go off anywhere with strangers—"

"He's talking to the police first," I said. "He knew about me already. About the… the box in my flat. So I thought I might as well call. Erin, maybe we can learn something. Maybe it'll help you to connect things? We can't just sit around doing nothing."

Erin's cheeks were pink with her building anger. She looked different than she did with makeup on, younger and more afraid. I guessed that was the point of all that eyeliner.

"Don't you think I know that? Don't you think I feel awful?"

"He might say more than he would to the police," I pressed. "Or maybe he'll just give us something to go on. Something that makes sense to you that doesn't to them?"

"You want *me* to talk to him?"

I thought of Adam's reaction when I'd mentioned the Father. "I think maybe he'll open up to you."

TWENTY EIGHT

Harriet

IN THE CAR ERIN didn't look at me, just stared at the black screen of her phone as we headed back towards Derby to meet Adam. After a while she reached into her pockets, pulling out her cigarettes. Then let out a groan.

"Fuck," she said. "I lost my lighter."

"Borrow mine. It's in the middle—"

"It must be in the hotel. Or on the goddamn floor somewhere. I can't fucking believe it."

"Hey, it's not the end of the world…"

"I really liked that bloody thing. I won't find another one the same—"

"Erin." I glanced over at her. Her eyes were filled with tears. "It's alright," I soothed. "If this is too hard, or if Adam doesn't want to talk to us, then we will leave. Okay?"

She blew out a breath, rolling her eyes.

"Okay?" I pushed.

"Alright," she said quietly.

We arrived at our location soon afterwards, a McDonald's on the outskirts of town. As we pulled into the car park Erin glanced up from her phone.

"*This* is where we're meeting him?"

"What?" I fought a smile despite myself. Erin didn't strike me as the anti-fast-food type. "You said you wanted to be safe. Where's safer than McDonald's?"

Erin pulled a face.

"I never would have guessed I'd catch you in a Maccies," she muttered, then shrugged. "But I'm not gonna pass up the opportunity for some chicken nuggets."

"It's not my usual go-to. But in all seriousness, they've got decent security. And it'll be loud enough that we can talk privately."

Finally Erin gave me a small smile.

"Whatever floats your boat."

Inside it was still quite busy despite being between the lunch and after-school flurries, but we managed to grab a booth so we could both see the door. I recognised Adam from his Facebook profile picture, and stood up to greet him. He was probably in his early thirties, green eyes and a strong jaw, but the exhaustion of the last few hours haunted him.

"Hi Adam, I'm Harriet. This is Erin. She's a—"

"I'm Jillian," she said, her jaw tense. "Chambers. Survivor. All that shit."

Adam froze. Like suddenly he came off autopilot and realised where he was. He sank into the booth, shell-shocked.

"Thank you for agreeing to meet us," I said. "I'm sorry about your mother. Has there been any news?"

He shook his head. "No. Nothing. They... I'm sorry, I'm such a mess. I left my husband at our hotel and I really – I want to get back. What do you think we can do to help Mum? You mentioned Oscar and Isaac before, and the police mentioned them again today but they were.... you know. Cagey. Can you tell me how they're connected?"

"I don't know exactly, but that's what I was talking to your mother about before she went missing. About what happened to them. Can I maybe ask you some questions?"

Adam was deep in thought but he nodded. "Like I said, it was a long time ago... But the police asked me some stuff today. What do you want to know?"

"What do you remember about the time around when they disappeared?"

"When they ran away, you mean?"

"Is that what you think happened?" I asked.

"Well, I don't know. Mum said they ran away at first, but then... she changed her mind, I think. They were seen at a bus station though. And they'd ended up in big cities before." He worried at his lip. "Do you really think... there's a connection? To you?" This he directed at Erin. Until now she'd been toying with her half-empty chicken nugget box, refusing to look at either of us. Now she locked eyes with Adam.

"Do *you* think it's possible?" she asked.

"I... I never thought about it until today."

"When they disappeared, was there anything weird going on at home?" I asked.

Adam shook his head. "I don't remember anything. Jonah – my brother – was often away at weekends because he did all sorts of sports. He ran cross country and played basketball. So I was home with Oscar and Isaac. Isaac was older than Oscar. He came to us first. He was moody; he'd had a really rough time. As soon as Oscar arrived they just clicked. Oscar used to follow him round everywhere. I think Isaac liked the attention, liked looking after him and feeling important. They were always colluding after that."

"So there weren't any fights that you knew of?" Erin repeated. "No reason they'd run away?"

"No, I don't think so. But they'd done it before, both separately at their previous foster homes, and Isaac ran away from his bio parents. They *did* manage to get kicked out of school, right before. I can't remember exactly what happened. I think Isaac stuck up for Oscar when some other kids were bullying him and it got out of hand, but I remember it being really awkward."

"Awkward how?"

"Mum had to take them to work with her when she couldn't get a babysitter. I remember her being angry because there was no support at the school for struggling students but they just dug their heels in and refused to help. Fixated on Isaac lashing out instead of dealing with the problem, I guess. And Mum had this cleaning service where she'd go clean people's houses, but it was very bitty. A day here, two hours there. Never consistent. So it was hard to find a sitter with such short notice."

"Do you remember any of the places your mum took

them?" I asked. "I know it's a long time ago."

But Adam was nodding. "There were loads over that couple of weeks, mostly regulars up near Stanshope. There was this one huge farm that had a bunch of collies. Oscar and Isaac were both obsessed with the dogs and wouldn't stop talking about them for days afterwards. And there was this fancy house nearby to that one. I remember them telling me that they got in trouble for running off and making friends with a gardener. And a big old place in the middle of nowhere, a small manor type house. *Dove* something, like the river."

Erin and I exchanged a glance. There were a lot of old abandoned houses around there, some derelict and left to ruin, houses with big grounds and a lot of privacy. The buildings were too expensive to keep and too precious to sell, and often they were left to rot like haunted relics. It wasn't far from where Erin was found. Was it possible that's where the Father had seen them, at one of these places? Chosen them then?

"The last one… Are you sure it was *Dove* something? That it was up in that direction?" Erin asked, her brows furrowed.

"Yeah. I remember Dana Wood who owned it, because Mum used to talk all the time about how pointless those trips were. Dana paid Mum to clean but the house was always spotless. We used to call her Neat-Freak Wood — behind her back, obviously. Some rich lady left the house and a bunch of money to her in her will — she was a carer or something — and I think she thought that it would be rude to let Mum see an untidy house, especially because she'd seen where Dana lived before, which wasn't nearly so posh. Actually, Mum took me *there* one time when I was off school sick. That was just a regular house – she never even sold it when she moved, I don't think. She didn't need to."

"Where was that?" I asked.

"She lived in Elby before, same as us, right down at the end of Elgin Road. Basically in the fields. Nice little house, but a bit out of the way."

"So, your mum took the boys up to the big house, this manor. And then your brothers ran away and – disappeared. Do you think you could find the address of the bigger house for us?"

I could almost feel Erin vibrating, her leg bouncing under the table. She'd pushed her left sleeve up and was scratching at her arm rhythmically. The skin was red and blotchy.

"Yeah. Uh, probably. I'm not sure. Mum used to keep meticulous records but it depends if I can find them. I think she kept all of her old invoices, though. She never throws anything away." Adam's expression shifted. "It's weird, actually. I asked her about taking the boys to Dana's once after it happened, because I thought maybe Dana might've said something that made the boys run away. Mum shut me right down, like it was the stupidest thing she'd ever heard, but it *is* possible."

"Why did you think she'd have upset them?" Erin asked. Her face was very pale now. "Did she upset people a lot?"

"Not really. But we knew we were meant to be nice to Dana if we ever saw her, just in case we upset *her*. I wondered if maybe Oscar had said something and she'd said something back. She could be quite scary."

"Why?" I asked.

"Uh, well, Mum told me she had two sons, and one of them drowned in a lake or something. She was *really* touchy about it."

Erin had gone quiet. I reached under the table to rest my hand on her leg, and she grabbed it tight. I was sure we were both thinking the same thing. Two sons. One dead…

"After that Oscar and Isaac left, and Mum packed up the cleaning business when they were gone. She did fundraising and stuff instead. I don't see how any of this helps. That was all over twenty years ago. Mum's gone *now*…" Adam's face crumpled. "I'm sorry," he said. "I think – I'm going to go. But I sent you my number…? I'll let you know if I find that address."

We watched him leave. Erin was trembling, still gripping my hand.

"Those houses…" she whispered.

"The police searched them. Talked to everybody."

"They could have missed something."

"Yes."

"But…" Shock made us both numb. "I don't understand how it all fits together… Maybe she had a husband? Could he be the Father?"

"Adam didn't mention one. Maybe the husband left?"

I tried to think it all through. "It couldn't be her, though. Right?"

But even as I said the words I knew that there was a sickening amount of sense in this crazy, blossoming theory. *The Father* – the name had come from the media. What proof did any of us have that this killer was a *man*…?

I thought about what we knew. Or thought we knew. Erin was probably drugged, and it made sense that other children had been too – or at least one from each pair.

Erin's dad had seen somebody who might have been small at the window that night. He couldn't tell if it was the children playing, or if he'd seen somebody else. But the abductions happened through open windows, so whoever took the children couldn't have been huge.

And perhaps they might have been less afraid of a woman. They could have been persuaded to go with somebody who looked like a carer, especially if she had a uniform, latex gloves and all…

If she was a carer, she might have been used to dealing with children, carrying dead weights too. I thought of the nurses I'd seen at the hospital when Dad was sick, constantly marching the halls, turning patients, lifting and helping to wash them… A lone carer would have to do all of that and more. And if she was a woman, she might be smaller, so getting in and out of windows wouldn't have necessarily been hard. Especially not with one child compliant to help the other. And she might have access to drugs, something that could reliably knock out a small child. And the insulin…

Erin jumped suddenly, knocking her coffee and nuggets back.

"Shitting hell," she swore. Then she lowered her voice, glancing around. "It's what Jenny Bowles was talking about."

"What?"

"*Siblings*. Protection. This woman had two children and she lost one. I wonder if… Could she have been taking children to replace her own? But like… as an audition? It comes back to the same question: What's important about siblings? But then my mum… she mentioned that Dad thought Alex said he would protect me. And Jenny said the same thing. *Siblings should protect each other.* And Isaac liked to look after Oscar. And Alex always looked after me. Do you think Dana was looking for a child who would protect her remaining son? Or one to look up to him? A replacement child for the one she lost – and one who would, if she engineered it, also have lost a sibling? Maybe that's why the children were never found together…"

We sat for a moment in the afternoon light, the restaurant getting busier around us. My chest felt like it was filled with barbed wire. Was it possible that we had just figured it out? Could this person – this *woman* – be the one who had killed Jem and Mikey? The one Erin had escaped from when she was seven years old?

THE FIRST TIME

Mother

LAST WEEK THE CLEANER'S babysitter had cancelled. Her boys weren't meant to be off school but there had been an emergency... She'd brought them to the house without asking. They'd spent the afternoon running around in the garden in jackets that were *just* too small and jeans that showed their ankles while Jenny cleaned the big bathroom – the one without the leaking roof.

Dana watched the boys run zig-zags on the lawn and felt a pang in her chest. The boys were adorable, so loving and protective of each other. It wasn't fair. Jenny, the stupid *cleaner*, had children. So many of them. She fostered and adopted and she was happy. It wasn't fair that Dana couldn't have that.

After Chris-Bear she'd tried so many things but each one fell through. The adoption agency said it could take *years* for anything to happen. Mouse didn't have years. He was getting more and more withdrawn every day; he refused to speak to her most of the time, ate alone in his room. She struggled to even get him to school – had even considered trying to teach him at home.

Jenny didn't know how lucky she was.

"Oh they drive me round the bend, duck," she'd joked.

How could she joke about such a thing?

Dana would never joke about her children again. She thought about Bear. How sometimes she had resented him when he cried, even just that little bit. How Mouse was best when he needed her, when he was poorly and she could look after him. The rest of the time he was distant and horrid.

She wanted to tell him she'd done the best by him that she could. Without Jack things had never been easy. Of course, she knew she'd probably driven him to suicide. Wasn't that what she was supposed to say? But no. He was a selfish prick.

She didn't like to think about the way she had found him, hours after he disappeared into the basement. She really had thought he'd just left, so that's what she'd told the boys. But he hadn't – or at least he hadn't left the building. His spirit had stayed, and now he haunted everything. Especially Mouse. Maybe that's why Bear had died. Maybe there was something evil inside her boy now.

Mouse was like his father sometimes. She thought of the cat. Her son wasn't happy. She wanted to give him another brother, one who needed Mouse as much as Mouse needed him. Then maybe he'd be happy again.

Tonight she'd left work early and was driving aimlessly. She was trialling a new childminder, but suspected that Mouse wouldn't like this one either. It was hard to find good ones who'd watch him for the hours Dana needed to fit around her job. Still, she'd make the most of it while she had one.

She liked to drive around like this when she could. She found winding country lanes, driving with her lights off for the thrill. Sometimes she followed buses, just to see where they stopped. Anything to stay out of the house. That was how she'd ended up at the bus station tonight, just out to the side where trees lined the road.

It was like God, or fate, had smiled down on her. She pulled in thinking she'd get a coffee, have a cigarette before driving to get Mouse at the agreed time – and there they were. Jenny's boys. It was late. She'd finished work at around ten. Dana glanced backwards and forwards, looking for Jenny's beat-up Honda. But the boys were alone. She thought of how she'd felt when she'd seen them playing last week. That jolt of longing.

She wound down her window. They recognised her, of course. The smaller one looked frightened but the bigger one was in charge. He asked, bold as brass, if she'd drive them somewhere.

"Where exactly are you going? Two boys, out here all alone – where's your mum?"

"She's not our mum," the big one said.

"We want to go to Birmingham," said the other.

"Birmingham is a long way away." Dana weighed up her options. It felt like a nudge, a push, even. They *wanted* her. They *needed* her. They were already frightened, and fear made children pliant. "What will you do when you get there?"

"We'll figure it out," said the big one.

These boys… Jenny didn't need them like Dana did. Like Mouse did. If Dana took the boys to Jenny's tonight, they'd only run away again. So… why not make the most of this?

Normally Dana liked to plan. If she'd learned anything from Jack it was that a well-concocted plan was like gold. She hadn't even known he'd killed himself for thirty-six hours because he'd designed everything perfectly – his tool-belt in hand, a rope waiting in the basement – and she hadn't asked any questions, hadn't even realised he'd been wanting to do it since before they moved into the house.

And yet, here was an opportunity. A ready-made plan. She could keep the boys in the house, downstairs. Or in the shed first, if she needed to make sure they wouldn't run. Later on she could fix it so they'd even have their own spaces, downstairs where the rooms were bigger than they needed to be.

She'd get them settled and then she'd go get Mouse from the childminder. It would be easy. They could keep whichever boy Mouse liked best. They might even keep both.

Then Mouse wouldn't ever have to be alone again.

"Come on then, boys." She unlocked her car doors and ushered them inside. "Best climb in the back. There are picnic blankets down there, I think. Make yourselves comfortable. Birmingham, here we come."

TWENTY NINE

Harriet

ERIN WAS OUT OF the restaurant before I could process exactly what had happened. What had started in my head as a vague inkling of a suspect had suddenly bloomed into something real, something tangible. And Erin was already gone.

I rushed to catch up with her. By the time I reached my car, Erin was fumbling at the lock.

"Where are you going?"

"I don't know," she snapped. She spun. Her face and hair were wild. She looked as though she was on the verge of collapse. I reached to steady her, grabbed her elbows. But she shook me off.

"Hang on a minute," I said. "Let's just wait. Take a second."

We got into the car. Erin collapsed into the passenger seat with her hands between her knees. She looked like she might vomit.

"Do you think it's true…?" she asked eventually. "Do you think it could be her?"

"I don't know," I said gently. "But if this woman was a carer and she travelled – that would give her access to all kinds of different people. Medicine too. Something like morphine maybe. That'd knock kids out easily enough. And I bet a carer could easily lift an unconscious, pliant child. The insulin, too – it wouldn't be hard to steal if she had diabetic patients."

"Do you really think she would kill, though, if she was a carer?" Erin clenched her fists a couple of times and then dug around for her phone.

"It's not unheard of," I said. I thought again of the Beverley Allitt case. Those true crime nuts might have been closer than they realised.

"There's got to be a reason, though." Erin was swiping angrily at her screen. I saw Google and then she leaned away. "For Monica, for Jenny. For everything that's happening now. For the candles and the doll. I just don't know what it *is* yet. All these little things make sense though, don't they? I just don't know what to do."

"Erin, we need to call the police," I said firmly. "That's what we need to do."

"I know that. I'm just…" She paused, still staring at her screen. "I can't see any information about her online, nothing about if she's still alive. Oh, but she's still on the electoral register with a local postcode. I think it's the one in Elby. The smaller house. Maybe if somebody else does live there they might have a forwarding address for the place near Stanshope."

"Erin—"

"I'm going to call the police. I think we should meet them at this Elgin Road house. I'm sure I can find it on Google Maps easily enough."

"Erin, have you thought about this at all? If she *is* a killer, and we just turn up at her house, what then?"

"It won't be like that," Erin said. She was still vibrating with nervous, almost manic energy. "We're going to wait for the police. Please, Harriet. I just want to drive over there and – see the place. We won't leave the car. It might jog my memory, you know? I can't just sit in that hotel room while the police…" She looked at me now, properly, and her expression was filled with hope and fear, and I felt myself relent.

"Erin…"

"Harriet, look, you kept asking me if I remembered anything at my house. Well, I remember that rubber smell and then being carried out of my window, and then I remember stairs and darkness, and a girl who might have been Jaswinder, and then I remember the woods. All I'm saying is, I don't remember a man. I've never remembered a *man*. What if this is the truth? I need to know. I have to remember. Please can we just go and see the house? I've got to be sure it's not…" She didn't need to finish the sentence, but I knew.

I need to be sure it's not where I was kept.

A hundred thoughts crashed over me at once. I was angry that Erin was putting me in this position, but I knew she didn't have a choice. She hadn't asked for this, and she didn't want it. But she needed to know what had happened to her, to Alex and Monica and Jenny Bowles. And I wanted to help.

"Okay," I said firmly. "But you call Detective Godfrey right now. We're not moving until you get her on the phone. And we are *not* leaving the car."

"Fine," Erin said. "I don't want to. I just have to *see*."

I drove on autopilot, fear churning inside me as I listened to one half of a conversation Erin reluctantly held with the detective on the phone. She explained everything slowly, everything Adam Bowles had told us and everything we had drawn from it. I couldn't tell what response she got but she maintained the same level of nervous energy the whole time.

"They're going to send somebody to meet us there," Erin explained afterwards. "Godfrey didn't give anything away. It's so hard to tell what she's thinking."

"That's probably her job."

I could just turn around, right now. I knew that. I could pull over on the side of the road and lock the doors, or I could drive straight past this little arrow on the map and keep going until we wound up back at the hotel. That would keep Erin safe, keep us both from getting hurt. But what if Erin was right? What if her memory was vital evidence? What if she held the key to conviction? I felt sick at the thought that I might stand in the way of that. I flicked my indicator and turned.

"I think we're almost there," I said quietly.

We drove a little further, at a crawling pace now. Ten miles outside of Derby. It wasn't even a village. It was so tiny, just a corner shop, a post office and a book exchange in a weathered red phone box, and then we were out into a wooded area, the smattering of houses stretched far apart between patches of greenery, little falling-down stone walls bordering the properties from the road.

I coasted right to the end of the hamlet, where Elgin Road grew winding and bordered by tall trees. There was one more house here. Tucked away so well you could only just make out the shine of a window through foliage that was all green and red and brown.

"This must be the one," Erin murmured shakily. "Adam said it was right at the end – this is the last one."

The car just about fit onto a muddy spot where I cut the engine. It was getting dark now, and much colder. We sat silently, staring into the dimness as the last of the sun cast golden rays in between the leaves. Erin twitched. From here you couldn't see the rest of the houses; there was just this one against the trees and the sky.

"There's nobody here," I said, as much to myself as to Erin. There was no Dana Wood as far as we could tell, no car or sign of life, but no police either. I locked the car doors just to be on the safe side. When I turned to face Erin she'd gone green. "Hey, are you okay?"

She didn't speak at first, just nodded slowly. Her eyes were wide as she took in all of the details, the small house and the ramshackle garden. The trees seemed filled with shadows.

"I need to get out," she blurted.

"Erin, no—"

"I think I'm going to be sick. Let me out. Let me out—"

Panic surged and I clicked the locks. Erin opened the door to lean out, and then bolted to a bush. She vomited, the sound wrenching through the still air.

I got out and approached her slowly, fear and anger and frustration still churning. I kept one eye on the house as I patted her back. When she'd righted herself she wiped the back of her hand across her mouth and swallowed with a grimace.

"Fuck," she said.

"Back in the car now," I said.

But Erin made no move to get back in. Instead, she stood looking at the house. The windows were dark, reflecting what was left of the daylight. I felt very exposed out here. There were no cars nearby, just the wind in the trees and the distant sound of cattle in a field out of sight.

"*Erin*," I warned.

She just shook her head and started to step towards the house. I reacted, holding out my arm and catching her before she could go any further.

"Are you kidding me? What part of 'wait in the car' do you not understand? Erin, you're obviously not thinking properly. Do you not understand how dangerous this could be?"

Erin shrugged me off but didn't push past me. "This house," she said. "I have this horrible feeling. I... What if somebody is in there?"

"Nobody is here."

"How do you know? What if... What if she's going to do it again? What if there's somebody else in there and she's going to hurt them? What if that's where she's keeping *Jenny*?" I hadn't thought of that and it filled me with dread. But if they were her fingers, if she'd bled a lot, surely she would already be dead...? That thought was worse.

"Erin, that's not your responsibility," I tried. "The police are on their way. We need to wait for them."

"Why? If they'll be here soon then we can at least find out if the house is empty?"

"I'm not just going to watch you walk in there on your own. For God's sake, Erin, don't you care about your own safety? What about me?"

"Of course I do!" she exclaimed. She flung her arms up angrily. "Fucking hell, this isn't just about us. I can't stand out here when there might be somebody inside. And anyway, what's she going to do? She's one woman; there are two of us and the police will be here any minute."

"That's no excuse to blindly march into danger." I folded my arms across my chest.

"If you're that afraid then you should stay here. I just need to make sure there's nobody in there."

"I'm not *afraid*," I snapped. "Well, okay. I'm terrified. But that's not the point. I just don't want..." *I don't want you to get hurt.* "I just don't know what we might find in there. It's not up to us. We're not prepared."

"You don't have to come!" Erin shouted. I'd never seen her this angry, all of that fear and frustration wound up together, and I hated that it was directed at me. "Just let me *go*. Jesus Christ, Harriet, you're not my mother."

"Erin, this isn't fair!"

"You think *any* of this is fair?" Erin let out a stringy laugh and I felt my stomach drop. My anger began to subside. Erin was right. The police would be here any minute. "*Please,*

Harriet," she said softly. "Please. The car's open; if anybody is in there we'll get the fuck out."

I didn't move. My whole body felt frozen with fear and indecision.

The air smelled strongly of autumn: cold wind, damp earth, and somewhere not too far away a bonfire tinged the air with its tell-tale scent. Through the hedgerow there was a little section of garden path – although the garden itself was badly overgrown and hardly contained by the old stone wall. Cracked concrete slabs marked the path to the front door, where pots of plants were thriving only due to their own scraggly hardiness.

"In and out," I said. "And I want you to know I'm only agreeing because I know I can't stop you and I won't let you go alone. Because I came to you. I dragged you into this. *I* found *you*. And I don't want you to get hurt."

We both stood very still for a moment. Erin's gaze was fixed firmly on the house. I felt a shiver start at the top of my spine. Erin's golden hair blew in the wind and she didn't push it back. This was a bad decision.

We headed for the front door together. My brain scrambled for a plan and I hoped to God Erin knew what she was doing.

I raised my fist and I knocked. Once. Twice.

Nothing.

Or, not nothing exactly. It was more like an absence of *something*. The birds continued to sing. The distant noise of a plane flying overhead hummed through the air. Somewhere a creature scurried back into the hedge.

Inside, though, was silence. There were no signs of life.

I looked at Erin again. She frowned.

"Nobody's home," I said.

Erin reached out, her hand snagging on the door handle.

"Erin!"

"I'm just checking," she said.

She pushed it and it didn't resist. The door wasn't locked.

"What if Jenny is in there?"

I didn't argue. I was almost certain there was nobody here, but what if I was wrong?

The house was dark. In the grey late-afternoon light I could see that the decor was sparse chintz furniture and dusty wood.

Erin pushed the door all the way back and we peered inside.

"Hello?"

Erin stepped through the door and into the hall. I followed. It was a small space, dim and quiet, splitting off into a lounge on the left that looked very square. It was a tight fit, but I moved quickly so Erin didn't leave me behind.

All of the surfaces were as dusty as those by the door, the side tables covered in a thick, uninterrupted film. The dark carpets were grey with it, too.

This place didn't just feel empty, it felt abandoned.

This thought made me feel more confident. Safer. I stepped ahead, picking through the room, cataloguing everything. There was a cabinet up ahead, just through into the small dining area with a table against one wall. The cabinet might have been lovely, once. The cherry wood was lush and glossy beneath the dust; the glass door had been decorated in the corners with little engraved swirls. There was a small golden handle.

I moved closer.

"Nobody lives here," Erin said distantly. She was somewhere behind me now. "I wonder if she's still paying bills…"

I didn't move. I couldn't. The cabinet grew before me, like something out of a nightmare. I couldn't tear my gaze away from its contents. And then Erin's silence told me she'd seen them, too.

The tennis ball, doodled on one side with a red heart; the silver harmonica, tarnished after so long behind glass; the Manchester United shirt, folded neatly on a shelf; the stuffed bear with a hole in its foot and a braided green bracelet around its wrist; the baby doll in her little pink dress – the letters *P A U* still branded on one foot… They were arranged like fine china.

I sucked in a breath at the sight of the teddy bear. Remembered what my aunt and uncle had told me once, about Jem's love of making friendship bracelets for his toys. My body vibrated as I wondered…

And then something else made me pause. A single flat pebble, a hole drilled at the top and a long black cord through it. It had black marker initials on it. JC.

"Erin…" I whispered. "Is that yours…?"

She was at the glass. She lifted her hand to touch it, but stopped herself just as I reached out to prevent her. Her face was ashen. She blinked slowly, taking it all in.

"Yes," she said. "Alex made it. I used to wear it around my neck. I must have had it… the night me and Alex were taken. It's… Why is it here?" She gulped air as if she was drowning.

"And that doll. It's like the one in my bedroom… except older. I think – I think I remember it. From – wherever she took us. Harriet, why does she – what are we going to do?"

"We wait for the detectives," I said firmly. "Don't touch anything."

"But what about the bitch who did this?" Erin spoke through gritted teeth. "Where is she?"

AFTER

Mother

THE RAIN POURED. DANA wondered with a small thrill whether the river might break its banks again. There was flooding elsewhere, so why not here? That would give the police something else to tackle. The house around her was empty. Silent.

For the first time in – God, more years than she could count – Dana had the place entirely to herself.

It was for the best, obviously. With everything that had happened she'd decided to go to the backup plan early. It was always meant to be a last-resort contingency, but in the years since she'd come up with it, technology had changed and so had she. She'd grown… Not more reckless. That could never be true. But perhaps less careful. Was that a fair distinction?

The girl had been… an oversight. If Dana had suspected they were both going to run she'd have done something. Mouse knew, or she thought he might have had an idea, but he'd thought it was a good test of their suitability. Well, he wasn't wrong about that. It had certainly split the wheat from the chaff.

Dana peered out of the curtains. The house was spotless – or just a little less than spotless. She'd cleaned the whole place, top to bottom. Made sure it was absolutely pristine. And then she'd let Mouse track in and out a couple of times with dirty feet, artfully arranged a plate of biscuits complete with crumbs. The house, this part of it at least, looked lived in, but tidy.

Over the years she'd become very good at keeping up appearances. People from her old life came to see her sometimes – dates in the diary well in advance, of course, and she never let them stay long. It was nice to take the risk, sometimes. To liven things up. But this was different. This time she would have to be really on the ball.

She hadn't slept. She'd been outside most of the night, checking the lay of the land. The rain hadn't stopped, and she could hear the rushing of the already-swollen river when she got close. The banks would be a mire, the planes alongside the narrower bits like a swamp. The air was thick with the scent of river water.

She headed deeper into the woods. She was looking for the traps she knew her neighbour often laid for the foxes. She'd always turned a blind eye before, wondering if one day they might be helpful. She hoped she would be right.

She knew she couldn't guarantee that any of the police scent dogs – she was sure they'd use them – would find a trap, but she *could* make it more likely they wouldn't notice them in the rain...

There were a few spots she knew the farmer used, down beyond the lake and into the woodland that way, where the land was still private. It was the way the girl and her brother had run. Sure enough, she found a trap there, not even hidden. She gathered armfuls of the leafy ferns that grew nearby, gently kicked up patches of the mulchy leaves, until the trap was hard to spot. Satisfied, she smiled.

She did this several times more, heading back towards the river and the roads, the way she had run last night when the children got out. All she needed was one accident. One police dog, caught in a trap because of the rain, the visibility. Then they'd call off any search until the weather improved, and it was set to storm up here on and off all week. She didn't care if *people* came. But dogs… she knew she couldn't fool them.

By the time she was finished she was exhausted, but she didn't care. She was filled with purpose. She didn't know how long she would have to wait, but her gut told her they would come soon.

When the police finally arrived, mercifully alone and with their dark coats dripping, their hats pulled low, Dana was ready. Showered, coffee in hand. Just a normal morning. Cautiously, she invited them inside. She was at her best, the perfect mother. A little frazzled, a little helpful, concerned and willing. They asked about Jack, were sympathetic when she told her story.

He left me when my boys were small. Now there's just us.

They asked about Mouse. She told them he was at a martial arts trial class this morning at their old village hall, which was true. She'd arranged it perfectly. Afterwards he'd go to the little house to check on the boys, but they'd be out of it for a while yet. And then, eventually, she'd be able to join them. But Mouse was a big boy and he could take care of them until then.

The police poked around – she let them. Wanted them to. It was vindicating, knowing that she was *better*. She had planned harder, for longer, and thought of everything. After the first pair of boys she'd learned how to do it perfectly. That was just patience. And this was the same.

They never found it. They passed the bookcase, wandered down the back stairs, searched the rest of the empty basement. They did not notice that those rooms were perhaps just a few feet shorter than they should be; they did not see the hidden corridors and small rooms that required additional access around the edges of the house. Her perfect little rabbit warren.

She was proud of the maze she had built with her own bare hands, starting the day she brought those first boys home. They hadn't been right – maybe they hadn't been brothers for long enough – but they had taught her how to do things. To be independent. To do what Jack had never done, and build a life.

The policemen went out into the gardens, where the wind was blowing a gale. The distant shores of the lake were a turmoil of mud. All of this – it had been God's will. Like it had been God's will when she hadn't chosen those other children, the ones the Lord showed were unsuitable, the one who woke up or failed her early tests. She knew that she would have been caught if she'd tried, and she always listened to her gut, that tingling of anticipation deep down in her belly. It had always been about trust.

That feeling was why she had chosen the boy and the girl, the autumn pair. Their window, it had been fortune. Open just when she needed it, even though she'd not been planning to take any more until next year. Even their escape – the wind, the flooding – was a sign that things were destined to go her way. A lesser woman might have been afraid, but not Dana.

That night, after the police had gone, she relished the silence. The whole, aching, haunted place was her own. She wandered each room, trailing every corridor with trembling fingers. It felt like she had spent her life building these walls, creating a *home*. And soon she would be back where she started, in the house she was glad Jack hadn't convinced her to sell. The one she'd hung onto, just in case. The boys were there now, the whole tribe of them. She was fiercely proud of Mouse. Finally he had stepped up. Tomorrow, or the next day, she would be Mother again, but tonight…

Tonight she lay in her bed, surrounded by familiar things. She inhaled the scents of the house, the dust and the polish and the lavender bedlinen. She breathed the darkness, and sent a prayer of thanks to Mary Brennan, the old lady who had left her this house when she'd died… There were some perks to the job.

Dana knew that soon this chapter of her life would be over. The thought wasn't entirely unwelcome; she was tired.

And ready to be safe again.

Nobody could ever find out what she had done.

THIRTY

Erin

EVERYTHING WAS WRONG. I looked at each of the items in the cabinet in turn, searching for anything else I recognised, but there wasn't anything of Alex's in there. I stared until I couldn't stare any more, and then I tore myself away. I stumbled, tripping over my feet in an attempt to keep going.

"Erin, we can't touch anything!" Harriet shouted.

"I won't. I just…"

I was still going. Harriet followed me, one step away from dragging me outside. But she was in shock, just like I was, and the house had to be empty. The layers of dust on everything were so thick I could taste them.

"We need to do it together, then." Harriet's voice was faint. She looked about as sick as I still felt.

The rest of the ground floor was as empty as the lounge and dining room. A small kitchen led out a back door and into a yard that was wild and overgrown with weeds.

I needed to know more. I needed to know *why.*

The house felt too empty to give answers. There was nothing here except the cabinet of morbid trophies, and I didn't even know who they all belonged to. Harriet might. Distantly I knew I wanted to ask her, but I couldn't bring myself to talk about them – about the children – in this place. Sickness roiled in my belly at the thought of the ghosts living in that little glass box.

I kept moving, driven onwards by the fiery anger burning up inside of me. Upstairs there was a small hallway, two bedrooms and a study. The bedrooms were sparse, the mattresses bare. The smaller bedroom had a double bed, and was decorated in shades of pale pink, with tepid, sun-bleached paisley curtains and two hideous faux-sheepskin rugs. Under the window there was a small set of shelves, bare but with streaks in the dust where something – or many uniform somethings – had once sat. Too identical to be books – videotapes maybe? There was nothing there now. There were no photos, no framed pictures, but I could see the spots on the walls where they had once hung.

I stepped into the twin bedroom. This room was larger, and the first thing I noticed was the desk under the window that overlooked the garden. It was just an ordinary, cheap table, but that wasn't what caught my eye. It was what sat on top: pools of wax that had melted off two pillar candles, red like blood. My body convulsed at the sight of them but I managed to steady myself.

"Erin, come on," Harriet said, trying to urge me away. "Let's get outside – I don't want to stay…" Then she noticed the candles too.

"Somebody has been here," she said, fear in her voice. "We need to go."

310

"They're covered in dust," I said, and I sounded more confident than I felt. "Look, there's plenty on there. She's not been here for a while."

Harriet backed out into the hallway, ignoring the two single beds pushed up against the walls to the left and the right, ignoring the entrance to the ensuite. But the door was open and my feet kept moving.

Inside, sitting on the cistern, there was an unopened pack of single-use latex gloves, a row of nail brushes still in their packaging, and a sealed bottle of rubbing alcohol. On the back of the sink sat packets of disposable razors, bin bags, bleach and duct tape, all new and unused.

Bile rose in my throat, threatening to spill again. I swallowed it down.

"Erin, please, stay with me." Harriet appeared behind me, her red hair like a halo. "What did you find?"

"It's like a – kit," I whispered. "For breaking into a house without leaving any evidence. But they're all new. Unused. I think I'm going to be sick…"

Wordlessly we headed back out into the hall. Harriet's arm brushed mine and I flinched. I couldn't bear the thought of being touched right now; the skin on my arms felt like it was on fire and I was desperate to scratch it.

"This is useless," I growled. "Fucking useless!"

"Erin—" Harriet tried to calm me but that only made it worse. I wanted to scream, cry and throw things. Most of all I wanted to run out of this haunted place, but I knew I couldn't until I'd seen it all. Just in case I never got another chance. Just in case the police missed something.

"Alex is still gone," I forged on. "Monica is still dead. Nobody knows where Jenny Bowles is – she's probably dead, too. We're no closer to finding the bloody answers, not really. We still don't know why Dana Wood's been doing any of this, or where she is now. Am I going to spend the rest of my life looking over my shoulder? Are *you*?"

Harriet didn't speak. She made to move towards me but I sidestepped, heading towards the only remaining door up here, presumably another bathroom.

"Erin, fingerprints—"

I attempted to stop myself, realising too late that she was right, that I was letting my emotions get the better of me, but the door was only loosely latched and when I leaned against the wood it started to open.

It stuck halfway, scraping against a carpet, which was spongey and swollen like moss. A smell began to seep into the hall, strong enough that I gagged.

"What the fuck…?"

Harriet recoiled. I felt sick – but I didn't stop. What if it was Jenny? Or worse.

A little voice screamed something else in the back of my mind, something crazy: *What if it's Alex?*

I pushed the door harder. Something had made the carpet stick and there appeared to be a layer of duct tape stuck to the bottom of the door; it felt like pulling a stick over a rotten log.

Harriet had her phone out.

"Where the bloody hell are they?" she said.

I shook my head. This door hadn't been opened in a long time; I doubted anybody was going to jump out now. I took a deep breath and stepped into the gap, which was just wide enough for my body. Inside, the bathroom was cloaked in darkness, blackout blinds pulled low to block the weak sunlight.

Everything was cast in shadow: the dark walls, the carpet, which was spotted with a patina of mould. The smell was stronger, but still I couldn't place it. Something old, something...

"Erin, what is—"

I stepped fully inside, gingerly twisted so Harriet could join me. The dimness was deceptive and the room was bigger than it looked. There was a bathtub, old and small with clawed feet, and a shower on the wall above it. Duct tape lined the gaps at the window, the air vents near the ceiling, patches of shining, ominous grey.

"Harriet..."

She came up beside me.

"We need to leave," she said. She grabbed for me but I dodged her. "*Now*, Erin."

"No, not until—"

Harriet tried to lunge for my arm again.

"The police—"

"Wait!" I yanked my arm back with such force that I stumbled, my trainers sinking into carpet which had once been so wet it had never fully recovered, the floor marshy and uneven.

There was something in the tub. I felt vomit rise into my mouth and I reeled backwards. Harriet grabbed me, dragging me away from the swarm of colours and shapes that made the vague outline of a body.

"Who is it?" I begged as we tumbled out into the hall. Harriet kept going. "Is it…?" Tears were on my cheeks. I was going to be sick.

"I…" Harriet whispered. "I think it's Dana Wood."

Somehow we were downstairs, outside, and vaguely I was aware that I was shaking. I didn't feel cold. I didn't feel much of anything except swirling confusion that made the weak light feel watery and the trees seem to close in around me.

I was hardly even aware of Harriet as she stood next to me. Detective Godfrey was somewhere in the house behind me. There were other people too, but I didn't know who they were. Police. Crime scene people. I tried to focus but I couldn't.

Harriet looked as haunted as I'd ever seen her, her skin so pale she looked like a ghost.

Without thinking I grabbed her hand and we walked away from the house until we reached the hedge at the front of the garden. We stood in silence for a moment. I cast my gaze towards the grey sky, watched as a small brown bird flew from tree to tree. As we stood, the numbness started to subside and I was left instead with a burning, itching feeling all up my arms and legs. I started to scratch but Harriet caught my hand.

"Why do you do that?" she asked softly.

I didn't want to look at her but it was hard not to. Her freckles were stark, like a constellation of tiny stars.

"Do what?"

"Sometimes when you're nervous you scratch your arms."

"It feels like my skin's crawling."

I huffed out a sigh, watching as some more people came and went. Detective Godfrey appeared in the doorway, her shoulders hunched against the wind. She looked for us, nodded when she caught me staring, and then popped back inside.

"It used to happen worse when I was a kid, but I got it under control – and then it didn't bother me. Until recently." I shrugged, realised Harriet was still holding my hand. I gave it a quick squeeze.

She held on for another minute, and then folded her arms against the chill.

"Do you think... it's definitely her?" I asked.

"I think so. I don't know."

"It looked like... she'd been dead for a while."

"I'd guess it happened longer ago than the stalking started," Harriet agreed. "Maybe she died in the tub, probably drowned given the mess of the carpet..." She avoided my eyes, picking at the skin on her hands. She was more affected by this than she let on. "Then, uh, I guess it was drained or it evaporated over time and she was left there. That might explain it. I bet the tub acted as a kind of natural shelter against the air, slowing down the decomposition, although all the science I know is from TV. But somebody didn't want the smell to get out, hence all that tape on the walls and the window. It might be the person who's been following you, who hurt – Monica."

I fought a shiver. Harriet took a deep breath, as if to settle her stomach.

315

"So… where does that leave us?"

"A copycat, probably." She glanced up, and I realised just how afraid she was. More now than ever before.

"A copycat?" I whispered. That felt worse, somehow. Like all of the rules had changed. "No," I managed. "It can't be… Not like that."

"If that's her, Erin——"

"What about the clues and signs and *everything*? The doll, the candles. Who else would do that?"

Harriet didn't move.

"*Somebody* has been here," she agreed. "The candles on the desk… Maybe there'll be DNA on them or something. I'm just saying it can't be *her*. If she's dead she can't exactly have been wandering around Arkney breaking into your house. What happened to those children might not have anything to do with what's happening now. It might just be about *you*."

The words were like a slap in the face. I was pacing, I realised, and I stopped dead as a look of apology flashed across Harriet's face.

"Christ, Erin. I didn't mean to say it like that… It's just——"

"Just what?" I blurted. "You think this is my fault?"

"No! Jesus Christ, Erin, that's not what I'm saying. I'm not thinking straight, okay? I'm fucking terrified. We just found another body, so I'm sorry if I'm a little foggy. I just wonder if it's possible that there's someone else behind this."

"What about the candles?" I snapped. "They triggered something inside me… some memory, *something*. They're important."

"You make candles, Erin," Harriet pointed out, but she had softened a bit. "You can buy them from anywhere. Maybe it's just a coincidence."

"And the note? Why hurt Jenny if it's about me? Why watch Molly? Leave gifts for Jaspreet?"

"Maybe somebody is using what happened to get to you."

I fought the urge to cry. Maybe Harriet was right. I reached deep into my pocket for my cigarettes before remembering I still didn't have a lighter. I didn't want to ask Harriet for hers. I didn't want to talk any more at all.

I shivered in the chill wind, felt the first sprinkle of rain on my skin. I felt like he, she, *whoever* was watching me – even now.

The front garden was small but the hedges were high and I started to feel claustrophobic. I stepped closer to Harriet, suddenly needing her warmth.

She pulled me into a hug, but the sensation of being watched didn't disappear. I closed my eyes tight, sucked in Harriet's shampoo smell and the scent of the garden. It wasn't possible, was it? That the man I'd been afraid of my whole life was a woman – and she was dead.

I clung to Harriet. With my eyes closed all I could picture was the room from my dreams. A basement room. Alex somewhere I couldn't see. I felt panic rising inside me and I snapped my eyes open.

A wet stomping sound made me jump away and turn back to the house. Detective Godfrey was heading across the unkempt front lawn, her face a mask of concern.

"How are you holding up?" she asked. It was different from

the tone she'd used when she'd arrived, her car screaming into the driveway spewing gravel and dirt. She'd been angry, then, but now she looked tired. A bit confused.

I shook my head. Shrugged. I had no words.

"We'll need to carry out a full, formal investigation," she said. "But it does look like there's a connection here. The house is owned by a Dana Harper. Looks like everything is in that name, but we're getting everything cross-referenced to a Dana *Wood*, like Mr Bowles said."

Harriet and Godfrey continued talking but I couldn't focus. I thought about the gloves, the razors, the unused items that might seem innocuous in any other house. I tried to remember, running through the dreams in my head. But all I could see was that basement room. Was any of what I'd remembered real?

"Is there a basement?" I blurted, interrupting Harriet and Godfrey. They both looked at me questioningly. "In the house. Is there a basement?"

"They're checking the perimeter now, but it doesn't look like it." Godfrey shook her head. "Should there be?"

"I don't know. I'm not sure, but I think… I think wherever we were taken, wherever she took us, had a − a basement or a storage shed or something…"

Godfrey made a note, then pulled out her phone and sent a text message.

I shivered.

"*Why?*" I asked.

Harriet and Godfrey looked at me again, pity and apology on their faces.

"Erin…" Harriet whispered.

I could see that they didn't know whether I was asking about now, or then. And I didn't know either.

"Why would somebody do this to me, to Monica, to Jenny, *now*? Who would want to, if not her? And who killed *her*?"

None of us had an answer.

Godfrey's lips twitched as she scanned the trees and the hedge and the coming and going of her colleagues.

Then she said, "There's a diary upstairs. We found it under the bed. I say diary, it's more… ramblings. A notebook just filled with – they're half unintelligible. But on the first page there's what looks like a poem, dedicated to 'My Lost Child'. Do you two know anything about that?"

"Yes," Harriet answered quickly. "Well, maybe. We think so. Adam Bowles told us that Dana lost a child, a boy who drowned in a lake."

Godfrey gestured back to the house. "The pages allude to something else. A brother. Do you know anything about him? Did Adam say anything to you?"

I clenched my jaw. Harriet held my arm, her fingers digging into my skin. I thought about what Jenny Bowles had said. Siblings. *It's always siblings.* Dana Wood was dead, but she had been abducting siblings for a reason, and with her gone who did that leave?

The boy who had failed to save his brother. The boy who might want to finish what his mother had started.

Her remaining son.

Father

MOTHER ALWAYS CHOSE THE worst ones. Some were better than others, of course. And sometimes it was fun to help her choose, like the time they'd been at the zoo and seen two little boys monkeying around. But Mother had long since stopped taking him with her when she went to hunt. More and more she left him home alone and came back having already decided.

Sometimes she made decent decisions, he had to admit that much, but they were like a lapse in her awful judgement. Morgan was fine – at least for a while. He'd thought about trying to explain to Mother what it was he wanted, but in truth he didn't know. And anyway, he couldn't stomach talking to her for long enough to describe it.

He found it funny that the news had started calling her the Father. Because they thought she looked after the children. He didn't think what she did could be called *looking after*. If anything he was the one who fed them, who made sure they followed the rules. If anybody was the Father, it was *him*. And if it were up to him, he'd choose different kids.

He liked that Morgan was quiet. Like him. And smart, too. She read books, and she had an arsenal of card games, which she taught him patiently. He liked that.

Mother said she was pleased, that Morgan was a good fit. She called her Otter, because she was cute and loved to swim in the lake – on nice days they'd taken to letting some of the children outside, for fresh air, otherwise they got all pale and sickly, but they could only do it once they were sure they wouldn't run.

Morgan was a strong swimmer but she never went far from the house. Mouse knew it was because she thought her brother was buried near the lake – because that's what he had told her. He'd even made a show of digging a grave where she could see him, because he *knew* she wouldn't want to leave Paul if she tried to run. Of course her brother wasn't worthy of being buried here, but she didn't have to know that. And Peter needed leverage.

Mother thought the Taking Test – which was actually a series of small tests – was enough. She said she watched them for days, sometimes weeks, to make sure that if, say, somebody scared them, or hurt them, or if they fell, that one sibling would protect the other. Sometimes she engineered the circumstances, but other times she just watched. She said that she knew straight away from how they acted whether they were good enough, but she always waited for a Test moment to be sure. She followed them, made sure she could get to them easily, and then used the drugs to knock one of them out. Once, maybe twice, one of the children woke up and she abandoned them – but they wouldn't remember her by morning, the liquid morphine saw to that.

Peter disagreed with Mother about the testing being enough, though. It wasn't as simple as that. Most of them, like Morgan, needed extra incentive to stay. He was tired of having to get rid of them too soon, simply because they tried to run. But that seemed to be unavoidable, no matter what tricks he used.

"Mouse, you're still *unhappy*," Mother sighed. She sighed a lot when she wanted to be dramatic. She wanted him to care. As though somehow when he cared about her she had power over him again. He couldn't bring himself to care. Instead he fed her crumbs of love, just enough to keep her from going completely mad.

"I hate when you call me that," he snapped. "For God's sake, I'm not a little kid any more."

"You'll always be my Mouse. Can't you go and play?"

That was the first day he'd slapped her. Right across the face with the back of his hand. He wasn't sure what made him do it, only that he knew it would feel good afterwards. She shrank back from him, her expression flickering between fear and disgust.

Fear won. But not by much.

"Get out of my room," he said, and his voice was solid ice.

He'd stormed to the library after that. Morgan was always in there. She had special privileges, because she'd been in the house so long, but Peter still didn't trust her. They all knew that Mother had only managed for so long because she was careful, and Morgan was making her less careful.

He snuck into the library that afternoon so Morgan wouldn't hear him. He wasn't sure what he wanted, maybe to catch her doing something bad, something he could punish her for. Then he could shut her back downstairs and Mother wouldn't whine. But when he got to the library, Morgan was just sat on the floor by the fireplace, dust motes swirling and a book in her lap. She looked pretty. When he tried to kiss her – just a kiss – she'd kicked him.

Rage took over. Boiled up inside him like molten lava, and he thought of Mother, the disgust on her face twisting Morgan's features too. He gripped his hands around her neck and *squeezed*. She fought back, and he realised he liked that. He liked other things, too, pinching and poking and scratching. She cried, but stopped fighting after a while. She just lay there. That's when he realised he was *bored*. Bored of her, and of this short chapter. He wanted somebody else. It was time for another pair.

He went to get the insulin.

Charlotte and Hazel came a couple of months later but he didn't really like either of them. They were both so *annoying*. Mother had wanted to try two girls, to see if they might be more submissive. She liked Charlotte, but Peter couldn't handle their collective incessant wailing. Randeep and Jaswinder were disappointing to say the least, but the brother-sister combination seemed to be a winner. Randeep was definitely protective, but of the wrong person.

Peter was getting desperate, but Mother was worse. Some

days Peter swore she'd gone entirely mad. She stayed out most nights after her shifts now she had deemed Peter was old enough to be in the house by himself, and sometimes she didn't come home at all. She was waiting for a chance, the right chance.

And it *was* chance that she found Alex and Jillian, on an especially warm October night. She told Peter she'd followed them expecting to come back again the next summer, but there was that open window, a sign from God above – and it was too good to pass up.

The business with Jillian was unfortunate. Sometimes he liked the feisty girls for a change, but this time it had backfired. She'd pretended for over two weeks to be quiet like her brother, but it had been a ruse. They'd almost lost them both. How had they managed to get out? It had to have been Randeep. This was what came from keeping him after they'd found the others. Three children were too many. Peter had wanted to get rid of him but Mother insisted they wait.

But now she was worried. Still in control, but definitely on edge. What happened if the girl led the police right back to them? The whole thing had been a mess from start to finish. Peter wished she'd never bothered to bring them home in the first place.

But there was something about Alex...

They'd found him in the woods not far from the house, his face tear-streaked, his pyjamas caked in so much mud you could hardly see what colour they were. They'd been looking for him for hours, and then, just like that, there he was.

Peter thought he'd have to get rid of him then and there. But the boy had looked at Peter and grabbed his hand silently, holding onto it. He didn't beg. He didn't cry any more. He just looked at him and Peter swore he heard him think, *Take me back to the house.*

There was some sadness deep down inside Alex that shone like metal and made Peter feel generous. So he decided to keep him.

For the next few hours he half expected Alex to try to run, especially with his sister still out there somewhere. When one sibling ran there was usually a pretty strong chance the second one would bolt too. But Alex didn't run. In fact, he followed Peter around like a little lost puppy. He watched silently as Peter and Mother packed up their things and cleaned the house from top to bottom. He didn't scream or cry when Mother carried him out to the car, unlike Randeep, who made himself sick over it. And when they got to the other house – the one Peter only vaguely remembered, where it would be safest to stay until they were sure everything was settled – Alex asked a question.

"Is this what you always do with them?"

Them. Not us. It was a sense of kinship Peter hadn't felt in forever. Alex asked other questions, too. Clever questions. *How do you choose them? Why do you take two? What happens if my sister and the police find the house? Will your mother send them away? Did you used to live here? How far away are the neighbours? Do my parents know where I am? Not like Dad cares. He saw us, he saw your mother, and he just went right back to bed.*

Alex was smart, yet somehow gullible. Not naive so much as eager to believe. Peter kept the boys locked in the little bathroom for a few days, while Mother stayed at the big house. He took the larger bedroom, which had once been his mother's, and he enjoyed the space. He talked to the boys from time to time, but mostly occupied himself with reading a few of the books he'd brought with him. But he couldn't settle. Everything felt too tight here, cramped. Peter dreamed of the lake, of the wide open spaces, of the dusty library and the basement with its cool, damp smell and the twisty corridors Mother had built.

Soon they could go back. But not until everything had blown over. Peter had no doubt that Mother would fix it all.

And in the meantime Peter couldn't allow himself to trust Alex too much. He'd been burned before. He knew he needed to test him, to see what his limits were. But he also knew he couldn't push him, not like he'd done with Morgan. He'd have to lead him, coach him. Be gentle. Peter wasn't used to being gentle.

But somehow it worked. Alex and Peter talked through the bathroom door while Randeep snivelled and cried and refused to eat. Eventually Peter let Alex into the bedroom. He tied him to the bed, just with a bit of old rope. Alex could have untied himself, but he was busy asking questions. Peter lit his favourite red candles, the ones he'd brought from home. They reminded him of the church service when they'd said goodbye to Chris. Alex said the candles had scared his sister when Peter had lit them in the basement. It was an offering, that piece of information. The first step.

For the next few days it felt like both of them were waiting for something to happen, but then it stopped feeling like living on a knife edge and it started to feel *normal*. Peter decided he wanted to keep the big bedroom. Mother wouldn't argue. He knew he could convince her. It could be *their* space.

After a week of the boys living on cheese sandwiches Mother finally came to the little house. She'd brought all of her tapes, her journals, her pictures, and purchased a new small TV. That's when Peter knew they wouldn't be going back to the big house, and the thought filled him with a nameless, twisting emotion. It was like sadness.

Randeep was still locked in the bathroom. He had been since they'd arrived, since he'd let Alex and Jillian run away. Mother had said they needed to figure out what to do with him, but Peter had some ideas.

Alex's sister was on the news almost non-stop. She had somehow managed to survive the cold night, the rain that must have soaked her to the bone, the fall that Alex had described down that long, muddy slope. She was feisty, just like Peter had thought. He shouldn't have underestimated her.

They didn't let Alex watch the news. Alex didn't talk about his sister, but Peter suspected he thought she was dead. Why else would he have come back to the house like he did? That made it easier in some ways, and harder in others.

It was hard to avoid the news, the interviews and reporters weighing in on Alex's abduction and Jillian's return, but Peter managed it. They only watched TV on Saturday mornings, for the cartoons, but Alex never complained.

Long weeks went by before Peter felt ready. After two months, he started to relax, to leave the channel when the news came on. Mother was still worried that the truth would make Alex try to run. But Peter wondered something different. He wondered and he wondered, until finally there was a news recap on the abduction, and he let the younger boy watch.

Alex's wan face flickered with the light coming off the television, his golden curls wild like a crooked halo. When he saw his sister, grainy footage of her being carried by their father into a dark building with a cover over her face – a cover that slipped, just for a second – Alex flinched. And then he looked away.

Peter recognised the emotion on his face. *Anger*. That same burning, white-hot anger Peter knew, hiding a hollowness beneath. The kind of fire that no water could douse.

He knew then that Alex was ready to take his final test. It meant Peter could tie up the loose ends.

He was excited.

Because what happened next would determine how long Alex got to live.

THIRTY ONE

Harriet

WHEN THE POLICE FINALLY let both of us go we headed back to the hotel. Neither of us wanted to be there – but then, I don't think we wanted to be anywhere at all. We moved in a numb sort of silence. Too sick to eat much, but desperate for the oblivion of a couple of bottles of cheap supermarket wine. We didn't talk about Dana Wood. About the cabinet full of trophies. About what had happened today, or in the past.

We hardly talked at all, only brief words here and there. When we walked into the hotel room Erin stared at the TV with longing. But we knew what we'd see if we turned it on. News appeals, press. I wanted to ask Erin if she was okay, but I couldn't. It was clear that neither of us were *okay*.

She phoned her Mum, as I had done, and their conversation was so stilted, so filled with pauses, that I fled to the shower where I could try to sort through my thoughts. But no matter how hard I scrubbed, I couldn't wash away the image of that body in the bathtub, the sheer horror worming inside me. That person… She was responsible for Jem and Mikey's deaths. She was a monster. And yet − I realised I was *sorry*. Sorry she was dead, sorry that we'd never get real justice, a chance to ask *why*, and sorry, too, that somebody had left her there alone. I scrubbed my skin harder; it felt like I might never be clean again.

When I'd phoned my mum she'd been distraught.

"You need to stop this," she'd said. "It's *dangerous*."

And all I could think was *I know. I know, I know.* I felt sick with it, my stomach swirling precariously. It didn't matter how many times I told myself otherwise, I knew that I had got myself into this mess. And I knew I couldn't stop now.

Around eleven we finished off one of the bottles of wine. We were both exhausted, and the alcohol coated everything in a fuzzy layer. Erin curled up on the bed, still dressed in her leggings, her phone unplugged and face-down on the bedside table. She hadn't even made it under the duvet before falling asleep.

I drifted to my laptop. I trawled through the pages of the book, the ones that I had written in fits and starts over the last few days. They felt alive, practically crackling with electricity.

Of course. They were about Erin.

I scrolled, watching as the tone of the words I had written changed. At first Erin was *Jillian*; she was standoffish, reluctant to speak and sometimes a little hostile. But as I'd written what had happened to her, to *us*, over the last days, I realised that everything had changed. Jillian had become Erin. Had become something else, too.

I continued reading, checking on Erin every now and then.

Something felt like it was growing in my chest. Something like a scream. I'd texted Adam Bowles earlier to thank him and ask for more information, a name for Dana's son. When he texted back his message was rambling and he seemed unsure. I tried to search for the name Adam offered, googling everything I could think of, but I got nothing. I didn't even know if Adam had remembered it correctly.

I turned back to my own words, finally noticing something that had become so painfully obvious that I was angry at myself for only just seeing it. It had leaked into every word, every page.

Suddenly I couldn't be in here any more. Jerkily, I got up, pulled my jacket on and grabbed my cigarettes. I was outside before I could stop to think what I was doing, the air refreshingly chill. I'd known something was growing between us, between Erin and me. That this was more than just blowing off steam. That it was more than just looking out for her. But I hadn't admitted it.

I had *feelings* for Erin. Romantic, not just sexual feelings. This was new, and entirely unexpected. I'd had physical relationships before, but nothing with any kind of emotional resonance. And I didn't know what to do.

I lit my cigarette and smoked it quietly. I'd chosen a spot where I could see the entrance to the hotel since I couldn't stand under the awning to smoke, and the trees overhead rustled with wind and dripped rain onto my shoulders.

The night was quiet. There was only the faintest hum of traffic, the leaves above my head. I listened to the sounds of myself: the beat of my heart, the way the cigarette seemed to fizzle on my tongue as I smoked it. It might have felt peaceful, once, but the shadows stretched and the quiet felt like an echo of something else. Something louder. Something like absence. The way a quiet room changes when another silent person enters.

I glanced towards the hotel again, but nothing had changed. The unmanned reception desk was dim. There were few cars in the car park, only the four I'd noticed earlier. I counted them again, just to be sure.

I'd have the cigarette and then I'd go back inside to deal with how I felt about the book, about Erin. I'd been stupid to come out at all. Whoever had broken into Erin's house, who had killed Monica and kidnapped Jenny, was still out there. They had probably killed Dana.

Could it be Dana's son? I was frustrated by how little I knew about him. There were hundreds, thousands, of Peter Woods. It wasn't exactly uncommon – if it was even the right name. I thought again about the message Adam had sent. I'd been thinking about it on and off for the last twenty minutes. His mother, he'd said, had thought that the Wood children were strange.

I've been thinking about it. The older boy, Peter, was a bit weird. Mum said he never spoke to her. But his brother was so cheerful. I remember him. By the way, I've managed to find this address. I think it's the right place.

I'd doodled the address next to my laptop, then googled it. *Dove Manor*. It was near Stanshope, which fit what he'd told us before. I'd wondered whether I ought to wake Erin up. But she needed to sleep. We could see if the detectives knew anything about it tomorrow.

I wanted to get Erin away. Maybe we could join Erin's mum in Skegness; anywhere would be better than here. I'd been too exhausted, too numb, to suggest it a few hours ago, but it was stupid for us to still be here.

I knew Erin wouldn't want to leave. It was as though she was determined to see this through, no matter how dangerous it was. And I… I could do more to help her, to protect her, if I was with her.

I shivered. The jacket I'd grabbed wasn't thick enough, or waterproof, and I was starting to get cold. I wondered what time it was.

I finished my cigarette quickly and was just scrubbing it under the sole of my shoe when a noise stopped me.

I glanced up. There was a man, standing just outside the doors of the hotel, dressed in dark clothes with his hood pulled up against the chill. I couldn't tell whether he'd recently arrived or whether he was leaving. He peered into the empty reception area.

"There's nobody there," I called.

He turned, spotting me with surprise and lowering his hood. I stepped from under the leaves of the tree, glad it had stopped raining.

"You have to phone the hotline or use a machine to check in."

He came a little closer. We met just before the shadow of the trees. I kept my distance, wary after the last few days, but he gave me a shy smile.

"Are you a guest?" he asked. "I've never stayed in one of these."

I didn't answer. Instead I inched round him, towards the entrance.

"Do you think you can help me?"

"Sorry?"

"To check in," he clarified. "I'm useless with machines."

He let me lead the way to the hotel. It wasn't until we were almost at the doors, just out of the little awninged space where the red light of the CCTV camera blinking was the only splash of colour, that I realised what had made me uncomfortable.

He had no bags – and there were no new cars in the car park.

I spun, but just as I did I felt something crash into my skull. Stars speckled my vision and my knees buckled from the impact, pain ricocheting through my neck and shoulders. I sprawled onto the tarmac, palms skidding painfully.

I was too stunned to even move when he hit me again.

THIRTY TWO

12 NOVEMBER 2016

Erin

WHEN I DREAMED, IT was of Alex.

We sat on cold ground. My arms were no longer bound; a piece of rope had been there, but it had fallen away. I reached up, gingerly taking hold of the piece of cloth around my face. When I peeled it back I was greeted not by darkness, but warm, buttery daylight.

I blinked. The room was thin and long and all of the walls on one side were made of glass. A veranda. No, a big, long conservatory that looked out over a garden.

I turned my head, wary of the pounding inside my skull. Everything was too tight and it ached. Alex was there. He was there and he was okay. His cheeks were pink and shiny, his blond curls stuck to his forehead. He smiled reassuringly.

"Look at these," he said. "Jilly, look at these."

On the floor — polished wood, so shiny that it looked like the surface of a pond — there was a plate of sweets. Cakes and chocolates, little pink and yellow fancies and a few small sandwiches, cut into triangles.

"Where are we?" I asked. It was my seven-year-old voice, high and

scared. I remembered the girl in the basement. She was dead. But this place was nothing like that dark place. Alex only shrugged.

"We're in the upstairs. He said it's so we can see what happens if we're good. We'll have to go back down there later so they can clean up after us. But for now we're in here, and maybe later we can come back. If we're good." He frowned.

"Did they hurt you?"

"Hurt me? No."

"What's going on, Alex?" I begged. I wanted to kick the plate of sweets away. "Why are we here?"

"Dad doesn't care that we're gone, Jilly. But we can stay here if we follow the rules. If not they'll dig a pit and throw us in."

"Why doesn't Dad care?"

Dream Alex shrugged and stuffed two fancies into his face. He was trying to be brave, trying to stop me from being afraid.

"Who are they?" I whimpered. He gave me a little yellow slice of cake, slid it right onto my grubby palm. Like an offering.

"We have to be good to each other. And to them."

"Dad will find us. He'll come and bring us home. He's not a wimp."

"What if he doesn't come?" Alex asked. "I don't think he will. And Mum won't come without him."

"Alex, you're scaring me."

"Good."

When I woke my mouth tasted sour and my head ached. I rolled onto my side, unconsciously reaching for Harriet's warmth.

Her side of the bed was empty. I groped sleepily in the darkness, the only light the small, winking battery on Harriet's laptop. I turned the bedside lamp on, expecting to find Harriet in the armchair, or even asleep at the desk. She wasn't.

I got up. Checked the bathroom. Empty, lights still on, as though she hadn't been gone long. I sighed, rubbed my hands over my face to push back the dreams. She must have gone out for a cigarette.

I checked my phone. It was almost four in the morning. Perhaps she'd gone to get a snack from the machine in the lobby.

Taking opportunity of her absence I wandered over to her laptop, casually grazing a knuckle over the track pad. The screen blinked to life.

I sat. The words in the open document swam for a second as I forced myself to focus.

It was a chapter from her book. The book I hoped she might have given up on. It started with *I first met Jillian Chambers on a cold day in November. She wasn't supposed to be there. I had arranged to talk to her mother, and I was nervous. But when Jillian turned up things went from bad to worse. She was angry at me, I think, for interrupting her life.*

She seemed closed off. Sad. Sometimes she makes everybody in the room feel like they're waiting for her to say something harsh, waiting for the other shoe to drop.

I felt my belly hollow out. Was this what Harriet thought of me? I forced myself to read on.

I first realised there was something wrong with Jillian that night. I was worried about her. Not because she was rude, but because she seemed frightened. Selfishly I chalked it down to my unexpected presence in her life — but I quickly learned there was more to it.

I scanned further. The mouse skated across the screen. I let the pages scroll. Two chapters more. Still the words *Jillian*, *the Father*, jumped out at me. Then, a few rare interviews, chapters with headings that were names I recognised: Jeremy and Michael, George and Jacob, Morgan and Paul, Charlotte and Hazel, Randeep and Jaswinder.

And then, *Erin, Erin, Erin*…

"It's all about me…"

The whole second half of the book. It wasn't notes about the other families, the other victims. Not like Harriet had told me it would be. Instead it was page after page of *me*.

I stopped reading. Stopped scrolling. I slammed the laptop shut, the rattling sound jarring my bones.

My heart battered in the cage of my chest. I was angry that Harriet had misled me. She'd told me the book wasn't about *me*. And yet… I realised I was also glad. Grateful. That she might have the courage to tell the story that I couldn't.

It had been almost half an hour. Where was she? I glanced around, looking for her handbag, her keys. They were still on the bedside table, where she'd left them. I stood up, kicking aside the plastic desk chair. I checked the bathroom again, even though I knew she wasn't there. I tried ringing her phone, but it went straight to voicemail. Beside her laptop I noticed an address, scribbled hastily. A chill ran through me. *Dove Manor.*

I felt sick. She couldn't have gone without me, could she? She wouldn't. Not without her keys. We'd driven here together.

I'd made it to the door before I spotted what was folded just underneath it. A plain white sheet of paper. My skin prickled as I realised that it hadn't been there when I went to sleep. I bent slowly, retrieving the folded sheet from the carpet. I unpeeled the two halves slowly, terror making my bones sluggish. I didn't recognise the handwriting.

I didn't think. I was already dressed in leggings; I shoved my feet into my trainers, which were cold and felt like cement blocks on my feet, and grabbed my jacket and my phone. I was out of the door and in Harriet's car in less than five minutes, my heart in my throat the entire time.

The words of the note spun in my head. I knew it. I knew it was all a game. I knew something was off. The looping words convinced me I'd been right before, about the Father. About Peter Wood.

Why haven't you come to visit me yet, Jilly? I left you all of the clues. Perhaps this will help. I've invited your friend to Dove Manor for a tour. I think you should come too. Come alone or I'll kill her.

THIRTY THREE

Erin

IT WAS STILL DARK. Half four in the morning just rolling around. I'd had too much wine to be driving. It was completely, impossibly unsafe, but I couldn't wait. Not without knowing if Harriet was in danger.

I only had a decent idea where I was going, blind hope driving me onwards. Dove Manor. Adam had said it was near Stanshope, so that's where I headed. I didn't have enough battery to get me all the way with Google Maps, and now I was in the middle of nowhere with five per cent and no directions. I knew it had to be somewhere on the other side of the woods Harriet and I had walked through only days before. And with a name like Dove Manor, it probably wasn't far from the River Dove. I just prayed that I could find it in the dark.

I also had no idea what I was doing. If I managed to find the house, what then? I should have called the police, Wendy, anybody, but even the thought of it sent a bolt of fear right through me.

If I turned up with police, sirens… he'd kill Harriet.

The note had made that clear. This had been his plan all along.

That was why he'd stalked Jaspreet and Molly. Why he'd killed Monica, taken Jenny and sent those fingers. It was why he'd broken into my house. To prove what he could do: he was unstoppable, and he cared nothing for human life. If I called the police and he found out, he *would* kill her. I believed him.

I could barely think through the fear. So I put my foot down and drove faster.

The country roads were narrow, trees and hedges closing in tight. I headed uphill, the valley and town below spreading like a stain, hollow yellow lights flickering. I started to doubt myself. Was this the way we had come before? I was sure I recognised the roads, but now I couldn't tell. I was about to pull over, to waste precious battery on scouring the map again, when I saw it.

It was a wooden signpost staked into the wet earth, in the image of a bird. A dove, complete with an olive branch – or what might have been, once, but the old wood was weathered and rotten and most of the branch had been chipped away by wind and rain.

In the darkness it was a portent. It was fortunate that I had even seen it, and something in the back of my mind trembled. I knew I'd seen it somewhere before. I pulled to a stop. There were no cars around, no people for miles. What the hell was I doing? Risking everything for Harriet, a woman I'd only known two weeks?

But I knew it wasn't just about Harriet. I wasn't just afraid for her. I was fucking angry at whoever was doing this. If I ran now, like I'd been doing my whole life, then this might never end. So far the police hadn't exactly proven themselves – and Harriet had. The anger inside me grew, directed at everything. I wasn't going to run away, but I didn't have to play completely into his hands either.

I got out of Harriet's car and dug around in the back, looking for something useful. There was a battered, empty gym bag, a small tool box – and a hazard triangle. That would do. I got it out and laid it at the base of the signpost. At least this way somebody might know to come and find me…

I got back into the car feeling nauseous but ready. The track was just about wide enough to drive up and there were no fences to keep me out. It was overgrown, my headlamp beams bouncing back to blind me. Water ran down the path in rivulets, from the rain in the night, the current so strong there must be a ford nearby. Vaguely I wondered if it might flood.

Something tugged at the back of my memory. Sounds, rather than sight. The sound of car wheels through water, the sound of panicked breathing, the steady tap of a restless thumb against a steering wheel. And then, another memory. Slick mud, flood plains marshy under my exhausted body as I dragged myself beyond the water.

Overhead, now, the trees were a cage of darkness blocking out the setting moon. The car crawled and my body was wild with panic. Then, *there*. A large ornate iron gate with gold spikes at the top. A shiny new padlock.

This was the right place. It had to be. The lock confirmed

it. This was all part of the game. I was meant to be here, but I couldn't go that way. Like an aggressive, dangerous session of hide and seek.

I got out of the car and the greyish brown leaves squelched underfoot. The air smelled of rotting wood and earth, damp as more rain started to coat everything in a fine white mist.

I was going to have to find another way in.

What on earth had Harriet been thinking, leaving the hotel room by herself? I was tormented with visions of her hurt, and they made my belly clench. And then anger again, white hot and slick like oil settling on water. How dare this man treat us like pieces on a chessboard.

I grabbed my phone, for all the good it was with its battery still draining – I'd switched everything off, put the brightness way down, but still it was seeping away, every minute that passed another moment closer to being totally, absolutely alone.

I left the car where it was, just off the path. The leaves were mulch under my wet trainers as I headed right, along the length of the fence that flowed out of the gate where an old track was still faintly visible among wild trees and undergrowth.

I kept my breathing even, my footsteps as regular and as solid as I could make them. It was still dark out, and the fresh rain was making it hard to see. I didn't want to use the flashlight on my phone in case it drained the battery to nothing. Or in case I missed something outside of its narrow band of light.

As I rounded a slightly firmer curve of the fence, one hand trailing against the metal and the other outstretched for trees and long tangled branches, I noticed something. I'd reached an impasse, a greyish black wall that stretched high into the trees. I stopped, my breath coming in short, sharp bursts. My forehead was dripping, water sneaking down the back of my jacket. I looked to the right.

The wall stretched into the darkness, but somewhere up ahead I could just make out something else. A patch of stone that was darker, like an opening. I hopped and wobbled my way over the uneven earth. I stumbled, catching my hand against the stone wall, cursing as I felt it bite into my skin. My weak ankle tilted and for a sickening second I was going to fall, but it held.

I sucked at the patch of skin on the pad of my thumb where the rock had sliced it. The blood tasted metallic and hot, the sensation in my mouth almost welcome as I realised how thirsty I was. Still drunk, too. Everything had the soft edges of drunkenness, even my panic. I knew that I wasn't thinking clearly, but there wasn't anything I could do about it.

The opening was an arch carved into the stone. It led through into an area that looked remarkably similar to the one I'd just left. Trees that reached high overhead, some with low-hanging boughs. I smelled rotten fruit, perhaps apples or pears like the trees that had grown in my parents' garden when I was a child. My stomach churned. Now it reminded me of something else. Dana Wood's body in the bathtub, that cloying pervasive scent. I forged onwards, hoping this was the way to the house.

It wasn't yet five-thirty but it felt like I had been awake for hours. My body ached but deep down the core of fear and anger kept me moving, the furnace inside me burning with uncontrollable terror that I fought to leash with long, confident strides.

The sight of the house broke the barriers. An icy wind whipped me to shivers, the cold in my bones already. And something else.

The house was… a *monster*. There was no other word for the hulking shadow that grew out of the trees. Two wings, sandstone, red brick and black slate twisted together to create the impression of a Bosch painting. And over to the right I saw something that made my blood sing and my memory thrash free of its shell.

Just like that.

Like the snapping of a cord, everything came tumbling out.

There was a small shack, an outhouse where somebody might once have kept innocuous gardening tools like spades and trowels. A wooden plaque above it – a dove carrying an olive branch. I knew, then, that this was right.

And I felt rather than saw the image that had hidden at the edge of my dreams for eighteen years.

I was seven years old again, being led from the back of a big car in the dead of night. Stiff-legged, wet-eyed, I had managed to pull up the blindfold – the one they'd put on us so we wouldn't see the front of the house, wouldn't see where the orchard ended in another high wall and the back gardens began. So that we couldn't see where they parked the car, in the small clearing in the woods.

So that even if we made it outside, even if we ever escaped, we would never find our way off the rambling grounds. We would never be able to find the car, or the path, or any way out of this maze-like place.

But I had seen it.

I remembered now. And I knew, with a clarity that felt like a bolt of lightning, that Harriet must be in that house. He – Peter – had her, and the only way to save her was to go inside.

I knew that this part of the house was older than the front. That the whole place was a cobbled-together monstrosity, Frankenstein's monster sort of thing: cold panelled hallways that didn't lead anywhere, oddly shaped doorways, and old, polished flagstones which looked like they came from two different houses. I knew that down there, to the right just beyond the trees, there was a lake. The one that Christopher Wood had drowned in.

I broke into a run. I scrambled up to the edge of the house, searching for a door. A door I remembered vaguely as being small and down a short set of stone stairs. I found it on instinct alone – just like I'd found the house – and once I was there I was confronted by the weathered wood and the brass knocker.

Alex's words were in my head now, his childish voice high and sweet. *"The front of the house is theirs. It's where they live. We live downstairs in the back. But if we're good we might be allowed upstairs, to use the bedroom."*

I'd known even then that it wasn't true. They would never let us loose in a house this size. Instead I remembered only darkness, concrete, cold stone and no windows. Except the conservatory. Two glorious hours of sunshine, before we'd been made to go back downstairs.

I pressed down on the door handle. It wasn't locked.

I slipped into the dark, cold room and inhaled the air that was equal parts dust and something else, something more human. The smell of a person. Sweat, maybe, but clean enough. Somebody had been here.

The room was so dark that I closed my eyes, tried to remember if I knew the way. I didn't, but I inched my feet across the flagstones, my heart stuttering at every brush of a cobweb. There were leaves in here too, carelessly left to fester. I heard their tell-tale autumn crunch and knew they were fresh.

I wanted to call out. I wanted to shout Harriet's name, but I didn't dare.

I hit the edge of the room. The wall loomed in the pitch darkness. The walls were cold and hard, my fingers scrabbling against bare brick for what felt like an eternity. I stumbled over uneven stones, jumped at the skittering of browning leaves as I inched forward, until finally I felt something that was not stone. It was wood. A door.

On the other side I finally allowed myself a moment of torchlight. The frigid space around me was illuminated in a clinical white light. Moving faster now, I hurried down the length of a hallway until a jolt of recognition stopped me in my tracks. It felt like the ground dropping out beneath my feet.

It was just an old bookcase, festering volumes on the shelves. But it sat away from the wall, a gap big enough behind it that I could just squeeze through. And there, instead of a wall, was a door.

And when I pushed it open, stairs. The stairs from my dream.

I paused for a second, listening. I could hear nothing but the sound of my own panicked breathing. The stairs descended into darkness, and with a sinking sensation in the pit of my belly, I knew where I had to go.

Down.

THIRTY FOUR

Harriet

PAIN LANCED DOWN THE right side of my face, my jaw, my neck. I could feel the muscles at my collarbone cording with effort as I struggled to consciousness. Every second felt like a fight at first. The darkness was cold, empty, smelled like dirt and musty old wood and something metallic.

I blinked. Tried to reach for my face. My hands were tied at the wrist; they rested in my lap, heavy like concrete. I opened my eyes wide, straining. It was so dark I couldn't see a thing.

I waited. The only sound was my breath, which was ragged. Gently I massaged my forehead with the back of one of my hands, checking for tender spots. The worst of the pain was at the back of my head.

Slowly it came back to me. The hotel, the cigarette, the man. I surprised myself when I realised that I wasn't afraid. But the numbness I felt instead was worse, as though my body had already given up.

I don't know how long I sat there. I was cold, shivering,

and aching all over. And then, eventually, I started to see. The walls of the room began to appear in shades of grey as my eyes adjusted to the dark; they were planks of wood, maybe, crooked and gnarled.

I was dazed. How long had I been here? It seemed like hours. I was freezing under my thin coat, which I noted I was still wearing. My whole body was stiff with cold, but I could move. I felt sick, my head pounding from the blow. It was still tender, but the adrenaline had worn off. I wasn't hungry though, and I didn't need the toilet, so I couldn't have been here any longer than a few hours. Slowly, stiffly, I let myself shift from the hard concrete floor, wobbling as my vision tilted.

I lifted my hands from my lap. They were tied together at the wrists, and then attached to the wall with a long piece of rope. I moved a little, to get a better look. The rope was hooked around a metal ring, bolted to the wood. Like you might use to tie up a dog if you had to leave them outdoors.

Now suddenly the fear hit me and I let out two panicked, gulping cries before I got my body back under control. Wild thoughts consumed me. Had Jeremy and Michael been here, once? I fought off the urge to sob again, imagining them in this place. Cold, afraid. Was this where they had died?

I thought about calling for help, but what good would that do? Whoever had left me here – was it Dana's son? Or somebody else? – might only be waiting for a noise from me and they'd come back. I thought about Adam Bowles, how his text had led me here. Could he have anything to do with this? But, no. I had asked for the address. It was Dana's son. It had to be.

I took as many deep, slow breaths as I could and tried to calm down. My head was thudding; it felt very heavy. I looked at my wrists more closely. They had been zip-tied, the rope running between my palms. Somehow this filled me with relief. I'd seen a video once, on how to break these sorts of plastic ties with a shoelace. I'd never tried it, but I set to work now, aware every second of the pain inside my head as it grew.

I pushed back questions of what I'd do once I was free. I couldn't think that far ahead.

Getting the shoelaces untied was the hard part, my fingers numb and fumbling in the cold. But I did it. I tried to force the laces between my hands, but the rope made it difficult. I dropped them. Cursed as they blended into the darkness.

Then I found them. I tried again, this time with more success. Once they were through I tied them together. And then, as I'd seen in the video on YouTube, back when I thought things like this were for *fun*, I began to move my legs, back and forth like I was riding a bicycle. The movement was painful, my thighs aching, my back stiff. But I kept going, using the laces to saw through the plastic until I was, suddenly—

Free.

The rope pooled in my lap, still tied to the ring on the wall. I resisted the urge to cry. Instead I lowered my legs, retied my shoelaces slowly, and let out a juddering breath. I reached up to touch the back of my head, feeling dizzy from even the slightest pressure. I thought I might vomit but I took deep gulps and waited for the feeling to pass.

Slowly, I climbed to my feet. I was unsteady, my knees

threatening to give way at any moment. But I held onto the wall, felt the rough-cut wood dig into my palm of my hand, and inhaled.

It was a small room, I realised. Maybe a shed. The door was a darker spot against the cracked and warped wood of the walls. Frantically I ran my fingers along its outer edge, searching for a latch or a handle, even a knot in the wood or a hook I could pull.

There was nothing.

I barely resisted the urge to scream. My head, God, it ached… I patted my pockets, but he'd taken my phone. My cigarettes and my hotel keycard too.

If he had the keycard – he had access to Erin. Would he be able to find out which room was ours? Panic coursed through me and I felt again like I was going to vomit, but I fought to slow my thoughts. That didn't make sense. All of that just to steal a keycard? He didn't want to hurt Erin. He wanted…

He wanted her to come here. To protect me.

"Oh, Jesus…" I whispered, dread making me weak.

For a moment I sat. I was exhausted, an iron-tinted taste in my mouth, like when I used to spar too hard in karate practice. I leaned against the wood and closed my eyes. If I didn't get out of here, this might be the last place I'd remember.

So, after a minute, I got up. I stepped back from the door, locating the weakest-looking panel. It was warped, twisted with the rain and the sun and years of neglect. I took a moment to focus, and then snapped my foot out as hard as I could.

The sole of my shoe was thick rubber but I felt the impact

right up in my knee and in the clenching of my teeth. It hurt. But the wood made a groaning noise so I did it again. And again. Until finally, something gave.

I tumbled forward, catching myself at the last second. I grazed my knuckles against the wall but ignored the pain. The board was loose, and I set about prying it off. Rusty nails, jagged, unyielding until my fingers were sore and bloody. But I got it off, and then set about the next.

It wasn't long before I was sweating. It stung my eyes, and the exertion made my head pound so badly that my vision swam. Gradually, the smells of the outside began to filter through the gaps. Grass and trees and fresh rain. I wanted to cry, I wanted to lie down and sleep, but I refused to stop until I had managed to climb out, scrambling through the hole I had created in the wall of the shed. Out into the dark. It wasn't as late as I had thought, still maybe only two or three in the morning, the moon still high.

It was only when I was outside, looking in, that I noticed it. The source of the metallic scent. I had dark brackish stains all over me. Old, gloopy blood. I'd lain in a puddle of it. More than one person could lose and live.

I knew I should be moving. Running. But my eyes were fixed to the spot. I couldn't move, and all the while my brain just looped *Erin Erin Erin*.

Was she here? Did he have her?

I had to find her.

THIRTY FIVE

Erin

"HARRIET, WHERE ARE YOU...?" I whispered.

There was another basement corridor ahead. I'd lost all sense of direction. The house was bigger than it seemed, a maze of hallways, as if an old, small cellar had been converted, twisted into something else. Some passages ended abruptly, while some became rooms and then corridors again without it seeming as though I'd crossed through. Everything was bare, windowless and dark. It was colder down here, the chill deep in my bones as my adrenaline ebbed away.

The effects of the alcohol were starting to wear off too and I felt heavy. I chose another hallway at random. This one – it felt right. There were doors that led off to the left and the right but I ignored them. I knew I would recognise the one I needed when I saw it. I had to...

I must have walked almost the length of the house. Suddenly I hit a sharp turn and my body reacted, muscles moving as though from memory. The ground sloped slightly and I felt my heart hammer harder. Yes, this was right.

And then: just a door, dark and wooden like all of the others. But I recognised this one. There was a big, long scratch mark down the front. It had looked like this back then, too.

Suddenly I was overwhelmed. I had been here before. I had been here during the worst nights and days of my life – and I finally *remembered*. Not everything, but I remembered Alex, and this room, and the conservatory, and I remembered – Dana. Stern, unsmiling, her hair scraped back in a severe bun as she gripped my arm hard enough to bruise. And a boy, Peter, solemn and arresting.

I was so wrapped in my memory, the fear uncoiling inside me and turning to anger, that I didn't hear it right away. The sound was faint, muffled by the door, but it was definitely human.

Was it Harriet? My stomach lurched with fear. I froze. What if she was hurt? What would I do? Or worse, what if it wasn't Harriet?

Seconds like hours passed as I stood. Then, without even realising I was moving, I saw my trembling fingers grip the handle. I was a puppet and my body was out of my control. I could taste the panic on my tongue, the bitter iron tang in my mouth. I swallowed.

Then I opened the door.

It was dark, but not too dark to see. I shoved my phone into my pocket and let my eyes adjust. The muffled crying stuttered and then died. I noticed the candles with a dull kind of shock, a handful of them on the floor, stood in their own red wax. There was a single bed, like the one from my dream. A cot big enough for an older child, with high bars at the back and an open front, the whole thing dirty and grey with age.

On the bed there was a lump of darkness. I recoiled, thinking of the girl from my dream, the hollow eyes, the twisted fingers. Jaswinder, already dead and rotting. The body was left there for long enough to scare Alex and me into silence before being taken away. Jenny's fingers – they were meant to remind me.

I fought the bile that rose in my throat.

The silence was as heavy as a lead-lined blanket. I begged my eyes to work faster, to take in the dimness, the flickering light, the shape on the bed. Was it a child? Was it *Harriet*?

No. It was too large to be either.

"Who are you?" I demanded. My voice didn't wobble and for that I was glad. "Where is she?"

The figure didn't move right away. When he did, he uncoiled with a slowness that betrayed years of abuse. He was probably around my age, a little older. He wore dark, ripped jeans and a plain t-shirt. He was pale, shadows under his eyes and hollows in his cheeks. A few days' worth of stubble darkened his jaw.

He was bound to the bed with a piece of rope, tied at one end and looped around his wrist. His other hand was free but he acted as though he was handcuffed.

My throat felt like it was full of wasps.

I didn't recognise his face. Not at first. But those eyes... I would recognise those eyes anywhere.

For a second all thoughts of Harriet were gone as the man struggled upright.

"Jilly…" he whispered.

"Alex?"

I stood rooted to the spot as though any second he might evaporate in a cloud of smoke. It was a trick. It had to be. But he didn't move either, as if he was afraid of the same thing. His golden brows dipped as he studied my face. I mimicked him, taking in the strong line of his jaw – like our father – and the dip of his collarbone beneath his baggy shirt. My eyes latched onto the dirt and dust on his jeans, the piece of rope that tied him to the bed, and a million thoughts raced through my mind.

What came out was, "What the fuck?"

He flinched, swinging his legs over the edge of the bed.

"*Jilly*," he repeated.

That single word was the solution that dissolved the glue holding me to the spot. I ran towards him, all cares gone as I threw myself at his feet.

"Alex," I cried. "You've been alive all this time? What have they done to you?"

I was crying hard, perhaps the most I'd cried any day since the moment I woke in that blinking, pale hospital room without him. I clutched his bony legs now, holding them close to my chest.

Alex seemed confused by the physical contact. He moved only to lay one of his hands on my head. It was a gentle touch, so gentle it felt like the beat of a moth's wings.

"Jilly," he whispered softly, his voice husky. "You came back."

My name from his lips was like cool water and I cried harder still. Slowly I came back to myself, felt the hard concrete beneath my knees and the snot running down my face, and the weird, unreality of the moment.

"We have to go," I said suddenly.

"I can't leave."

"What? Why?" I gestured to the rope. "It's just a bit of rope. I can untie it." I set to work on the knot, which wasn't tight.

Alex tensed but didn't move away. The knot was fresh, clean and not matted. The thought that Alex had been tied before, probably more times than I could count over the years, made a fresh wave of tears clog my throat.

"Have you been in the house all this time?" I asked. "The police... What about when they came here?"

Alex shook his head, mute, although I saw a bolt of panic in his face at the mention of the police.

"Why didn't you run?" I asked.

Nothing.

"Alex, where is he? Is he coming back? Are you *hurt*?"

Alex said nothing. He just watched as the rope fell from his wrist, trailing on the concrete just beside a puddle of red wax that had melted from one of the candles. They couldn't have been burning more than an hour or two. What did that mean for us? For Harriet?

"Alex, we need to go. Can you stand?"

He massaged his wrist gently. He was like a baby bird, fragile and unsteady. I fought the unease as I thought of Harriet. Was Peter with her right now? Would he hurt her?

Did he leave Alex here for me to find, to distract me?

"Can't we talk for a minute?" Alex asked gently. "Just for a minute."

I stared at those candles again, watching the flames dance. How many times had I lit a warm candle to soothe my nerves? How hard had I battled to overcome my fears? Had it been because of this? The way they had left us with candles, down here in the dark? The puddles of wax were growing. Harriet was still out there somewhere.

But this was my *brother*.

"Okay."

I listened with horror as Alex stuttered about Peter. *Peter*… How he had lured his own brother down to the lake in the middle of winter and let him die. How Dana had watched from the house, too far away to help as one of her sons killed the other.

"He didn't like most of the children that she brought home. He told me. He wanted a brother but he liked hurting the girls. He didn't like the really young ones, or the loud ones. They tried to come up with tests to see what Peter actually wanted, tried to find one who'd care about him. He talked about Jacob a lot. Morgan – she was okay, too. He liked her for a long time, but eventually he got bored…"

Morgan. The girl whose untold story had haunted me like a ghost my whole adult life. The girl who I had always been afraid of becoming. I would have thrown up if there was anything left, anything other than the hollowness deep inside me that threatened to turn me to stone.

"Did he tie her up too?"

Alex shrugged.

"Are you saying you've been here since… What about later? When the police came to look for you? Were you here then?"

"It was too late when they came. Dana made us move to the little house. She was worried about the police following your trail to get here. She said if they found me I'd have to go into care, because Dad didn't want me any more."

"Of course Dad wanted us."

"No, Jilly. He wanted you. He didn't want me. I was always getting in the way, trying to stop you setting him off. He…" His lip trembled.

There was something unspoken between us, then. A small space that opened up, reminding me of how different we were now. How much I didn't know about him. I hadn't managed to save him, and so he had stayed with them. They had lied to him.

I had never had a nightmare that was as bad as this.

But there was Alex. He was here, *alive*.

"Did he – did they… hurt you?"

Alex shrugged again.

"Not really."

"Are you sure?"

I wanted to touch him from head to toe, be sure that he was okay. But there was something about this man that wasn't like the Alex I knew. An animal wariness in the back of his expression that told a story of a life he hadn't shared with me.

"Can we go, please?" I asked when Alex didn't answer. "My friend. I think he brought her here. To get me to come. She might be hurt. Do you know where she is? Where he might have taken her?"

Alex's eyes widened but then he shook his head.

"You shouldn't worry about her so much. She'll be oka—"

"She's got to be here somewhere," I cut him off. "I have to find her."

I started to edge towards the door. Alex was a grown man; he could follow me. I wanted to grab hold of him and drag him but I didn't think I could. Even as thin as he was, he could take me if he decided to put up a fight, just like when we were children.

"Come on," I said then. "You know this place. Can you help me find her?"

I was aware I was talking to him like a child. He *was* a child to me. When he shrugged he only made it worse and I had to blink to clear the image of him at nine years old, clutching my hand somewhere in the cold, clammy dark.

I reached the doorway.

"Don't leave me." It was barely even a whisper. So quiet I didn't hear it for a second and by the time I understood what he was asking I was already in the hallway.

A shriek erupted, exploding through the silence, a sound that was verging on animalistic. I froze in place, my head snapping back. Alex was still in the same spot, his hands at his chest, the wail coming out of him in increasing volume as he rocked back and forth like a child.

Without thinking I darted back into the room. I ran to him and wrapped my arms around his shoulders. He was a head taller than me, his arms thin but surprisingly strong. I felt the muscles in his back tense at the contact and then melt again as I held him.

The sound stopped as suddenly as it had started.

"I'm sorry, Alex," I whispered.

The hug was awkward. He smelled foreign and complicated, like earth and detergent and sweat and rain. My brain was in overdrive. I thought of Harriet, of Peter Wood and the fact that he could come back any moment, and still I held Alex in my arms. I wanted to burst with joy and sadness and horror and everything in between.

"Shh," I crooned. "I promise I won't leave without you."

THIRTY SIX

Erin

IT TOOK A MINUTE for Alex to calm enough to talk again. When he did he was pliant, exhausted by his tears, and I was able to guide him out into the hall.

But he was on guard, glancing every way multiple times before taking several steps and then stopping to do the same thing again.

"I have to find her," I said as we reached the bottom of the stairs. "Do you understand, Alex?" I didn't want to talk to him like he was stupid, but eighteen years in this place, with those people, had changed him. Ruined him. He had never been back to school, never had any friends. Just him, and them. All that isolation, that loneliness, that fear.

I remembered the bathroom at Dana Wood's other house, Godfrey and Harriet saying that the woman who had abducted so many children seemingly without effort had probably been drowned in her own tub... The oil slick of emotions in my stomach reminded me that I didn't know *this* Alex. Perhaps

Peter had done that to his own mother. Perhaps Alex had seen Peter do it. What would that do to a person?

"Do you understand that I need to find her?" I pushed.

Alex stared at me.

"We don't have to leave," he said uncertainly. "She's safe right now."

"How do you know, Alex? I can't trust that. Peter could be anywhere—"

"They're always safe as long as they don't run."

"He tied you up. He kept you here all this time. The police are at the other house. If he goes there, he'll see them. He'll panic. He'll think I brought them there. He said no police. I didn't call them because – because he said not to." I fought the tears that rose in my throat. "I need to get Harriet home."

Alex's gaze narrowed. "This is my home."

"Alex…" I couldn't keep the despair from my voice. "This isn't anybody's home. Nobody has lived here for a long time."

"I have," Alex said.

I didn't know what to say to that so I didn't reply. If I could just get him out of here, back to civilisation, I could call the police…

"Alex, where are you going?"

Suddenly he was running. I raced to catch up. He bolted up the stairs like a gazelle, his long legs taking the steps two at a time, and I struggled behind.

"Wait!"

He skidded to a stop at the top, slid around the bookcase over the doorway, and I panted after him, my legs burning.

Then he ran again, into the house proper.

I finally caught Alex after another flight of stairs, another corridor I didn't recognise. It was shorter than the others we had come through and I could smell the rain outside.

Alex was hardly out of breath but his nostrils flared in and out as he glanced about.

"Alex, what's going on?"

He pointed. Up ahead there was a room. I had lost all sense of space. There were more windows here but I had no idea where we were.

"What's in there? Is it Harriet?"

Alex just inched closer. I listened hard but heard nothing but the gentle patter of the rain and the gloomy shifting of long curtains half obscuring a view of grass and trees. The rest of the passage was dark and still.

Enough time had passed that a weak grey light was visible around the edges of the door ahead. I followed Alex, a few steps behind. I glanced around for something I might be able to use as a weapon if Peter found us, but short of breaking up some furniture I couldn't see anything.

"Alex." I reached out for him. He dodged my grip but I tried again, this time snagging the sleeve of his t-shirt. "*Alex.*"

"Jillian." He turned and his eyes were wide, the whites almost grey in the shadows, the blue that deep ocean colour I remembered.

"Help me out here," I said. "This is fucking weird."

He stood completely still, like a ghost.

"You think it isn't for me?" His tone was clipped. "You

think this is normal? You think I haven't dreamt about this day? I've waited and waited and now you're here and you can't wait to leave again."

His face was so impossibly sad. I felt my heart shatter, the pieces piercing my belly, my lungs. I wanted to collapse into his arms again, let him hold me, careless of the years that had passed since I saw him last. But I knew he couldn't.

"Alex," I repeated his name again, the word on my tongue sounding foreign and heavy. "Did Peter tell you where he was going? Did he tell you what he did with Harriet?" *Did he tell you to distract me?*

Alex shook his head and his shaggy hair bounced. I wondered how long he had been in that room downstairs. How long those candles had been burning. How long we had left before Peter found me here. He must be here, somewhere. Biding his time. This was all part of the game.

"You wouldn't understand," Alex said. "Things aren't black and white."

He yanked his arm away from me, his focus snapping to the room ahead.

Watching Alex walk away broke something inside me. The fear I'd felt on reading that note slipped under the hotel door, that blinding, tongue-clenching terror, slowly subsided. I'd found Alex, and now I could find Harriet. I needed to let somebody know where I was. So, as Alex – this stranger with Alex's face – opened the door ahead, I slipped my phone out of my pocket. My battery was way into the red, 3%. There was one bar of signal. I found Wendy's name in my recent call list. The battery wouldn't manage a call, but a text might be okay. If I could get it to send. *I'm at Dove Manor*, I typed. *Send help. Emergency.*

"What's taking you so long?" Alex turned. There was something about his expression that was unfamiliar.

"I'm coming."

I shoved my phone back into my pocket quickly.

"Hurry up," he said.

He led me into a bedroom. The floors had once been polished or waxed and still shone in patches where footsteps hadn't worn the surface to dullness. There were two single beds with metal bed frames, their white bedsheets now grey. One bed had a teddy bear on it, well-loved and missing an eye. The other one was empty, but its sheets were mussed.

"What is this…?"

I turned, my eyes drinking in the sight. The undecorated walls, the plain white sheets, the early morning light around the edges of the curtains making everything look ghostly. It looked like a sick ward. Like an orphanage. *Orphanage.* My brain latched onto the word and the shiver returned so hard I felt bedbugs crawling on my skin. I rubbed at my arms.

Alex caught my movement and he frowned.

"Don't you know?" he asked. "Don't you remember? This was going to be our bedroom."

How could I tell him that I had hardly remembered anything at all until an hour ago? How could I tell Alex I'd forgotten what had happened to us, to him?

"I don't…"

Alex held his arms out as though this was a ballroom or grand library worthy of showing off.

"*Look*," he said.

I noticed the mussed-up sheets again, saw the disturbed dust on the floor, a set of footsteps tracking to and from the bed, and the pieces clicked together.

"This is your bedroom," I said. "This is where you've been staying."

Alex started to shake his head.

"You said it was going to be *our* room," I carried on quickly. "Did we ever stay in here...?"

"Our bedroom," he repeated instead of answering. "Look."

He wandered towards the huge window. I followed, slower. There was a radiator that was long dead; the air was icy. He swept the curtain back, releasing a flurry of dust motes.

He pointed. The sun was rising, red like blood. The garden spilled out below. A gentle slope down to the lake. The same landscape I had seen an hour ago.

Only now I knew its secret.

"Why did she take us?" I asked.

"Family," he said, simply. "She wanted a family. Peter had to approve. Siblings are best because they stick up for each other. You can figure out if they'll protect each other, choose the brave ones."

Alex didn't look at me as he said this but I felt my heart stutter in my chest. Did he remember that night? Did he remember what I had done? How I had gone on without him? How I had never gone back? I could almost taste the dirt in my mouth, feel the grazes from the leaves on my bare stomach, my back, my knees. Feel the throbbing in my head, the blood in my eyes.

"Why *you*? Why did they keep you all this time?"

Why aren't you dead?

"Because…" Alex sighed. It was a long sigh, a heavy one that seemed to carry years of questioning. The same question I had asked, only in reverse. What did Alex have that I didn't? Was I a coward for running, even though he told me to? Or was I a coward for not coming back? But how could I?

"Peter chose me." Alex swallowed hard. His eyes were wet and I wasn't sure whether it was from fear or sadness.

"You were special," I said softly.

"You have to understand, Jilly. I made a choice. I decided to live."

I understood that. Probably better than anybody. I thought of the verge. Of how I had let him push me, and how, when I had woken there alone, I had left him behind.

"I understand."

"I knew they wouldn't let both of us leave. I knew that if you stayed, you would die. So I made the other boy help us, and we ran. And then… I knew we wouldn't make it. You were too slow. I needed you to go faster. I thought if you went ahead, that would help. And when you fell… I thought I'd hurt you. I panicked. I didn't know what to do. I came back here and they were *nice* to me. This room was… Do you really not remember the promise they made in the beginning?"

"I—"

"They were going to let us live here. And we wouldn't have to go to school and we wouldn't have to deal with Dad any more."

"Alex, why do you keep saying that about Dad?"

Alex shook his head. "You wouldn't understand," he muttered. "You never did."

"I don't remember…"

Alex pointed again. Just to the left I could see the little potting shed; it had been so ominous in the darkness and now it was just a wooden shack. "They took us there, first. From the car to the shed. We were terrified. Do you remember the darkness? They blindfolded us."

"Dana and Peter?" I asked.

"They left us there. For hours. Until we had calmed down. They needed to make sure we wouldn't run straight away like some of the others did. And then, when we stopped crying, when we were calm enough, they brought us inside."

I couldn't remember it exactly, but I recalled the blindfold and peeking at the house and feeling Alex's hand in mine.

"They took us to the basement first, to show us what would happen if we didn't behave. That's where we stayed, downstairs, until we were good. And then they brought us to the conservatory. It was so warm even with all that glass. So different from the shed. Everything was better then. We had cake and rules and… That's what we were going to get if we kept being good."

"That doesn't make it okay, Alex. Just because they promised us nice things. That woman took your childhood—"

"Jillian, don't you understand what I'm trying to say? She

was trying to offer us a different life. We would never have to go to school; we would always have a friend. We just didn't *all* deserve the life she offered."

I tensed. Alex's tone had changed. He was gripping the ledge of the window, his knuckles white. I saw fresh scratches on the back of his hand. Four of them in a jagged row, marring the pale, hairless skin.

I trained my gaze back on the shack, suddenly aware of how close to him I was standing. The smell of him. The size. He was skinny, sure, but I could see, again, that quiet strength I had felt in our embrace, and, for the first time, I was afraid.

"What did you do," I asked eventually, "that made Peter put you in the basement today?"

Alex turned to me, his expression deadly serious.

"Nobody put me in the basement. I was upset so I went down there. The rope grounds me, helps me to think. It's like Dad's 'naughty step' – you remember the one he'd put us on when he was watching TV and we got too loud? Or – was that just me?"

"What about Peter?

"We should go." Alex nodded towards the window; outside the rain had finally stopped and a glorious morning was dawning. I felt sick, thinking of Harriet, somewhere on these grounds alone. I had been so sure she was in the house, so sure that Peter had her, was using her to get me. But now I didn't know.

"Do you know where Harriet is, Alex?"

"Come with me."

And I did. Somehow I was still glad that I wasn't alone, that no matter what he had done to Alex I wouldn't have to face Peter by myself. That Alex was alive, that he was *mine*.

Whatever they had made of him, Alex was still my brother.

THIRTY SEVEN

Harriet

I CONTEMPLATED MY OPTIONS. The woods, or the house.

I didn't know whether to run, whether to try to get to a road and call for help. But… it was still dark. The sun hadn't even started to rise yet. The ground was uneven, and I didn't have a torch. I glanced around, at the grass and the trees, the woods stretching beyond the greyish-black line of water that might be a lake, and I doubted that I'd make it. My head was pounding, I felt woozy. Faintly, I thought I must be concussed.

I glanced again, back and forth. The woods or the house.

I thought of Erin's face. The way she wrinkled her nose, the way she'd kissed me. Would I even see her again? If I was a sacrifice – just a way for Peter to get to her – what then? If Erin was here, would I even know? How would I find her?

Then a thought struck me. It came so fast I almost laughed. If Erin was here, I knew, there was only one place she'd be. *Remember last night when I said I'd never take the woods again, even over certain death? Next time hold me to that.*

Woods or house? House.

And maybe, if there was a God, the house still had electricity and it might have a phone.

I started walking. I ignored the fear that the man who had knocked me out, brought me here and tied me up might be inside. That he might already have Erin. That I was wasting valuable time. That I was walking into a trap.

I ignored everything except the thought of Erin's face.

I suspected that this was the house where Dana had brought the children. The place where Jenny Bowles had cleaned and where Dana's younger son had died. It had that sort of feel to it. Empty, abandoned. The bushes and plants in the garden around the shed were wild, overgrown and tangled. The house loomed out of the foliage like a monster.

And yet towards it I went.

I tried to move silently. It was hard. My legs and arms were aching from scrambling to get out of the shed. I caught my foot in a tuft of grass, felt my knee go weak as I fought to right myself.

The door to the house was down a flight of stone steps that I could hardly see in the dark. I stumbled again, flinging my arm out. The door was ajar.

I took one last look at the garden, at the shed, at the sky that was still prickled with stars, and then I stepped inside.

The whole place felt empty, haunted. I stumbled through the darkness, passing the odd window that limned abandoned rooms in moonlight. Everything was dark and grey and shadowed, old and creaking. I reached a foyer. Some stairs. There was a small table at the bottom, polished wood shining through the dust, but no telephone.

I avoided catching my eye in the mirror that hung on the wall. I didn't want to see what he had done to me. The pain in my head was blinding.

I tried the stairs. They creaked a little under my weight, but were quieter than I feared they might be. I poked my head into room after bare room. Windows were broken in some of them, graffiti sprayed on walls, empty beer cans and cigarette butts on the floors.

I found nothing new. No clothes, no electronics. I was desperate for a phone. There must be one somewhere; I just wasn't looking in the right place.

I reached the end of a corridor. The walls boxed me in. My body contracted. But there was one final room here. I don't know why I hesitated, but something slowed me. The door was closed tight, unlike most of the others, but more than that it just *felt* different.

I made myself open it. There might be somebody in there, but there might be a phone. I needed a *phone*.

The room was huge. It had a window that looked out over the blue-tinged grass in the garden, the curtains open to let in the weak moonlight. I stepped inside, closing the door quietly behind me. This had been somebody's bedroom.

A four-poster bed dominated the space, its old sheets moth-eaten but beautiful. Silken flowers, birds, butterflies. A large vanity took up one wall, a cluster of framed photographs sat on the left corner, their glass free from dust. Two boys, one blond and one dark. In the first photograph they were younger, holding hands solemnly. In the second they had grown. This one looked like a newer addition, its frame plastic instead of wood. I picked it up to get a better look.

At least, I *thought* it was the same boys in the second photo, but in the dim light it was hard to tell. The brown-haired boy was the same. He went from solemn to cheerful, a small smile on his lips in the second picture, the shape of his mouth changing his whole face. The other boy seemed to get older very quickly. In the first he seemed cherubic, perhaps four years old and smiling. The second photograph had been taken in a park or a garden, both boys looking away from the camera and towards each other. The blond boy was now haunted by dark hollows in his cheeks and eyes.

Something tugged at me, something about that second photograph, but I wasn't sure what it was. Perhaps the blond boy wasn't the same one in that second picture at all.

My eyes strayed to the other wall, where there was an old television mounted in a wooden cabinet. The shelves below were filled with VHS tapes. More tapes than I could count, neatly piled and lined up in rows, uniform in size and shape.

I tiptoed closer. Each of the tapes was labelled carefully in a cursive, looping hand. The white labels had yellowed, the black ink long-faded to brown. Some of them were impossible to read, but others I could make out.

DANA HARPER IN *THE SWEETEST DARK*

DANA HARPER IN *THE FOLLY OF YOUTH*

The television was the kind I'd had growing up, small with an inbuilt VCR. Without thinking, my fingers chose a tape at random. *Kiss Her Goodbye*. I started to pop it into the machine.

I knew it was foolish, but I couldn't help myself. Curiosity overwhelmed all of my senses, and after locating the mute button I tried to push it in.

Nothing happened.

Of course it didn't. There was no electricity. No power. I cursed myself inwardly, wanting nothing more than to find out what, exactly, these tapes contained. It was clear the woman was Dana Wood. Perhaps she'd been an actress before she got married. Maybe Harper was her maiden name, and that's why we'd never found her before. I pictured the life she might have had, once.

What would make a woman go from actress to carer? I wondered if it was her marriage. Her children. Whether it had been her choice or whether she'd been forced. What had made her take the next step to killer?

It didn't matter. It confirmed my foolishness. Even if there was a phone here, there was no electricity and it wouldn't work. I wanted to kick myself. If I'd left the grounds half an hour ago I could have been a mile away by now. I wasn't thinking. My head…

But as I was beating myself up, I noticed something else. It was a small floral journal. It sat on the vanity as though it had been placed there temporarily, right on the edge. As though it was waiting for somebody to come back to it.

I steadied myself against the TV stand and then stumbled over to it. It was damp, but clean, its covers soft and well-thumbed. My fingers recoiled from its tepid pages, but I forced myself to pick it up. It was about the size of my hand. I opened the cover and saw that the first page might have once been filled with the same cursive hand as on the tapes, but water had smeared the ink, leaving it mostly illegible.

Godfrey had said she had found a journal containing poetry and diary entries in the little house. I wondered if it might have been like this one. If Dana had kept more than one. Perhaps… The thought made me squirm, but perhaps Peter had brought it back here after he'd killed his mother. Like a trophy.

I flipped through the pages, my brain stuttering over odd phrases that made any sort of sense. *Mouse is home again. The doctor says he needs rest. He wasn't very happy with either of us. I think we need a new doctor.* And then, a few pages later: *Mouse is different without Bear. Withdrawn. He won't talk to me except to yell. Yesterday he bit me. I think I'm going to homeschool him. Jack wouldn't have let this go on, but Jack isn't here and I am and I know I can figure this out. I have to find a way to make this better.*

I could see no dates on the entries, no thread that connected them together either. Sometimes the pen was different – darker, its point pressed harder into the paper – and sometimes the words were so faint I couldn't read them at all. Sometimes the pen changed halfway through a page, as though a thought had been left half-completed until maybe days or weeks later.

I felt my mouth go dry. These were the ramblings of a mad woman, surely? I saw names, but they weren't names I understood: Mouse, Bear, Chicken, Duck. *The new one is an Otter.* Like people were animals. Were these – the children?

I continued to flick through, finding paragraph after

unintelligible paragraph. *Mouse likes Otter. She's more confident now that Squirrel is gone. She's smart too. Maybe she's the one we've been looking for. She can keep Mouse occupied for hours. He just stares and stares at her. We're even going to let her sleep in the bedroom upstairs. She already spends hours in the library – I don't think she'll run, not since she thinks Squirrel is buried by the lake. Mouse was right about that.*

As the entries progressed the writing got sloppier. Like the writer was drunk, or not paying full attention. There were crossings out, underlined passages. Whole sections gone over and over so much that the letters merged into one another.

Right at the back there was a single page where the writing was legible. The water stains had smeared some, but not all, of the words. *Can't be too careful. Of course I care. But Mouse comes first. And we'd never bury them near the house anyway. Too risky.*

Gecko – allenton, near new car park on may st

Lamb – favourite playground, mulberry chase

*Chicken – back alley near church, edmonton lane BG ** found*

*Monkey – foremark, by the water at east edge, near tree that looks like lightning ** found*

*Sparrow – river derwent, near statue that looks like a horse **found*

And then, nearer the bottom:

Squirrel – ridge near carsington water, ½ mile from first car park

*Otter – abbey park, river near the grove of trees ** found*

My whole body convulsed and I nearly dropped the book. *Monkey. Chicken.* Michael and Jem. Their bodies were found near a church and a reservoir. I tried to breathe but my chest hurt. I wanted to cry.

I forced myself to look again.

Sparrow. Was that George? He'd been found near the Derwent… I gripped the journal as I noticed another location further down the list.

Otter. Abbey Park. That must be Morgan. Her body had been found, not even well-hidden, on a bank of the river near a cluster of oak trees in a park in Leicester. I'd asked her mother about it during an interview, and Vera had just repeated *Why there, why then?* as though I might know the answer. It had been as though Dana wanted her to be found.

I swallowed hard. There were other names, other animals, locations I didn't understand. My eyes grazed over them again and again, drawing the words out as though they might begin to make sense.

It was a list of where the children had been buried. Did she want some of these children to be found? Was she pleased when they were? I found myself looking at the little asterisks next to some names. They'd been added in different pens, different colours, probably at different times. Like a journal of her success.

Did she want to be caught? Or was it gloating? I couldn't tell.

I was so trapped in my thoughts, the disgust roiling inside of my stomach, that I didn't hear the footsteps until it was too late. I shoved the journal down the back of my trousers just as the door swung open.

There was nowhere to hide. It was him. The boy from the photograph, but he was a man now. He was the one who had hurt me. I felt my skin prickle as realisation swept through me like electricity.

"I thought I might find you here. Though I did hope you'd wait until we had company. Have you had your fill of my mother's shrine? I made it myself." He had a small smile on his face. When I didn't answer he added, "Didn't anybody tell you that it's *rude* to touch other people's things?"

THIRTY EIGHT

Erin

"FASTER, ALEX."

We reached the ground floor of the house. Tension made my movements clumsy, but so far I had seen no evidence of Peter. I fought the panic that was clinging to my spine, keeping my back ramrod straight. I needed to stay calm.

"Alex, I need to find her and get out of here. *Now*." I was a broken record, I knew, but Alex didn't seem to understand.

I walked half a step behind him, still amazed at the quiet strength housed inside his skinny body. This was the big brother I had cuddled and argued with – and yet he was a complete stranger. I didn't recognise anything in his mannerisms, the little head toss as he turned to check on me, the shrug of his shoulder that was neither Mum nor Dad.

"This way." His voice was hoarse, full of emotion.

He wasn't one for words. That much was still the Alex I had once known.

We came to what must have been the conservatory. I

flinched, not wanting to see the room that I remembered from my dreams.

"We don't have to go in there, Alex. I don't need to see it—"

"How come you don't remember anything, Jilly?"

Alex had stopped dead in front of the doors that led into the conservatory. I could see the bars of pale light through the strip of glass, could imagine the early morning cold before the sun had a chance to warm it. I didn't need to see it. I didn't want to.

"I hit my head…"

"Didn't you ever think about me?" he asked.

"All the time."

"Why didn't you come back? Why didn't you… bring people sooner?"

"I…" I felt shame burn my cheeks pink. "I tried. But the hospital – the dogs, my head… I couldn't find you."

Alex shook his head, as though that was the end of that conversation, but as he opened the door to the conservatory and ignored my plea for us to go another way, he spoke again.

"I just want to show you one more thing," he said.

"Okay…" This was Alex and I would do anything for him. I would. It was just hard to remember what it was like to have a brother, to think of what he needed, like he had always done for me. And what if Peter came back before we found Harriet?

But he was my *brother*.

The conservatory was different from in my dream. Sparse, a few small chairs and a table. I located the corner, though, where the two of us had sat.

"It was good, sitting here," Alex said. "Then – she came. She told us what had happened and that she'd look after us. About Mum and Dad. Do you remember?"

"I…"

I remembered the cake. But Alex was so desperate. I could see the gleam in his eyes.

"Jilly, do you *remember*?"

If this was the price I had to pay for my brother…

"Yes," I lied. "I remember."

Alex slumped in relief, a long breath shooting out of him.

"And you remember what happened afterwards? Outside? When we ran and ran after the other boy helped us?"

The other boy.

"I…"

I did remember. A stolen key, cold and heavy in the palm of my hand. That was why Alex had brought me here. To the conservatory. I scanned the wall of glass until I saw the panel that was actually a door, the handle brass and solid…

"Randeep gave us a key," I said. I recalled long limbs, trembling fingers, and a boy who had already lost everything and was willing to lose more to help us.

"*Go now*," he'd whispered. "*Go and I'll keep them busy. Tell somebody about Jas.*"

And then Alex had grabbed my hand and dragged me out across the lawn and we ran as the sky darkened and the sun began to set. It was so cold, our bare feet frozen and sore, our new nightclothes soon caked in mud from the torrential rain. The dark swollen clouds overhead, the rushing sound of water…

"Oh, Alex…"

"You do remember," he whispered.

"Come with me again, Alex," I said. "We can go home. Mum – oh my God, Mum will be so happy to see you. Dad – Dad's gone."

I'd never allowed myself to acknowledge it before, how Alex had always borne Dad's drunken moods, how he'd let himself be needled and put down because it took the pressure off me. How he'd always spirited me away to a different world. But now I saw it – and it was too late.

Alex's throat bobbed as he swallowed his tears. I reached for him but he yanked his arm back.

"Why won't you stay here with me?" he said. "It's not so bad. It's… it's a bit cold now. Not like before. But we can stay here. We still have some money; it's hers but nobody needs to know. It's not perfect but it's *good*."

"Alex, you're not making sense. He'll come back," I said. "Then what?"

I didn't want to tell Alex about the threats, about the break-ins and Monica and Jenny. I didn't want to scare him. Somewhere along the way he had stopped being my older brother and now I felt like I needed to look after him. I wanted to protect Alex from Peter because I couldn't do it before. Alex was playing right into the psycho's hands.

"Alex, I don't understand why you feel safe here. Children died. Dana and her son *killed them*."

"No. They didn't. It wasn't like—"

"They *did*, Alex. Jaswinder. The girl who died right before

385

we got here? Don't you remember her?" I saw her hollow, slack face swimming before my eyes. Red candles around her like a shrine, one snuffed out.

"*No*," Alex repeated.

His footsteps stuttered on the wooden floor. I thought suddenly of the potting shed. Could Harriet be in there? I couldn't wait for him any longer, not with freedom, escape, so close.

Suddenly I couldn't rein it in any more. The frustration and fear burst out of me, and the volume in this glass room was shocking.

"Alex, for fuck's sake snap out of it!" I shouted. "I need to find Harriet and if you won't help me then at least tell me where to look."

I yanked on the door to the conservatory, finding that it wasn't locked, and then I was stumbling outside, and very briefly I wondered if I was still drunk because this wasn't making any sense. I should have called the police, taken the risk. Harriet might already be dead.

Alex followed me outside silently, watching as a blackbird shot out of a tree and into the sky at my exit. He seemed more wary out here, his shoulders hunched against the cold wind. In his t-shirt he must have been freezing.

"This way, then," he said.

We cut across the grass at a jog. Alex led me past the potting shed, which seemed bigger down here, and I shivered at the memory of the darkness, the wetness, the blindfold... I hated that it only came back in pieces. I wanted to grab my brain and shake it. I made myself look at it as we passed. It wasn't the same now. It was older, damaged, a jagged maw torn in the panelling. It was dark inside. I went cold as my memories surged again.

We ran for a minute or so, Alex surprisingly fit.

We were out of sight of the house in just minutes, the trees growing around us as we reached the end of the wild lawn. I could see the lake between the edges of the trees, glittering in the morning light.

Suddenly Alex branched left. I skidded on the wet, ropey grass, my breath coming short.

"This way…" Alex was muttering, and I couldn't make out his words. Then his pace quickened again and we ran between tall silver birches that seemed like ghosts standing watch.

And then I saw where we were heading, and my skin was on fire and my heart was bursting out of my chest. I stopped dead, just short of the small clearing. Alex kept going until he reached the middle, and when he turned his grin was triumphant.

He was stood by a well. I knew it. I *remembered* it. I felt sick.

"Jilly, look."

He started to push the cover off. It was heavy, corrugated metal that screamed as he tilted his weight into moving it to one side. I knew that the disused well was not filled with water. Not any more. Somebody had filled it in, a long time ago. Now it was sand and dirt, maybe five feet deep – although it had seemed like much more back then.

I knew because we had both been inside it.

"*Alex…*"

I couldn't move.

The darkness had been absolute. The moon was out by the time we'd made it here that night, terrified and panting. Alex gripping my hand the whole way. A little part of both of us wanted to go back to the warmth of the house. To the nurse lady and her son. But we had both needed to rest, to plan. We weren't ready to face the woods. Neither of us wanted to die.

"Jilly, come look."

Alex's voice brought me back to the present and I inched closer even though my whole body was screaming to run. I moved one hand slowly to my pocket but nothing there could comfort me now.

What if the well wasn't empty? What if it was Harriet in there? I couldn't hear anything. No crying, no tears of pain. My bowels turned to water.

"It's a bit dark in there, actually. Here."

Alex reached into his pocket.

He pulled out my lighter. The one I'd lost in the hotel car park.

"No," I whispered. "What about Peter?"

His expression didn't change.

"Peter's gone," Alex said. "He isn't coming back."

I could see it now. I finally understood. Peter was gone. Like Jas was gone. Like Dana and Monica were gone. What about Harriet?

"I'm trying to show you. So that you *remember*—"

Peter was gone and only Alex was left.

"Alex," I said, my blood curdling in my veins. "What have you done?"

AFTER

Alex

DANA WAS AFRAID OF Peter. Alex could tell, by the way she spoke to him, by the way she bought him only the best clothes and toys and gave him the biggest bedroom, but also by the way she refused to touch him. She recoiled from him as though his skin might poison her.

Perhaps it would. Alex had been touched – more than once in the last few weeks – by those surprisingly delicate hands, and every time he felt a little bit less like the Alex he was before. It was as though something had snapped deep inside him when he'd watched Jilly tumble down that hill and land in a heap at the bottom. She had looked so small, so helpless, even though she had always seemed so strong. He hadn't meant to hurt her. He'd wanted to save her. And now he could never go home – not knowing what he'd done.

He knew he'd hurt her, because if she'd been okay she would have come back for him. She'd have sent help. But she hadn't.

The morning after Jilly escaped, the sky still dark, Dana

and Peter made a start. Alex watched them both wipe down the length of the conservatory where he and Jillian had sat just a week or so ago, the smell of bleach strong inside his nose. Peter was the one giving the orders, his mother nodding as though they'd done this before. But she did as he said. She had been outside most of the night. Whether she was looking for Jilly or doing something else, Alex didn't know.

Alex was terrified, but he was also fascinated. At home Dad was the one who made the rules, and it was like nobody noticed how unfair they were so long as Alex was the only one they hurt.

Dana and Peter weren't like that.

After they'd cleaned up they tied Alex and Randeep to the bottom of the stairs while they filled the car. Books, candles, clothes. Nothing big, but all of the essentials. Bathroom things, Dana's scrubs, bin bags, razors. Alex knew that Dana shaved her hands, her arms. He'd felt how soft they were, how smooth, when she'd brought him here.

Every time Peter passed Alex on the stairs, he smiled. Alex hated that smile. So, to distract Peter, Alex started to ask questions. And to his surprise, Peter answered them.

Randeep was silent. He'd been crying for hours and now he was completely frozen. Alex had been so grateful, yesterday, for the key. So he and Jilly could escape. But now he was angry at the other boy. Why didn't he make any sort of effort? If he carried on like this he'd get himself killed.

Alex tried not to think about Jillian. He tried not to think of the alternative future where she might have led the police right to him so he could go home. That hurt too much.

When the packing was done, Mother blindfolded Alex and Randeep and carried them both to the car. Peter told them to lie in the back under heavy blankets. But he let Alex take his blindfold off. Just Alex, not Randeep.

"Don't tell Mother," he said.

Alex knew he should try to run. But he saw the way Peter and Mother looked at Randeep, as though he was already dead, and he couldn't do it. Without Jilly he wasn't brave.

It still wasn't quite light out when they stopped driving. The whole way Alex had felt Randeep trembling against him, but he felt numb. He had no idea where they were, now. Dark trees, a stone wall, a little house.

Inside they locked him and Randeep in the bathroom. Then he heard a car engine again, and Peter knocked on the bathroom door to get their attention.

"Mother's gone to deal with the police," he said.

Alex knew that the police would never find the basement rooms behind that bookcase, not unless they knew they were there. And Peter's mother was clever.

But Alex could be clever, too.

So he started to tell Peter a story. He told lies about Jilly. About how she'd *made* him run. About how he never wanted to go. And by the end, he didn't know how he was supposed to feel any more. He thought about that a lot over the following days, and weeks.

He realised he was angry. Angry at himself, for pushing Jilly. And… he was angry at Jilly, too. It filled him with a sick feeling but he was so angry that she hadn't been strong, that she had been hurt. Maybe the anger masked something else, but anger was safer than sadness, so he let it grow.

But he also felt relieved. Peter and Dana had accepted him again, as though he hadn't nearly ruined it all. He wasn't like Randeep's sister, who had died. He wasn't like Randeep, who had given up.

After a long while in the bathroom, Peter let him out. Just him, not Randeep. He let Alex watch TV. Things were almost... normal. Until one day, they were watching while Dana was at work and the news came on. Peter let him watch. And Alex saw Jillian.

Alive.

Alex felt that anger flare again, but this time it was so hot, so white, that he saw nothing but sparks. She was alive, Dad was holding her, and she had never come back for him. She had let him believe she was *dead*. Alex could hardly breathe, but he fought the anger and looked away.

Later on Peter came to him. Silently he handed Alex a syringe filled with a clear liquid. The lid was on but Alex was still worried he'd accidentally stab himself.

"He has to be punished," Peter said. He took Alex aside with an arm around his shoulders, and led him into the bedroom. Alex was allowed into the whole upstairs of the house now, as long as he didn't go too near the windows.

"You told me you knew Randeep would try to run, like his sister," Alex said. "You thought he might try to get Jilly and me out because he was angry."

Alex thought about Jas, who had died before he and Jillian

had even come to the big house. Somehow he felt nothing, as though they were just stories in a book, not real people.

"I did," Peter agreed, "but he still shouldn't have done it. He failed the test. I mean, look what happened to your sister. It's his fault she didn't come back. He scared her. If we don't punish him we're as bad as he is. If Mother had punished Chris more after Father left – like she punished me – he would still be alive and none of this would have happened. Because of Randeep we had to leave Dove and now we can probably never go back. Because of him and your stupid sister."

They went into the bathroom. Randeep was barely conscious. Alex wondered how much of the morphine Peter had given him to keep him calm. It was liquid, like the kind people used in hospitals, or on old people. That's what Peter said. You just squirted it into their mouths and it chilled them right out… Alex had seen the cabinet where Dana kept all of her medicines, in a little black box with a combination lock, opening it only when she stole a little more. But Peter knew the code.

Randeep's head lolled back, his body sprawled on the floor. He glanced at Peter – older, wise somehow beyond his years.

"You gonna do the honours?" Peter asked.

He gestured to the syringe in Alex's hand. Alex looked down at it dimly, and then back at Peter. This boy was his only chance. With Jilly gone, who else did Alex have? Dad had seen them, that night, and he hadn't even found a way to help. And Jilly – she was alive and she still hadn't come back for him.

Alex knew he could hang on. Maybe the police would find him one day. But he didn't know how long Peter would be patient. Wouldn't it be better to have Peter as a brother than to be dead like Jas?

"You want *me* to do it?" Alex asked.

Peter shrugged as though he didn't care either way, except they both knew he did.

"It's easy," he said. "You just pinch some skin – there – and put it in at an angle. Then push it down. You don't have to do much, it's fine even with your little hands."

Alex looked down at his hands. The fingers were skinny, the palms small. He tried to imagine them pinching Randeep's skin, pushing the pale liquid in through the needle.

"Come on, Alex," Peter chided. "You know he can't stay in the bathroom forever. And we'll never be able to trust him now."

Alex looked at the syringe again and then at Randeep's face.

It wouldn't be that hard. Just put the needle in and push the top down. The other boy wouldn't feel it. And really... *I have to do it or else it'll happen to me.*

The words were crystal clear in his mind.

"It's his fault your sister is gone," Peter said again. "If it wasn't for him she'd still be with us and we'd still be in the big house. We could go swimming in the lake and read in front of the fire and pick apples in the orchard. And now we just have this tiny, crappy little house. He needs to be punished."

It was this or death. Alex couldn't die without talking to Jilly again. Not without finding out why she hadn't come back. Not without being sure she hadn't forgotten him.

"Okay," Alex said.

It wasn't as easy as Peter said, but he did it.

THIRTY NINE

Erin

"I WANTED TO TELL you, Jilly. I wanted to ask you why you never came back, but I couldn't find you. And then, when I found you, you didn't even notice me – you were always so *busy* you didn't even see me." Alex held my lighter between his thumb and forefinger, the distance between us closing as I inched towards the well.

"If you hurt Harriet…" The threat sounded empty even to my ears. I had nothing to bargain with. No sounds came from the well and I felt fear worming deep in my gut. If she was unconscious – or worse, *dead*… "How long has she been in there?"

"Oh for goodness' sake! It's always about other people with you. See for yourself."

The animal was back. Alex flicked the lighter towards me and it landed in the dirt.

"I thought you'd be pleased to have that back. You dropped it outside your hotel, you know. Anybody could have picked it up."

Finally I was close enough to peer into the well. I didn't

reach for the lighter – didn't want to give him a chance to catch me off guard. Instead I let my eyes search the darkness for Harriet's red hair, her pale skin.

Vomit rose in my throat. It wasn't Harriet. My body went cold, my knees buckling.

"Why, Alex…?"

Jenny Bowles was dead. I could see the waxy colour of her skin, that absolute, final stillness. My belly turned somersaults, but I was too bewildered to fight the spike of relief – *it wasn't Harriet*.

"Why her?" Alex asked. "I needed you to remember. And I could tell she was starting to crack again. She told me – how she was sure Peter killed her boys. How they didn't run away. He *didn't*, you know. And they *did* run away. It was just that Mother found them. Jenny saw Peter a few years ago. She recognised him, and she started saying she was going to tell. We had to threaten her. To make her shut up. It was fine until your friend called her. She started to panic again, blew things all out of proportion. I went to see her and she said that was it, it was over, she wasn't going to be afraid any more. So I fixed it."

"Alex—"

"If you'd have remembered faster I wouldn't have had to do it."

"Don't—"

But he was on a roll. "You forgot about me. You pushed me so far from your mind that you *forgot* it all."

"I didn't!" I shouted.

Alex watched me carefully, like a lion might regard its prey. His eyes were on my face. I wondered if he could see what I meant. I never forgot about *him*.

I inched my foot closer towards the lighter, until my sole was pressing it into the dirt.

"I'm sorry," I whispered. "Okay? Is that what you want to hear? Why don't you just kill me?"

"Sorry?" Alex let out a barking laugh. "Sorry fixes everything, right? Your 'sorry' takes away everything that happened? You didn't come back, and they made us leave the house, and now look how it's falling down. While you've been *moving on*, buying a nice place, a car, I've been having to go back to that shitty little house to get warm, to think, sleeping in the cold, stealing stuff I can't afford. Mother is dead and her savings are the only money I have left. You don't think about these things, do you? So yeah, Jilly, I'm angry at you. But I never wanted to *kill* you."

"Then what do you want?"

"I want – *you*." He made a sweeping gesture with his hands. "I wanted you to know I was still here. I wanted you to know that I *survived*. I wanted you to be my sister again. Is that too much to ask?"

"But all that death, those threats... Why?"

Alex frowned, his eyes going blank.

"People just... they just moved on. I followed Randeep's mother, Jacob's mother. Peter told me all about them. How they'd forget about us, how they'd just go about their lives as though nothing ever happened. Peter was right. They never cared about any of us."

"Alex, it's been years. They have memorials, they get

together to remember. That's what healthy people do—"

"No they don't!" Alex shouted. A muscle bunched in his neck. "You don't *move on*, Jilly. You should never forget."

"I didn't forget about you!"

I wanted to grab the lighter. If nothing else maybe I could throw it at his head hard enough to distract him while I ran. But what then? I felt cold terror seep into my very bones. I was trapped and he knew it.

"I can see it, Jill. In your eyes."

"But if it's about us, about *me*, why kill Monica?"

"She was a fucking distraction!" This laugh was so loud I jumped. "Jesus, you've got no idea. I was there, the whole time. I followed you. I waited on street corners, outside that stupid bar. And you never even *saw me*. So I got rid of her. And the writer."

Harriet. My body began to tremble.

"What did you do to her?"

"Don't worry," he said, rolling his eyes again. "She's safe. Insurance. Not that I need her any more. You were so *slow*, Jilly. I had to get you up here somehow. So I put the cow in the well and thought, well, if I could recreate things for you a little bit then you might remember. You might come home."

Home? The word filled me with dread. But Alex was getting tired of talking. I needed more time to plan, to figure out what I was going to do. I had to keep him distracted.

"After I was gone, they looked after you, didn't they?" I fumbled for the words. "They made you a part of their – family? A new brother, for Peter… is that right?"

He didn't answer.

"What happened, Alex? Did they tell you that we wouldn't miss you, that Dad didn't love you? When he died the last thing he said was your name."

"It doesn't matter now," Alex said coldly. "You're here now. We can be a family again."

As he said this I realised, truly, what was happening. He'd lost the family he'd created, one way or another. Dana was dead. Peter was gone too. Now he wanted me back. But Alex didn't know what family was any more.

"That's right," I said slowly. "I'm here. You don't need Harriet if you've got me. We can explain that it's a misunderstanding and I'll stay here with you. I have money. We can do whatever you want, fix this place up…"

He relaxed. He wanted for all of this to go away, for it to be me and him again, like before.

"You can help me to remember—"

"Stop it," Alex said wearily. "Just stop."

"Will you take me to Harriet?"

"I will," he said, "if you'll shut up."

Then Alex turned his back, as though he knew I wouldn't run – and he was right. But quickly, I bent to the ground and picked up my lighter, shoving it in my pocket. And I slipped my phone out, found the text to Wendy, and hit send. There was still one bar of signal. Hopefully the message would go before my battery died.

* * *

The trek back to the house seemed to take much longer. It was as though Alex had been fighting, before, to seem normal. Now he didn't care. Demons swarmed between us, ghosts of what had happened, what *hadn't* happened, and the years that had passed since we'd last been together in this place.

Alex's hands were in his pockets the whole time, his shoulders hunched against the brisk wind. Eventually the house loomed back into view. The bricks looked ice-cold even in the sunshine that now lit the building from one side.

I stumbled and Alex's hand whipped from his pocket – a small switch knife in his grasp.

"*Be careful,*" he grunted.

I bit back the fear that surged.

"Where are we going?"

"Back inside."

I tried to focus, to push thoughts of Harriet from my mind. Inside I might find a weapon. A chair, a lamp, anything heavy or solid…

Alex shoved me back through the open conservatory doors. Into the dim house, towards the bookcase, which he pulled back. It was no wonder the police never found anything. How could they have known? But Alex didn't wait for me now and I had to hurry to keep up.

Then we were back in the dark warren of corridors and passages.

"Stop."

We had reached a dead end. I wasn't sure if I'd been down this hallway earlier, but the passages all looked the same, long and narrow, some with doors just on one side but others opposite each other where the corridor narrowed. The doors were plain, dark wood, adorned with—

Shit.

"Why are they all locked?" I asked. Four doors, and four shiny dead bolts were screwed onto the outsides. Locked from the outside.

Alex barely looked at me. "It's just the way it is."

"You said you'd take me to Harriet."

My brother, still holding the knife, pulled back one of the bolts. The door opened onto a small room, large enough for a bare single mattress and a bucket with a little room either side. It was so dim I could barely see anything except the books that were piled haphazardly against a wall, their pages yellow and mildewed. Against another were several metal jerry cans.

"What are you doing?" I asked.

"In there." Alex pointed.

"I'm not going anywhere until I see her."

"Get in the room and you can see her," he snapped.

Then I heard it. A muffled tapping. It came from the room opposite.

"Harriet?"

"Erin?" Panicked, tired. "Is that you?"

"Harriet—"

"Get in the fucking room, Jilly."

I stood, indecision burning, before I finally did what he asked. I stepped into the open room, not far in but far enough to feel the claustrophobia sink in. There was a battery-powered light by the door, like a camping lantern, which cast the opening in a dim white light. He waited until I was far enough in and then, still gripping the knife, he reached over to the other deadbolt opposite.

"I'm going to open it – for a second. So you can see her. If you try to run I will kill her. Do you understand?"

"Yes."

Alex unlocked the door. He pulled it open, just a little. Harriet was on the floor in a room that was so small her knees were tight to her chest. A cupboard.

"I had to restrain her. She's *fine*," he said.

"Are you okay?" I asked. Harriet's face was pale, blood smeared down one side. She had bruises under both of her eyes as though he'd hit her very hard. "All that blood…"

"Most of it isn't mine. It's from the shed where I woke up. I think he killed somebody in there."

"Jenny," I said. "It's – it's going to be okay. This is Alex. He was just explaining how we got it all wrong—"

"I'm not stupid," Alex cut in. "I know she's not going to let this go."

"But you said you'd let her leave!"

"Yes. Well. Once we're gone she'll have all the time in the world to get herself out."

And then he swung the door shut and slid the bolt home. He turned to me, his eyes shining.

"I'll go and get the car ready." He stepped in, pushing me further into the room. I noticed a metal loop on one wall, a piece of rope attached.

"Wait!" I exclaimed. "Where are we going? I thought we were staying here?"

I was frozen to the spot as he grabbed the rope, knife still pointed at my chest. The only time he let it drop was when he tied the rope to my wrist. I should have run, but I *couldn't*. I wanted to launch myself at him, I wanted to claw at his face, but I couldn't make my limbs obey.

Alex pulled the rope hard, so hard it grazed my skin. "You stay there," he said. He went to the wall and picked up one of the jerry cans — it looked like the ones I remembered my dad throwing away when we were little. I remembered how Dad had struggled to lift them when they were full, and yet Alex picked this one up as if he was used to the weight.

"I'll come and get you in a minute. I wanted things to work out differently, but it's clear we'll have to go to plan B. Good job I had multiple plans. 'Always have a backup,' that's what I was taught. That's why I took these."

He held up one hand, and glinting between his thumb and forefinger were Harriet's car keys. I'd forgotten about them, but Alex hadn't. When had he taken them? My brain stuttered with panic.

"Alex, wait!"

But he was at the door already. He turned back to me and shook his head.

"No, Jilly. I've waited for eighteen years. It's your turn now."

FORTY

Harriet

"ERIN? ERIN, ARE YOU okay?"

The man had locked the door again and left me in darkness, but I could still hear them talking, their voices charged with emotion. *Alex*, Erin had said. Alex. Her brother. So it was true. The blond boy in the second photograph hadn't been Chris, after all. It was Alex.

"Erin, answer me, please?"

After a moment I heard her voice. "I'm sorry, Harriet." She sounded like she was crying. "This is all my fault. I can't believe—"

"You need to calm down," I said firmly. "He might come back at any minute. We need to get out of here."

"How?" she wept. Her voice was muffled behind two doors but I knew she was freaking out. "He took the car keys. I didn't even call the police. He said if I told anybody we were here, he'd kill you. Harriet, nobody is coming for us."

I felt my stomach drop but fought the fear.

"Are you hurt?" I asked.

"No."

I could picture the new terror on her face. If I didn't get a handle on this she'd spiral into a full-blown panic attack like the other night.

"Good," I said calmly. "Have you got your phone? He took mine while I was unconscious."

"I – he didn't take mine. I think he wanted to… Trust me? But my battery—"

"One step at a time. Are you tied up?"

There was a scuffling noise, like trainers scrabbling for purchase on a floor. Then something rolling.

"Not any more."

"Good. Send a text message – don't try to call, it'll take more battery."

"I tried to send a text before. I don't know if it went." Another pause, then a screech. "Fuck, Harriet. My phone is dead. I don't know… I don't know if Wendy got the message. I should have sent it sooner!"

"Okay, Erin." A wobble of fear shook me but I fought it again. "It's okay. It doesn't matter. We need to focus. Listen to me, we can fight this. We're together, aren't we?"

"Yes." Erin was silent for a moment. "What are we going to do? There's nothing in here. Mattress, bucket…" Then she stopped. "I don't know what's in these."

"In what?"

"These metal jug things. Jerry jugs? They look – I'm not sure." There was a metallic sound, and then, "It says flammable on the side. Smells like – petrol? But they're basically empty."

"For his car." The pieces fell into place. "He's been living off the grid, I guess, probably keeps the fuel so he doesn't have to go to a petrol station around here. Because of the cameras… Are they heavy?"

"Yes, pretty heavy."

"Can you use one of them to knock the door handle out? The bolt isn't too much higher, you might be able to reach it."

"I don't know. I can try…"

"Good," I said. "Good, Erin. Please try."

There was a clanging, thudding sound, like metal on wood. Then scraping. Then something else and Erin's muffled curse. And then, nothing.

"Erin? Are you okay?" I tried in vain to see, forcing my face up against the crack in the door but it was too thin, and there wasn't much room to move. "*Erin?*"

And then another noise. Footsteps. I felt my heart lurch. Surely he couldn't be back already, could he? I scrambled upright, knees bent, ready to kick out at him if he opened the door again.

It did open, and—

"Ow!"

My feet connected with Erin's thigh.

"Jesus, Harriet."

She clutched her leg, stood before me like some sort of dishevelled angel. A strange, confused frown on her face.

"God, Erin, I'm sorry." I looked behind her. The door, and the lock, were still intact. "You didn't have to break anything?"

"He left the door unlocked."

A look of understanding slowly dawned on her face. She offered me a hand and I took it, feeling my body ache and tremble. My head was still pounding.

"Why would he—"

"It's what Peter did. To… train them? If they were good, they wouldn't leave. It's like he's testing me. He didn't tie me up properly. The knot was tight but he left one hand free…"

She saw the look on my face, the barely disguised disgust at what he had endured, and her expression shifted.

"I know," she said.

I wanted to hug her, wanted to feel her solidness to remind me that this was real. She was here, and he had been foolish enough to put us together. But Erin kept her distance and I could tell she was trying to formulate a plan.

"What now?" she asked dully. "What the fuck do we do now? He's got the car keys and we'll never get out of here without a car. It's miles to the nearest public road. The woods… I can't go back in there…"

"We've got to come up with some sort of plan."

Erin let out a quiet, incredulous laugh.

I stepped into the corridor and looked around, taking in the darkness. The rooms with their deadbolts. There had to be something.

"Can we use one of those jugs in your room to knock him out?" I asked.

Erin bit her lip. "Maybe, but I don't think it'll do much good. They're empty but they're still hard to lift, and it's going to be difficult to aim it because they're so unwieldy. And he lifted that other one so easily, and that one wasn't empty... He's stronger than he looks. I don't want to take the chance."

I continued searching while Erin talked. The first locked door led to another empty room. "Fuck."

"Harriet, we have to make a decision." She looked stronger now, as though running out of options had given her some steel back. "He's going to come back any minute and he'll take me with him. If the police don't get here in time, if Wendy doesn't get my message... I wanted to protect him. From Peter." She shook her head. "But he's not my brother any more. He's a *monster*. I'm fucking done worrying about him."

"Okay," I said. "Let's think logically. What have we got?"

I glanced around again. We had empty petrol cans. A corridor. Some rooms. A little time. We could run, into the woods, but Alex was stronger than both of us, and I'd seen the knife he was carrying. If he caught us, at least one of us would end up dead.

I opened another door – and pointed.

"Erin, look."

There were more petrol cans inside. Two of them. The first was empty, but the second – easily three quarters full. But what good was petrol without...

"Erin, what else have you got in your pockets? You normally have cigarettes and—"

"My lighter!" Erin crowed. She fumbled in her pocket, pulling out the beat-up plastic thing triumphantly. It was filthy, covered in mud and grass, and I wasn't sure if it would still work. But it was better than nothing.

"Okay. I think I have an idea. How brave do you feel?" I asked.

"I... I don't know. Oh Jesus, do you know what you're doing?"

I shook my head. But Erin had moved closer, ready to listen. If we couldn't run, that would mean we were going to have to fight.

An unspoken question hovered between us: *how badly are we willing to hurt him?*

FORTY ONE

Erin

I CREPT THROUGH THE hallways like a lost child, trying to calm my thumping heart. I didn't want to do this – any of it. Finding Harriet, seeing her boxed up in that tiny room, had set something loose in me, something both wild and resigned; I was *so tired* of feeling like I was teetering on a knife point.

But I kept going because of Harriet, too. I was afraid – of my own brother. I was afraid that he would catch me, like he always had in the games we played as children, and that once he had me, he wouldn't let go.

I hurried out of the labyrinthine maze of dark corridors, sliding out from behind the bookcase and making sure I pulled it well away from the hidden door. Sweat dripped down my back from the exertion.

When I came to the conservatory the daylight was a surprise. It felt like years since I had been out here, since Jenny and the garden and the well… I couldn't believe she was dead and he'd just left her there. The thought made me feel ill, sickness rising above the fear.

I hoped Harriet was right about this, that she knew what she was doing. I hoped that she could be quick, and that I could be convincing enough to make it work.

I followed the faint tug of memory towards a patch in the woods where Dana had kept her car. I recalled the sensation of lifting my blindfold, seeing the thin path cut in moonlight around to the side of the house. A clearing beyond the trees. It wasn't much different now, only this time it seemed much closer.

I stepped forward. Everything in me screamed that I should be running *away* from my brother, not creeping towards him, and yet I took another step into the tree-line. Another—

Crack.

The sound of my foot snapping the body of a twig reverberated in the quiet. My heart leapt – it was too soon. I hadn't meant to do that. For a second I froze, breathed, tried not to break down into tears and wait for death.

And then my brother appeared around the edge of a tree. He had a duffel bag in his hands, and the empty can of petrol sat nearby. Our eyes met. He dropped the bag just as I let out a little involuntary wail.

I wanted to run. I needed to. But I was frozen. I was prey, trapped in his vicious sights, and all my traitorous body could do was tremble.

"Jilly? I told you to stay put."

"I…" Panic. I could barely see straight, a screech in my ears yelling *run run run!* But still I didn't move. I was back to being his little sister again.

"I wanted to help you. Where – where are we going?"

"It's not important. Jilly, what are you doing out here? Where's your friend?"

"I…" I knew I should lie. I must be able to make something up; I'd had years of practice of telling people I was *okay*. It couldn't be that hard! "I…"

My body jerked.

Alex threw himself forwards, as if expecting me to bolt. I screamed, dropping to my knees in the dirt and raising my hands over my head.

"Alex, please," I sobbed. "Don't make me do this. I don't want to go!"

He was close now, within reach. He could grab me and throw me in the back of that rusty old Land Rover and there would be nothing I could do. He was stronger than me, bigger, faster.

"Please, just let me go. We don't have to do this."

"You said you wouldn't leave me again," he said. Spittle flecked his words. "Jilly, you *promised* me."

"I didn't think—"

"You didn't think we would have to leave? We can't stay here now, can we?"

"Alex—"

"This is all your fault. If you'd just remembered me, if you'd just come back…"

He was right.

"I'm sorry."

"Right. You should have stayed in the house. I'm disappointed that you couldn't even pass that one little test."

He paused. "Well. Since you're here, we might as well make a move. *Sorry*."

My own apology repeated back with such a vicious edge was the final straw. It was an armour built of courage, bolted like a metal plate over my heart. Alex was never going to be the brother I'd lost.

So I nodded. As if resigned. And then I waited, just a second, watching for the sloping tilt of Alex's shoulder as he relaxed a little. Just a little – that movement, at least, hadn't changed. And then I sprang up from my position on the ground, and broke into a run.

But Alex was ready for me. His arm shot out faster than I would have thought possible, his fist connecting with my jaw so hard I felt it in my belly. I scrambled in the dirt, knees and elbows and fingers. Alex grabbed my jacket, but I kicked out. I managed to wriggle free. Instead of running, this time I threw myself at him, tackling him to the ground.

Alex was taken by surprise. I heard the solid *oomph* of air rush out of him as his back hit the wet grass and I leapt to my feet, already running. I pumped my arms and legs as fast as I could, darting across the lawn with speed that shocked me.

In the conservatory I threw furniture against the doors, just enough to slow him down. Alex was still a few hundred yards behind me, clutching his mid-section. I hurtled down the dark hallways, through the hidden door, panic bringing an iron taste to my tongue, until I was back opposite Harriet's little room. She wasn't there. I looked around, wildly, eyes scanning the dimness. She was meant to be back by now. She was—

Alex was behind me. He was filthy, panting. I felt myself go cold. I couldn't let this happen.

I was trapped. My back to the room he'd shut me in.

"Oh, Jilly," said Alex.

Where was Harriet?

AFTER EVERYTHING

Alex

THE FIRST TIME HE had the thought he ignored it. He knew it was just the changes talking, adjusting to a new life. Dana had said it would take some getting used to – for all of them. They all had to take it slow.

Alex was trying to move on. Even though he had only lived in that big old house for almost three weeks, he knew it would impact him forever. Sleeping in the basement, the promise of that bedroom with a view of the garden, it had really changed how he thought about things.

The little house wasn't bad. It was about the same size as the one he'd lived in before, with Jilly. And Mum and Dad. But it couldn't have felt more different. Here he shared a room with Peter instead of Jilly. And there was no *waiting* for Dad to lose his cool. If anything, Dana was more worried about Alex and Peter than they were about her. She even let them keep the big bedroom.

The house was old, but Dana had kept it nice when she

415

got married. Her mother had lived there for a while. Dana had enough money saved to keep paying the bills after her mother died, and she had continued to clean it once every week without telling anybody. Now they were all glad she had.

Slowly, a routine started to develop.

Alex couldn't stop thinking about how he'd seen Jilly on the TV. They'd talked about her 'escape' from the Father, how she'd risked her life to get away.

But Jillian *hadn't risked anything*. That had been Alex, all Alex. He thought about the way she was, even now, using him to protect herself, and his anger towards her grew. He had felt so guilty. He had mourned her. And it had been a lie.

The rest of the world was just the same as before. But what wasn't the same was Peter. And Dana. And everything Alex had done. He felt connected, now, in a way he never had before. Not even with Jilly, who always thought he was a bit soft, a bit weak, *cute*. She had never seen the way he felt when Dad picked on him. When Mum told him to stop being so sensitive. He'd hidden it from her, but she still should have noticed. Peter and Dana, though, they knew how capable he was.

And, Peter said, Alex was like them now. He would be tied to them forever, or risk getting put in jail himself. Alex knew that was true.

After a while Dana said she wanted the boys to interact with other children, but she never stopped working, probably hunting too, just watching other children now, old habits hard to break. The boys didn't mind; she left them to do whatever they wanted, and they both knew she wouldn't bring home another one. Alex was the final child she'd ever need.

They didn't want to go to school. Alex had never liked school anyway, and Dana didn't make them go. Alex wasn't sure how he'd get into a school even if he wanted to, how anybody wouldn't know who he was. And eventually he realised he didn't want to be found, not any more.

But the boys couldn't settle in the little house, no matter how hard they tried. It felt safe, sure, but not special. That early connection between them was never the same as in those few days when Alex had first been allowed out of the bathroom. Before Randeep. Before Alex found out about Jillian.

"I feel like I'm dying," Peter confided years later. Alex didn't know how long exactly. He'd sort of lost track. Days, weeks, didn't mean anything any more, especially when they kept having the same conversations. Peter always confided in Alex, never his mother. Alex wasn't afraid of him like Dana was. Not after what had happened with Randeep all that time ago. He'd learned, since Randeep, that there were worse things than Peter. Monsters that lived inside you like dreams until they were nightmares.

"It's like somebody has unplugged us," Alex agreed. "And we've slowly been running out of battery since we left the old house."

"Exactly. I can't focus. I can't sleep. I'm going crazy. I need the house and the lake and the fields and the woods…" Peter got that wistful look on his face. Alex loved this expression the most; it was Peter's most beautiful one. His dark hair and pale skin made him look like an angel.

"You're not going to die," Alex said. "You can't die just because you're bored. It's not possible. Why don't we get Mother to let us take the car this weekend, you can teach me the gears again? We could even go up to the house, look around."

"Don't tell me it's not possible to die from boredom," Peter said, ignoring him. "It's like being without oxygen. Her decisions will kill us both eventually. If we'd stayed in the house after what happened, things would be fine now. The police would never have found the door anyway. We could move back any time, but she won't let us. It's all got to be on her damn terms."

And that's when Alex had the thought: Peter and him, wouldn't they be better off without Dana?

The second time he had the thought it was more intrusive. She came home with three shopping bags filled with cakes and chocolates – a gift for them. The boys had tried to work through some of the schoolwork she'd left them, which they usually did diligently. Alex missed school these days in the same way that Peter did; he missed the books, the learning, but not the people. Even though Alex was sixteen now he still yearned for it sometimes, the real teaching that Dana's lessons never quite captured. He couldn't believe he'd ever hated it.

But when Dana got home that night she was disappointed – in something or other that they'd been working on so hard all day – and she left their treats on the kitchen table instead of giving them to Peter and Alex.

It was such a small thing, but here it meant everything. It

meant a storm was coming. Peter went into one of his quiet rages. He disappeared into the garden, stalking out into the autumn night without even his jacket, leaving Alex alone with her.

Even after all this time he hated being near her without Peter. He understood his brother; they communicated without words, sometimes on such a basic level that they went days without speaking at all. Dana was different. She was distant, selfish to the point that he could see nothing beyond her desire to be the perfect mother – even at the expense of being a decent human being. It was always the way things looked on the outside that mattered. How people in the village looked at them, even though it had been years, whether they paid too much attention to the boys, whether Alex's blond roots were showing again. She didn't care how anybody felt so long as things *looked* right.

When Alex and Dana were alone together, something always shifted. The power, the balance, it all felt wrong. And Alex didn't like it.

Wouldn't the world be better without her? Without her they could go back to the house, back to the freedom of that comforting quiet. He knew how to do it, too. Peter had told him all of the tricks for not being caught. The gloves, the shaving, the ritual. He could do it so easily.

He was sure Peter wouldn't mind.

The third time Alex had the thought it was a long time later. Years had passed. The big house was a distant memory, but it still haunted his dreams – like Jilly did. Then Dana came home later than usual one night. Somebody had finally accused her of stealing patient medicines, and although they hadn't been able to prove it, the stain had stuck.

Alex had preferred it when she was out of the house all of the time. He and Peter would sit and smoke weed, sometimes do the odd job here and there to earn some cash, steal Dana's bank cards and go on spending sprees. Peter's favourite thing to do was to draw out cash using his mother's card and hoard it like dragon treasure – just because he could. Just because he liked the way she panicked, every time, that he was planning to run away.

After Peter taught him how to drive, Alex liked to take the car into other towns on Dana's days off and pretend he was somebody else. It was like a game. Dana and Peter didn't worry about him by then because nobody ever recognised him. The world thought he was dead.

But he realised that the best part of these trips was coming home at the end of the day. Peter waiting for him with a cold beer. They trusted each other and there was a thrill in that.

With Dana home all the time, things were different. There was a tension in the house. All she did was smoke and drink and talk about all of the precious things they'd left at Dove Manor. She talked about the films she'd starred in, about the lady who'd left her all of her money and the house. How she'd once been wildly wealthy. Alex and Peter didn't give a shit about *things* and they didn't care about *stories*.

And this one night, when Dana came home, she was already drunk.

"The jobs are gone, boys," she sobbed.

Peter couldn't get another word out of her, but Alex – after Peter left to shoot beer cans with a BB gun – managed to get her to tell him a little more. She'd been caught stealing. Again.

"We could move back to the house," Alex said. He pleaded – he never pleaded any more. "Couldn't we? Start over?"

"What would that solve? The money won't last forever and neither of you two is good for anything."

"It would be better, there. Like Peter said it was before."

"No," Dana slurred. "For God's sake, boy. *No*. I've told you. We are never going back to that house, never ever *ever* again."

Alex didn't try to fight the maelstrom that rose and battered his defences like a tide. It had been years since Randeep, but he still remembered how it felt. The relief after it was done, like picking at a mosquito bite so hard that it bled.

He turned to her, to his mother, and said, "Okay, Mother. I won't bother you again. Why don't you go and get changed, and I'll run you a nice, hot bath. Sit with you a while, like when I was little. We can talk about your movies."

"Oh, my Bear," she said. He never knew why she called him that, only that it never felt quite right. "You're a good boy. Yes. A bath sounds like just the thing."

When Alex had the thought this time, he didn't reason with it. He didn't ignore it.

He listened.

1 SEPTEMBER 2016

Alex

IT HAD RAINED IN the night. The earth was spongy underfoot, the dirt clinging to the soles of his boots. He didn't come out here much any more – it reminded him too much of the time he and Peter had picnicked on the sand at the end of the long grass near the water. That was about a year after they moved back into the house, and the tension hadn't quite boiled over yet.

That day had been hot and they'd carried a rucksack full of beer and sandwiches down to the lake. They lived on sandwiches in those days. The bread was cheap if you got it discounted and you could always toast it over a fire when it started to go stale – which it did, often, without a fridge to keep it fresh.

They'd lounged until they were hot, frustrated. Everything was piling on. The broken windows, the graffiti that wasn't theirs, the teenagers who disturbed their peace. They would go to the little house sometimes, just to have a space to think, or sometimes to read. Peter had used some of their meagre cash to join a gym, just for the shower, and it drove Alex mad.

They didn't talk about it but it was there, in every inch of their conversations. Or lack of conversation. At some point they would run out of money, they would stop being able to live like this, camping in the old house without drawing attention to themselves.

Peter was angry that Alex hadn't redirected Dana's savings to a different account, that he hadn't thought about electricity or council tax or how they'd be paying for that little house for the rest of their lives because it was in Dana's name and nobody knew she was dead.

That day, on the beach by the lake, something had split. One minute they were drinking beer and the next they were sprawled in the sandy dirt, clawing and elbowing, knees in soft flesh and spittle flying. It ended with Alex's broken nose, Alex holding Peter in the water for a second too long.

That's when things had started to go wrong. And then, just like today, they'd been talking about Jillian. It was always fucking Jillian. Peter would say something casually, something mean, and Alex would retaliate. It was the one thing they hadn't beaten out of him.

Alex dug his heels into the damp earth now, sucking in the evening air. There were gnats out, an autumn haze of them around his head. He wafted at them half-heartedly but his focus was elsewhere, on the earth under him and the mound of dirt.

Jillian didn't know the damage she'd caused when she hadn't come back for him. It had splintered him in more ways than he knew at the time – and only now did he appreciate the mess he'd made. Dana was long gone and he didn't regret that. Not really. But the stuff with Peter…

He tried to sort through his emotions. He'd had a drink too many, which was unusual, and he couldn't get his brain to kick into gear. He thought of Dana, of her gin-and-tonic smell, and wrinkled his nose. She had always got drunk to soothe her pain; he drank because it made him bold. It was different. It didn't make him like his father.

His thoughts kept circling back to Jillian. She was Erin, now. One day, months ago, he had been at the soup kitchen that had sprung up in a community centre in Arkney. Arkney was his favourite place to drive to, the winding roads on the way, the quaint sort of feeling to everything – just close enough to civilisation to feel like an escape from the country. He went to the soup kitchen whenever he could; it was a free meal and they didn't ask too many questions. Besides, nobody had ever recognised him. He was a ghost. And any money he could save on food was grand.

And as he was leaving – he'd seen her.

His sister.

It was like a jolt through his heart, like a defibrillator that sent him into a tailspin before the rhythm evened out again. He would have known it was her even if she hadn't spoken, even if he hadn't heard the same upward lilt she'd always talked with. She had his face, only wider, and his shoulders. Their dad's jaw, just like Alex. He didn't spare a thought for his parents – he tried never to think of either of them, especially after Peter told him how they'd always talked of Jilly, only Jilly, during all those bloody press conferences in the early days.

How glad they were she was alive. She was a miracle. They were so *relieved*...

And Alex, whenever he thought of Jilly, always tasted that bitter anger on his tongue. She had never come back for him. He refused to admit that he missed her.

Refused, until the second he saw her. She was skinnier than he'd thought she would be. Her hair was darker, especially at the ends. Her nose was very fine and pointed and she wore sunglasses that dwarfed her face. But God, it was *her*. And she was walking out of the bank with her phone to her ear and she looked... fine. Normal. Happy, even.

Alex couldn't begin to explain the rage that blossomed within him. Rage and impossible sadness that made him dizzy. The scent of the air was stuck in his nose and he swore he could smell her perfume and the anger boiled over.

His parents had let him go. They didn't care about him. But here was Jillian and *she* should have cared because he had always loved her and protected her. Suddenly he saw his life for what it had been: gold leaf over tin. A lie. A substitution.

The anger was a monster that he could not fight. He held himself together long enough to see where she went next, hanging back with his hood drawn up over his face just in case.

Over the next few weeks, he began to follow her more and more. It was laborious progress, but it gave him something to do. He found a few of the parents, too, from the old notebooks and journals he and Peter had brought back to the house. Dana had documented her life in fits and starts, but it had felt important to keep them.

He liked to follow Jaspreet Singh because she reminded him of Randeep. Of that feeling of power. And that other lady, George and Jacob's mum. Peter had always liked to talk about the way she'd broken down at her press conference after her sons were taken, and again when only one was found. Alex thought she, of all of them, would still be sad.

Yet they were the same as Jillian. He had hoped to find these people in tatters – some memory of their dead and missing children in their faces, the way they walked or talked. But everywhere he looked the families of the children Dana and Peter had taken were simply *moving on*. His own mother – he'd seen her with a man. Alex's dad was gone. Probably dead. Good fucking riddance. But his mum looked… happy.

He visited Jillian again, just to be sure. He found out where she lived, where she worked. He stood on pavements – right there in the middle of the street – and waited for her to notice him, to look up from her goddamn phone and see him.

But she never did.

For the first time, it became a chore to go home to Peter. Peter didn't understand. And then, today, things had changed.

He felt it the second his brother came out of the kitchen with a bottle of beer in his delicate hands. Alex could barely speak. So many emotions rushed up and crushed his voice. But Peter noticed. As he always did. He could read Alex like a book.

Alex had thought of that day by the lake, when for once Peter hadn't been stronger than him, and it had fuelled him with belief. With a need to make things right.

It started with an argument; Peter was being stubborn, as usual. He said there was no point dragging up the past. Alex disagreed. He wanted to do something about all of this, to make Jillian remember him. Why couldn't Peter understand that?

It ended with Alex panting by the kitchen door, his bloody hands gripping the broken beer bottle and Peter – beautiful, broken Peter – bleeding on the grass outside.

Alex shook his head and started to fill Peter's grave. He knew none of the children were buried out here, but it was right for Peter to be near the water. He wouldn't have wanted to be buried anywhere else.

As Alex dug, a song trilled in his ear. Old words, a rhythm he'd long forgotten, rising back to the surface. They were built on anger, on sadness, on wishes.

Make it right.

To do it he would need to go back to the beginning. Then maybe Jilly would understand what she'd done to him. Maybe she would see that now, even after everything, he still needed her. He needed them to start all over again.

FORTY TWO

Erin

FOR A MOMENT NEITHER of us moved in that dim hallway. I noticed something on the outskirts of my vision, a dark shape against a darker wall. Relief flooded my veins – and then Alex darted forwards.

"I wouldn't," I said. I stood my ground. I gestured to one of the jerry cans – it was almost empty, but not quite. I nudged it with my foot and the sound of the liquid sloshing inside drew Alex's attention.

"Jilly…" His voice was all warning but I caught the plaintive note, right there at the end. "What about our trip?"

"There will be no fucking trip. Let me go or I'll burn your home to the ground." I used the word home intentionally. He flinched – but less than I expected, as though he had already reconciled with the idea of leaving this place behind.

"I'll give you one last chance," I said as calmly as I could. "You let me tie you up. You give me the car keys. You wait for the police. And I leave."

"Or what?" It was a genuine question, like he was weighing up his options. Choosing whether to take the risk. I wondered if that was how he had survived all these years. Always choosing between obedience and death.

"If you don't let me go you'll lose me anyway. And the house. You'll have nothing."

Alex stared at me and for a second in those blue eyes I saw a glimmer of the boy he once was.

"Jilly, please," he said. "Don't leave me again."

"No."

He snarled, then, and the little boy was devoured by the animal.

"You won't start a fire," Alex sneered. "You can't convince yourself that it doesn't scare you."

"I'm not the girl you remember."

"Jilly. Come on. Come away with me. Be my sister again."

"You stopped being my brother the minute you hurt somebody," I said. "Why won't you admit this isn't all my fault. You could have come with me, Alex. Why didn't you run?"

"I couldn't!" Alex wailed. "I had to go back. I thought you were dead!"

I let this wash over me. I had believed for years that I hadn't been good enough, that I had failed. But he was the one who made sure I had to make it on my own. Pain lanced through me, but underneath it a hot current of anger.

"You could have left later. Once you knew I'd made it." I was calm now, strangely detached. "There must have been times you could have got away. Why didn't you just come back to me then? Admit it: you *liked* it."

Alex's eyes shone. Barely suppressed memories flitted across his expression.

"Yes," he said. Finally. An admission.

This time I was the one who lunged first. But he dodged easily, then spun and careened into me. He slammed my head back against the wall as the jerry can tipped, petrol dripping from its open top. I fought back, dug my nails into the side of his face.

He was heavier, faster. I scrabbled for something, crawling into the room where he had tied me up. The *rope*. The rope was on the floor, somewhere. If I could just… But Alex, blind with anger now, grabbed me by the back of the head, his fist curling in my long hair as he smashed my face down on the floor.

I saw stars. I let out a long screech, determined not to let Harriet down. I was worried she might try to intervene – it would ruin our plan. But she didn't. I waited until Alex and I had rolled towards the far side of the room, my hands scrambling, searching for the tell-tale lump of my car keys in his pocket and then—

"Now!" I screamed. "Now! Now!"

Alex was on top of me. One fist still in my hair, he pushed the other against my neck. The force was almost more than I could bear. I couldn't breathe. My nose was bleeding, too. Tears and bloody snot ran down my face.

I wriggled as hard as I could, but Alex was strong. His bones dug into my soft flesh and I screamed again. He twisted the hand in my hair to slap it over my mouth. His breathing was hard, fast, and I could smell the animal sweat on him and I bucked harder, my hips wrenching against him.

I couldn't see into the hall. Couldn't hear Harriet. What if it didn't work? What if nothing happened? I'd told her to run, but what if the lighter didn't work? If she couldn't start the fire? Would she try to help me?

And then it happened. There was a creeping realisation as we both noticed the smell, the sound of crackling fire. Alex was less prepared for it and for a second his grip loosened. I bucked once more, hard, using my entire weight and years of anger and self-loathing to throw him off. His head hit the wall and he dropped, stunned.

I scrambled to my feet. The jerry can was right there. I grabbed it, tossing what was left of the petrol towards my brother. I didn't stop to see if my aim was true; I was out of the door in seconds flat. I slammed it behind me – and slid the bolt home.

In the hallway Harriet was already running. I caught sight of her as she turned back to check on me, her face glowing with the light from the flames that already licked at the mattress we had dragged out of the room. The flames spread, devouring the faded curtains we had torn from the entrance hall as they went up like a funeral pyre.

Her eyes were wide and I could see her clutching at one of her arms as she gestured to the petrol path she had laid, which soon the flames would reach, like a treasure hunt of pain leading out of the house.

We ran.

I tried not to think of the petrol that had splashed as Harriet had poured it, the puddles of it I had run through to get here… Alex hadn't even noticed that the trap was already laid.

The halls felt like a labyrinth. It wasn't long before I could taste the smoke, acrid and hot and turning the dust to soot as it devoured the bones of this old house. The air was filling with dark smoke and soon it was hard to see where we were going. I relied on my memory. My blessed fucking memory.

The flames were as fast as we were. Faster, maybe. I was surprised at the speed with which they took over, made this house theirs, latching onto the petrol that Harriet had poured at other points through the house. They devoured the offerings we had left in their path, curtains and paintings pulled off walls while Alex had been outside packing for our new life together.

We did not belong here any more.

The hallway to the conservatory felt endless. My brain kept looping *We didn't have to do this. We could have just locked him up and waited*. But those locks wouldn't have held him. We had to make sure we were far, far away before he got out.

I stumbled. Harriet reached for me, her steady, capable hands wrapping around my arm and yanking me upright. But I was slower than she was, body still freshly smarting from my fight with Alex, my weak ankle hurting. And there would be furniture in the way of the conservatory door. I shouldn't have tried to slow him down.

"Go!" I yelled. "Get it out of the way!"

Harriet gave me a last look as I limped after her, before racing ahead to do what I asked.

A sound made me pause. I spun – and Alex was there again. He was bloody now, knuckles bleeding, his face sooty and streaked with sweat, one of his shoulders hanging loose in its socket as though he'd used it to ram the bolted door down. He rounded the corner like a wraith silhouetted against the fug of smoke that crept along the passage.

"You said you wouldn't leave me, Jilly. You promised."

I inched backwards, testing my right leg. I had twisted it again when I stumbled, and now it shuddered under my weight. *Fuck*. I held my hands up.

"Alex, just let me leave—"

"I won't lose you again. You went once before and I had Peter, but now I have nothing. You *won't* leave me."

His growl echoed in my bones. Then I realised that it wasn't just Alex; the whole building was growling. Groaning. Aching as the fire damaged its core. The wooden panelling on these walls was burning, smoking, and with a great, creaking crash something gave on the floor above.

Alex and I looked up together, but I wasn't going to hang around long enough to find out if the ceiling would hold.

I ran – as fast as my leg could carry me – down the corridor and out into the conservatory, just as a screeching sound of falling timber and plaster made my ears ring.

"Jilly!" Alex's scream was raw. My belly lurched at the sound and I spun.

It had happened. Rotten floorboards and fire, and what

looked like a statue, an armless, headless woman, falling right through the ceiling. I stood, half-paralysed, unable to decipher the plaster dust from the smoke, the rubble and fire from my brother's outstretched arm.

The whole building might come down if the fire got hot enough. I felt a shudder. I should go to him. Help him. I didn't want him to *die*—

But even as I thought it, I was moving. Out towards Harriet and fresh air and *freedom*. Alex wasn't my brother any more, and I couldn't risk my life to save his.

Harriet wasn't in the conservatory, but the door was open. I prayed she had made it out. And then I was on the lawn. The air was cool and I sucked it into my aching lungs.

Somewhere, Harriet coughed.

Seconds after I stumbled into the garden the house shook as something else collapsed. I heard a tinkling of glass somewhere. Perhaps there had been other cans of petrol stored somewhere else, ready for more long drives in a dead woman's old car.

Harriet was stunned. She sat on the grass, cradling her arm, which had a long, slicing cut down the middle, still bleeding. She gazed up at the house in shock.

"We need to go," I said. "Your car—"

I fumbled in my pockets, but the keys were gone. Tears made my vision blur.

Just then another thundering sound made the ground

shudder. I could see the fire now. The flames licked through windows that had cracked in the heat; it had already spread beyond the first floor. I helped Harriet to stand and she said nothing as we moved, but gripped my hand tightly in hers.

"Alex has a car," Harriet said. "Right? Maybe he left the keys inside."

We reached the side of the house. The old rusted Land Rover emerged like a spectre through the trees. Time was like water; I let the ticking seconds soothe me as I held Harriet's hand. The driver's door was still open. The keys were still on the seat, Alex's bags on the grass.

I turned to look back.

Flames. Red, gold, glorious. I felt them on my skin like a kiss from the sun and I inhaled deeply, the smells of ash and smoke and something sweeter, too. How much petrol had there been in that house?

Behind us the wind whipped up and the trees rustled and the crackling, burning sound was replaced by screaming my brain knew but failed to recognise. The fire was soothing the pain – so unlike the tiny, broken flames from Alex's candles. It was an inferno. And now Alex was in there; he was burning.

I fought the urge to crumple to the ground, to weep out a maelstrom of grief and anger – and, buried deeper, the relief that he was gone. That it was over.

"Look, Erin."

I felt Harriet's hand, gently, on my shoulder. She turned me to face the driveway that led to the front of the house. The fire was hot at our backs, and the drive sprawled ahead and there, in the distance, were the gates. The screaming wasn't Alex.

I saw blue and white and bright, stark yellow jackets and the sound grew.

"Police."

FORTY THREE

24 JANUARY 2017

Harriet

I'D BEEN AWAKE FOR hours. My eyes were gritty, my head heavy. But it was a peaceful kind of tiredness, my body aching from a long night at my desk – a *satisfying* kind of tiredness.

Erin stirred in the bed behind me. She'd stayed in the spare room with me, sleeping on the lumpy futon instead of a proper bed because I couldn't drag myself away. She was wrapped, sleepily, in some of the blankets I'd made. She always liked to nestle herself in, like a cat. And she peeped out now.

Outside there was a faint shimmer of white where snow had fallen in the night and was now melting, slick and silver-grey on the building across the way. Erin shivered.

"Morning," she said.

"I finished it."

There was a moment of silence. Digesting. Waking up a little more. I might have waited to tell her, but I couldn't. I'd wanted to say something since the second I finished the first draft – three hours ago – but I couldn't bring myself to wake her.

"The whole thing?" She scooted upright in bed, her expression caught between excitement and dread. She'd only read parts until now. And I'd edited since then, written a lot more, turned it into something with a solid shape.

Ignoring my old tutor, I'd allowed even more of myself to leak onto the page. I wrote about my relationship with my brother, about how he had always encouraged me to explore my feelings. I wanted to show his kindness, his love, as I wanted to do for all of the children out there who had died because they wanted to protect their sibling. I'd spent more time thinking about Jem and Mikey than I ever had, and allowed myself to reflect on how that had affected me growing up. I didn't want it to seem selfish, and I was worried what Erin might think.

"It's ready," I said.

Erin looked haunted for a moment, perhaps reliving – as I had – that day at the house. And every uncertain day since. But every day was one step away from what had happened, a step towards the future.

I'd since told her all about my family. My aunt and uncle, and my cousins – as much as I knew of them. She'd met my brother and his fiancée when they flew in for Christmas, and had been warm and welcoming despite the feelings I'm sure it all stirred up.

Erin smiled, then, and the spell was broken, her face lighting with a tired sort of happiness, pride at her own bravery. And, I thought, she looked proud of me, too.

"How does it end?" she asked.

I climbed off the chair at my desk and onto the bed,